ALL FOR LOVE

Beverly Wells

Dawn,

With warmest

wishes,

Always,

Bev

All For Love by Beverly Wells
Copyright© 2014 Beverly Wells
Cover Design Livia Reasoner
Prairie Rose Publications
www.prairierosepublications.com

All rights reserved.

This is a work of fiction. The characters, incidents, and dialogues are products of the author's imagination and are not to be construed as real. No part of this book may be used or reproduced in any manner whatsoever without written permission of the publisher, except in the case of brief quotations embodied in critical articles and reviews.

An extremely big thank you to Cheryl Pierson and Livia Reasoner at Prairie Rose Publications for their guidance, encouragement, and believing in me and my story. And to all my fans, family, friends, and fellow authors who continually offer support and incentive—this book wouldn't have happened without you. Love you all.

In loving memory of Tadd; you are forever in our hearts.

CHAPTER ONE

Toleman, Wyoming 1886

Thwack!

The well-aimed object impacted dead-center between Lorelei Webster's shoulder blades. Knife-piercing pain stabbed deep as flames sizzled across her skin. Its bite didn't begin to match her humiliation, or the warning behind the insulting attack. Braking her foot on the first step up to the walkway, she fought to catch her breath. And inhaled the odor of tomato.

Whoops of male laughter pierced the stifling air, triggering tears to cloud her vision. Juice oozed through her cotton blouse and across her tingling skin as a chunk of pulp plopped to the ground with a muted thud. She prayed the steps would open up so she could sink below. Refusing further disgrace, she sniffled back the sudden weakness, raised her chin and squared her shoulders. *Unmannered, ignorant bastards. All of them.*

"Take that Miss Neb-nose," Sam Ahearns bellowed from across the street. "That's what we think of your damn meddlin'." Raucous mirth rose from his cohorts.

"Yeah, maybe now y'all know to keep yer unwanted snoot out of affairs that don't involve ya," Andy Piedmont's voice thundered worse than she'd ever heard.

*Oh my, I've riled them but good this time. One, two...*she silently counted to ten, striving for any kind of dignity she could muster. *Don't*

5

let them see your fear. You're right in doing what you believe in. You are! She hoped her wide-brimmed bonnet hid her distress.

Gathering courage, she held her back taut to brace against another assault and, hesitantly but determinedly, lifted her left foot to the next step. She focused on her original destination straight ahead, yet the bank seemed a mile away. If her rubbery knees did not fail her, maybe, just maybe, she could make it inside with a smidgeon of poise.

"Okay, you men, break it up." Michael Pearson's voice had never sounded so good. "You've had your fun, done enough harm for one day. Get moving before I lock you up for roughing up the lady."

She wished he *would* lock up the entire bunch of imbeciles.

"*Lady?*" Sam Ahearns sneered. "Sheriff, you lost your mind? She ain't no lady. She's a neb-nose, stickin' her nose in where it don't belong. A trouble maker and a damned nuisance. She best keep her big snoot outta our business if she knows what's good for her. We'll—"

"That's enough, Sam," Michael roared. "Button your lip, or I'll be forced to put up with your company all afternoon. And you won't be sitting on my side of the bars playing poker with me either. All of you owe Miss Webster an apology."

Lorelei grasped the upright pole to the railing to thwart her shaking. Her blasted legs refused to lift her leaden feet.

"Throw shit too, and bad apples, I say," Tom Burdock spat. "Sam's right, Sheriff. She stuck her nose in too far this time. Ain't no sayin' otherwise. *She* owes *us* the apology, fer Christ's sake. Town shoulda never hired her after Gilbert took off."

A slight breeze stirred the bright September day. Yet, it felt more like a June sun as it blazed down on her sticky back and radiated clear through to her face. Would the enraged men have hung her from the nearest tree if Michael hadn't arrived? They were not merely angry. They were downright vengeful.

But dammit, they were in the wrong. Tom Burdick had beaten his wife to resemble the tomato now lying in the dirt. She couldn't stand by and watch another defenseless person be abused. Not if she wanted to live with herself. Not if she wanted to sleep at night. At the age of ten, she had witnessed suffering, first-hand. She had stood there horrified and angered beyond belief at the senselessness. She had held her tongue that day. But no more.

"That's enough profanity on the street for today," Michael's voice rose curt, yet composed. "All of you get out my sight before I take you in and toss away the key. Now, scatter."

Lorelei's throat felt as parched as the baked earth of Main Street. Frozen in place, anticipating another go-around, she listened to the stomping of heavy feet as the men dispersed.

The muffled, sputtered cusses sawed through her chest, yet she sighed in relief. Pulling her sweaty palm from the post, she wiped it on her blue gingham skirt. Her hands trembled. What would they do next time? Undoubtedly, there *would be* a next time. She knew herself all too well.

"You alright, Lorelei?" She flinched, startled by Michael's voice over her shoulder.

She pivoted, and plastered on a composed smile to hide her fear and embarrassment. Rivulets of perspiration trickled down her neck to pool into her high laced collar.

"Yes, thank you. I apologize for again causing such a ruckus." She wanted to say more, but knew if she did, she would wither into a glob of jam.

The handsome stranger standing at Michael's side merely added salt to her wound. He stood an inch or so taller than Michael's six feet, his dark brown eyes almost level with hers as she stood on the raised stoop. He wore a black serge suit, its knee-length frock coat straining against broad shoulders, and a black string tie at the neck of his white high-collared shirt. His knee-high boots gleamed as if he had just spit-shined them for hours.

With hat in hand, the sun splayed across his nut-brown hair to highlight golden threads. His eyes, almost black, regarded her as critically as the others.

Clean shaven like Michael, his lips thinned slightly, and she realized with mortification she had been assessing him quite thoroughly. Was it a cocky grin he held back, or one of disgust at her ill-manners? Her face flamed and its scalding seeped down her neck. Why, she had near been drooling.

Apparently oblivious to her discomfort and brash behavior, Michael asked, "Lorelei, have you met the doc? I remember you missed our welcoming party when you were down with the influenza."

"No, I haven't," she managed without stammering. How had she not seen him in the two weeks he had been here? He looked very distinguished. Not the typical saddlebag doctor. *He could treat her anytime. It might be worth suffering another malady.*

"Guess I better make introductions then. Lorelei, meet Seth Taylor. I'm surprised you haven't run into him before now." Michael laughed good-naturedly. "Guess we've kept him running between babies and fixing up broken bones too much."

How utterly humiliating to be introduced to him—now. With tomato clinging to her back. *Good gracious.*

"It's so nice to meet you, Doctor Taylor. Toleman isn't very big, but I hope we have enough families to keep you busy so Cheyenne doesn't lure you away." She leaned forward and extended her hand, praying it remained steady; that he did not realize she was babbling.

When he hesitated, she felt more disgraced from his condemning stare than from the irate men. She could well imagine the stories he had heard. And most likely, they had not included the nasty little secrets kept behind closed doors. Oh, no. The men would not have offered those despicable tidbits.

He clasped her hand as several people crossed the street, and others walked along the far end of the boardwalk, their heads slightly bowed as if reluctant to reveal they had witnessed her fiasco. Was the doctor as embarrassed to shake her hand?

Michael seemed to notice nothing out of the ordinary as the doctor's large, warm hand clasped hers. "Seth, this is Miss Lorelei Webster, our schoolmarm."

Michael laughed again. His whimsical attitude grated on her strung-out nerves. Sometimes Michael could be obtuse, no matter how good a friend.

"And…I should add, our Toleman defender of righteousness."

Lorelei's muscles pulled taut at his flippant remark. *And at other times the jackass could be downright obnoxious.*

"It's a pleasure, Miss Webster." Doctor Taylor's deep voice did funny things to her insides. Little flips and skips.

He looked far from being overly pleased if the hasty withdrawal of his hand, the widening of his eyes, was any indication of the degree of pleasure. He acted as if she had some contagious disease. His smile looked forced, his eyes appraising, as if he were cautiously observing a black widow spider.

She had hoped the new doctor, a pillar of the community who shared her deep concern for people, would augment her ammunition against the town's corruption. He did emit an aura of strength and confidence. She had wholeheartedly believed he would be an ally in her mission. Undaunted by her negative first impression, she resolutely banked the notion she could sway him.

Yet discouragement seeped into her pores as his lingering, all-condemning scrutiny shouted otherwise. She highly doubted he would be the comrade-at-arms she had counted on. *No strong cohort here. It'll take diligent work in order to enlist this one.*

Michael bounded up the three steps to her side. "Come to my office so I can sponge that mess off your back before your blouse is ruined."

She could deal easier with Michael's look of pity than his usual star-struck one. She regarded him as a good friend, yet knew if she encouraged him, he would leap at the chance to take their relationship further. How funny to realize Michael's gaze did not affect her. But, oh! She had felt a definite thrill when she had looked into the doctor's dark, compelling eyes.

Unsure she wanted Michael to sponge off the evidence of her fracas, she eyed the bank's door with indecision as it opened.

Doris Piedmont stepped out and flashed an abashed, sympathetic look before nodding. She scurried down the long, weathered boardwalk, the click of her hard-soled heels fading as she fled. Seemed even Doris dared not speak to her after this calamity. At this rate, she wouldn't have a friend left. With an ache in her chest, she blinked back tears and clenched her teeth.

"I—"

"Come on. It'll save your blouse and give you time to cool that temper of yours before it steams off again."

Steams off? She opened her mouth to voice her indignation.

Michael howled. "Come on, save your spouting off for inside unless you want another audience."

She bit her lip to remain silent, for now. She could do without another audience, thank you very much. Cupping her elbow, he led her past three doors to the jail. The doctor's even strides followed. *Curse the man for not going his own way.*

****

Seth eyed the slender waist of Miss Webster as she marched stiff back and chin high and obviously quite miffed at the lawman's remark. He watched her skirt sashay back and forth; her softly rounded hips sway enticingly with each and every forceful footstep. She definitely had a nice, firm backside.

Whoa! Why the hell did he view anything remotely appealing about the woman? He had heard from more than a few men about how she butted her nose into family matters that didn't concern her. And now he had witnessed just how extremely explosive she could rile them. If it wasn't so important he talk to the sheriff right now, he would head in the opposite direction.

He did not condone spousal abuse any more than she did, but that matter was best left between husband and wife. She had even struck a sour note in him by inciting memories he had fought long and hard to bury. He would be damned if he would allow her to dredge up those atrocities. He did enough of that on his own.

As they entered the office, the aroma of strong coffee and stale tobacco permeated the small room. No sooner had Seth shut the door than the sassy woman lambasted the sheriff.

"What do you mean 'steam off'?" She stood like an avenging angel, elbows bent and fists shoved firmly into her hips. "I do *not* simply rant. I try to right the wrongs in this damn town. Actually that should be your job, *Sheriff.*"

Pearson grinned as he soaked a small towel in a basin of water and wrung it out. He glanced at Seth. "Have a seat Doc, I'll be with you after I've unruffled this witch's feathers."

"Unruffled—"

The lawman's booming chortles bounced off the walls. Miss Webster's proud stance jolted from stiff to rigid. She ought to put her efforts into woman's suffrage, Seth mused. As he settled into the chair, he had to force back a grin. God, she was all spit fire. Hell on wheels, to be precise.

"Now, don't get so lathered up. You know I'm on your side," Pearson said. He ambled to her side, turned her around by her shoulders and began dabbing at the red stain.

"On my side?" she huffed, twisting her neck around to glare. Seth figured they had forgotten all about him.

She untied her bonnet and slid it off. Her hair, the color of spring wheat and pulled back in a tight bun, shimmered like fine threads of silk. His breath caught.

"Those men think they have the God-given right to treat their wives any way they want. They don't treat their children any better either. And they dare to call themselves fathers! They don't know the meaning of the word. They only know how to beget them. You all think with that thing between…"

Her gaze flew to where he sat. Her rounded eyes burned potent and brilliant as blue flames. Suppressing another grin, he watched her swallow, her face flush as if her words had just registered. She broke eye contact and looked over her shoulder as Pearson rinsed out the cloth then returned to his chore. Seth wondered just how close these two were; how long her hair would be if she removed the pins; and why he couldn't stop admiring her.

"I haven't seen you or any other men lift a finger to protect them from their suffering, Michael."

"That's not fair," Pearson protested, trying diligently to remove the stain while merely smearing it worse. "Last week I talked to Henry Jacobs about not taking the switch to Bobby."

She stopped her tirade as if mulling over what he had said. She took a deep breath, exhaled slowly. "Yes, you talked to Henry," she said, her voice calmer, "and I thanked you for trying. But that's not good enough. They don't listen to words."

"What in the blue blazes do you want me to do? Lock each one up every time they mistreat their families? They have the right."

She twirled around faster than a spinning top. "They have no right to verbally or physically hurt others. Not their wives, especially not the

11

children. No one has that right."

"Be reasonable, Lorelei." Pearson seemed to be losing patience as well as the argument. "I'd have half the town in the cells and no one to run it."

She gave a snide smirk. "That's correct. Half the damn town would be locked up where they could do no further harm. And if your jail isn't big enough to hold all of them, you could ship them off to Cheyenne. I understand they have plenty of room."

"You're being ridiculous."

"Oh, Michael," she sighed and shook her head. "That's where you're wrong. That's why we don't see eye to eye."

Whoever fathered this feisty, pert woman, should have named her Bold, Seth mused. By God, she'd even cursed without a hitch in her breath or giving it a second thought.

He had vowed a long time ago to lead a mundane life, engross himself in his life's devotion. He wanted none of the havoc, no reminders of the cruelties life could dish out.

Though he found Miss Webster's backside tempting, her silky hair and cornflower eyes all too enticing for his peace of mind, he had accepted long ago he had no business pursuing any woman.

And at that very moment, he made another firm vow: To stay way the hell away from the troublesome, meddlesome Lorelei Webster.

CHAPTER TWO

Seth turned to the sheriff as soon as Miss Webster breezed out of the office, her feathers still more than a bit ruffled. Pearson's attempt at salvaging the blouse had been fruitless, other than removing a few clinging seeds and strings of pulp.

Seth needed to discuss Purdy and be on his way. He wanted to forget the flighty woman yet found his mouth disobeying his stymied mind. "What'd she do this time?"

Pearson's carefree grin compressed into a tight thin line.

"Last night she barreled into The Silver Dollar, marched up to Tom Burdock and tongue-whipped him for beating his wife." He swiped his hand across his face.

"Would've been bad enough had she faced him alone. But the saloon was full. Even interrupted a heated poker game." He shook his head again, sauntered over to the kettle of coffee on the woodstove and poured some into a tin cup.

"Want a cup?" He glanced his way.

"Sure, why not. What did Tom do?" Seth asked, unable to hold back his inquisitiveness as he strode toward the sheriff.

Pearson poured another cup and handed it to him. "Hell, he became madder than a peeled rattler is what he did. He called her every vile word in the book. If I hadn't stepped away from the bar and dragged her outside, he might have done more."

Pearson pulled his chair back from the desk and plunked down in it. Seth remained standing, amazed at the hot situation the schoolmarm had created.

"Doesn't she realize she can't humiliate them that way? Good God, doesn't she have any common sense when it comes to pushing them? Especially in public?"

"Who the hell knows? She's smart, but when she gets her dander up, she sees bright red." He sipped the steaming brew.

"Can't you make her see some sense? You two seem pretty close. Won't she listen to you?" Seth took a seat in the oak chair adjacent to the desk.

Pearson gave a rueful laugh. "You saw how well she listens to me. When it comes to defending the abused, she listens to no one, but her heart. She might be twenty-eight, but at times, I swear, she thinks and acts like a child."

Funny, Seth had not thought about Miss Webster having much of a heart. Only haughty boldness, colder than a witch's tit come Sunday when it came to anything other than determination to incite havoc. She, for some reason, maybe an unconscious death wish, had a willful desire to stir up trouble. A brazen drive to right the wrong. Was it heart-felt? She wouldn't have a heart left for long if she continued to harass those twenty-odd men the way she did. No, he doubted the woman felt one lick of remorse.

Pearson toyed with the cup's handle. "We're not as close as you might think. Not where she's concerned. Wish she was."

Seth couldn't hold back his laugh. "You mean you'd actually want more of a relationship with the feisty woman? I pegged you for having more sense."

The sheriff's eyes gleamed. "Can you blame me? Just think about all that passion she's got wrapped up in one tidy package. Hell, if she's half as energetic in bed as she is in fightin' for her cause, she'd be worth it. I'm not talkin' commitment here. Heaven help any man to think that way. But all my courtin' seems to be barkin' at a knot in a tree. She dang well keeps it just friends. Now, don't get me wrong here. I count her as a *good* friend. She's got a good heart down deep, and I'd help her out in a minute, but she's way too much effort for any man to try to tame."

To Seth's complete surprise, Pearson's sexual interest in the woman rubbed him the wrong way. So, the sheriff wanted to bed her, but wanted no ties attached. Two to one, the brash woman was not innocent, yet the man's flippant attitude more than bothered him. *This isn't your problem, stay out of it.*

He forced himself to change the subject. "You're not going to like what I have to tell you about Dan Purdy,"

"Yeah? I figured as much. If he'd died in his sleep, you'd have said so outside and left it at that. What'd you find?"

"He was strangled."

"Strangled?" Pearson's eyes widened. He leaned back in the captain's chair with a loud sigh. "Shit, there wasn't anything that looked like he'd been strangled. No evidence of a struggle. You sure?"

Seth took no offense at his doubt. "I'm sure. It wasn't obvious right off the bat to the others. But by the time the men carried him to my place, discoloration had set in. After my examination, I have no doubts. He was strangled by someone with big hands, hands as strong as steel. His neck was broken."

Pearson gaped at him as if trying to find a logical answer on his face. "Could be half the town if that's my only lead. Makes no sense. Everyone respected ol' Dan. If it was an outsider, there'd have been some sign of robbery, maybe a struggle, something out of the ordinary." He shook his head, pulled out a cigarette. "It just don't figure."

"Whether if figures or not, that's what happened. Could you have overlooked something? Something at the bank?"

"Hell if I know. I went over everything with a fine tooth comb. Nothing seemed out of place in his home. A folder with some recent land contracts and loans were on Dan's desk at the bank. Most likely he planned to work on them in the morning."

It was none of his business to question the sheriff as to his findings so Seth dropped the matter. Would the folder hold answers to this puzzle? That was the sheriff's job to pursue it, not his. Sticking his nose in where it did not belong was the last thing he wanted. Unlike Miss Webster, he avoided that kind of involvement if he could help it. This time was no different.

Seth set the cup on the desk and stood. "I better get going. I promised the Harrises I'd take another look at Jethro."

Pearson struck a match on his boot heel, lit a cigarette, and exhaled a cloud of smoke. "How is the little tyke? Heard he was pretty bad off there for a while."

"Yeah, he was. He was doing a little better two days ago. He's still plastered from head to toe with measles and spikes high fevers at the oddest times, but he's holding his own. He's a tough five-year-old, even if he looks like he's three." Seth smiled as he thought of the youngster with the cherub face and short, pudgy legs. When healthy he was a holy terror. God, how he loved to watch the little ones grow. He opened the door.

"Give my best to the Harrises for me. And thanks for telling me about Dan. 'Course I don't know why I'm thanking you. Now I'll have to dig deeper. Don't even know where to start."

Start by going over everything in front of your nose, you fool. At times Pearson demonstrated he could be the conscientious sheriff. Other times he just sat back and let the world go its merry way as long as it didn't rattle his lackadaisical mood.

"I'll give them your regards. Good luck with your investigation."

****

As Seth rode west to the Harris's, he questioned whether he should have settled in Toleman. It had seemed like a nice, peaceful town. Not big and hectically busy like Cheyenne, or San Francisco where he'd said his last good-byes. He needed peace and quiet where he could practice medicine the way he wanted.

Now all he saw was a sheriff who half the time did his job, the other half of the time he sat on his duff and joked about trivia; a town where a good share of men abused their families, or drank and gambled to all hours, much to the distress of their wives; and a schoolmarm who did not have the God-given sense to keep her mouth shut, and who most likely would end up on the wrong end of a noose if she failed to learn her lesson soon.

****

Arriving at the Harris farm, Seth dismounted, grabbed his bag and looped the reins around the hitching post. He wouldn't dwell on the things wrong with the town. He would concentrate on the beauty of the land, his growing practice, and the hordes of good folks. They had been too long without a doctor.

As he strode toward the cozy-looking slat house with its soft-lit amber windows, his mind played havoc. He envisioned sun-kissed wheaten hair, round alluring hips, a luscious full mouth. A woman he so desperately needed to avoid.

Shit, you're a fool for letting your lust dream dreams. Especially when that enticement will add upheaval to your life.

Seth knocked on the door. Hell, it had always been easy to resist a pretty woman, he thought with a smile. She was bossy, meddlesome and overbearing. Not his type at all.

But by the time Mrs. Harris opened the door, his smile had vanished. Somehow, for some unfathomable reason, he knew resisting Miss Webster would be as hard as hammering a nail into a rock. He didn't relish being tempted. He could hardly afford the heartache that would come with it.

I'm not good enough for the likes of any woman. Even the loud-mouthed, so-called neb-nosed Miss Lorelei Webster.

CHAPTER THREE

Three days later, Lorelei dipped the corner of a cloth into warm salt water and applied it to Fannie Allen's swollen cheek. The woman's left eyelid and cheek bore the dark purple, mostly black, evidence of her husband's most recent temper.

Yet that was not why she had come. She silently fumed in disgust. A more serious matter existed here.

"Fannie, you can't even move your arm. How can you care for your children? You have to let me take you to Dr. Taylor."

Fannie's eyes widened. "That Mable Gillis should never have told you. Please, Lorelei, I can't. If Claude ever found out I spent money for a doctor, he'd…"

"Horse whip you?"

Fannie hung her head. Lorelei figured she'd come pretty damn close to the truth. She knew she had to use well thought-out words to coax the reluctant woman to seek medical help. Fannie's fear was ingrained as profoundly as a fossil in stone.

"Fannie, listen to me. Mable was right in seeking my help. I know she's a busybody sometimes, but she only wanted to help. Clara can watch the younger children while I take you in my buggy. Claude won't ever know. Just tell Clara I need you to help me hang curtains that I can't do by myself. You know Claude won't be home much before midnight. It's only seven now, so we have plenty of time. There's no way I can fix your shoulder. You need a doctor. It's dislocated, possibly broken. Don't worry about the cost. I'll see to it he gets paid."

Fannie's mouth dropped open. "Oh, I could never have you pay for

18

my care. I—"

"Hush, that's what friends are for. I'm only thinking of the children. You have no choice if you're going to do for them."

Lorelei watched varied emotions spread across her face. Fannie attempted to move her arm, grimaced then shuddered. She undoubtedly tried to deny the situation.

Knowing she had hit below the belt when she used the children to jog Fannie's resistance, Lorelei felt no regret at her tactics. The lady needed help. She was it.

"Please, while it's still dusk, call Clara in and let us be on our way. Dr. Taylor can set your shoulder and we can be back before the children are asleep."

Fannie cast one more doubtful look, her eyes a weary, pitiful shame for a woman the same age as she. Much too young to look so withdrawn and defeated. How many nights had Fannie endured Claude's wicked temper and cried lonely tears? A gripping fist twisted within Lorelei's chest. It was not fair or right.

"Alright, but you have to promise we'll hurry. I can only be gone for a short time with Clara in charge. Those five can be a handful."

"I'll have you back before the sun fully sets."

Lorelei glanced outside. Could she keep her promise? The sun would set in an hour or so. Fall was approaching fast and nights came upon them now by eight thirty. It would take a half an hour just to get to Dr. Taylor's.

****

At the knock on his door, Seth laid down the medical journal he had been reading in his study and hurried to the door. The knocking grew louder as if the person's patience knew no bounds.

"I'm here," he barked as he whipped open the portal.

Lorelei Webster, eyes round as saucers and her mouth agape, stood with her fist raised to pound the thick wood to sawdust.

"Miss Webster, I should've known only you would try to bash in my door." He smiled, hoping he made her feel contrite. She looked more annoyed. Good. He was equally annoyed at having thought about her eyes and hair throughout the day.

"I…wasn't sure you had heard me, and we're in a bit of a rush." At her words, he peered around her to see who were the *"we're"* she referred to. Though dusk cast only a muted gray to the evening, he couldn't see anyone with her. Had she finally lost her mind?

"*Is* someone with you, Miss Webster?" He slapped on another complacent smile.

She scowled, turned her head and looked flabbergasted. She spun around. "Oh, for heaven's sake, Fannie, he's not going to bite you. And the sooner we get in there, the sooner we can be on our way. Now, come here."

Expecting a shy child to come forth, Seth was surprised when a woman stepped from the sidelines. He had seen the brunette in town, but didn't know her. Her slumped shoulders and bowed head spoke a thousand words. He opened his mouth to tell Miss Webster to cease her harping at the poor soul. The chance never came.

"I apologize for coming here so late, but Fannie—oh, this is Mrs. Fannie Allen—is in great need of your service."

At her words, Fannie raised her chin. He noted bruises on the left side of her face. Her eye was just about swollen shut.

"Please, ladies, come in. I'll see what I can do."

Once inside, he retrieved the oil lamp, led them across the living room, down the hall and through the second doorway to the infirmary.

"Please have a seat, Mrs. Allen." Fannie sat on the wooden chair he indicated. Figuring he would get more answers from Lorelei, he turned to her. "Was cold applied for the swelling?"

"Yes, and afterward I applied a warm compress of salt water. But her face isn't why we're here. She can't move her left arm."

Only then did he note how Fannie held her left arm bent at the elbow and drawn tightly to her waist. "I see. Can you move it at all?" he inquired, as he sat on a rolling stool in front of her. He kept his voice low to calm the skittish woman.

"I don't think you do see," Miss Webster huffed. "You have to fix it without asking a hundred questions."

With her impatient attitude, he was amazed she had stopped the horse and buggy long enough to have anyone even look at the blasted shoulder, never mind care for it.

20

He swiveled to face the irritating woman, fought his own sarcasm. "Miss Webster, might I remind you, *you* are the one who came seeking *my* expertise. If you want it, I need to ask necessary questions in order to treat her."

She appeared at a loss for words for a fraction of a second. He wondered if this might be a first. She undoubtedly was not accustomed to someone speaking curt words in a monotone. Only combativeness and bodily attack.

"I apologize," she said, her voice sheepish.

Praise the saints above! She looked contrite. Something he had not expected in a million years.

"But we have to hurry. Claude, Fannie's husband, is at the saloon. If he finds out she's here, he'll do worse to her."

"You can't be serious." He turned to Fannie. She bit her lip, lowered her chin and scrutinized the floor. *Miss Webster had been serious.* His dander rose at the thought of anyone denying someone medical care. No wonder Miss Webster was flustered. Hell, he felt flummoxed.

"And Fannie's oldest daughter, Clara, is watching the other five children until we get back."

"I'm sure they'll be fine," he reassured Fannie. "I want you to try to move your arm, just a little, if you can." He watched her move it no more than an inch. She gasped and grimaced.

"We need to slide your arm out of your dress."

Fannie blushed, but nodded and Miss Webster came to her side. With a few mewls, sighs and squirming from Fannie, they managed to free the arm of the long sleeve. Though Miss Webster tucked the dress around Fannie so only her shoulder and arm were exposed, Fannie's cheeks flushed. Seth concentrated on acting as professional to allay her threatened modesty.

When Lorelei stepped back several steps to allow him better access, he rolled his stool closer.

"I'm going to press on your shoulder, Mrs. Allen. It'll be uncomfortable, but I'll try not to cause you too much pain."

With eyes leery, Fannie nodded. Seth palpated her shoulder, immediately feeling the head of the humerus popped from the socket. Totally dislocated.

He tried to distract her concentration on his manipulation. "You have six children. That's wonderful." He applied more pressure as he checked the ligaments. "How old is Clara?"

She grimaced as his thumb pushed deeper into the joint. "She's…eight."

He fought the urge to spring back. *Eight?* And she was watching five younger than herself? "I see." He continued to check the surrounding muscle and tissue, and threw a contemptible scowl Miss Webster's direction.

Miss Webster had the good grace to look reprimanded for a split second. Then the uppity, snide attitude fell into place.

He leaned back and looked at Fannie. "Your shoulder is dislocated. I'm going to have to pull on the arm in order to put it back into place. It'll hurt like crazy, but will only take a minute." She nodded. Her set jaw said she would brave the storm. She had more spunk than he had expected.

"Miss Webster," he glanced over his shoulder, "I'll need you to hold her right shoulder tight against the chair so she can't move away from me."

"Alright." She took her position behind the chair, and placed a hand on Fannie's right shoulder.

The woman never cowered from anything. *Amazing.*

She patted her friend's good shoulder. "It'll be over before you know it, Fannie. It might help if you hold onto my arm with your right hand and squeeze for all you're worth."

Her sincere offer seeped deep inside Seth like a cup of soothing tea. He had been wrong. She did have a heart.

Fannie clenched her teeth. "Would you like laudanum, or a shot of whiskey?"

"No, thank you. I'd rather have nothing. Just do what has to be done. I can bear it." She forced a feeble smile.

He grabbed a thin towel from the stand, twisted it taut to resemble a rope and held it to Fannie's lips. "Bite down on this. It'll save your teeth and actually lessen the pain."

She opened her mouth and he inserted the rope across her tongue. She bit down hard. He placed his left hand on her shoulder, held his right arm parallel to hers and gripped his hand around her upper arm. He would have to pull straight down with every ounce of strength he had; then, with utmost caution, ease the bone back into position.

"Ready?"

Fannie nodded. Her jaw squared as she bit harder.

"Hold her as securely as you can, Miss Webster. She'll want to fly out of the chair when I pull. I can't have that." He glanced upward. Miss Webster's jaw resembled a vise. Ten times more rigid than Fannie's.

"You do your part and I'll hold Fannie so you won't even feel her flinch." Miss Webster pressed her left shoulder against Fannie's shoulder and anchored her right arm across the woman's chest. Either she would crush poor Fannie to death, or push all of them over backward, chair included. Unwillingly, he found himself smiling at her fortitude.

Seth pulled down on the arm, regretting the severe pain he caused the woman. He saw tears gather in her eyes, felt her try to escape. Miss Webster pressed harder, immobilizing Fannie in a death grip. He wished he could see the other's expression. True to her word, he had to give Miss Webster credit.

With mastered expertise, his muscles taut with strained tension, he pulled down, held the arm in alignment, and allowed the head of the long bone to ease back into proper position within the socket. It took less than the proclaimed minute.

"You can relax your hold, Miss Webster. I'm finished." She straightened, stepped away and stretched her back.

He rolled his shoulders, flexed his arms to ease out the kinks, and then returned his attention to his patient. He removed the cotton rope. It looked as if it had been compressed in a wringer. Thin rivulets of sweat ran down her parchment-like face.

"You alright, Mrs. Allen?"

She sucked in a deep breath and rested her neck against the chair. "I...think so. It was...more painful than I expected." She drew in another long breath.

"It's not a very pleasant experience, but you were superb. I'll need to bandage it for a few days to hold it in place while the muscles regain strength."

Fannie sprang straight up in the chair, her eyes rounded with panic. "No. He'll know I was here!"

Seth felt baffled. Never had he been in this situation where a husband would deny his wife aid.

Miss Webster took Fannie's hand in hers. "Tell him I did it. That I knew you were in pain and insisted on wrapping it for comfort. He'll believe I wouldn't take no for an answer."

For the first time, Fannie Allen managed a wisp of a smile. "Then he'll be angry at you."

"Oh, and I'm shakin' in my shoes." Lorelei shivered and flayed her hands out in front of her. Her eyes did a circling dance Seth had never seen the likes of. "Can you imagine any man in this town being angry at me? For shame." Lorelei's guffaw must have originated from the tips of her toes. Deep. Hearty. More than infectious.

Seth laughed with the two of them at her ridiculous antics and words. As he chuckled, he watched Lorelei Webster...

And felt as if he had been flattened by a herd of buffalo.

The haughty, stiff-backed troublemaker had blossomed into a jovial, devil-may-care, compassionate woman. One with genuine humility. She had helped a friend, and now offered to add another check to the list of her transgressions by taking the blame.

It should have pleased him to realize she possessed a heart. But it didn't. Instead, her sincerity touched him way too deeply. He would rather deal with the brazen, arrogant, mouthy woman.

"Dr. Taylor?" Miss Webster asked, sounding provoked.

"Yes?" He tried to pay attention where attention was due.

"I asked you if you'd please wrap the shoulder. We don't have much time to waste." Back was the staunch face.

Good, he could deal easier with this Miss Webster.

CHAPTER FOUR

With Fannie's shoulder wrapped and her dress refastened, Lorelei shuffled her to the door for a quick exit. Fannie, still pale from the excruciating ordeal, paused and turned around at the open door. The night's chill swept past them and she gathered her shawl tighter around her, using her good hand.

"I don't have money to pay you, Dr. Taylor, but somehow I'll get it." She looked so disheartened that Lorelei wondered how the woman kept going each day with such a tyrant of a husband.

Dr. Taylor smiled and Lorelei felt it clear down to her toes. He should always smile, she thought. His eyes sparkled to make him look years younger; the thin crow's-feet deepened to add to his masculinity. Her heart thrummed faster. She knew better than to let herself be drawn to any respectable man with any kind of sense. Especially one who did not seem fazed by her presence.

"Don't worry about it, Mrs. Allen. How about a couple of chickens? That would suit me just fine." His smile could like up the sun. Lorelei could not take her eyes off the man.

"Oh, dear, I couldn't do that," Fannie countered, looking totally flustered. "Claude would wonder where they went to. I—"

"I told you not to worry about payment, Fannie. I made you come, so I'm responsible." She glanced at Seth hoping her smile seemed spontaneous. His impervious grin made her feel awkward.

"You have chickens, Miss Webster?"

She found her smile impetuous this time. "I'm sorry, but no. I'd have to slaughter them if I did, and that just wouldn't do. I'll pay you cash. I'll stop by tomorrow, if that's all right."

He remained silent, intently studying her as if she had grown horns and a tail. Maybe he half-believed she had them, she thought with a heavy heart. He might be one of the most handsome men she had ever seen, but she did not forget for one second he thought of her no different than half the men in town. No good.

"That'd be fine, Miss Webster."

"Thank you, Dr. Taylor. And thank you for helping Fannie. We best get a move on." Not wanting to confront Claude should he come home earlier than expected, Lorelei ushered Fannie through the darkening night toward the buggy. The soft glow from the opened door and windows illuminated their way.

"It was my pleasure, ladies," he said, following them.

Lorelei took Fannie's good elbow, prepared to assist her up.

"Allow me." Seth stepped around Lorelei.

She drew back and watched him assist Fannie up with ease. Without further thought as to his gallantry, Lorelei scurried around the back of the vehicle to her side.

"Again, allow me." Not realizing he had followed her, she flinched. In one fluid motion, he lifted her, more than assisted her. His warm touch upon her waist blazed right through her coat. Lorelei's heart leaped within her chest. It had been a long time since any man treated with her so much respect. Even Michael's attempts at courting didn't match this man's courteousness.

He stepped back. "Good night ladies, have a safe trip."

Lorelei's blood raced as she commandeered the horse down the road, the Luna moon paving the way with silvery beams. It must be the moon that flustered her so. Why, the man acted as if he preferred to be as far away from her as possible. She berated herself for thinking him as anyone other than the town doctor.

****

Seth watched them until they completely faded into the curtain of darkness and he could no longer hear the wooden wheels clamor over the hard-packed earth. Turning towards the house, he rehashed Lorelei's words. *"I'd have to slaughter them if I did, and I'm afraid that*

26

just wouldn't do."

There could be no other reason than meaning she could not stand the thought of killing an animal. A smile stole across his face as he closed the door and returned to his study.

Relaxing back in the comfortable threadbare chair, he rested the medical volume on his lap. Miss Webster might appear hard-nosed and callous, but inside dwelled a soft, little kitten. She not only shied away from killing an animal, she had offered payment for a friend to receive medical help.

Seth found her generosity and compassion surprisingly touching. He'd had conflicting thoughts about her the day they had met. Now, they puzzled him more. Who was the woman who wore a mask of boldness, staunch perseverance and a scalding tongue, yet hid behind a veil of empathy and genuine caring?

Good Christ! Where the hell had that kind of gibberish come from? He had no proof she possessed any of those good qualities. Could only assume. And if he wanted to maintain the uneventful life he sought, had to sustain he corrected, he would have to stay far away from the friction-rousing woman.

"She's a trouble maker, an instigator," he said without much conviction. For deep inside he longed to be able to respond to her alluring charm. His mind pictured her sweet smile as she offered Fannie comfort and words of encouragement; her hair glistening like fine threads of gold and silver in the soft glow of the burning lamps; her appealing scent of lavender.

Stop it, you fool. You'll drive yourself insane if you let her get under your skin. He gripped the thick book, clenched his teeth in frustration, until sweat covered his face. He had fought the desire in the past. Lorelei Webster was no different. Could be no different.

He was dirt; the filthiest scum on the earth. He could not allow himself to forget his ugly sins for one moment.

He sprang from the chair and hurled the book across the room. It met the barrister bookcase with an ear-piercing crash. Glass splintered and flew. "Damn you, Father. Damn you to hell and back if you're not already there."

****

The last day of September brought a brisk chill to the air. The children, more than ready to call another end to their day, raced towards town, their books bobbing through the air like balloons and book straps flapping behind them as they darted.

Lorelei closed the schoolhouse door and surveyed the surrounding hills. The riot of bright reds, flaming oranges, and deep golds brought a smile to her face. Autumn was her favorite time of the year, closely followed by the beauty of spring. Deciding to walk the mile to town on such an invigorating day, she pulled her shawl tighter around her shoulders.

She inhaled the fresh crisp air, her feet springing in a jubilant gait. She would pick up the sugar she needed, then go pay the doctor. He lived at the very end of town so it would not be out of the way at all. And she owed him.

Inside Miller's general store, she ambled through the long aisles, inspecting various ribbons and material. Though she had no use for such a frivolous yard good, she reverently fingered a bolt of rich blue velvet. She didn't often loiter, but today seemed a perfect time to dedicate a few minutes to herself.

Turning to Charles Miller's monotone as he conversed with a customer, Lorelei eyed Andy Piedmont. The short man's muscles across his back bunched beneath his flannel shirt as he hefted a sack of flour onto the counter.

She had seen a few men in town yesterday, but they had gone out of their way to avoid eye contact. And she had been just as happy they had. She had not encountered any trouble from them in the past few days, and wanted to keep it that way.

Quietly retreating to the back of the store, she pretended to inspect the various hoes leaning against the wall. Eyeing the two men at the counter, she stepped back to go around a grain keg. Her knees collided with a warm solid form.

"Oh!" She swiveled around to see who she had almost trampled. Squatting down in front of several shovels was none other than Seth. With a hand braced against the wall, he shifted his feet to maintain his position. He looked none too pleased.

"I beg your pardon, Doctor Taylor. I didn't see anyone back here." She peered down at her full skirt blanketing his bent legs and felt her face flush. She took a hasty step back.

"I suggest from now on that you watch where you are going, Miss Webster. A person could get killed if they got in your way."

If at all possible, she knew her face flamed ten shades deeper. Would she ever give this man any other impression than she always caused havoc of some sort? Most likely not.

"Are you hiding back here too?"

At her question, his eyes went from questioning to smiling. His lips thinned as if he held back a laugh. "Actually, I was choosing a shovel to purchase. Are *you* hiding, Miss Webster?"

At his close scrutiny, she felt more self-conscious than ever before. And here she had thought she had made a better impression on him last night. What a complete fool.

"No, Dr. Taylor, I am not..." His dark eyes drilled into her. Accusing, even before she voiced her lie. She refused to add lying to her transgressions. She had enough of those without adding more. "Yes, I was. If you must know, I didn't want to confront Andy Piedmont." She lifted her chin, proud she had told the truth. So be it if he thought her a coward.

"I believe you have just ruined any chance of that, Miss Webster." He pushed against the wall and levered himself up.

"What?"

"He's coming this way with Charles," he whispered.

Lorelei's back stiffened of its own accord. *Oh no.* Surely Andy would know she had deliberately skulked in the back to avoid him. She would be the laughing stock for the entire town besides being the labeled busybody, neb-nose and whatever else.

She glanced at the back door, yet knew it was too late for a beeline exit. Tears clouded her vision as she thought of the humiliation she would suffer in a few seconds. It had been hard enough to hold her head up lately. Just wait until the others heard she had cowered in a corner from one of them.

Footsteps against the wide planks grew louder, nearer. Her knees shook, sweat beaded across her brow and her eyes filled.

"So, Miss Webster, you really think this one is better?"

Lorelei blinked back the tears and gaped at him. What in the blue blazes? In a flash, she realized his intent. Bless the man. She'd give him a big kiss if this worked. Well, maybe not. If she became *that* forward, he would elude her more than he already did.

"Definitely, Dr. Taylor. That shovel has your name on it." To her amazement, her voice did not squeak. With no idea which shovel he had referred to, she kept her hands at her sides. She watched the men come down the aisle. Her knees turned to water.

"Well, now, I didn't see ya come in Miss Lorelei," Charles said, scratching his bald head. "Couldn't figure out what in tarnation the commotion was back here. Ya wantin' a shovel, Doc?"

"Sure thing. And Miss Webster offered me advice as to which one would better suit."

"Humph! She's always got some kind of advice for somebody," Andy Piedmont scoffed, his mouth pulled in a satirical smirk.

"Sorry I disturbed you, Charles. I'm afraid I just about knocked over several of them while picking one out," Seth lied, avoiding Andy's statement as if he hadn't spoken.

"No problem, Doc. Just wanted to make sure ya was all right back here. Thought maybe ya'd clunked yur head or somethin'. Ya need any more help?"

"No, none at all. I believe I'll take this one." He picked up the broad pointed one and held it like staff. He turned his head toward her. "Thank you for your help, Miss Webster."

Her throat was so dry, all she could do was nod.

Charles nodded and smiled. "Good choice, Doc. It's the best one I've got. Ya goin' to do some gardenin'?" He retreated up the long aisle, talking over his shoulder in a raised voice.

"No, just weeding. But I might put in a few shade trees."

They all reached the counter and Charles tallied Andy's bill. "Put it on your account?"

"Yeah," Andy grunted as he hoisted the sack of flour over one shoulder. "I'll be back after awhile when you got the rest of the list put together." He gave one contemptible glance over his shoulder at her, then lumbered out the door.

Lorelei knew where he would be heading, did not doubt it for one minute. Straight to the saloon for his afternoon ration. She took her leave from the two men, walked to a nearby table and haphazardly leafed through the material. Out of the corner of her eye, she observed the doctor. She could not help herself.

He leaned the shovel against the counter, removed the tin lid from the glass jar on the counter and grabbed a handful of hard candy sticks. "Put these on my tab, too."

Charles chuckled, his thin shoulders bucking as he put the sticks into a small paper sack. "Sure thing. Ya sure like those sticks don't ya, Doc? Never saw anyone go through so many sticks of sugar. Your goin' be sweeter than an apple pie if ya don't watch out. The women will be after ya like they're starvin' for honey."

Seth smiled good-naturedly at Charles's jest, a pink hue staining his neck. Lorelei's pulse fluttered as she again found herself more than a bit affected by the man's devastating smile, the twinkling of his chocolate eyes. And to think, he even blushed. He was more bashful than she had thought.

"It'd take a lot more sugar than these few sticks to sweeten me up, Charles. I'm afraid the ladies will have to pick on somebody else. These are for my young patients." He grabbed the shovel and his brown bag, and turned in her direction.

Lorelei instantly glanced down and fingered an ugly drab calico. She felt her face redden. And heard him draw closer.

"Good day, Miss Webster. Thank you for your help. But might I make a suggestion?"

Baffled and more than leery at what his suggestion might be, she gazed upward. Gone was the smile. Would he expose her folly to Charles now that Andy had left?

Embarrassment surfaced. She couldn't utter a sound.

"That material is definitely not your color. I suggest something more vivid, bolder, maybe flamboyant." He kept a straight face, not a smidgeon of a smile, turned, and exited without even so much as a by-your-leave.

She felt as if her face had ignited. If he had worn just a fraction of a grin, she could have laughed at his teasing. But he had meant it as an insult. No denying it.

She raised her chin. So, he thought she needed clothes to match her overzealous personality, did he? He had let her know exactly what he thought of her. Well, so had the rest of the town, and that had not stopped her. His opinion would not change her stance, either. She would continue without his earnest support.

Then, why did she feel so disheartened?

CHAPTER FIVE

Seth elevated the barbell over his head with a grunt. Sweat dripped from his chin, coated every inch of his bare torso and arms and dampened the waistband of his old trousers.

"Forty," he huffed, holding his arms rigid and supported the bar without a single waver. Yet, his arms screamed for respite.

He inhaled before setting the heavy weight down with a thud. He had been faithful in the daily ritual for the past sixteen years. Since he had been sixteen, he had honed his body to become a sinewy mass of taut muscle, refusing to allow his body to resemble the gangly weakness it had once been. If he needed brawn, he would have it in reserve, ready and able to be tapped.

Unwelcomed visions of his father's fists, his sardonic smile, clouded his mind as he grabbed a towel off the chair. He swabbed his arms and chest then donned his shirt.

"Damn you, Lorelei, for making me remember." His curse ricocheted off the walls of the den he had converted to a weight room.

He stomped to the kitchen, poured a glass of water and gulped it down. He sighed as the liquid soothed his dry throat and aching lungs. His hand fisted around the glass as he, for the hundredth time this week, thought of the annoying woman.

She had not raised the men's hackles lately. All remained calm on the viable front, yet he knew it could change in an instant. Like a stick of dynamite with a slow-burning fuse.

Her mere presence as she passed him on the street or waved from the schoolyard when he journeyed to outlying homes forced him to recall a past he tried to bury as deep as the surrounding hidden mines.

Yes, simply seeing her set off a string of fireworks inside him that singed him to the core. He remembered the warmth of her fingers as she placed coins in his hand for Fannie's payment. *Maybe he should leave this town.* If the returning nightmares did not subside soon, he would have to think about that possibility.

The thought of turning his back on this community that counted on him, of his running away like a scared child, soured his stomach. He needed roots, needed to learn to block out the past. But it would not be easy.

With a firm resolve, Seth squared his shoulders and forced himself to focus on more pleasant things. He went to the window and surveyed his recent labor of love. Boxwood and junipers skirted the front of the house, their deep green bathed by the setting sun. Two thin red maples now graced the front lawn, adding a bit of hominess. In years to come, they would offer shade to his home. One he took pride in. He didn't want to leave.

He scowled at the very person he tried to push from his thoughts as she approached his home.

"Damn." And she had the Cooper boy by the hand. Even from this distance, he could see the reddened eyes of the teenager. He noted the boy's obvious reluctance to accompany his teacher, if his tight-lipped frown was any indication.

Without further thought to the annoying woman, Seth strode to the front door, intent on treating the youngster if need be. He certainly did not have to drum up business. Not with Lorelei Webster around. As much as he wanted to avoid her, he smiled.

Seth opened the door as the two trod up the porch steps. "Well, hello," he said, hoping his greeting would belie his restless feelings. He would rather meet a snake than confront Lorelei right now. He needed to push her and the memories she stirred up out of his mind.

"Good evening, Doctor Taylor. Might you have a few minutes? We need some professional advice." Lorelei's smile beamed as sunny as he had ever seen it. Her eyes appeared bluer; her hair shimmered in the sun's soft rays. What would that hair look like if she let it hang down? Would her high cheek bones be as prominent?

Jamie shuffled from one foot to the other and stared at his shoes as if reluctant or embarrassed. Seth's heart warmed.

What was she involved with now? He wanted to lead a sedate life, needed to avoid hassles so the past would lay dormant.

"Certainly. Please come in. How are you Jamie? It is *Jamie*, isn't it?" He'd often seen the boy working the Coopers' fields.

Jamie shuffled once more before lifting his head. His eyes were rimmed in red, sorrowful yet cautious, and stained with embarrassment. "Yes, sir. I'm Jamie Cooper."

Seth smiled and extended a hand, hoping to allay the boy's anxieties. "It's nice to finally meet you, Jamie."

Exuberance flashed across the boy's face. It vanished just as quickly. In its place lurked a dismayed, faraway look no young man should bear. Yet, Seth understood that look. It had stared at him from the mirror a thousand times when he had been Jamie's age. Only, his own reflection had held more self-loathing.

Jamie let go of Lorelei's hand and took Seth's outstretched one in a firm grip. The youngster swallowed as if a large ball of cotton had wedged itself in his throat. An unsettling feeling crept through Seth as he pumped the boy's hand.

Seth pulled away and held the door. "Please, come in."

For all Jamie's woeful expressions, he stepped back to allow Lorelei to pass. Seth smiled at the boy's good manners.

Once they were sitting comfortably in the living room, Seth decided he better come right to the point. If Jamie needed his advice, he would offer what he could. But he would not entertain Miss Webster all evening. The town would most likely find out about it and stone his house to ruins.

"What can I do for you two?"

Lorelei sat up straighter, flashing a quick glance at Jamie. Jamie's eyes seem to plead with his teacher before they sought the floor for escape.

"Jamie was thrown out of his house this afternoon."

Rather than explaining further, she left it at that. Did she expect him to take in Jamie? He hadn't handled his own youth well, how could he do any better for the boy?

"I fail to see what that has to do with me, Miss Webster. I'm a doctor. I heal, not patch up family arguments."

His words sounded curt, harsh, even to his ears. He could imagine how they sounded to the booted-out young man. He cringed at his hasty comeback. He knew all too well what it had been like to hang his head in shame, to not be wanted by a father who...

His insides shook as he battled away the horror. Damn, she had done it again. Made him remember. His temper flared and he struggled to hold back a sizzling expletive. He clenched his teeth, fisted his hands to squelch the anger.

Her eyes widened. He had not thought she would be shocked at anything anyone said or did. And he regretted his words.

Her shoulders slumped, but she raised that pert little chin. "Yes, I understand that, Doctor Taylor, but we're here because of the reason *why* he was kicked out."

Again she left her words hanging. Pulling explanations out of her was harder than pulling out a loose but obstinate tooth.

"Come to the point, Miss Webster. I'm not following this conversation."

Jamie, hands clasped, stared at the floor.

She inhaled as if needing extra air in her lungs. He doubted the hot bag of wind she blew in town ever lacked for a refill.

"Jamie wet the bed again last night."

Stunned by her remark, he eyed Jamie's bowed head, the quivering shoulders. More than likely, Jamie expected him to laugh. He could well imagine the boy's shame.

"I see. You think Jamie might have a medical problem?"

"No, you don't see at all," she informed him. "It's not Jamie's fault. He's told me that he doesn't usually have a problem. It only happens when his father comes home drunk. If you had a father as mean and contemptible as his when he's drunk, you'd realize Jamie's bed wetting is due to nerves. And he can't go home until he promises not to...have another accident again."

Seth scrutinized Lorelei. His innards twisted violently as flashbacks of exactly what kind of father he'd had stormed his mind. The air suddenly turned heavy, hotter as if a blast from the wood stove swept

36

the room. He found his hands mirroring Jamie's shoulders. He did not like it one bit.

Pull yourself together, man. Think of Jamie. He needs you. As always his potent urge to help overrode his mind.

"His father is abusing him as much as if he'd beaten him. It's not fair. It's not right." Her hot-tempered declaration should've reinforced her hell-fire attitude. Instead, her strong conviction to right the world tempered Seth's rattled mind.

Despite his better judgment, he smiled. "There's no fair or right about it, Miss Webster. Only facts. And the fact is, no matter how much Jamie can't tolerate his drinking, or how much he frightens him, he's not going to change him. And neither are we."

She looked crestfallen as her shoulders slumped. Jamie sat with a wide-eyed stare.

"What is it son?" He wished he could turn away from this hopeless situation.

"I ain't scared of him," he mumbled, fixing his gaze on the far wall, his chin lifting in a good attempt at bravery.

"I am not afraid of him," Lorelei quickly corrected.

"Yeah, that's what I said," Jamie answered, his focus glued to across the room.

Seth eyed the boy. "Of course, you're not. I worded that poorly. Forgive me." The boy seemed intent on each one of his words, though he ogled the same focal point on the wall.

"What is it you feel when he comes home from the saloon?"

Jamie's shoulders stiffened visibly and his eyes finally shifted to him. They held eye contact as Jamie's mouth trembled. "I wish he'd just go somewhere else and sleep it off."

The implication of Jamie's words hung in the air like a tangible force. Clearly, an inebriated Miles Cooper did not treat his family well. The tall man had a barrel-chest like a stiff bag of hard grain, and his biceps resembled ham-hocks. His wrath would be one to reckon with.

"Can you and your family just pretend to be asleep and avoid him when comes home that way?" Seth knew how hard that was to do. He felt his collar dampen at remembering the sounds of stumbles followed by profanity, furniture being overturned and clattering to the floor. Of course *his* father, more often than not, had not had to be drunk to dole out his viciousness.

"Sometimes." Jamie's forlorn reply erased Seth's reminiscence. He needed to deal with Jamie's problem, could entomb his own later.

"I know what I do when I want to block out something that I don't want to think about." Oh, he sounded so on top of things. Yeah, he was really on top. *If they only knew the truth.*

"W...what do you do?" Jamie leaned slightly forward, his eyes full of inquisitiveness. Hope.

Would his tactics be successful for Jamie? They had worked to block out thinking about what was taking place. He would not divulge that they failed more than not. And unfortunately, the same plan did not work on nagging memories any longer.

Seth leaned forward and rested his forearms on his thighs. His eyes met the boy's eager ones. "I force myself to think of something wonderful. Something I really care about or love to do. I concentrate so hard that it blocks out what's happening." Seth almost laughed at his words. How easy it sounded. What a laugh.

"I...I tried that. Didn't help." His eyes lost their luster.

"Then you didn't try hard enough." He glanced at Lorelei as she eyed Jamie. Her doubtful eyes shifted to him, then returned to the boy. And wonders above, she remained silent.

"Jamie, listen to me. You have to form a picture in your mind, not just think. You have to let yourself see that picture, a vivid picture. Let yourself feel the feelings that you would feel when you put yourself there. Immerse yourself in it."

Jamie looked baffled so he tried another method. "I had a dog, Buster, when I was your age. How old are you?"

"I'm thirteen, sir."

"Yes, just about your age. Anyway, Buster was my best friend. He was big and black with long ears and a long pointed tail. I could tell him anything and he'd listen and, I believe, he understood. We went everywhere together. So—" he chose his words carefully to tell only the tip of the iceberg, "when my father came home angry or drunk, I thought about Buster."

The boy didn't blink, just waited for him to give him that one thread to hang onto. And Seth longed to give it. He avoided looking at Lorelei.

"I want you to close your eyes and picture what I'm describing. Try to visualize what I am seeing and *feeling*." Jamie closed his eyes and Seth could feel the boy's anticipation.

"Buster and I are running through the half-grown wheat fields, free like two birds, without any rules, without anyone else in the world." Seth glanced at Lorelei. Her eyes were shut as if she too wanted to see. He smiled at how relaxed she looked. A far cry from moments ago.

"I'm running, running fast, barefoot and shirt sleeves rolled up. The afternoon breeze feels cool as it rushes across my face, brushes my bare arms, yet the sun shines bright overhead. Out ahead, I see Buster's ears flopping and flapping as the big black dog bounds up and down through the tall golden fans. His tail looks like a big black stick wagging and waving just above the swaying wheat as he leaps farther ahead. He barks and I run faster, knowing he's telling me to stop lagging and catch up.

"As my feet hit the earth harder, I smell the freshness of the wheat, the rich fertile soil. I feel the warmth of the sunshine as it surrounds me. I feel alive, healthy, good and happy. Just me and my dog. I race faster to catch him. And when I do, I wrestle him to the ground and give him a bear hug for being my friend. And he returns that friendship with big, slobbery kisses all over my face."

Seth paused a moment, content to see both of them entranced, their eyes closed, listening and waiting. Oblivious as to what his hand was doing. "Now open your eyes."

In unison they sat up straighter and opened their eyes. Jamie's eyes immediately went to Seth's hand. Lorelei's followed suit a fraction of a second later.

"What are you doing?" Jamie looked perplexed by Seth's thumping on the table with his knuckle.

Seth smiled. It had worked. He hoped Jamie had something meaningful so he could immerse himself in its fanciful picture.

"When I took you to the wheat fields, did you hear me tapping?" Seth watched as comprehension sunk in. The boy's eyes grew enormous as a smile lit his face. A sly glance toward Lorelei said she, too, realized what he had done.

"When did you start tapping?" Lorelei asked.

"Right after I started telling you what I felt. Neither of you heard it?"

They both shook their heads. Seth peered at Jamie. "If you can not only think about something that really means a great deal to you, but actually form that picture as life-like as you can, the rest of the world will fade. At least, most of the time. Sometimes, nothing helps, except to tell yourself another day will dawn, and with it, there's hope. Hope for a better day."

Jamie leaned back as if in deep thought. Seth watched a myriad of emotions cross his face. So disjointed, he could not read them. He had hoped to see a bit of elation, some sign that Jamie felt more confident in facing his father's wrath.

He glanced at Lorelei. Her eyes fairly shone with gratitude. "That was quite remarkable how you brought us into the story with you. You're a very good story teller, Doctor Taylor."

Her radiant smile sent his pulse bounding in his throat. As much as he knew, she or any other woman was forbidden to him, he still yearned to lose himself in the blue depths of her eyes. His loins grew heavy. Over the years, he had mastered the ability to resist, so he gathered his wits and pushed all fantasies away.

"Thank you. I just hope it offers Jamie a way to handle his situation better." He turned his attention to boy who still looked more than skeptical. Well, he had tried, and it had been the only suggestion he had, at the moment.

"Do you think it might help?"

"I dunno," he shrugged his small shoulders.

"I do not, or don't know," Lorelei corrected. Jamie nodded.

"All you can do is try it next time, son." Seth suspected Jamie questioned if it would work. He hadn't instilled the positive attitude he'd hoped for. "If it works, you can breathe easier. And hopefully you won't we…have another accident. Or maybe you can think of a better way to distract your thoughts."

"Maybe." The discouraged ring in his voice twisted in Seth's chest like a tight rope. He longed to reach out, tell him to keep his chin up.

He could not afford to get in over his head. He had done his part. He had talked, even admitted his father had come home drunk. That was as far as he could extend his involvement, far more than he had ever confided in anyone. If he allowed himself to give more, Miss Webster would have more on her hands than Jamie wetting the bed.

He lived with knowing he was dirt under people's feet. He did not need to recall the graphic memories. Even for Jamie.

CHAPTER SIX

Over the next week Seth lost more sleep than he had in his entire career. He had delivered Mrs. Ellis's tiny girl who had refused to leave the comfort of her mama's womb until three a.m.

After a drifter had been shot at the saloon, Seth worked through two nights repacking the non-stop hemorrhaging of the chest wound. Despite his skill and effort, the loner had succumbed.

Now, his heavy footsteps thudded across his porch. For forty-eight hours he had tended Blair Keeper after he had fallen down an abandoned mine shaft. To Seth's dismay, he had to perform a below-knee amputation to Blair's mangled right leg.

Opening the door to his house, he failed to appreciate the unusually warm and sunny October afternoon.

"Bed, just give me a bed." Depositing his black bag and coat on the sideboard, he trudged to his bedroom. He hit the mattress full-force, face down, and collapsed in exhaustion.

****

A pounding jarred Seth from deep slumber. He blinked to clear his sand-filled eyes, to orient himself. Moonlight beamed passed the open curtains of the otherwise dark room.

"Doc, Doc, you in there? Come quick, Doc."

Seth literally flew out of bed at a man's frantic voice.

"Christ, now what," Seth mumbled as his feet hit the floor. Light-headedness had him wheeling. He staggered to the dresser, splashed water over his face and wiped it as he dashed down the hallway and through the unlit living room.

Silhouetted by moonbeams, a man stood in the open doorway, cradling a small adult or child in his arms. Two others stood behind him. Acutely recognizing disaster, Seth's fogginess vanished as adrenaline pumped through his veins.

Without further hesitation, Seth lit two oil lamps on the closest table. Muted light filled the room. "Follow me," he said, grabbing a lamp in one hand, his bag in the other.

In the infirmary, he set the lamp and bag down and lit three more lamps.

"Lay him on the table. What happened?" he asked, grabbing his stethoscope from his bag and finally peered at his patient.

Seth's throat constricted, cold knotted in his stomach.

Jamie Cooper.

He scowled at the lifeless, pale youngster as Fred Harper deposited the sodden-clothed boy on the padded exam table.

Usually, he prided himself for his steeled composure in an emergency. Yet he shuddered with trepidation; it nearly rocked him from his feet. *No, not Jamie!*

Taking two quick steps to Jamie's side, he felt for a carotid pulse. Slow and thready. *An ounce of hope, thank God.* The boy's respirations were shallow, barely evident. He sighed in relief, his hands trembling against the stethoscope as he auscultated the lungs. Rhonchi and harsh rales throughout both lungs indicated he had swallowed quite a bit of water.

"What happened?" he barked, heedless of his curt impatience. A pasty duskiness hued the boy's face. As the youngster labored to exhale, wheezing and crackles filled the still room.

Seth rolled Jamie over so his head and shoulders hung over the table and began pushing against the lungs.

"I asked what the hell happened. Anyone got a tongue?" He diligently worked on saving the boy and glanced up.

Tom Burdock and Stanley Freemont looked too horrified to speak. Fred shifted his feet, stared at Jamie, but answered.

"We was down by the river. Had...somethin' we needed to talk over. We heard a splash, but we couldn't see nothin'. Then Jamie's dog started in barkin' and we knowed somethin' was wrong. That dang flea bag don't go in the water no how, but he sure was flustered. Runnin' circles he was along the bank."

Continuing his ministration, Seth looked up to see Fred's hands twisting together non-stop, eyes fixed on Jamie. Fred's usual rosy cheeks were as ashen as Jamie's.

"He gonna be all right, Doc?"

Jamie gasped and choked. A small gush of water streamed from his mouth onto the floor; his shoulders shook from the effort. Still unconscious, skin like ice, yet he failed to shiver from the sodden clothes. But he breathed on his own.

A knot big as a fist lodged in Seth's chest. "I don't honestly know, Fred. But I'll do everything humanly possible that I can. Go on." Seth focused on manipulating the child's back.

"We ran over to where the dog was yappin' thinking maybe Jamie had jist gone for a late night swim. Sure didn't think it was too smart. Not with it being so cold. Then we seen the back of his shirt, white as snow it was, shining in the moonlight. Like he was jist floatin'."

Seth heard Fred's feet shuffle. Jamie coughed feebly and gagged. Seth wiped the phlegm and water from the boy's face, then again kneaded his back.

"We waited to see if he'd start swimmin', but he didn't do nothin'. We yelled, but he still didn't do nothin'. That's when Stanley jumped in and pulled him out."

Seth glanced at Stanley, for the first time noticing the man's dripping clothes, his shoulders shaking as he shivered. Fred brushed his face with a trembling hand. "Damnedest thing, Doc, Jamie's like an otter in the water. I've seen him swim with nary a struggle, even when floodin' turned the current wild."

Eeriness crept over Seth at Fred's words. Had Jamie deliberately tried to drown himself? Chilling fear sent goose bumps over him at the thought. No, he was jumping to conclusions.

"Think he hit his head, Doc?" Stanley asked.

Considering the possibility, Seth turned Jamie's limp head and inspected it. No bruising, swelling bump, cuts, or scrapes.

Damn. Had the boy tried to end his life? Because of his father's tirades and boozing? Seth felt a tug on his heartstrings. They were more kindred spirits than he'd realized. But Jamie was stronger. Seth had contemplated suicide when he had been Jamie's age. But he had chickened out. Yes, Jamie was stronger, if indeed, he read the writing on the wall correctly.

"It's possible. Or maybe he got a cramp." He tried to act nonchalant in his fabrication.

Again Seth auscultated Jamie's lungs. They sounded better, yet too many rales and rhonchi rattled throughout the lobes. He was not out of the woods by a long shot. He slid the child back so his cheek rested against the table and turned to Stanley.

"You did a wonderful thing tonight, Stanley, and should be proud of your good deed. But you better go home and get into dry clothes before I have to treat you for pneumonia."

Stanley quivered and glanced at the floor as if embarrassed by Seth's praise. "Ain't no good deed, Doc. Just did what any God believin' man would do for anybody. I just hope he's okay. He don't look so good. Ya think he's got any chance?"

Seth rolled the unconscious boy over and began divesting him of the wet clothes. His skin was clammy as death.

"I hope so, Stanley. I'll get him dry and warm and try to get some medicine down him. Then pray. You men better get home. You're wet as well, Fred." He reached for a towel on the nearby stand and swabbed the boy's hair, bare chest and arms.

"One of you needs to stop at the Coopers to tell them."

"Sure thing, Doc," Fred said as he helped Seth pull down the soggy trousers. "I'll have Johanna come right away."

"Thanks." Seth dried the thin legs. "Tom, before you leave, hand me that blanket on the trunk. And one of you grab the pillow on the cot and put it on top of the other pillow on the bed. He'll need two to elevate him so he can breathe easier."

Tom retrieved the woolen blanket, unfolded it and laid it over the boy. Fred fetched the pillow.

Seth tucked the blanket around Jamie, lifted him, and carried him to the bed at the far wall. Gently setting his charge on the thin mattress, he arranged the pillows so Jamie lay in a semi-reclining position. Jamie's breathing remained shallow, though he labored with each small breath.

"Someone should tell Miss Webster. She's pretty close to him. I'm sure she'll want to know."

If the room had been silent before, it now turned quiet as a tomb. Seth glanced at the three. They stood statue-like, each wearing a mortified expression.

"She has the right to know." He went to the counter, opened the cupboard and retrieved the antibiotics he needed to get into Jamie as soon as possible.

Fred's Adam's apple bobbed up then down as if he'd swallowed a piece of coal. "Maybe she does. But I ain't a-goin' to her place. She's the reason we was talkin' out at the river."

Seth's hand froze as he surveyed each of them. They looked like children caught smoking corn silk out behind the barn.

"What's so important, or should I ask, what's so *secretive* about Miss Webster that you had a meeting by the river?"

Fred dug the toe of his boot into the carpet and stared at it. "She's been a thorn in our asses since she came a year ago. We ain't had no trouble with our womenfolk before she come. Now, she fills their heads with all sorts of ideas about their rights. Two days ago, she told my Eleanor how to make sure she didn't beget another kid. Can you believe that? I say, if'n I want to put another brat in her belly, then by God I have *that* right. No woman's a-gonna tell me different."

Seth almost laughed as he thought of how Miss Webster had stirred up more trouble. From protecting children, to fetching help for an injured wife, to counseling in pregnancy prevention, she stuck her unwanted snoot into anyone's affairs. The woman, most assuredly, sought a road to self-destruction.

"What were you men planning to do? Tar and feather her?" Mixing the decoction in a beaker, he forced himself not to smile. These men were infuriated enough, he need not mock them.

Tom Burdock snorted. "She be a good teacher, we don't deny that. She teaches our children real good. But we don't need her sticking her nose into every part of our lives. She ought to get herself a man. A man would take that piss and vinegar out of her. Yeah, that's what she needs. Someone to put her in her place."

Seth almost shuddered at the thought of any man leg-shackled to the willful woman. She'd most likely walk all over the poor soul, or send him to any early grave. Yet, he had seen her compassionate side with Fannie. How she'd sought help to relieve Jamie's frustrations. She merely approached things the wrong way.

She'd humiliated Tom at the saloon, and Tom harbored a grudge a mile wide. He couldn't blame them. But he didn't like them ganging up against her. Not if they meant her harm.

"Yeah, and we can get another teacher just as good," Fred added. His vehement words jarred Seth's further reflections.

"Another teacher?" Seth went to the oak cabinet in the corner and retrieved an extract of elecampane. If he could get it down Jamie it would help him expectorate some of the phlegm and water in his lungs. He'd add a bit of brandy to stimulate the child's heart. He reached for the aconite to allay the mounting fever sure to come, and the few items to make a poultice.

"Yep," Fred volunteered. "If we find us another, we won't need her. We'll advertize in the Cheyenne paper. Then she won't have reason to stay. Out she'll go, long nose and big mouth, too."

She had stuck her nose in too deep this time, Seth thought. Yet, as he pictured her small nose and her gentle smile, he formed an all together different picture of Miss Webster. *Damn.*

"It might not be that simple, Fred. I understand it took a long time to find Miss Webster."

"Yep, you're right, Doc. It did. But we'll be awaitin', no matter how long it takes."

Seth wanted to argue the point and found it surprising that he would defend Lorelei. He thought better of pursuing the issue and decided he best pay attention to Jamie.

"I need to get this medicine down Jamie and a poultice applied. No reason for you men to stay." Seth did not have the heart to ask the shivering Stanley to go to Lorelei's and wondered if he held her in such contempt as the other two.

"Doc, after I get out of these wet clothes, I'll go by Miss Webster's. It ain't far." Seth thought of the small three rooms attached the schoolhouse.

"Thanks, Stanley. Thank you all for helping."

47

****

An hour later, Seth sat by Jamie's side watching the uneven breathing as he sponged the child's limbs with witch hazel. Beads of sweat ran down his sunken cheeks from weakness and an inevitable fever. Gray semi-circles on his lower eyelids marred his youthful face. An unhealthy pallor clung to his skin.

Johanna Cooper had rushed in, a genuine mother's concern causing hysteria. Once he had assured her all was being done, that presently Jamie held his own, and that he would stay by his side, she calmed and had returned to her two daughters left alone. Miles, as usual, was not home.

Seth took a sip of brandy, having poured himself a jigger as well as adding some to Jamie's decoction. He had been able to trickle a fair amount down the boy's throat. Though Jamie had coughed from its bite, he had not awakened.

Relaxing in the slatted-back chair he had positioned by the bedside, Seth's eyes closed in fatigue. The hours of sleep he had obtained hadn't been nearly enough. Especially after being drained from Jamie's ordeal. He let slumber take hold.

****

Lorelei knocked several times before she peeked through the window at the steady glow of the oil lamp in the living room. When Doctor Taylor did not answer, her worst fears leaped upon her. Had Jamie died? Had Seth gone to console the family? *No! No, dear God in Heaven, don't let it be.*

She returned to the door, her hand shaking as she lifted the latch and pushed the portal open. She should call out, yet the tightness in her throat prevented her uttering more than a squeak. Heart pounding in her ears, she walked to the infirmary. The door stood open. Witch hazel stung her nose as she hesitantly peered in. Anticipating Jamie lying under a head to foot covering, she held her breath, almost afraid to look.

Jamie lay on the bed, snuggled under a mound of woolen blankets drawn up to his chin. Seth, head drooped, his chin nearly resting on his chest, slept in a chair. Lorelei clutched the door casing as dizziness swept over her, so great was her relief. Tears trickled down her cheeks.

She heard Jamie's harsh breathing, first alarmed by its wheezing; but then, more than thankful he lived. Gingerly, she crossed the room to reassure her he wasn't in distress. At his side, she fixated on the slow up-and-down movement of his chest under the blankets. She glanced at his face.

"Oh, Jamie," she whispered as a deluge of tears let loose. His skin looked like wax. She fought to hold back a whimper. An iron fist seemed to squeeze her chest.

Why had he been swimming at night in the cold river? The answer that had materialized in her mind at Stanley's recounting again rose up like a lamentable demon from hell.

If Jamie had tried to commit suicide, it was Miles Cooper's fault. Him and his drinking, the suspected beatings of his wife, his sharp and foul scolding of his children, his humiliating mocking of Jamie at every turn. Miles Cooper didn't deserve the family he had. Not by any stretch of the imagination.

Lorelei fisted her hands until her nails dug into her palms. She didn't feel the intensity. But she did feel the agonizing pain Jamie must have felt; so desperate to want to end his precious life. Outrage threatened to make her head explode.

"Someday you'll get your just rewards, Miles. And I pray it's soon." When Seth stirred, she started and realized she'd spat the words through clenched teeth. With eyes closed, he stretched his long legs and leaned his head against the slats.

He looked uncomfortable and exhausted with his broad shoulders slumped; dark circles under his eyelids marred his handsome face. A shaft of wavy hair lay across his forehead to make him look younger, almost vulnerable.

Careful not to wake him, she removed the tipped glass from between his fingers and laid it on the nearby table. She eyed a pillow and quilt stacked on a cot across the room.

Tip-toeing, she fetched them and returned to his side. Cautiously, she eased the pillow behind his head, and then covered him with the soft quilt. Her blood heated as her hand brushed his well-muscled outstretched thigh.

She scolded herself for being so affected by a man who could barely tolerate her. She knew by the way he looked at her, how he tried to avoid her except when he made a common-courtesy greeting. He thought her far too imprudent for his liking.

Maybe she did flirt a bit with Michael and enjoyed his attention. Sometimes. But she had never been interested in the opposite sex for more than needing their brawn, or lending support in whatever stand she pursued at that moment. Now, she felt drawn to a man who was as blind as a bat to her charms. Most likely, he did not think she had any. Disheartened, she shook her head at the futility of her thoughts.

CHAPTER SEVEN

Jamie's whimpering woke Seth with a start. In his sleep, the child thrashed his head back and forth and mumbled garble.

Seth leaned over and felt the boy's forehead. Thank God, the raging fever had lessened to low grade. He should not have imbibed those few sips of brandy, not as tired as he had been.

Disgusted, he rose to stretch his cramped muscles. And halted when a pillow and quilt fell to the floor. *What the hell?*

He scanned the room; felt his heart flutter as he stared at Lorelei Webster. She lay on the cot, curled on her side, her feet tucked beneath her blue dress. Her arm pillowed her head while her high-top button shoes rested on the floor.

She looked so peaceful, so innocent without the lines of indignation or fire-breathing reprimand. One pretty lady.

Foolishly, he took a moment to appreciate her beauty. He may not want a relationship with the hell-fired woman, yet again found himself fascinated with her hair. Tied with a blue ribbon at her nape, it hung almost to her waist. He liked it down; itched to run his fingers through the silky locks. His obsession had to stop. *She can never be anything to you and you know it.*

He marched to the wash basin, then kept busy by sponging Jamie and forced more medicine down. Yet, he found himself stealing glances at the sleeping beauty. Felt a pull deep inside.

****

Morning came with its sunlight beaming through the windows. Lorelei stirred and felt the thin canvas stretch beneath her. Her eyes

51

flew open. Last night's episode rushed back.

She flung her feet over the side and scanned the room. No Seth. Going to the bedside, she sighed in relief at seeing a tinge of pink had returned to Jamie's cheeks.

"His fever stayed low most of the night," Seth said as he walked through the doorway. She turned at his uplifting words and the tantalizing smell of coffee.

A mug in hand, wearing the rumpled clothing from the night before, he ambled to her side. "If the congestion lessens by tomorrow, he just might be out of the woods."

Amazing. Even disheveled, he looked good; no, much better than *good.* With the top three buttons of his shirt undone and shirt sleeves rolled to his elbows, she feasted on the brown curly mat on his chest, the straighter hairs on his muscular forearms. He was one solid mass of taut muscle. Her heart flitted and her cheeks flushed as if she'd slugged down that hot coffee.

"Do you really think he'll make it?" She brushed back a few wisps of hair that clung to her cheek. How rumpled *she* must look.

It didn't matter, she thought with more dismay than she should. She could be wearing a queen's gown and a hairdo styled to perfection and it wouldn't faze him.

"The men got to him just in time. I have high hopes he'll mend readily. Would you like some coffee?"

"Ah…yes, please. But I can get it."

"There's sugar on the counter and milk in the ice box."

"Thank you." Lorelei couldn't get out of the room fast enough. That partially unbuttoned shirt did things to her insides she'd never experienced before. Good Lord above but she could swear a bird was twittering and flittering within her chest.

Returning to the infirmary, Lorelei prayed her shaky hands wouldn't spill her coffee. The few minutes it took to pour a cup, smooth down the wrinkles of her dress, finger-comb her hair and refasten her dress at her neck hadn't stopped the thrumming.

She watched Seth sponge Jamie's face. The muscles across his back flexed under his shirt as he leaned from the chair. She had never noticed Michael's bunch and cord like that. If she had, her pulse had never responded as is it did now.

"Jamie, open your eyes; it's Doctor Taylor."

Jamie eyelids twitched, his mouth contorted in various shapes as if he resisted waking up.

Lorelei set her cup on the small stand, crossed the room, and squatted down at the bedside. Almost bumping Seth's knees, she shuffled to allow more space between them. He didn't seem to notice. What had she expected?

"Jamie, it's Miss Webster. I'm here with Doctor Taylor." Lorelei laid her hand on Jamie's forearm and rubbed it gently. "Jamie, please wake up so we know you're all right, sweetheart. We want that very much. I love you, and want you well."

Seth scrutinized Lorelei's hand on the child's arm. Her sincerity, just as he had witnessed with Fannie, rocked him. Again. Through to his core. Maybe because it seemed so out of character for her...as to what he had originally thought.

Her soft words of genuine love choked his throat as if he was a turkey with gravel lodged in its gullet. If he didn't watch himself, he'd be under this witch's spell in a minute. Along with all her troublesome shenanigans.

Jamie's eyes fluttered opened. He blinked several times, then wet his lips with his tongue. "Thirsty." He gave a weak cough.

"Oh, Jamie, Thank God." One, then two tears streaked down her cheeks. Her quivering lips smiled before she pressed them together as if holding back a heart-felt sob.

Seth felt his eyes tear at the boy's response. Felt a quaver not only at Jamie's impendent recovery, but equally at his reactions to Lorelei. He longed to embrace her, hug her tightly as elation swept through him. He vacated the chair, strode across the room and filled a glass with water. He blinked several times to clear his vision and to quell his strange reaction toward Lorelei. Returning to Jamie, he sat on the bedside, supported the boy's shoulders, and offered him a few sips.

Jamie rested his head back down, a fearful look in his eyes. "Guess I'm in trouble."

"Oh, no, sweetheart, you're not." Lorelei again touched the boy's arm. "Everyone will be thankful that you're safe. Don't think about anything but getting well. Do you hear me?"

His thin mouth curved up slightly. "Yes…ma'am. Thank you…thank you…both." His eyelids drooped.

Seth patted the boy's shoulder. "You're welcome. Go back to sleep now. We'll be right here if you need anything."

Jamie closed his eyes as if drained from the slight exertion. Seth tilted his head, indicating he wanted Lorelei to follow. They went to the corner and gathered their cups.

"I have a feeling he wasn't just swimming," he informed Lorelei, expecting her to gasp.

Instead, with her mouth a grim line, she nodded. "I agree."

He should have known she was too bright for her own britches, and too open-minded to let the incident ruffle her feathers.

"He'll need a day or two to rest before one of us approaches the subject. But it must be dealt with. Most likely, he's already realized that's not the answer and won't try it again."

She looked appalled. "I know Jamie. If he tried it once, he *may* try it again. I'll talk to him."

"Good. Thank you." He didn't believe her about Jamie trying it again. The boy was smart. Surely, he would see it wasn't the solution. He felt certain of it. He wondered if the relief he felt was due to the fact that he wouldn't have to deal with the situation, or that Lorelei would be leaving soon, and he could get on with his normal life.

"I need to go home and freshen up. But when I return later, I'll sit with Jamie so you can sleep. You must have been up half the night. On Saturdays, I usually only clean and that can wait."

Seth preferred she not come back at all. But that would be asking too much. He needed to gather his thoughts, to regain his perspective on his life. How in the holy hell would he find sleep with her sashaying those curved hips around his house?

He eyed her hair. The gentle waves curled under at the ends and hung half way down to her tiny waist. That strong need to feather his fingers through its shimmering softness invaded his senses until he thought he might go mad. He swallowed. *Dammit to hell and back.* How could he tell her not to visit Jamie?

"That would be fine, Miss Webster."

****

"Later" came in about four hours. Lorelei Webster arrived at his door with biscuits and chicken soup in a wicker basket. For Jamie's recuperation she had said, while she smiled ever so sweetly, assuring him there was ample for him too, if he liked.

Seth couldn't flee fast enough.

She spelled disaster. Tempted him way too much. Entering the safe haven of his bedroom, he wondered why out of all the women in the world he might have been tempted by—if he deserved a good, sensible one—would he fall prey to Lorelei Webster. They were as opposite as night and day. Did opposites really attract?

As his eyelids turned heavy, he welcomed sleep. Anything to stop thinking about her. Anything to stop him from remembering his past. And Miss Lorelei Webster conjured up that past every time she made him feel the attraction to her.

"Damn her soul."

****

"Miles is furious, Lorelei. He won't come and see Jamie." Johanna hung her head in despair.

Lorelei had tip-toed through Seth's home after he had gone to his room. She had been amazed how neat and clean he kept everything. She had not heard of anyone cleaning for him. The entire house was well-furnished with expensive pieces of furniture, Aubusson carpets, and decorated in soft browns and blues giving it an elegant, yet cozy atmosphere. In the hall, she had noted the cabinet displaying numerous hand guns and rifles.

Now, she felt like taking one to shoot Miles Cooper. He would not visit to assure himself of his son's health? The man was insane. She wished she could pack up Johanna, Jamie, and the two girls and send them to far corners unknown.

"Why does he turn his back on Jamie, Johanna? I don't understand." She kept her voice down so as not to have it carry across the room to where the three siblings chatted.

Johanna remained silent, watching her daughters sitting cross-legged on the bed. It was nice to see the three so loving. Jamie didn't get any of that from Miles. And Johanna, as much as she liked her, lacked the fortitude to offer any extra affection to Jamie. Most likely, she feared Miles would take it out on her.

"He's hard on him. Ever since…Jamie stood up to him."

"What do you mean?" She'd always known Jamie possessed spunk. *Good for you, Jamie.*

"Oh, it was nothing." She shrugged as if she tried to convince herself of her own words. "One night, awhile back, cause he don't do it no more much, Miles got rough with me. He'd been drinking and didn't mean it. But Jamie came in and fought him. Miles, he's not forgot that night, or forgiven Jamie for it."

Lorelei knew Johanna lied through her teeth. There was no way on God's green acres anyone could convince her that Miles did not beat her, or the children. Johanna merely hid the bruises and masked the pain in her eyes better than some.

"He should've been proud that Jamie tried to protect you." *Were you, Johanna? Are you at least proud of your son, or have you shied away too, defeated by your husband's cruel hand?*

"He doesn't see it that way. Never will." Her gaze fell to the floor, obviously avoiding eye contact.

"Mama," Jessica half-shouted, half-whispered, drawing their attention across the room. The five-year-old scooted off the bed, her short, chubby legs propelling her toward them. Grabbing a handful of Johanna's skirt in her tiny fist, the blue-eyed, carrot-top stared upward with a pout. "Mama, Jamie fell asleep while I was talking to him. Is he still so very sick?"

Johanna squatted down and lifted the petite child into her arms. "No, pumpkin, he's almost better. The doctor said he'll be much better by tomorrow, and after a couple more days of rest he'll be able to come home. He's just all tuckered out, so we have to let him sleep as much as he wants so he can come home. You want him to come home soon, don't you?"

"Oh, yes, Mama! Missy does, too. She cries at night cause she misses him. Then…I cry too, cause I miss him tucking me in, and pinching my nose and calling me 'little carrot'."

Lorelei turned from mother and child at the child's words. *How*

56

wonderful to have someone love you that much. Miles did not count, but Johanna and the three children shared a bond Lorelei longed for. Her heart ached from it.

It had been years since Lorelei's mother had died from pneumonia. Since then, she had never known that kind of gentle caring from anyone. Oh, she had had some close female friends, but their relationships had not been that deep seeded. As for men in her life, they either shied away because she spoke her mind, or they felt threatened by her knowledge and independent nature.

She thought of Michael with his flirtatious courting—if that's what it could be called—but knew he did not truly care. He put on a good show, and maybe he cared a little. But deep inside, he lacked the understanding, the respect for her that came with a meaningful relationship. She didn't fool herself for one minute.

She valued his friendship. But she had never felt any pull toward him otherwise. He had kissed her passionately, long and almost possessively, but it had failed to stir her senses, or her heart. It had been pleasant. But somehow, she knew a kiss should be more. Unfortunately, she didn't know what *more* was.

"Lorelei, what about you? Will you be leaving too?"

Lorelei startled at Johanna's question, bringing her back to the present. "Ah, I'll stay until Dr. Taylor awakens."

Johanna smiled and released Jessica. "Go tell Missy we're leaving, pumpkin. And speak softly so you don't wake Jamie. We'll come back tonight."

The child tip-toed slowly toward the bed with exaggerated prudence. Lorelei found herself yearning for a daughter as vibrant and darling as little Jessica. Her smile vanished with the realization of that possibility being as far away as the Milky Way. *You're wishing on a star, with little hope for such a future.*

CHAPTER EIGHT

"Stop!" Lorelei screamed from her buggy. She pulled hard on the reins, appalled at the whipping within the Aiken's corral.

Paying her no mind, Tom Aiken laid another cruel flog across the work horse's shoulder. The horse whinnied, digging its wide hooves into dirt and pulling back in earnest on the bridle that Tom held in his meaty fist.

"You have no right to harm him. Stop!"

Tom ignored her protest. She fumed at the ill treatment the man doled out to the bedraggled horse. Without a second thought, she leaped from the vehicle and rushed through the partially opened gate.

Tom did not even turn his head as she dashed forward. He again raised the vicious weapon, struggling to hold the bridle within his grip. The horse, eyes frantic, danced and struggled against the man's restraining force. Again, to no avail.

Lorelei raced up behind Tom. She had to jump to grab his forearm with both hands as it started its descent. She swayed in the air as if dangling from a thick branch. Her weight on his arm didn't faze him. But it did curtail his inflicting another slash.

Tom flung his substantive arm much like one would to dislodge a pesky bee from a shirt sleeve. She hung on, her body suspended in limbo, her feet flaying every which way in an attempt to hold her perch.

"Get away from me you damn bitch. He's lazy and stubborn. I'll do any damn thing I want to get some work out of him." He thrust his arm outward with enough force to jar her teeth loose. She bit her tongue, tasted rustiness in her mouth.

Lorelei's head snapped back. A sharp piercing pain speared down her neck and across her shoulder blades. Her skirt billowed one way, then another, as if a strong wind had gusted from the open plains. Yet, she hung on, clawing her fingertips more firmly into his flesh. The horse neighed, tugging and sidestepping to break loose. Tom pulled cruelly against the horse's bit.

"Enough, you crazy bitch!" He released the leather strap and the horse wisely retreated to a safer place. Lorelei's feet skimmed the ground and she thanked God for the reprieve. With one quick move, Tom bent his arm to bring her within inches of his hostile glare. And raised his other fist.

Lorelei saw the mound of power come at her. Instinctively, she released her hold and ducked. But not quite quick enough.

It connected with her jaw. The impact sent her reeling through the air. She landed on her backside with a jarring thud. Stunned from the blow and the hard landing, she blinked several times to clear her foggy vision. Her chin throbbed, her right hip screamed. She felt as if the horse had trampled her.

Her entire body shuddered. She didn't know if it was from the assault, or fear of what might come next. Either way, she hurt and trembled with genuine fright. Vomit threatened.

Her vision slowly cleared, and she stared at dusty, worn boots braced two feet apart, not two feet in front of her sprawled legs that lay exposed up to her knees. She tugged her skirt down for modesty. To hell with modesty. She needed to get out of his way.

"I told you to stop, but you wouldn't listen, would you?" Tom snarled. She wondered if he would spit on her, or beat her to a pulp. If he had just listened and realized what he had been doing to that poor, decrepit horse. She knew she had acted irrationally, but how else could she have made him listen?

She braved a glance upward. The giant loomed over her, his arms resembling thick tree trunks, his dark scowl menacing. He still held the whip. She flinched and prayed for mercy.

"I should beat you. Flay you till you can't bother us anymore. You're damn lucky my fist only brushed you."

His words sent a chill down her spine. She forgot about any pains.

The misplaced blow had been more than enough. Had his fist met its true mark, it would have likely killed her.

"I…couldn't watch you hurt that poor horse…no matter if he refused to do your bidding or not." She swallowed, the dusty dryness preventing further words. Terror throbbed in her throat.

"Poor horse, my ass. That, little *lady,* is none of your business. He's *my* beast. I can treat him any way I please."

She wet her lips with her tongue, tasted dirt and blood. "He's an animal. God put him on this earth, like you and me. He shouldn't have to suffer such treatment, no matter who you think you are. He has feelings. He feels pain, just as we do."

He looked taken back for a moment as if actually considering her words. Had she made him see the light? *Oh, God, yes, please.*

"Feelings, shit! He ain't got no feelings. He's a cussed animal. If he did the work he should, I ain't got no reason to whip him. If he ain't goin' to, he'll learn what he gets."

Enough for shedding any light, she thought in disgust. Hoping their few words had tempered further rage, she drew her knees under her and pushed up with one hand, intending to leave with any dignity she had left. Vertigo hit as bile threatened to erupt. She inhaled deeply, blinked two times before her eyes focused. The churning in her stomach subsided to dull queasiness.

His out-stretched hand came into view. Stunned, she looked up. His face looked chiseled in stone. She clutched the offered hand, wondering if he would fling her across the corral. He assisted her up, then jerked his hand away. She fought to find solid footing as the earth collided with clouds overhead. She swayed, nausea rolled. The bright afternoon grayed as if a mist covered the land. Gradually, the world returned to its axis.

"You should be doin' your schoolin', mindin' your own damn business. You shouldn't be stickin' your nose in where it don't belong. Now, get off my property and don't come back."

"But—"

"Jist get. Next time, I won't be so neighborly. And my punch won't miss its mark next time, either."

Neighborly? Thinking better than to push her luck, she decided she best leave. She was not up to another battle. Plus, she'd promised Jamie she would visit after school. With luck, he could go home today and Johanna expected her to bring him home.

****

In less than ten minutes, Lorelei arrived at Seth's. With nerves still shaking, soreness screaming from head to toes, she trudged up the steps. Her chin felt like a bruised peach, and her lower lip and tongue throbbed to match her bruised hip.

She knocked on the door. Maybe she should have gone home first to repair some of the damage. Seth would be appalled at her dishevelment. Well, his opinion of her matched half of the men's, so why should it bother her? Yet, it did.

Thinking better of it, she turned to leave. Hinges creaked as the door opened. *Oh God!* Her foot faltered on the first step.

"Miss Webster?"

Coward! Without turning, she answered. "I just membered I need to go home before I visit Jamie. I'll be back sortly." Lord, her lip must resemble a beef steak. How embarrassing. She could barely enunciate. She descended another step and winced as her right hip protested. She clung to the railing for support.

She inhaled to steel herself, and then raised her foot for another jarring step downward. His booted heels clapped across the porch. She cringed, knowing she couldn't make a run for it.

She sensed him at her right. She averted her face.

"What's the matter? You act like...Good Holy Christ! What happened?"

Oh, why couldn't it be night? Why couldn't he accept her mutilated words and leave well enough alone?

She thought of lying. Of convincing him she had fallen down a stairway, been attacked by a ferocious dog, trampled by a runaway wagon. But lying was not in her. She had a hundred faults in his eyes. She would not add lying to the lengthy list.

"I gueth you couth say I stuck my nouth in too far again." She wanted to see his reaction so bad she could almost taste it. Even with her swollen tongue. But she dared not look. Instead, she kept her face

61

turned away, praying he would be disgusted and let her go her merry way. She wasn't so lucky.

He took one step past her and turned. She glued her eyes to the newly planted maple. His fingers touched the left side of her jaw and gently guided her face toward the right.

She didn't want to look at him, but her eyes, curse them, had a mind of their own. Their gazes met. His eyes widened, his expression neither repelled nor disgusted. Her eyes filled with tears of embarrassment and total humiliation.

Without facial or verbal emotion, he asked, "Who did this?"

Trembling attacked her weak legs, and then migrated to her shoulders and hands. Though it hurt, she raised her chin and fought for any poise. Right! She focused on his collar.

"I deservth it." She almost gagged on the lie. She hadn't acted any differently than any other decent person would have.

He remained silent while she concentrated on his broad shoulders. He was as large as Tom Aiken, younger and far more handsome. Yet for all his muscularity, his easygoing attitude negated any impression he could be made of sterner stuff.

She almost laughed at the train of thought. She opposed cruelty, yet found herself wishing he would demonstrate more assertiveness or aggressiveness, so she could respect him more. It was his one lacking quality. Yes, she thought with surprise, she actually fancied a man with more mettle.

"I asked who did this." God love him, he actually sounded angry. Her eyes darted to his. She had not thought he had it in him. Maybe there was hope for him yet.

"That's noth imfortant." Lord, it hurt to talk.

"Let's get you inside. I'll decide what's important." Now, he sounded disgusted. When he took her elbow, she went willingly. At least he could patch her bruises. Well, most of them. He was *not* going to touch her backside. Oh no. He might lack that mettle she so adamantly wished he possessed, but he was a man. Too handsome to touch any of *her* private parts. No matter how much she hurt.

With his hand at her elbow and his other arm across her back, he guided her inside. With every ounce of fortitude she had, she walked to the infirmary as upright as she could. She prayed he wouldn't realize how much the hip hurt.

She also prayed he couldn't hear her heart madly pounding. His hand at her back sent strange, but warm unsettling feelings through her. Feelings she knew she should not allow. His faint woodsy aftershave, more than alluring, assailed her as he sat her down on the hard chair.

Stabbing pain shot through her hip. She squirmed to get comfortable as he crossed the room to a wooden framed partition with white muslin inserts. He rolled it, the wheels squeaking, until he positioned it between them and Jamie.

"This will give you privacy should Jamie awaken." He scowled and she flinched. Most likely, he detested having to fix her up. Of having to touch her anymore than he already had.

"I can go home and put a compreth of warm tea on my chin. I'm sure the swelling will go down whith it. My mama used to—"

"You have blood all over your chin. It may require sutures. Not to mention whatever else may be wrong." He sounded exasperated with having to treat her. He probably thought the men would boot him out of town if he helped her.

"I don't want to be of any boder." But she did, dang blast it. Well, maybe not a bother. But she wanted something from this man she could not explain. Maybe she merely wanted his respect, his friendship. Yet, she continued to show him what a nuisance she could create rather than her good side.

His brows rose as he gave her an incredulous look. Then his lips pursed into a thin-lipped smirk that clearly stated she was indeed a bother. He crossed the room, retrieved a small white cloth and basin of water and returned to stand in front of her.

"I want to hear what you did this time, Miss Webster," he said matter-of-fact as he gently sponged her chin. She stared at his chest to avoid his condemning eyes.

"Did you barge into the saloon *again* or merely burst into someone's home?"

She wished the floor boards would open and suck her under.

"Neither, Docthor Thaylor." She glanced upward. He appeared to be holding back laughter.

"Really?" He smiled as he continued to cleanse her cheek and neck. "You didn't get this purple goose egg on your chin or the fat lip by singing Sunday hymns on the church lawn, Miss Webster."

She flinched as he pressed harder.

"Sorry, I didn't mean to push so hard. There's no open injury on your face, just a lot of swelling…and quite a bit of color. Stick out your tongue." He was going to laugh, dang his soul. His eyes were already laughing.

She stuck out her tongue. Not for his inspection, but because she felt like sticking it out at him. *Curse the man.*

He did laugh at her child-like antic, keeping his chortle muffled for Jamie's benefit. She felt like socking him in the jaw to see if his would match hers.

"You do have one nasty gash on your tongue. But I'm afraid you'll have to let that repair itself." He ambled over to the table, grabbed another small cloth and returned to her. "Here, place this on the tongue while I wash your left hand."

Lorelei did his bidding, surprised to see the scraped skin on her hand. That was the least of her worries.

He first washed the hand, then dabbed it with a clear liquid that stung like fire then proceeded to wrap the abrasion.

"Here, let me see," he said as he procured the cloth from her hands. "The bleeding stopped. I advise you not to drink or eat anything too warm for a day. Stay with cool or cold liquids so it won't start up again."

Lorelei nodded in acquiescence.

"I'll be right back with some ice." When he left, Lorelei peeked around the screen. Jamie remained deep in slumber. She leaned back and winced from the pain in her hip. She would be sore for many days ahead. She no sooner had righted herself to a half-way comfortable position when Seth returned.

"Here hold this on your chin. I need to check the rest of you." He handed her the ice pack made of a fist-sized chunk of ice wrapped in a flannel cloth. She applied the parcel to her jaw gingerly. His nearness and scent lessened the soreness ten times more than his actual expertise.

With fingers as gentle as a child's, he prodded lightly along the rest of her jaw and neck. He turned her neck one way, then the other, cautiously. His feathery touch felt more like a soft caress than exploring for injury. Her pulse quickened, and she swallowed the lump growing in her throat.

"Everything seems in order. You'll be very sore for awhile, however." That was an understatement if she ever heard one.

"Now, while you tell me what happened let's get you on the table so I can check that hip that's giving you so much trouble."

"Oh, no! You don't need to. I—"

"Miss Webster, surely with your…ah ways, one doctor checking your derriere will not cause you the vapors." He, none too gently, pulled her from the chair. Her face flamed with humiliation. He probably enjoyed every minute of this.

"Come, Miss Webster," he said with arrogant decorum, his eyes twinkling as if he thought this a joke. She resisted, much the way Tom's horse had. And did not fare any better.

"No need to be shy. I'm merely a doctor checking one of my patients." Placing his hands on her waist, he hoisted her up onto the table before she could offer any kind of further protest.

The pain in her hip screeched. Of all the blasted times for him to find that dang mettle. He was not just any doctor. And her derriere was not just anyone's. It was *hers*, dammit.

CHAPTER NINE

Lorelei turned every shade of red imaginable as Seth eased her to a prone position. He had expected her tirade. He knew she felt mortified. He wanted to howl.

It was about time someone ran buckshot over her. Served her right, he thought, without any sympathy to her embarrassment. Maybe a few times in an uncomfortable situation would teach her a lesson.

Who was he kidding? This woman would never cower when it came to instigating trouble.

"Keep that ice on your jaw while I make sure your ribs and hip are all in one piece." He lightly palpated her ribcage, noting her trim midriff. "Any pain here?" When his thumbs lightly brushed the lower curve of her generous breasts, he felt as if they had been seared. He retracted them.

"No…not there," she whispered, keeping her eyes shut tight.

He swallowed, feeling as if he was dying of thirst. *She's just another patient.* Yet, the feel of her softness through the thin material sent his pulse racing like a gun-shy horse.

He inhaled the tantalizing scent of lavender as his fingers glided over the rest of the intact ribs. *Lord, help me. Not this woman, please.* He had always held himself in check, cautioned himself from being tempted by any women other than the few who offered their charms for a charge. And Lorelei was his patient.

Composing himself to proceed as a concerned physician should, he trailed his hands down to her thin waist. He experienced the sudden urge to encircle that waist to see if his hands could span it as easily as he thought. She wore no corset.

Pull yourself together. He had to clear his tight throat. "How about here?" He pushed inward at her waist.

"No…ah, just a little on the right," she said, flinching as he palpated a bit harder and towards the hip.

"How about here?" He pressed against the top of the femur.

"N…no." She kept her eyes shut, and he felt her quiver.

"I need you to roll to your left side."

Much to his astonishment, she obeyed without objection. As she rolled, she jerked in reflex and muffled a gasp. With her back ramrod stiff, she quivered to hold the position. Her hair, a once-neat bun, hung in haphazard tangles down her back.

"That was quite painful?" He peered over her shoulder to see her lips pressed tightly together. She had grit.

"Uh-huh," she managed to murmur.

He smiled at her strong constitution. Seth gazed at the roundness concealed by the soft folds of material. He felt the room heat, a fine sheen of perspiration surface across his brow. He did not want to touch that delectable backside any more than he wanted a gun fight with a known gun slinger. He swallowed and cursed his insistence to check for more injuries.

The thought cleared his muddled mind in one second flat. She had been hurt, and he felt compelled to check the extent of those injuries. For God's sake, he was a doctor! With that in mind, he reached out and touched the shapely curve of her buttocks.

"Ow!" She nearly lifted off the table. He watched her fingers turn white as she gripped the edge of the table.

There was no way he could examine her through the many folds of her petticoat and skirt. He felt fine drops of sweat turn into rivulets and run down the side of his face. He had never been embarrassed before like this. *Damn.*

"I have to raise your skirt to examine that hip closer."

Dead silence filled the room. Had she heard him? "Miss We—"

"I heard you, Dr. Taylor. Just…just get it over with."

A minute ago he'd had no sympathy for her abashment. Now he did; painfully so. It was not easy for a woman to expose private parts to most doctors. And, knowing this woman, though however briefly, he knew this would be more disconcerting to her than many others.

Having no other recourse, he lifted the yards of blue skirt and white ruffled-lace petticoat to her waist. He pulled his gaze from her long, shapely calves. Expecting to view knee-length cotton pantaloons, Seth gulped, totally unprepared for the sight before him. He blinked to make sure his eyes were not playing a tortuous game.

And stared at red silk drawers.

Not drawers at all, he corrected in astonishment, but tiny, skimpy panties. They encased her firm buttocks, just past their roundness. And frilly black lace trimmed the frivolous garment, to boot. *God Almighty!* She might be a brazen woman, but never had she struck him as one who would wear such feminine attire.

If her skin did not remind him of alabaster and feel like satin, if the voluptuous curve of her hip and shapely taut derriere did not set his pulse to bound, he would have laughed.

She was more of an enigma than he had imagined. Just looking at that enticing bottom enveloped by that skimpy cover of femininity caused his loins to react violently.

Holy hell! I have to touch it. His mouth salivated while his throat went dry. Embarrassment was *not* his problem.

With shaky hands, he drew the scrap of silk down. His fingers grazed the baby-soft skin, smooth and warm as fresh cream. He inhaled and felt as if the air had thickened. Flames shot through his veins. God help him, he longed to reach down and kiss the pink softness with his lips.

He stared at the dark black-purple hematoma that spread from one side of her delectable right cheek past her hip bone. His raging yearnings ebbed as he lowered the fabric further.

"Good God! It's a wonder you could sit in that chair." Only when she gasped her dismay, did he realize he had spoken aloud.

"Is...is my hip broken?"

"I—just a minute." He took a deep breath to get his libido back where it belonged. "It's going to be uncomfortable while I prod this area." *And just as uncomfortable for me, believe me.*

"Just do it. Just get it over with."

Whether disconcertment or impatience caused her to become the stern Miss Webster again, he didn't know. But he *did* know that she became as brisk as they came when she felt vulnerable. Was that her defense when cornered or nervous?

Rather than dwell on that curious assumption, he checked for further damage. Though visualizing the injury and knowing she suffered, he again felt his loins tighten. He was depraved.

Lorelei bore his exam like a tough cowpoke. She gritted her teeth and held back a whimper, though she stiffened from more than one manipulation.

"Nothing is broken. But you're badly bruised. There's severe bleeding into the tissues. I'm going to get more ice, and you'll need to lie here for awhile so the ice can do its job."

Seth grabbed two pillows from the linen shelf and propped them behind her back.

"There, you can lean back a bit so you won't have to hold yourself so rigid."

She eased back. The pillows offered her needed support, yet allowed the hip to remain upward.

"Better?" he asked.

"Yeth, thank you." She sighed, and her shoulders relaxed.

"I'll be back in a few minutes with more ice." He exited the room, keeping his back toward her, his erection more than uncomfortable and potently obvious. Maybe *he* would use the ice first.

****

Feeling composed after a shot of brandy and several minutes away from her, Seth returned to her side. Glancing at the peeled down red and black silk, he placed the flannel covered ice pack on her hip. Simply viewing the bruised and battered backside discharged lust to his loins again. He positioned another pillow behind her hips to hold the cold pack in place, then retrieved a thin blanket and covered her from his wayward eyes.

He peeked around the screen to make sure Jamie remained sleeping, and to help calm his rising staff yet again. He pulled up a chair in front of her. "Now, tell me how this happened."

She repositioned the ice to her jaw and studied him for a moment. He could see indecision in her eyes.

"You might just as well tell all. I'll hear about it sooner or later from the men. I might as well as hear your side of the story."

****

Lorelei considered his words. Better she defend herself now before he heard the worst. And if he could act like he had not taken full inspection of her backside, so could she—though she continued to feel her heated face. And what must he think of her underwear? *Oh dear saints in heaven. Of all the days to wear red.*

"I wath coming here to see if Jamie wath ready to go home. I thought I could savth Johanna a trip into town if he wath. When I past Tom Aiken's farm, he wath whipping hith work horsth."

"Whipping his horse?" Seth looked appalled. For once, at least, it was not directed at her. *Yet.*

"Worsth than whipping. It looked like he meant to filet the horsth's skin wide open at the rate he wath going. And that horsth must be as old as my long deceased grandma." She knew she sounded pious. She couldn't help it. The barbaric scene materialized before her eyes, infuriating her all over again.

"Go on." He looked leery of what she might say next as he stretched his long legs out in front of him.

She explained how she had hollered at Tom to stop. How he paid her no mind. How she latched onto his arm, finishing with her landing on her backside on the uneven hard ground.

For a moment, Seth just peered at his boots. When he met her gaze, she sucked in her breath. She had expected condemnation at her irrational interference. Instead, his eyes showed appreciation, almost a respectful admiration.

"You could've been hurt much worse. I hope you'll use some logic from now on before you act so impulsively. I don't approve of the means with which you try to change the world, but you deserve a 'thank you' since the horse can't say as much."

Though he failed to agree wholeheartedly with her methods, Lorelei's mouth gaped at his approval.

"I don't abide any man treating an animal that way. I'm sorry you had to suffer because of your good intentions."

"Thank you." She still couldn't believe her ears. "But why when I defend a horsth do you approf of it, and yet when ith's women and children, you turn your head, just like other men do?"

She was every bit that brassy woman he had accused her of being to ask such a direct question—and she knew it. Most men would tell her to take a flying leap in the manure pile if she confronted them like she had just done him. Would he be the same?

He smiled, and she felt its warmth clear down to her toes.

"You can't right the world by yourself. Men have jurisdiction over what's theirs. Their children and wives are their property. And it's none of your business."

His words sent her head spinning, her blood boiling. "Horsths are a man's property too. Why do you feel differently about that?" *So much for his compliment.*

"I don't. I think your efforts, whether for an animal or a person, are gallant. But I also think it's none of your business. Especially the way you go about it. Rather than reason, you rant. Rather than compromise, you storm. There's a saying, 'you can't put out a fire with fire'. The phrase says it all."

The man was as *loco* as half the town. Her heart wept because he lacked more spunk, more initiative to be a driving force she could respect. It was a damn shame for a man to be as intelligent and handsome as he, yet lack that all powerful force.

Well, she should be thankful they were on friendly terms. She could never expect more. And she would not want more if he eluded taking a harder stand on issues she took to heart.

He had managed to avoid several town meetings. How could a man so dedicated to medicine, to healing the sick and caring for those in need, shuck his community duty? She simply could find no reason for such a gaffe. Yes, it was a damn shame. Such a waste.

And as he would say, 'not her business'.

CHAPTER TEN

After two hours of on-again-off-again ice to her bruises, Lorelei insisted she felt fit to go home. From behind the screen, she adjusted her clothing, her backside feeling fifty percent better since it had turned numb from the cold and lessened in pain from the medicine Seth had given her. She listened to Seth explain her tussle with Tom Aiken to the now-awakened Jamie.

She trudged around the partition to be greeted by Jamie's gasp and wide-eyed expression.

"Wow, Miss Webster, you sure do look like you took a good right." His face contorted and his nose scrunched up with a scowl. "Must hurt a lot, huh?"

Lorelei hobbled to his side and brushed a lock of hair off his forehead. She managed a weak smile, her face too stiff to offer more. "Yes, it's sore. But it was his left that got me."

Jamie's eyes widened further as he gawked at her swollen jaw and lip. "You're sure lucky it was. It's his hard right he's known for, that's a known fact."

Lorelei breath caught at the child's words. She had felt lucky Tom's fist had missed a direct hit. Now, she felt absolutely blessed. Of course, her body didn't attest to being so lucky.

"I'm going to take Miss Webster home, Jamie," Seth said, moving the partition back against the far wall. "I'll be back in no time flat. Do you need anything before we leave?"

"You don't have to do that, Doctor Taylor. I can manage." She refused to cause him further inconvenience.

Seth's eyes met hers. "I know you could probably *manage*, but I insist. You already look drowsy from the medicine. Jamie will be fine by himself for awhile. Won't you, scamp?"

Jamie grinned at the doctor. "Sure thing, Doc. Take your time. Am I still going home today?"

"Jamie, it's Doctor Taylor. You—"

"It's all right, Miss Webster. I told him to call me, Doc. We're more than patient and doctor at this point. And since we're such good friends, *Doc* is just fine." He glanced at Jamie. "And yes, Jamie, I'll take you home as soon as I get back." He smiled down at the child, placing his large palm on the boy's shoulder to give a slight squeeze.

Lorelei noted genuine caring in Seth's eyes. She again wondered at the workings of his mind. Just when she had labeled him standoffish, a loner of sorts, she saw another side of him.

"Come along Miss Webster. I'll tie my horse to your buggy while you say goodbye." As he exited the room, Lorelei bid Jamie farewell and puzzled over who Seth Taylor really was.

****

The trip was uneventful back to her small apartment attached to the school house. Seth offered to cancel school for her for the next two days, explaining that way she would have Thursday and Friday as well as the weekend to recuperate. Hesitantly, she agreed. There was no way she could sit all day in her straight back chair, or chase after the little hellions at recess.

After he had taken her horse and wagon into the small stable and tied his horse to the hitching post out front, he joined her inside the tiny, but more than adequate, three-room dwelling. He also insisted on having one of the women stop by the next day, instructing her to send word if she needed him.

"I want you take two of these tablets and go to bed. They'll help the pain. You can take two every four or five hours as needed," he said, holding out the packet.

"Thank you." She took the small brown envelope he offered. "Just a minute, and I'll pay you."

His grin dazzled her. Her heart fluttered. She was not easily swayed by a handsome man's smile or a small kind gesture. But *his* smile did strange things to her, no matter where or when.

"No, Miss Webster. You paid me for the other night when I treated Mrs. Allen. I didn't do that much for her then or you today, so let's just call it even."

"That isn't right."

"The way I see it, it's right as rain, Miss Webster. Besides, protecting that horse is payment in itself."

Oh, how she wished he would call her Lorelei. But that seemed as far-fetched as hoping it would not snow this winter.

He turned and descended the two steps that served as her back entrance. She stood in the doorway and watched him untie his Palomino from the post. He looked up and nodded.

"You get some rest and let me know if you need anything."

"I'll do that. And thank you again."

Lorelei watched until he became a blur down the road.

"Why do I feel so empty now that he's gone?" she whispered as she made her unsteady way to the bed. Sitting down, she reflected on the man who troubled her mind so often. He was intelligent, pleasant, and courteous to everyone. He had manners, undoubtedly from a good upbringing. Obviously, he felt total dedication to his profession, and he had the skill to go with it.

Yet, so many times she had seen him deliberately avoid getting involved in any upheaval taking place. She had heard others comment that he was not rude, but merely a loner.

Oh, he attended church, unless he was out treating someone. And he frequented the town hall for the town or school board meetings. But that was it. If a heated discussion arose or any real trouble brewed, he seemed to extract himself.

Maybe he did lack a backbone. Surprisingly, she found she did not want to believe that. She recalled two occasions when he had taken charge and fired back with authority. Once when he set her in her place as he treated Fannie, and again when he ignored her protest to get up on his table for his examination. He had taken down her underwear.

"Lord, what had he thought?" Her face burned. Thank goodness she had not seen his expression. Her one vice in life was soft, pretty, feminine undergarments. Now, she cursed herself for it. *And he had inspected her rear end.* It amazed her she had been able to look him in the eye afterward. He had not acted any different than if he had looked into her throat. Thank the good Lord. Yet, knowing even her most private parts failed to affect him brought a raw, hopeless ache to her chest.

"You're being foolish. Thank goodness he *didn't* think anything of it." Again, the knowledge pierced deep inside.

But why did he shy from any strife? Recalling his talk with Jamie, she wondered if it stemmed from his father's drinking. Had it caused him to avoid confrontations, to lack initiative to go out on a limb?

She kicked off her shoes and cautiously curled onto the bed. She would sleep, maybe later take the pills. She would rather think about Seth. He intrigued her, attracted her like a moth to a flame, though he had strange ways. She shook her head in despair. The first man to ever catch her fancy and it had to be someone who evaded any community matters other than everyday humdrums.

He acted the helpful friend when she brought him an abused person. He had been kind and polite to her as manners dictated. But would he ever see her as anything more than an acquaintance? A tear slowly ran down her cheek as she acknowledged the hopelessness of any more between them. There could never be anything more concrete. She knew it as sure as she knew that her right hip screamed in agony. She was much too bold, too vocal for the calm, uninvolved doctor.

She yawned. Her eyelids grew heavy as she accepted the cold, hard fact she ought to thankful for at least his friendship.

CHAPTER ELEVEN

Seth saw Jamie home, then cantered his horse back home after Johanna had insisted he share supper with the three children and her since Miles was not there to eat his portion.

With his belly full of chicken and biscuits and warm apple pie, and knowing Jamie had fully recovered, he should feel content. But he didn't.

Lorelei Webster plagued his mind. Seeing her in pain had shaken him. The fact that she had been injured because of her meddling continued to rattle his senses. His mind conjured up hair-raising pictures of what could have been more disastrous.

"Damn fool woman. Doesn't know when to leave things be. Nor will she ever," he huffed, settling his horse into the stall.

Once inside his home, he removed his topcoat and poured two fingers of brandy into a glass. He gulped it, welcomed the fire burning a path to his stomach. It did not stop the worry inside. Desperate to suppress the unwanted concern over the woman, he felt tempted to slug back another shot. Not one to take a second drink, he instead threw the glass across the room. It hit the wall with a bang, shattering into thin shards.

He stared at the remains sprinkled over the carpet, feeling no relief from his misplaced temper. *And misplaced it was.*

"She's not my concern. She's digging her own grave, so let her lie in it." His voice bellowed through the silent room, sounding ridiculous to his own ears. For as much as he wished he could look the other way when it came to the impetuous Miss Webster, he knew he couldn't.

She was like a bee stuck to honey when it came to his shedding

76

thoughts of her. Not only did he realize he loathed the thought of her being hurt from any man's retaliation, but he conceded he felt a growing attraction to the meddlesome woman.

"This is ridiculous!" Disturbed by his train of thought, he strode to the window and glanced across the lawn. Shoving his hands in his pockets, he stared outside, unmindful of the peaceful setting. But his thoughts played a riotous discord he didn't know how to stop. His heart yearned for something so far out of reach that his throat constricted and his chest tightened.

Logically, he told himself, any relationship with Lorelei would be absurd. There would be heartache on both sides if they were to allow anything to grow between them. He would suffer, knowing he would never be worthy of her love. She would be devastated if she ever found out about his past hideous sins.

He forced his mind to eradicate any silly notions regarding the woman. He could not count the times he had resisted others. Now would be no different. Could not be any different.

Yet, this time his heart ached as if weighed down by a boulder. And all because of a woman who possessed a personality so far from his own that he questioned his sanity.

"We would never suit," he said with less conviction than he felt. He turned away from the window and sauntered through the empty house, feeling more disheartened than he ever should allow.

"I won't let you get to me, Lorelei. I *can't* let you, for both our sakes." He tried to convince himself he could resist her charm. He needed to keep away from her so his memories stayed buried, for his own peace of mind. But, as he entered his study, he knew it would not be as easy as he tried to tell himself.

****

Four days later, Seth crossed his porch after treating the Harper family for dysentery. He spotted the note attached to his door and yanked it down.

He read it twice, crumpled it in his fist, and went inside. He threw his bag and the note onto the davenport, removed his coat and went to the basin in his room. After splashing cool water over his face, he peered into the mirror. Droplets of water dripped from his cheeks and chin.

"A meeting, huh?" There could be only one reason for a town meeting for *men only*. Lorelei Webster had done it again.

"What the hell have you done now, Lorelei?" He shook his head and dried his face, his grin spreading in spite of himself. When would she ever learn?

Visiting ill families throughout the surrounding farms over the past three days, he'd had no chance to do more than nod at anyone on his way from or back to his home. Dysentery spread like wildfire when it hit—and it had hit hard, this time.

Though Tom Aiken had assaulted her, and the others lashed out verbally, and of course there had been the tomato throwing, he figured the men would not intentionally do bodily harm to her. Tonight, they would rant about whatever mischief she had created, but he seriously doubted they would form a lynch mob.

He did not want to attend tonight. Let them rant. Yet, an uneasy feeling knotted in his stomach. He would do extra lifts with the weights tonight…to ease his troubled thoughts.

****

The sun had long set by the time Seth sat finishing his tough steak dinner. Doctor he was, chef he was not. As he pushed the last soggy peas around his plate, he glanced at his watch.

Five of nine. Five minutes, and the town hall would rumble with condemnation over Lorelei. Maybe they had another topic. Maybe Ned Potter's livestock had trampled the others' fields again. Yes, that could be it. Somehow, he knew different.

That uneasy feeling settled in his stomach again. Maybe it could be the beef, or his cooking. He knew better. Too many maybes about this night set his stomach to churning.

Against his better judgment, he found himself retrieving his coat, dousing all but one lamp, and going out the door.

****

Seth heard the heated voices before he ascended the steps of the Methodist church that served as the town hall. He opened the door and wedged himself through the doorway, taking a place to stand against

78

the back wall. The filled-to-capacity room droned to a low muffle at his entrance. Half the men sat, half stood, lining the other walls. Tom Aiken, Tom Burdock, Andy Piedmont, Claude Allen, Fred Harper and about ten more. He knew the ones who were not there were home with the trots.

Sam Aherns stood before them, arms held up in the air looking like an avenging evangelist. "Hey, Doc. Glad you could make it." Sam nodded and continued as he strode back and forth.

"As I was sayin', she's got to go."

Damn, he had been right.

Seth spotted Michael standing near the front, a smirk on his face. He found himself wanting to punch the sheriff right in the nose. The bastard thought this all a joke.

"There ain't no two ways about it," Sam raved on. "As soon as we can get us a new teacher, she needs to be sent packin'. I intend to be the one to boot her out, physically if I have ta, but I need you fellas to back me up on this."

"What did she do now?" Seth had not wanted to ask the question, but his unruly mouth refused to listen.

Sam's cheeks puffed up, his face turned ruddier. "That bitch stuck her nose in too far, is what she done. She tol' my little Ellen not to give me none, no way, when that time for gettin' caught was near." Sam's eyes glared, bulging as if they might pop out of their sockets any second.

"I tell ya, Doc, there ain't no way no bitch got the right to interfere with that. If I want it, then I got that right. Ain't no law against a man takin' his fill when he wants. And no bitch's goin' ta stop me. Don't care if she gets in the family way fifty times, it ain't none of Miss Neb-nose's business."

Lorelei had done the same thing with Fred Harper's wife and he had been angry. But Sam was more than riled.

"Sam, why not just talk to your wife? Make her forget what Miss Webster said." Seth felt compelled to break Sam's momentum. To calm the storm before it blew through town with a vengeance.

"It ain't that easy, Doc. I had to jist about plead with Ellen. Ain't no man should have to do that. Ain't no way. Lorelei Webster has to go."

Sam eyes roiled with a hateful glare.

"Do you have another teacher yet?" Seth asked, keeping his voice calm in hopes of keeping the talk rational and reasonable.

"Not yet, but last week we sent an ad to the Cheyenne paper. They're sendin' it to other towns, too. As soon as we get us another, she goes. Hell, if I had my way, I'd send her packin' now, but the rest jist said they don't take a likin' to that. The womenfolk would be breathin' down our throats, for sure."

Thank God for the others' logic. Seth had not thought the men would really follow through with obtaining another teacher, but they sure meant it now. He needed to defuse this group before Sam had them changing their minds. He did not want any harm to come to Lorelei, or to see her booted out of town.

That would solve your problem. Without Lorelei in town, he would be free to live his ordinary life. Mellow, with no upheaval, without memories of his sordid past creeping up at every turn. Yet, gaining that life at Lorelei's expense soured his mouth. And damn, but he would miss her... and her nosiness.

Seth took a step forward, scanned the crowd. "I think you're right. The children would suffer from no schooling, and your wives would never forgive you if you sent her away right now. I know she's a nuisance to you all, but she can't really change anything by a few words if you don't let her. And that's all she's got. Words. Go home, talk to your women. Stand tall and tell them you won't put up with it. Just live your lives, and forget her."

"*Forget her*? Every fuckin' morning I see red when I wake up because of that bitch. Ain't no way I can *forget* her." Sam's voice roared throughout the room as several others mumbled under their breath to the ones seated next to them.

Seth had hoped his words sounded convincing to the others. He caught Michael's disapproving eyes and wondered at the man's outlook on life. Instead of Michael defusing this situation, he seemed to want to let the men get riled and vent their anger. Well, if that was allowed, maybe by chance it might work. But if it did not, then all hell might break loose. He couldn't afford to let that happen. Michael seemed oblivious to that concept. A volatile situation could erupt and he needed to douse it. *Now.*

"Like I said," he raised his voice over the growing cacophony. "Don't let a few words from her get the best of you. Go home to your families, forget she exists. When she sees her words don't make any difference, she'll stop." He wished he could forget her as easily as his proclamation to the others sounded.

Andy Piedmont stood and looked over the crowd. "I agree with the Doc," he yelled to be heard over the renewed harsh din. "She's only got words, just like the Doc said. They set my teeth to grinding just as much as the rest of you, but he's got a point. Let's not take anymore of her lingo. We can show her no one will listen. Maybe he's right and she'll give up."

Seth wanted to shake Andy's hand. Irritated grumbles filtered through the room, but the men seemed less hell-bent as they had been. Sam looked none too pleased as several of them stood up, nodded in agreement and made ready to leave.

"Have I got your word from the lot of you to boot her out if and when we get a new teacher?" Sam asked loudly over the murmurs and turning backs.

"I'm in," Tom Burdock replied over his shoulder. "But let's try Doc's way for now." Others followed suit, offering Sam support.

Thank God! He had placated them for now; but he had not won any battle. Hell, most likely, it had not started yet.

Why in the blue blazes had he tried to protect her? If truth be known, he had just defended her. She wasn't a bitch as Sam called her. And the man's label for her irritated the hell out of him. But she *was* a witch. He would stay as far away from her as possible before he did something they both would regret.

He would talk to Michael, to see if anything had been uncovered in the Purdy case.

Anything was better than to think about Lorelei Webster.

CHAPTER TWELVE

On Saturday evening, one week later, the chilling winds howled. Lorelei glanced out her bedroom window and watched tiny flakes swirl in a riotous white blur, yet very little accumulated on the ground.

Turning away from the havoc outside, she reached for her blue dress. Nothing was going to dampen her spirits tonight, even the threat of frigid temperatures or a little bit of snow.

"Just one dance, Doctor Taylor. That's all I want." She smiled, thinking of what it would be like to be in his arms. Warmth filled her veins at the mere thought.

She prayed he would at least make a short appearance at the annual Harvest Dance. And if so, she would somehow coerce him to join her on the dance floor. She had arrived the week after last year's event, so she had never attended the festivities. But from what the women said, this night was the biggest gathering at the town barn. Everyone tried to attend, dressing in their best attire.

She thought of the other social she had missed when she had been down with that blasted influenza. Her nose had been so red, her eyes so watery that she had not wanted to be seen by anyone. Of course, she had not wanted to infect others either. And, at that time, she had not known Seth Taylor.

She scowled as she remembered the women relating how Seth had attended for a short time, conversing cordially with everyone, but had failed to ask any woman for a single dance. Tonight, he would not get away so easily. Not if she had her way.

Smoothing down the folds of dress, she peered into the cheval mirror. A multitude of hues from grays to peacock blues shimmered across the indigo brocade. The scooped neck and long sleeves added femininity while remaining quite modest. She liked the way it conformed to her bosom, snuggled her waist. Most of all, she loved the way the many yards billowed at her feet. She had bought it in Cheyenne, not knowing if she would ever wear it. Tonight would be her night.

"Now, for the hair." She wrinkled her nose staring at her image. A tight bun would be much too severe. But if she wore it down, she would look like a young girl of seventeen. Not quite as seductive as she had in store for the good Doc.

"Oh, Lorelei Webster," she laughed at her thoughts, "no matter how hard you try you'll never be seductive. Maybe pleasing to the eye, but never that appealing."

Recalling the stunning hairdo of Lilly Tillman last week, she pulled her long locks to the top of her head. Lorelei had envied the saloon girl's upsweep with two wispy curls dangling past each cheek as she strode smartly down the stoop.

With a relish, foreign to her, for she had never been one to prim and fuss over any man like this, Lorelei set out to create her duplication. And, thank goodness, the discoloration on her face had lessened enough to hide the tinges with light powder.

****

Having brought two pies and a bean casserole, Lorelei assisted the women with setting food on the long pine tables that had been covered with white tablecloths at one end of the huge barn. Children shrieked and giggled, chasing each other, stirring up the straw-covered hard ground. Men, dressed in their Sunday-go-to-church suits and string ties, congregated in groups, drinking and laughing, adding to the deafening din.

Cotton streamers, dyed gold and russet, hung from tall beams to drape across the lofty peak. At each corner and every tall post stood hay bales and tied clusters of corn stalks surrounded by mounds of pumpkins. Oil lanterns glowed brightly above each decorated area. A large wooden platform in the adjacent corner housed several chairs and instruments awaiting the men who would offer their musical talents. Miles Cooper added a few more logs to the blazing fire in the massive fieldstone fireplace.

"The decorations are beautiful. I had no idea this place could look so festive," Lorelei said, scanning the milling crowd.

Fannie Allen smiled and patted Lorelei's hand. With her injuries forgotten, she seemed to be as lighthearted as Lorelei felt. "The men outdo themselves every year. They put everything they've got into making this a special celebration. Our harvests were good again this year, and it's their time to howl."

"Yeah, and howl they will, just give 'em time," Ellen Ahearns spat as she peeked into Lorelei's covered casserole then replaced the lid. "Mm, smells delicious." She looked at Lorelei, a sadness clouding the previous twinkling of her eyes.

These were some tough ladies to tolerate their corrosive men.

"They do their part all right," Ellen continued, her anger surging to the forefront. "But by halfway through the night, they'll decide to celebrate as hard as they've worked, and by tomorrow, none of them'll remember going home."

Lorelei wanted to say something, yet it would be a shame to ruin what should be a lovely time. No sense in adding turmoil tonight, or dampening the jovial mood. She held her tongue.

Spotting hay bales in the form of a large square in the farthest corner, Lorelei glanced at Fannie. "What's that for?" As she asked, she noticed ten round tin tubs inside the square.

Fannie laughed. "The tubs are for the children to bob for apples. Later, when they tire out, they can curl up and sleep. They don't last too long once things calm down. The younger ones hardly make it to when the dancing starts. Here, pass me those breads and I'll put them at the end with the others."

Lorelei handed her the fruit breads brought by Sarah Piedmont. As she did, she searched the crowd. Still no Seth. Her heart plummeted to the pit of her stomach. Would he not show up? Would all her time fussing and pruning go to waste? Most likely she wasted her time hoping for something that would never be, anyway. He had not shown any attraction to her before. Why should one hairdo and a pretty dress make any difference? He had seen her backside and it had not turned his head one bit.

"I must say, Lorelei, that dress does wonders for your coloring. I do believe your eyes have become a shade darker. You look lovely. You'll not want for any dancing from the single men tonight. Of course, maybe Michael will hog you for himself. Hmm?"

Fannie's mention of Michael jolted her. Did everyone in this town think they were sweethearts? Several other women had made comments to the same effect time and time again.

"Michael is a good friend, Fannie. We've shared a dinner or two at the hotel or at Jacob's eatery, but that's all."

"What about the church social two months ago? He seemed mighty smitten then," Mable Gillis intervened as usual. Nothing went past the woman's ears.

Turning to Mable, Lorelei bit her tongue. Mable was no more outspoken or meddlesome than she. Who was she to harp at the gray-haired biddy? And half the time, she meant well.

"We're just friends. Michael could never stand by and allow me to stir up trouble the way I do. And I could never abide his overlooking things that go on and not taking any action. We would probably kill each other the day after we married."

"Yes, sir, you got a good point there, Lorelei." Mable's whoop of laughter sounded like a cackle. "You need a man who can look the other way at your ways and be just as strong spirited as you. Nope, I don't think there's a man around these parts who *could* fill those shoes." Mable shook her head and hobbled away, her arthritis making her look older than her fifty-odd years.

The widow's word sliced her heart in two. Seth would never tolerate the commotion she caused. Dismayed by the thought, she knew she could never respect him, or truly love him, if he failed to show more mettle when faced with life's challenges.

Yet, she found herself again searching the crowd. Something about him drew her to him; Something more than just his dazzling smile, or his warm eyes when he allowed himself to relax his cool attitude. She recalled how he came to her aid at Millers', saving her from disgrace. It brought an appreciative smile to her lips, a tenderness to her heart.

Squaring her shoulders, her eyes scanned the crowd to no avail. She would not give up on him. Not quite yet.

****

The dancing had been going on for over an hour; the children had bobbed for apples and had been rewarded treats for their good efforts. Lorelei fumed, and still, Seth Taylor made no appearance.

Michael, for the fifth or sixth time, glided her across the straw-covered dance area, twirling her and being ever so attentive. At least it passed the time and helped her mask the crestfallen mood invading her once-uplifted spirits. She admitted she preferred to dance with Michael rather than having her toes trampled by Wayne Botley, the single foreman at Harper's ranch; or handsome and polite Steve Whitley. He had not stepped on her toes, but he had terrible halitosis—so fetid, she had been hard pressed not to end the dance before it finished.

She followed Michael's easy steps, the softly played waltz adding to her disappointment. Why had Seth not come? Did he think he would be obligated to ask her to dance? Did he stay away because of her? Surely, he had not been thinking about her. She wished she had that much influence. She knew otherwise.

****

Seth accepted a beer from Charles Miller and glanced at the many dancers. It took not a minute to spot Lorelei in the arms of Michael. Not only did the colorful gown stand out in the crowd, but her hair made her look like an angel as she floated across the floor. She was the most beautiful woman here. The most alluring female he had ever seen. Lorelei Webster might be an instigator, a verbal shrew, but tonight she was an enchantress.

She laughed at something Michael said and Seth's heart thudded against his ribs. He felt a tightening in his stomach as he watched the sheriff pull her closer, stroke her back. His anger shook him at seeing the other man touch her so familiarly.

Jealousy? Good Holy Christ, what was happening? How could he feel such an efficacious feeling about her? He was not even sure he liked the woman. Yet...he admitted he felt jealous. Lorelei was a strong, powerful force, one to reckon with; and with it, she extracted that same potent reaction from him.

He would be wise to slug down his beer and say good night. *Hightail it right out of here, now.* But his eyes had a will of their own. They insisted upon devouring every detail of the beauty that hovered so gracefully nearby. Her waist appeared smaller, her bosom fuller. Her hair shimmered like moonlight. His fingers itched to feel the softness of the delicate curls gracing the sides of her rosy cheeks. A lump lodged in his throat. He took a needed sip of beer.

Stop it, you fool. She can never be anything to you.

Yet, his gaze not only held him spellbound, but his heart refused to accept what he knew to be fact. It ached beneath his breast bone, desperately yearning to be near her for a fraction of a second. To have her bestow a smile for him like the one she had offered Michael. Then, he would go back to his sheltered world, behave himself as he knew he must. That's all he wanted; one brief moment to share with such an angel.

What could a mere second or two harm?

CHAPTER THIRTEEN

The waltz ended, and Lorelei decided she better mingle instead of feeding into Michael's misunderstandings. And misunderstandings they were. She was not naive enough not to recognize his heated glances, or the irritating possessiveness.

She had not meant to lead him on, or intentionally hurt him. And, she would, if she led him to believe their dancing meant more than fun. She had solely intended to have as good a time as she could without Seth's presence. She took a step back, allowing a respectable space between them. Another melody began.

"Thank you, Michael. You're a wonderful dancer. But I better see if Fannie needs help. People are swarming around the desserts." She smiled, and hoped she sounded sincere.

She turned toward the tables not twenty feet away.

And there stood Seth. Her heart tripped, her pulse bounded. He stood by Fannie as she cut wedges of pie and laughed. He laughed too, but his gaze now focused on her.

Their eyes met. He nodded as a smile curved his lips. She felt her face flush. The room turned much warmer and cozier.

"Hey, there's Doc. He must have just got here," Michael said, holding up a hand and gesturing to Seth. "I'll go with you so I can talk to him." Without waiting for an answer, Michael touched her elbow and directed her to the set of tables.

Fannie said something to Seth and he turned his head to the side to answer. They both laughed. When he glanced her way again, her pulse raced. She had to will herself not to hold his gaze. Otherwise, she knew she might swoon. Her feet faltered after a few steps, and Michael steadied her.

"Steady there. Guess all that twirlin' has given you sea legs." Michael chuckled and Lorelei wondered if he would laugh so easily if he knew why her legs were so boneless.

"Yes, I believe it has," she managed as they drew closer.

"How ya doin', Doc?" Michael asked, extending a hand to shake Seth's. "Good to see you finally made it. Hope you weren't out making a call till now."

"No, I wasn't. I had to take care of a few things before I came." Seth shook Michael's hand and glanced at Lorelei. Her heart felt as if it would push right through her breast bone.

"Good evening, Miss Webster. Enjoying yourself?"

"Yes…yes I am. And I'm very pleased you could make it. It's been a wonderful night so far." *It's more wonderful now that you're here.* For the first time in her life that she could recall, she felt at a loss for words. *Dear Lord, have mercy.*

She usually saw him in a suit. But tonight, he looked far more debonair with his boots highly polished, a longer black string tie, a gray satin vest, and a snugger-fitting black pin-striped topcoat.

His wide shoulders seemed broader, his height taller, his distant attitude a bit more mellow. And she drank it all in like a woman dying of thirst.

The atmosphere turned stilted. She knew she should say something. Instead, she held his gaze as the fluttering in her stomach rendered her mute.

"Miss Webster," a soft voice from Lorelei's side broke the unnerving lapse in conversation. She felt a tug at her dress.

She looked down at Nilla Jacobs. Her cherub face was tipped upward, her big brown eyes seeking and threatening to spill tears as her tiny fist clutched a fold of the brocade gown.

Crouching down, Lorelei took the child's hands within hers. "What is it sweetheart? Why aren't you asleep with the others?"

The child's lips quivered and she looked as if she would cry any minute. "I counent get to sleep. The hay makes me itch. I counent find my mamma or papa."

Lorelei wrapped her arms around the five year old and gave her a consoling hug. "Well, now, that's nothing to worry about. I believe I can fix you right up." Lifting the child in her arms she balanced the feather-weight on her right hip.

"See over there?" Lorelei pointed with her left hand to the far corner. "There's your mamma and papa. You just couldn't see them. As for that nasty old hay, how about if I lay my cape down and you can sleep on it?"

The child's teary eyes brightened while a smile spread from ear to ear. "Really, Miss Webster? You'd let me useth your cape?"

"Yes, sweetheart, I'll let you *use* it. Can you try to say that word again for me? Then we'll get you all snuggled up."

Nilla's forehead creased and Lorelei knew she was giving her best effort to think through the process of forming the word. The poor child looked exhausted. Lorelei regretted making her concentrate. Such a sweet child, and always eager to please, Nilla had made good progress over the past months with her enunciation. It had a ways to go, but it was nothing like the previous garble.

Nilla swallowed and then smiled shyly. "Ush...use," she said in a clear voice. "May I use your cape?"

Lorelei hugged Nilla tighter and kissed her forehead. "You most certainly may. And you said *use* perfectly. Thank you." The child beamed as she rested her head on Lorelei's shoulder.

Turning to the two men, Lorelei noted Seth's intense scrutiny. A thrill shot through her. "If you'll excuse me, I'll settle her in and be right back."

"That's all right," Michael offered as if he didn't have a care in the world. "I need to talk to Seth anyway about the Purdy business. You take your time. We'll be right here, Lorelei."

"Do you need any help?" Seth sounded so sincere and looked so intrigued by the little girl that Lorelei felt stymied by his fluctuating personalities. And what was the *Purdy business*?

"No, but thank you." Before her insides could play games with her mind, she crossed the room to retrieve her cape.

****

Seth watched Lorelei steer through the crowd, pausing when someone made a comment until she became swallowed up by the milling mass. He turned to Michael.

"What about Purdy?" He did not want to talk to the sheriff. He sure as hell did not want to discuss the Purdy case tonight. He wanted to feast his eyes on the delectable Lorelei. Should he ask her for the dance he longed for? Would holding her in his arms really sate his appetite? Or would it tease him more?

"Can't find a thing, that's what." Michael strode to the front of the table. "Let's have dessert while we wait for Lorelei. I'm still starved."

Seth's stomach rumbled, attesting he hadn't eaten tonight. Food remained on the tables, covered to keep it reasonably warm. His hunger was not for food. Not by a long shot.

"Pie sounds good. So what are you going to do about Purdy?"

"Hell if I know. I'll wait, see if anything pops up." Michael eyed the pies, glanced at the cakes and cobblers, then fixated on the pies. Michael's failure to delve into the strange case frosted Seth. It was the man's job. He did not do it well.

"What would you men like?" Fannie asked with a contented smile and a silver spatula in hand.

Lorelei Webster, if you please. Stop it. You can't have her.

"I'll have the apple please," Michael answered. "No, make it a slice of blueberry *and* a slice of apple."

Fannie laughed, placing a piece of each on a plate. "Nothin's ever going to fill your bottomless pit, Sheriff."

"Probably not. But I try, ma'am." Michael grinned, accepting his plate.

"How about you, Doctor Taylor? What catches your fancy?"

Lorelei Webster. "A piece of that lemon meringue, please."

"Good choice." Fannie nodded and cut a large piece of his favorite kind. His mouth watered as rich lemon wafted in the air.

He accepted the plate and dug in as Michael finished off the wedge of berry. The first bite was heaven. Not too sweet, not too tart. Creamy, and so lemony that he swirled it around his mouth, reluctant to swallow it down. The tall, golden-tipped meringue melted in his mouth, smooth and succulent.

"That's Lorelei's specialty you've got there, Doctor Taylor. Bet you haven't ever had one that good."

Lorelei's. He was doomed. As only doomed could be.

"Sure can't say that I have, Mrs. Allen. This is delicious."

"Delicious? It's downright decadent is what it is. I have to have a piece every time she makes one. And please, call me, Fannie. *Mrs. Allen* makes me feel like I'm doddering in old age."

Seth laughed. He had meant to be respectful. And as far as anyone knew, they hadn't shared an evening while he tended her wounds. "Only if you call me Seth."

"Now, that isn't right. But I would call you Doc, like so many others do, if that's all right."

"Right as rain, Fannie, right as rain."

Michael ambled along the table and asked Ellen Ahearns for a piece of cake. Fannie scooped out desserts as if she ran a restaurant. Seth indulged in savoring each and every bite.

Like her pie, Lorelei boasted a little sweetness, a bit of tartness. He had marveled at her attentiveness with tiny Nilla. Just like with Jamie and Fannie. All sweetness and patience. Yet she had a sharp, curt tongue that could bite and sting like a snake's. She had compassion when it came to people's troubles and injuries, yet gave as good as any man when facing the opposition.

Bold, brazen, opinionated and fearless when it came to defending others. Out to conquer and right the world of all its wrong. That was Miss Lorelei Webster.

Beautiful, intelligent, caring–and more seductive than was good for her own good, or his. And a mighty fine baker. That was Miss Lorelei Webster.

What a calamity. A hodgepodge of fire and ice, sugar and vinegar. How the hell could he ignore such a woman? How could he fight his feelings that grew day by day, by leaps and bounds?

But fight those feelings he would. *I have no choice.*

"I see you have some of my pie. I hope it's not too tart."

Seth started at the voice of his musings. He had been in his own world. He glanced up. Their eyes met.

"Are you fishing for a compliment, Miss Webster?" He could gaze at her face and soft lips all evening and be quiet content.

She laughed and shook her head. "No, Doctor Taylor, I'm not. To tell you the truth, I usually use a pinch more sugar in the lemon, but I ran out and had to make do."

Seth studied her. One thing, he knew, for sure. Lorelei Webster spoke her piece. And when she did, she told the truth. Honest as the day she was born. If she liked something, you knew it. If she did not, by God you knew that too, even if you did not want to hear it. And damn, but he liked that about her.

"You couldn't prove it by me. This is the best lemon meringue I've ever had. And believe me, I've had my share." He took the last bite and set his plate on the corner of the table.

A blush crept across her cheeks. He yearned to touch its heat. *As if you need more heat. You'd burn to a crisp.*

"Thank you, I'm glad you enjoyed it." She turned her attention to the dancers as if embarrassed by his compliment.

"Well, here's the little lady." Michael's voice grated on Seth's nerves. He had hoped he could talk with Lorelei before they were interrupted by others, especially the sheriff.

"Yes, I'm back." Lorelei smiled and Seth noted her strained expression. Had she also had enough of Michael for one night? Seth liked Michael, as a friend; but, as a sheriff, he failed to quite fit the bill. He was too nonchalant, too complacent. What were her feelings for Michael? *It shouldn't matter one damn bit.*

The invigorating music ended and numerous couples vacated the dance area, catching their breath as they ambled by. Others kept their places, waiting for another tune to start.

A waltz began and Seth felt more nervous than when he had stolen his first kiss from fourteen-year-old Patrice Benton. He needed to leave while the leaving was good. Knowing Michael would ask for the dance, Seth turned to her.

"May I have this dance, Miss Webster?" Why had he asked?

Surprise registered in her eyes. Yet, her smile was as sweet and pleasing as the meringue that topped her specialty. And it literally knocked the wind out of his lungs.

God, what have I done? Her twinkling eyes were too disturbing; her mouth too tempting. If he held her, her nearness would drive him insane. *Please say you need to sit this one out. Please, God, make Michael protest.*

"I'd be delighted, Doctor Taylor."

Michael grinned. "Go to it, Doc. Have a good time."

CHAPTER FOURTEEN

Reluctant to touch her elbow and escort her as etiquette demanded, Seth followed Lorelei to the dance area. He would have to touch her soon enough. What had he gotten himself into?

Hell, I've danced with many women. She's no different. Holding her at a respectable distance would not amount to a hill of beans. It would be an insignificant dance. Nothing more.

She stopped and turned. "Is this far enough?" Her warm smile seeped right into his bloodstream and wrapped snugly around his heart. Funny, she didn't look so brazen or so feisty right now.

"Perfect," he said, forcing a smile. The second his left hand closed over her soft one and his right made contact with her slender waistline, his heart leaped to his throat. His fingers burned, as if scorched by flames.

Don't think of how good she feels. Yet, he noted her soft skin, tiny waist, pleasing smile, her shimmering hair. Lavender invaded his senses as he glided with her across the floor.

"Miss Webster, may I give you a word of advice?" He should have asked about Nilla. Would she take offense and scurry away? That might be a relief from this torture.

Her eyes widened as her feet followed his with ease. "Certainly." She sounded skeptical, though she smiled.

"The other night I went to a town meeting. The men have had enough of your meddling for a while. You need to watch yourself."

She looked baffled. "I hadn't heard of a meeting."

"It was for men only. I don't imagine the women heard about it."

Her back stiffened and her fingers tightened within his.

She glanced to the side as if watching other dancers drift by, yet he knew she was mulling over what he had said.

"The meeting was about me?" She focused on the others.

"Yes. I'm afraid it was." He had meant to warn her, not to scare her, or make her feel ashamed.

"I see." She kept her eyes averted, yet he saw her lips quiver, her eyelids blink briskly several times.

The possibility she would shed tears nearly bowled him over. His throat tightened and his chest ached. He pulled her closer, needing to protect her from further hurt. She did not resist.

"You should be used to them talking about you." He tried to sound glib to lighten her spirit as he spun them around.

Their gazes met. Her chuckle sounded sweet as music. "Yes, I should. But…a meeting…they must be angrier than I thought."

"That, they are. And that's why I wanted to warn you. They sent an advertisement for a new teacher to Cheyenne."

Her eyes widened and her mouth fell agape. "But, I do my teaching well. Why would they do such a thing?"

Lord, how he wanted to hug her tighter, to tell her everything would be all right. He should have stayed out of her and the men's affairs. But he had told her. He was not like Michael, to let unfinished business get lost in the shuffle.

"You do an excellent job at teaching from what I've heard. Even they admitted it. But they figure if they get a replacement, then they can boot you out of town."

She stared at him. Her lips did not thin in anger or tremble with dismay. She looked like a confused child who had lost her way. His chest constricted further.

She hung her head. Was she embarrassed?

"I told you so you would watch what you say or do from now on. I told them…" He could have bit off his tongue.

Her gaze shot up to meet his. "What did you tell them?"

He could lie. Yet he felt compelled to let her know what he had said, what he had hoped for.

"I told them if they ignored your protests and ranting, you'd see it

96

did no good and you'd stop. I'd hoped that would be the case. Then they'd be happy, and you'd retain your position."

She searched his eyes. A tiny grin surfaced and her eyes twinkled. His heart hammered.

"Why did you even bother to say that to them? I would've thought you would've stayed out of it entirely."

Her comments surprised him, yet he found himself returning her grin. "I most likely should have. But they were so hot under the collar that I feared they might do something foolish. They needed to think rationally, and cool down."

When the music ended, he reluctantly released her.

She smiled, and he drank it in like a thirsty dog. "Thank you for trying to ease the situation. I appreciate your concern, and for telling me. I only hope I can change my ways. I've tried to sit back and approach things cautiously, but I've always failed. My daddy said I was too impetuous for my own good—and I am."

Her admission of her overzealous nature touched him more deeply than he knew he should allow. But how could he stop the tender feelings she invoked? He saw a different side of her at every turn. And each one contradicted his first staunch opinion.

He had labeled her an instigator; he had been wrong. Rile, irritate, aggravate, yes, but she did not instigate. She did not purposely annoy people, but acted in the defense of others who lacked the ability or means to defend themselves.

Another waltz began and he jumped at the chance to hold her again. Without glancing to see if Michael might claim the dance, he asked, "Would you care to dance again, Miss Webster?"

She did not hesitate. "I'd love to, Doctor Taylor." She placed her hand in his and they started easy steps to the side.

She felt so good in his arms. *Too* good. Sheer torture, knowing he would never be able to have more than a lasting friendship. Strange, how at first, he had thought to stay a million miles away from this hellacious beauty. Now, he valued her friendship far more than any other member of the community.

"I take it you got Nilla settled down?" Remembering how motherly Lorelei looked as she hugged and carried the child tugged at heartstrings he fought so desperately to hold intact.

"Yes. She's such a sweet child. I enjoy her at school."

"I have a feeling you enjoy all your pupils."

She laughed. "Yes, I do. I love children. But, I must confess, although I make them mind and do their work, I also love to spoil them."

How he loved to hear her laugh.

"You'll make a good mother someday." He spun her slowly.

Now, she laughed louder. "I truly believe there isn't a man on this earth who would want to father a child with me. Most men stay well away from my flapping tongue and head-strong ways. Surely, you know that."

"What about Michael?" A sour taste filled his mouth at mentioning the man, yet he longed to hear her answer. It would make no difference who she set her cap on. He couldn't have her.

Michael lacked honorable intentions toward her. Maybe he merely wanted to protect her, needed to prevent her from being left in the cold when Michael finished with her. Then, why did the idea of her with any other man pierce his heart?

"Michael's a good friend. He's…well sometimes lackadaisical in his job and half the time doesn't follow through. We'd be at each others' throat if we were around each other very long. He means well, but we can never be more than friends."

Thank you, Lord. Relief swept over him at knowing she would not be ill-used by Michael. But what about someone else? The thought unsettled him. He should wish for her happiness with someone who could give her the children she desired. He certainly had no right.

"What about you? Did you leave any broken hearts back in San Francisco that you pine for? Have any of the few single women in town caught your eye?"

The question rocked him, his right foot faltering for a second. Resuming his steps, he plastered on a meager smile.

"Not yet. I'm afraid as much as Michael is negligent in his duty, I'm dedicated to mine. I don't believe I could handle a wife, too." The lie slipped off his tongue as easily as pouring water from a pitcher. For years, he had used the same excuse.

Lorelei's heart sped at hearing no woman held Seth's heart. Of course, it was sheer nonsense to think he would ever view her as a candidate. He had stood up for her at the meeting, but that did not mean he would strap himself with a bold, mouthy woman.

No, Seth Taylor would choose a woman all soft and sugar sweet. One he could be proud of, who would be the epitome of femininity and poise, graciousness and gentility.

Well, at least she had his friendship. Somehow, when they first met, she thought they would be worlds apart. And, in a sense, they were. Yet, they had an easy camaraderie. She brought him her victims, he patched them up. Soon she would go broke if it kept up, though he charged her half the amount that he should.

Discouraged at knowing they would never be more than friends, she felt elated they shared that much. Yet it hurt, knowing she might never be held within his strong arms more than sharing an occasional dance. Never taste those tempting lips.

While in his arms, she drifted in heaven. All warm inside, as if a candle burned softly within. His large, calloused hand felt so strong against hers; his other palm feeling so very right as it held her as close as decorum allowed.

She would bask in this much for tonight and treasure it forever. As farfetched as they seemed, she would cling to her unattainable hopes and silly dreams. That's all she had.

Would they be enough to carry her through all the tomorrows?

CHAPTER FIFTEEN

Lorelei leaned against the railing. She always enjoyed watching the students release their youthful energy as they kicked the large ball and gave chase. Yet, her mind strayed.

For the past week, she had barely caught a glimpse of Seth as he rode through town, or when he passed the school while she supervised the children playing outside at recess.

Her hopes of their friendship taking a step further seemed fruitless. Either she was teaching, or he was off devoting himself to another patient. If wise, she should settle for friendship. Why should she pursue more? He might set her heart to pattering, yet his cool, leave-me-to-my-own attitude when it concerned the community continued to weigh heavy in her mind.

Pushing her confusing thoughts aside, she focused on the children playing tag. Concern set in as she watched Jamie.

He ran and chased, yet his eyes were dull, his movements sluggish. His smile looked forced, as if he was fatigued or depressed. He could be coming down with a cold, but Jamie was rarely sick. Most likely, his father had been indulging again. She would watch him closely.

Feeling the chill seep through her woolen coat, she waved the hand bell to call a halt to play time. The students readily ceased their game and flocked toward the schoolhouse.

Missy Cooper rushed to her side. "Miss Webster..." she caught her breath"...did you see? Johnny won again. He got the most tags."

"He certainly did, and he'll get his ribbon when everyone is at their desks." Lorelei smiled at the eight-year-old as she darted to catch up with the others. Missy had a child's crush on the handsome blond. At sixteen, Johnny Piedmont had long, muscular legs. No wonder he claimed the most ribbons, even if he did try to lose half the time.

Missy mirrored her brother, all politeness and sharp as a tack. Yet, sad anxiousness lurked behind her eyes, unless she was talking about Johnny. *Damn Miles Cooper. His besotted ways affected his children.* She would like to ring his thick neck.

Like soldiers, ranging from five to sixteen, the children trooped up the steps and returned to their seats. She followed, her thoughts drifting to Seth once more. He plagued her mind, and filled her dreams at night, leaving her yearning for more by morning.

It puzzled her that she wanted to overlook how he lived in his own sheltered world. It would be wise to listen to logic. Yet, her libido and wishful heart overruled. She needed to push harder, fish deeper. And prayed he would take the bait.

The time needs to be right. And when it was, she would reel in the line. But patience was not one of her strong virtues. If it didn't happen soon, she might go raving mad. How odd to finally pine for a man after resigning herself to spinsterhood. The depressing thought, though she concealed it behind the veneer of bold, self-assurance, curled achingly around her lonely heart.

****

Drying the last dish from supper, Lorelei jumped at the loud pounding on her door. The bowl bobbled as she fought not to drop it. No one visited after dark. The hairs on her nape bristled.

"Miss Webster, come quick. You in there?"

Johnny Piedmont's shrill voice froze her in place. She clutched the bowl against her pounding heart. She had told Seth and promised herself she would not rile the men unless absolutely necessary. If Johnny's voice was any indication, she might again end up at Seth's. She longed to be with him, but not at the cost of disaster. Yet, disaster usually struck out of the blue.

She raced to the door and flung it open. Johnny's eyes were wild, full of stark fear, his hair plastered to his sweaty forehead. He panted as if he had run a mile. His usual unshakable confidence didn't appear to

101

be so sturdy right now.

"What's happened?" Hands shaking, she snatched her coat from the peg by the door.

"Oh, Miss Webster. It's Jamie. You gotta come quick." Johnny bent at the waist and gulped in air.

Lorelei's heart plunged to her feet. A fist seemed to squeeze her lungs. Dear God, not Jamie. What had Miles done now?

"Where is he? What happened?" She sped down the steps. His horse stood silhouetted at the hitching rail.

"He's at Doc's. He's sick, Miss Webster." He unloosed the reins to his horse and faced her in the silvery darkness. "He took some of his mamma's pills. He don't look so good."

Her mind spun. It would take too long to harness her horse. "Can you take me on your horse?"

"Sure thing, Miss Webster."

"Let's go."

They raced to Seth's, Lorelei clutching Johnny's thin waist from behind. Clumps of dirt flew up from beneath the light layer of snow, the horse eating up the distance at break neck sped.

"Is Johanna there?" she yelled above the pounding hooves.

Johnny turned his head to the side. "Not when I left. Doc said to tell her he needed time without anyone in his way. She had to get the girls out of their bath…so she told me to go on."

Only a dim light lit Seth's living room as they approached. A slice of moonlight and a few stars illuminated the porch steps. The minute Johnny pulled the horse to a halt, Lorelei paid no mind to her dress hiking up to her knees as she slithered down.

She flew over the steps, across the porch, barged through the door and bolted to the infirmary. Fear had her as winded as Johnny had been. She skidded to a stop at the open doorway.

Jamie, white as a ghost, lay on the exam table. He looked so small, so much younger. Seth stood at his side staring at the boy. *No!* She wanted to ask if he was ali…

Words clogged in her constricted throat. Her ears buzzed, and she fought dizziness. *No, no, no. Not Jamie. Dear God, no.* She clutched the casing for support.

"Come in, Miss Webster. He's very ill, but still with us."

Lorelei took a deep breath and realized she had been unable to do so since coming to the doorway. The pungent stench of vomit assaulted her. Her whole body trembled, her bounding pulse drummed in her ears. She dug her nails further into the wood. *Still with us,* repeated in her clouded mind.

"Thank God." Tears flooded her eyes. And for the first time in her life, she truly thought she would faint.

"Easy does it," Seth's controlled voice filtered into her jumbled mind, soothing her; his warm hand upon her forearm provided comfort. Their eyes met through a blur.

Who reached out first, she didn't know. She didn't care. She sought only reassurance that everything would be made right.

His strong arms encircled her. She wrapped hers around his waist and held tight to the solid security. His nearness, the warmth of his embrace transmitted strength into her numb limbs.

There was no passion. She wanted none; she needed none. Only comfort, the feel of another sharing a moment of grief, of stalwart hope, of communicating an unspoken fortitude to see them through the next phase of this harrowing experience.

Seth leaned back, keeping one hand at her back and gently brushed back a lock of fallen hair from her face. "Better?"

She nodded.

"Good girl." She liked the term he used. It calmed her.

When he glanced past her and pulled away, Lorelei turned. Johnny, almost as pale as Jamie, shifted his eyes from his motionless friend to them as he gripped the door casing.

"Johnny, thank you. I appreciate you going for Mrs. Cooper, and Miss Webster. Come in. I imagine you want to see Jamie."

Johnny hesitantly took a step into the room. Lorelei stiffened, almost afraid to again look at Jamie. Yet, she needed to touch him; to assure herself he was, indeed, all right. Her face must have registered her anxiety.

"The drugs heavily sedated him before I could rid his stomach of what hadn't gone into his system. But he's breathing easier. Be thankful Johnny found him in time." He reached up and helped her remove her coat. She felt helpless as a lamb.

Lorelei glanced at Johnny, wanting to ask more questions. But she needed to go to Jamie's side. Answers could wait.

Forcing herself to walk to the table, she called for every ounce of courage she possessed. It was one thing to see a battered wife, harder to witness a bruised child. Her anger always overrode becoming distraught. Later, when finally alone, she would allow herself to fall apart. But seeing this earth-shattering scene of a child so still, so close to death's door, had her trembling, forced tears— and tore at her very soul.

She focused on Jamie's chest. From under the thin wool blanket it rose and fell slightly. Seth's words hummed in her ears. *'Be thankful Johnny found him in time.'*

How easily death lurked around the corner. How quickly it could claim its victim. Without Seth's expertise, Jamie would be lost to them. Guilt riddled her. She fought the raw emotion.

She turned her head and tried to smile at Seth. He stood across from her, his hand on Johnny's trembling shoulder. "Thank you," she whispered. "Thank you for being here. For saving him."

Seth didn't gloat or return the smile. "I did what I did because that's who I am, what I am. I try to save lives. I don't always succeed. In this case, I hope I'm lucky."

Her eyes rounded at his answer. She tenderly stroked Jamie's face. Seth sounded so humdrum, so business-like. Did nothing ever rattle him? Could almost losing a young boy's life not unsettle him? She would do well to borrow some of his placid emotion.

"Lucky?" she asked, clutching the child's cool hand.

"I induced vomiting to rid the stomach contents. I've administered stimulants, but the effects of the laudanum may be too potent for him to withstand. Its toxicity may injure his organs. It'll be a while until I know if he's out of danger."

Lorelei's heart lurched at his stark explanation. She should be grateful he had not given her false hopes. But his blunt, professional jargon wreaked havoc with her rattled nerves.

Footsteps scrambled in the hallway. All three turned as a blanched-faced, panic-stricken Johanna, clasping the hands of the two girls, rushed into the room.

"I...came as soon as I could," Johanna said in a choked voice, her face dotted with beads of perspiration despite the night's chill. Lorelei felt the woman's anguish tear at her own heart.

"Is he—is he..."

Seth strode across the room in four quick strides, bringing him to Johanna's side. "He's alive."

Johanna swayed and closed her eyes as her fists tightened visibly on each of the girls' hands. "Praise the Lord."

Missy stared at Jamie, her red-rimmed eyes dry, yet full of fear. Little Jessica whimpered and tears flowed down her pudgy cheeks as she craned her neck to see her sibling.

The three moved closer to Jamie. Lorelei stepped to the end of the table to give them room. She felt like an outsider, but part of her screamed Jamie mattered just as much to her.

Johanna released the girls' hands and gazed at Jamie. She neither lifted a hand, nor changed her stoic expression. Large tears silently slid down her cheeks as she viewed her only son. Lorelei's tears escaped, her throat aching at seeing Johanna's despair, of feeling her own torment. Guilt raged at her that she had overlooked this happening. Clearly, she had not been in tune to Jamie's warning signs. The air became too thick to inhale.

Lorelei wiped her cheeks with the back of her hand, and fought to remain strong for the others. She glanced at the girls. Missy grasped the table's edge as if suppressing a howl of agony. Jessica, bless her heart, stood several inches back, tears easing down her face while she peered up at her beloved brother.

Lorelei took a step toward Jessica so she could lift her up to see Jamie better. Her feet froze when the howl came.

Johanna's mournful wail shook Lorelei to her core. Pitiful. Heart-wrenching. Johanna leaned over and gathered Jamie's torso in her arms. She rocked back and forth, embracing him.

"My sweet son, my precious son. I love you so much, do you hear me? We all love you." Her sobs turned muffled as she crooned to the unconscious boy in her arms.

Lorelei couldn't stand it. She had shed buckets of tears over the years, been disheartened and distressed hundreds of times by various crises, but she did it privately. She knew she would break down and wail as loud as Johanna if she stayed. And that would never do. She prided herself in remaining strong for others while they drew from her strength.

The rank odor again curled Lorelei's nose, its acrid bite adding tears to her eyes. It was the means to her escape.

She bent down, lifted the offensive pewter basin off the floor and held it out at arm's length. "I'll take this out and dump it," she muttered, managing the few words past her constricted throat.

Seth scowled. "Miss Webster, you don't have to do that. I—"

"I need a bit of fresh air anyway. I'll be back shortly." She averted his gaze and prayed her words brooked no argument.

Pan in hand, she fled outside and welcomed the chill that nipped her flushed cheeks. She dumped the pan's contents over the porch rail. The tension of the disturbing scene eased a fraction as she inhaled the crisp air. Leaning against the rail, she allowed the pan's last remains to drip out.

Guilt burdened her mind, ate at her stomach like churning acid. *How could she have been so foolish?*

"You'll freeze out in this cold." She started at Seth's voice. Peering over her shoulder, she saw he carried her coat. He came to her side and placed it over her shoulders.

"Thank you." Unable to force a smile, she turned back to stare across the twilight that blanketed the front lawn.

"I'll do everything I can to save that boy."

At his sincerity, a smidgeon of a smile surfaced. He thought her distress stemmed from Jamie's precarious illness. In a way it did, but also because she had lent to its cause.

"I know you will. And I pray your efforts are good enough."

"What else is bothering you?"

His keen perception gave her pause. She turned to glare at him, more angered at herself. She averted eye contact.

"I let this happen. I could have prevented it if I hadn't been so gullible." She dared a brief glance at him.

His brows rose. "You, gullible, Miss Webster? I hardly think so.

Why would you say that?"

"Because I'm the one who talked to him after the swimming incident. I believed what he said."

He clasped the railing with both hands and leaned over a bit as if studying the lawn. Was he perturbed with her for her oversight, or at the lengths Jamie had taken?

"What exactly *did* he tell you?"

She hesitated, dismayed he would bellow at her stupidity in believing Jamie. She deserved it.

"He said he'd been tired and should've known better than to swim in the cold water. He told me he got a cramp and wasn't able to fight it." She stiffened, anticipating his tongue lashing.

"Sounds reasonable. He was a good convincing liar. He knew how much you wanted to believe him rather than think otherwise."

"Thank you." Surprised again at this unpredictable man, she sighed with relief that he had not reprimanded her like a ninny. Still, remorse festered within her gut, dismay riding heavy on her tired shoulders.

He straightened and turned. His eyes searched her face. They held no anger, no reproach, only intense scrutiny.

He cleared his throat. "I need to check Jamie. Stay out for as long as you like, but don't catch a chill."

She watched him walk through the doorway, the click of the latch sounding heavy in the stark silence. He puzzled her. How unlike her to feel such powerful reactions each time she saw him.

Well, no wonder, she thought, trying to give reason to her strange attraction. He was tall, muscular and very handsome, especially when he smiled. What woman would not feel a tug? She was no more immune to his appeal than any other female.

She thought of how he avoided certain situations. And that forced the disturbing craw. Though he walked with an air of confidence, taking charge when matters involved him, he nevertheless possessed that flaw. And, in her book, it was a big one. If she told herself to forget him because of that fault once, she had told herself a hundred times.

She could no longer deny her attraction, or that she longed to be the one to claim his heart. One he would lavish with affection. Her heart sank, her chest ached. What a silly dream.

107

No man in his right mind would find her attractive. Not with her rambunctious, zealous ways, her big mouth and large meddling nose. For years, she had accepted the fact she would never find a man who could overlook her faults. Why should she think *he* could?

Seth Taylor could have his pick of any single woman in town. Why think otherwise? Yet, hold her dream she would. No harm could come of dreaming. But, she reminded herself, dreams were for children.

And neither of them were children.

With the despairing burden of knowing she should have prevented Jamie's second attempt, plus the dismay at acknowledging Seth was out of her reach, her chest felt weighted down, her life no more than a mired bog. She slowly turned away from the darkness and returned to join the others.

CHAPTER SIXTEEN

"But Doctor Taylor, you need your sleep too," Johanna said without much conviction.

Lorelei noted the toll Jamie's harrowing escape had taken on the woman. She looked worn to a frazzle.

Mixing powders with a mortar and pestle at the sideboard, Seth smiled. "I know you want to be with Jamie, but the girls look ready to drop where they stand. So, I'll make you a deal."

Johanna's listless eyes fixed on Seth. "A deal?"

"Tonight's the most critical time. Whether you stay or not, I'll need to tend him more often than not. It's likely I'll wake all of you." Seth poured a liquid into the mix and stirred.

"I'll care for him tonight while you three go home and get some needed sleep. By morning, I'll definitely need rest. You can take over then. If his condition changes drastically through the night, I'll send word to you immediately. I promise."

"I…don't know. I should be here when he wakes." Indecision on the woman's face made her look all the wearier.

"I know how you feel, but believe me, you'll be of much more benefit to both Jamie and me tomorrow than tonight."

"But how will you send word? You sent Johnny home. You won't be able to leave him if he worsens." Johanna looked as if she might start crying all over again.

Lorelei shifted Jessica to her other hip as the child rubbed her heavy eyelids, fighting sleep with another big yawn.

"I'll stay here if that will make you feel better, Johanna. School tomorrow should be cancelled in light of this. I can come for you if Doctor Taylor feels you should come during the night. And tomorrow, when you relieve the doctor, I'll go home."

For a moment, Lorelei thought Johanna or Seth would disagree with her offer. But the exhausted woman managed a meek nod. Seth turned back to devote his attention to pouring the potion into a brown bottle.

She hoped she had not been too presumptuous to think he would allow her to stay. At least, he had not refuted her offer.

Johanna sighed. "I know you both are right, so I'll take the girls home. But I plan to be back at dawn. I can put a note on the schoolhouse for you, Lorelei." Johanna grabbed Missy's coat, handed it to the girl and then reached for Jessica's.

"A wise decision, Mrs. Cooper," Seth said. "You'll feel much better, I'm sure. Again, I won't hesitate to send Miss Webster should the need arise, I assure you."

Lorelei held Jessica while Johanna pushed the little arms through the sleeves.

"I thank you, Doctor Taylor, for all you've done for Jamie. I can rest a little easier knowing he is in your hands."

"Thank you, Mrs. Cooper. I'll continue to do all I can."

Readjusting her coat, Johanna turned to Lorelei. "Thank you again, Lorelei. You're always there when I need you. I don't know how I will ever repay you for your kindness."

Lorelei felt herself blush. She never liked being on the receiving end of compliments. It made her feel awkward.

"Don't be foolish, Johanna. What are friends for if they can't help in time of need? And you know I care about you and your children as if you're my own family. You go home and sleep so you can show that pretty smile to Jamie come morning."

She purposely made no mention of Miles. He could go to Hell. It would be the highlight of her day. She felt no remorse at such a thought, though she prayed forgiveness for the harshness of it.

****

Lorelei poured fresh-made coffee into two mugs at the kitchen counter while Seth tried to ease more medicine down Jamie. She added a spoon of sugar to hers before returning to the two males who played such a big part in her life.

Entering the room, she watched Seth carry Jamie to one of the metal beds and set him down on the thin, tick-mattress as if he weighted no more than a toddler. Jamie was tall and solid for his age, his muscles attributing to adulthood fast approaching.

She'd been so distraught over Jamie's condition she had not paid much attention to Seth's lack of suit jacket or vest. With his shirt sleeves rolled up, she now noticed how the muscles of his broad back flexed and bunched under the white cotton shirt. How his powerful biceps pulled taut against the fabric. Her throat went dry while her mouth salivated with gusto.

She noted his sinewy forearms covered with dark fine hairs as he pulled the brown woolen blanket to Jamie's chin.

He straightened, took a step back, and turned. He smiled as he reached for the cup of steaming coffee she held out.

"Thank you. It smells delicious. I'll probably need ten more." He took a sip.

And how absolutely delicious *you look*, she thought, unable to draw her greedy eyes away from the curly, dark hairs exposed below the two undone top buttons of his shirt.

"I'll keep you in a ready supply." Her heart fluttered so profusely, she wondered if she would be able to swallow hers.

"Sounds good. Let's sit for a minute."

He walked to the narrow bed behind her and sat. "Have a seat, Miss Webster. It's going to be a long night." Holding the mug in two hands he leaned against the wall and stretched out his long legs till his boots heels rested on the floor.

Lorelei surveyed the bed. Indecision at propriety made her hesitate. When he chuckled, she felt more self conscience at the awkward predicament. Had she ever felt so hesitant or unsettled, or so very aware of a man's masculinity? *Courage, girl.*

"It's a bit late to worry about your reputation."

Her face heated. "You must know I have no reputation to protect. They'll talk about me whether I'm here or not."

He laughed again as his eyes focused on her. "Then, if it's not your reputation you're worried about, don't tell me you're afraid to sit by me. I'd never believe you afraid of anyone."

"Of course I'm not afraid of you." Would her hasty reply make him realize she lied through her teeth? Now that she had him right where she wanted him, indecision stymied her. She felt ignorant as to how to charm a gentleman.

"Then, sit so I can rest my neck. It's too damn tiring to hold my chin up. It's been a helluva day, and I'd like to relax, if you don't mind. Take the chair, if you'd be more comfortable."

No one had ever called her a coward. But he had almost insinuated such a thing. *Well, she was no coward.*

With the poise of a well-bred lady sitting down to afternoon tea on an elegant settee, she sat, intending a reasonable, proper distance. Instead, the thin mattress, slanting under his weight, forced her to slide against his thigh. She gulped.

He moved first. Balancing his coffee, he adjusted his position until a few inches separated them. She felt heat from his all-too-close thigh. Would her cheeks ever cool?

Clutching her cup, she wiggled back so she too could lean against the wall. Her feet left the floor. She needed a diversion. *Talk about anything.*

"What made you come here from San Francisco?" Oh great ghosts! For sure, he would think her meddling again. Embarrassed, she scanned the room.

"I lived just outside the city. But the havoc of the large city made my decision. A smaller town sounded better."

Lorelei sipped the cooling brew. It felt foreign to be so tongue-tied, so ill-at-ease. His nearness had her insides buzzing like a swarm of bees trying to escape. Yet, warmth seeped through her veins, an unfamiliar yearning begging to be fulfilled.

"And is Toleman to your liking so far?" Had he heard her voice quaver? Frustrated, she kept her head against the wall.

She heard him swallow a swig of coffee. "Yes, as a matter of fact. Too bad you don't find it as rewarding."

Lorelei dared a glance his way. He scrutinized her. No smug smile,

112

no frown, just a stare. How inept she felt knowing he was sage to all her misfortune. She had only herself to blame.

"That's where you're wrong. Though I've raised many brows and tempers with my meddling, I'm partial to this town and the good people here. And I love my time with the children. My teaching is extremely important to me, and I believe I've accomplished quite a bit. I wouldn't give up my position for all the—" How stupid. Very shortly she might be forced to give it up.

"Gold in the world? You may not have to, but you may have to give up this school if you don't watch yourself, as I told you." His smile seemed condescending, almost mocking.

How utterly foolish to think he could be attracted to her. He had formed the same low opinion as the others.

"You said, yourself, only a hand full of men want me gone. The others will see I'm not ousted just because a few are angry." Why didn't her words register any clout in her mind?

Tears, unbidden, swam before her eyes. She blinked several times and eyed Jamie as he rolled to his side, rather than look at Seth and see his pity. She took another sip of coffee to ease the sudden dryness of her throat.

"Have you always been so driven to right all the wrongs in the world?"

She glanced his way, the tormenting memories vivid in her mind. "Since I was seven, though I didn't actually take a hard stand until I was older and believed I could make a difference."

"What happened when you were seven?"

His eyes showed such compassion, she went on. "I watched my friend's drunken father push her out of his way. She toppled down a flight of stairs. Her arms and legs were paralyzed for life. He'd often abused his family when drunk, but no one ever did anything. I vowed that day if I knew someone suffered at the hands of others, I'd take a stand to prevent them further harm."

His empathetic expression almost undid her composure. Whenever she thought about little Sarie, her heart twisted. Guilt gnawed deep because she had been unable to prevent the disaster.

As if sensing her distress, he nodded and thankfully changed the subject. "You came from Cheyenne?"

"Yes." So, someone had filled him in on her background.

"Why did *you* come here?"

"I saw the advertisement. My mother died when I was five and my father was dying from smallpox when I returned from my schooling. I also prefer a small town, but taught in Cheyenne so I could care for him. His heart finally gave out."

"I'm sorry about your father."

She looked up to his contrite eyes. "Thank you, but we weren't all that close. He had wanted a son from the day I was born. Instead, he got a girl who was stronger in will and mouth than he could barely stand. We loved each other, but because of our different natures we merely tolerated each other."

He laughed at that. A pleasing sound, deep, rich, and heartwarming. "I'm sure you did."

Jamie coughed, forcing them to direct their glances his way. He stirred, then nestled his head into the pillow without waking.

"Will he be all right?" Her gaze met Seth's. How very dark his eyes were, almost ebony, so very compelling. Again, tears threatened. What a night. Tension had literally drained her.

"I hope so. Morning will tell. Thank God Johnny got him here so soon." Fatigue and worry etched his face as he eyed Jamie.

"How did Johnny find him? I didn't think it wise to go into it when Johanna and the girls were here."

Seth bent forward and set his cup on the floor, then leaned back to rest his head against the wall. Closing his eyes, he inhaled deep, as if remembering caused him anguish. This man cared. Deeply cared. Then why did he hold himself back from the community? He puzzled her as much as she infuriated the men.

He opened his eyes and peered at Jamie. "Johnny said they often meet by the river to talk. I have the feeling his life isn't much happier than Jamie's. They must confide in each other."

He glanced her way, his eyes clouded by a dull sheen. She shared his weighty heartache at rehashing Johnny's arrival.

"When Jamie didn't come as planned, Johnny rode toward the Coopers thinking he'd meet him. He said he'd turned to leave outside the house when he heard a thud against their barn door."

Oh God! Jamie. Her heart tightened in her chest.

Seth shook his head, rubbed his hands down his pant legs, and turned his attention back to the sleeping boy. "Johnny found him lying just inside. When his boot struck a pill bottle, he realized what Jamie had done."

He looked at her, his eyes now masked his emotions, his voice steady and reserved. Anguish tore at her chest as she thought of Jamie, all alone. Simply giving up. How could Seth relate this and not show what he must feel? She had seen sadness—earnest caring in his eyes— minutes ago.

"He didn't take time to tell Johanna. He just dragged Jamie to his horse, threw him over the saddle, and rushed here."

"Thank goodness he thought so quickly. Dear God, what if you hadn't been here?" Tears trickled down her cheeks. She felt no embarrassment at her weak display. A child had almost died. She could not hold back her emotions any longer, even if he could.

"You know the answer to that. I don't need to say it."

At his stark words, a chill shivered up her spine. How could he speak so apathetically? No matter how hard he tried to act detached, or why, she knew otherwise. He definitely cared, for Jamie who had whittled his way into his heart.

Lorelei swiped at the wetness on her cheeks as she set her mug on the floor. She tried to hide her escaping yawn.

"You better catch some sleep. I don't want you falling off your horse if I have to send you after Johanna."

Lord, please don't let that happen. "I rode with Johnny. I'd have to use yours." She yawned again, cursing how unlady-like she must appear. Her eyelids felt ready to droop to her toes.

****

Seth should have known Lorelei never did anything plain and simple. He grabbed the pillow to his right and motioned her to lean up. When she did, he stuffed it behind her.

"Go to sleep before you collapse." The second he spoke, he regretted his gruff voice. Yet she didn't seem to notice as she settled back. As soon as her eyes closed, she fell asleep.

Thank God for small miracles. Her nearness alone played havoc with him. The familiar, gentle lavender scent drove him wild. And if those two things weren't enough to cause him pain below the belt, her tears had torn viciously at his heartstrings.

He could not afford for that to happen. Not in a million years could he let down his guard. How many times had he reminded himself? More often than not since meeting this bold woman.

He needed sleep. To bury fanciful thoughts along with his past. When she came near, his past sprouted up like an annoying burdock. It stung deep till he felt raw and agitated enough to bellow. It haunted him, mocked him at its irony.

The more he was with her, the more he yearned. Though why his libido reacted with such force over such a woman escaped his comprehension. And the more he longed for her, the harder his sordid past bit him in the ass.

He fought memories with closed eyes. Yet visions of his father's rabid eyes swam before him. He remembered the feel of calloused hands. Shame and utter humiliation swirled in his head while a cacophony screamed in his ears. His gut twisted taut. Bile churned and rose till he nearly gagged on its sour taste.

Seth's eyes flew open. A cold sweat beaded his forehead, clung to his palms.

Forget the past. Concentrate on helping Jamie. What you'll say to Jamie. Only Jamie.

CHAPTER SEVENTEEN

Lorelei awoke slowly, feeling cozy and comfy, as if warm bricks lay under her pillow, the quilt a secure embrace.

She snuggled deeper, only to stiffen at hearing a distinct *lubdub*. Her eyes flew open; the rest of her froze.

The oil lamp in the far corner burned low, bathing the room in a soft golden glow. Jamie slept soundly on the narrow bed to her left. The evening's events came crashing back. She realized not what she rested against, but upon whom.

Her heart thrummed within the confines of her chest, drummed in her ears. She flexed her fingers ever so slightly and felt the firm chest beneath his shirt. His embrace felt comfortable and secure. She feasted on his scent; soap and potent masculinity.

"You're awake."

Lorelei jerked back, yet remained within the circle of his arms. Did he think her brazen as usual? Their gazes locked.

A hint of a grin curled his lips. Then it vanished, leaving his expression blank. She felt flustered.

"Y-yes. I must've been sleeping hard." How ridiculous she sounded. *Could you not have said something logical?*

He did smile at her reply. A smile that brought sparkles to his eyes. Her heart thudded, her blood rose several degrees.

Their gazes held. Could he tell how content she felt being in his arms? Could he read the sheer dreaminess in her eyes as romantic notions and rising desire curled around her heart?

His eyelids lowered half way; his eyes darkened, if that were

117

possible. He, too, felt something; she could see it, feel it, as his arms tightened slightly.

He's going to kiss me. Her heart danced as she struggled to resist leaning toward him. She would not act as bold as she wanted to, not if it meant he might shy away at her advance. How dark the stubble looked on his face. Would it feel rough against her cheek? She welcomed the thought.

She waited with the eagerness of a child on Christmas morn. Potent desire soared. Oh, how she had longed for this moment.

As if he just realized what he intended, his eyes widened. His arms fell slack as he leaned back. He appeared rattled by what had passed between them. Emptiness lambasted her. She had never experienced such potent loneliness. *Curse the man's reluctance.*

Knowing she best ignore the shared intimacy—though it had been much too brief—she repressed tears and asked, "How is he?"

As she glanced at Jamie, she caught anger brewing in Seth's eyes. Was it directed at himself, or her? She stole a sideward glance. His eyes softened as he peered at the boy.

"He's resting well. I got more liquid and medicine down him a while ago, though he never fully awakened. I think he's over the worst." Seth stretched his legs and arched his shoulders.

Lorelei sighed at his optimistic remark. Had she seen anger? Yes. And most likely it had been aimed at her. "Thank God."

She glanced his way, praying she could act as if nothing was amiss. *But everything is wrong. Why didn't he kiss me?* Did he find her unattractive? Or was it her bold ways?

"Can I do anything for him or you as long I'm awake?"

When his eyebrows rose, she realized what she had said. Her cheeks heated. She looked down, busied her hands by smoothing down the wrinkles and folds of her skirt.

"I could go a cup of coffee, if you're offering."

She glanced upward. His grin set his eyes to twinkling again. *I'll take that much for the time being, thank you.*

"I've been longing for some for awhile, but didn't want to disturb you by getting up again."

Where she got the nerve to speak, she didn't know. "I apologize for leaning on you. I had no idea I'd done that."

"No apology necessary, Miss Webster. It was my pleasure."

Sure, as much pleasure as when we first met and you said those exact words. You didn't mean them in earnest then, and you sure as hell don't mean them now.

Discomforted by the awkwardness, she knew she better get that coffee. She would reason this out later.

Seth started to get up, apparently to assist her as she pushed upward. "Please, you just relax and let me get the coffee. At this point, we can certainly forget etiquette."

He nodded as she stood. "Do you want it black again?"

"Yes, please, I always take it black."

With stoic movements, she walked to the doorway. Just as she reached it, his words stopped her.

"You didn't lean on me. You kept tilting to the side and were going to fall over. I brought you back to lean on me."

She dared not turn around. Her satisfied grin was a mile wide. His confession marked the first gesture of more than mere politeness. Did he realize it? Undoubtedly not.

He may have resisted the kiss for now, but how long could he hold out? She hoped not much longer. A woman could die from the hunger for a man of her choosing. And even with his one annoying fault, she wanted him more than she thought possible.

****

Lorelei hummed while pouring coffee into each mug. *I brought you back to lean on me.* His words lulled her like a soft melody of spring, like the gratifying sweet scent of a rose. Her heart danced to a lively tune.

Why had he resisted? Her question brought her elation to a screeching halt as she lifted the mugs. The tone had been set, the atmosphere right and she within his arms.

Did he still view her as nothing more than a troublesome woman? The thought pierced her heart, sending a deep ache across her chest. She wasn't beautiful, but not ugly, either. Her meddling had to be the reason. The reason he could not overlook.

She watched steam rise from the coffees as she entered the infirmary and recalled Michael's words in his office. Did Seth think her full of steam? Her hopes plunged to her feet. Of course he did.

Seth avoided any sort of confrontation unless it involved medical assistance. He would never burden himself with a woman who could not keep her mouth shut longer than two seconds and raised the hairs on the necks of half the men. And their tightened fists, if truth be told.

With laden footsteps and a heavy heart of defeat, Lorelei crossed the room and handed one mug to Seth.

"I'll sit by Jamie for a while," she said, forcing a meek smile. Knowing she wore her heart in her eyes, she avoided eye contact. If she saw what she knew she would in his, her tears would not stay at bay long enough to turn her back.

She sat in the chair at the bedside, set her mug on the washstand, and then smoothed the hair back from Jamie's forehead. She welcomed the soon-to-come dawn. Yet she yearned for the time with Seth to linger. She didn't know her own mind anymore.

****

After finishing his coffee, Seth had fallen asleep. Lorelei glanced over her shoulder as she had done so often over the past hour. He plagued her mind, yet she coveted the time to thoroughly study him. His dark lashes fanned his high cheek bones, a lock of hair lay across his forehead. She longed to smooth it back.

He looked serene, yet his well-muscled body attested to a tower of power and strength. His knowledge and expertise as a physician exceeded superb.

He could have pickings of any woman he desired. Most assuredly, he did not want her. He had made that abundantly clear this morning. She would never be the one to find a place in his heart. Her dreams were as silly as thinking a man could reach out and touch the moon. Her chest constricted.

Jamie stirred turning Lorelei's attention. He mumbled in his sleep, moving his arms under the heavy blanket.

"I'm going to give you some water, Jamie," she whispered so as not to disturb Seth. She picked up the spoon resting in the pewter cup of water and slipped a few drops between his lips as Seth had instructed her to do every so often.

Jamie's eyes remained shut though his throat rippled as he swallowed the offered small amount. Over and over, she repeated the gesture, careful not to rush him and cause him to gag.

When Lorelei heard the rattle of wheels outside, she realized daybreak had dawned though the window's curtains hid it well. Johanna, true to her words, marched in with the two girls at her side a minute later.

At seeing Seth sleeping, the three tiptoed across the room. When had she started thinking of him as Seth and not Doctor Taylor? She liked his name, enjoyed thinking of him as such.

"Good morning. How has he been? Did he awaken at all?" Johanna whispered, concern etching her face. Both girls, eyes wide in anticipation, stood like miniature soldiers.

"Good morning to all of you," Lorelei whispered as she set the cup and spoon down. "He slept all night. A few times he moved, but he never woke. He's been able to swallow sips of water and broth off and on. Se…Doctor Taylor feels encouraged."

She needed to use caution with the familiarity of his name in front of others. No sense in feeding the rumors that would fly if others found she had been here again by herself. She almost laughed at the thought. What was one more flame in a fire?

"Thank goodness," Johanna sighed as she bent over and placed a kiss on Jamie's forehead. She straightened, removed her coat, and walked to the exam table and laid it down. "You girls take off your coats and set them with mine, please." The two began to remove their coats as directed.

"Good morning," Seth said in a low voice as he stood and stretched his shoulders.

Watching his maneuvers, Lorelei became tongue-tied and skittish as a new born colt.

Lorelei averted her gaze, reluctant to look at him after what had passed between them. Of course, it had been one sided, and he probably had not thought anything of it. *Get your wits together, girl, before you make matters worse.*

121

Johanna fairly beamed at him. "A good morning to you too, Doctor Taylor. Lorelei tells me you think he had a good night."

"Yes, much better than I expected." He walked to stand several feet to Lorelei's right. Unable to stop herself, she peered at him. He smiled at the girls as they piled their coats on the table, and ran his fingers through his tousled hair. Oh, how she would love to do the same with her fingers.

"And how are you young ladies this morning? How pretty you both look in your fine dresses. When Jamie wakes, he'll be very happy to see you two."

The girls grinned shyly; Jessica's eyes lit up in awe of the man's compliment while Missy blushed.

He glanced at Lorelei. She wasn't quick enough to avoid eye contact. Their gazes met, and for one heart-stopping moment, she thought she saw dismay in his expression. Then, it vanished.

"You should go home now, Miss Webster, and get some sleep. I appreciate you staying." His polite dismissal tore at her heart.

Lorelei blushed in embarrassment, realizing she had slept a good portion of the night in his comfortable arms. Lord, but she wore a perpetual blush lately. At least, in his presence.

"I'm not that tired since I slept off and on. If there's anything else I can—"

"Please," he held up his hand. "You did more than your share already. And we all appreciate it. I caught some sleep too, but neither of us really slept well. We both need more rest."

If you only knew how very relaxed I was in your arms. She turned to Johanna. "Do you need anything before I leave?"

"No, nothing. I brought muffins for Doctor Taylor and soup for later. As he said, we more than appreciate you staying here last night. Please, go home and get some rest."

Without further reason to remain, Lorelei stood. She picked up their coffee mugs. "I'll put these in the kitchen."

Wishing she could stay, yet knowing Seth needed his rest, she placed the cups on the kitchen counter and turned.

Seth stood in the doorway holding her coat open. Was he being polite or rushing her on her way? The latter thought pierced her very soul as if a knife had plunged into it. She forced herself to take the few steps across the room.

"Thank you." She turned and stretched her arms through the sleeves. She pulled the coat tight around her. He stepped back.

"We'll see you later?" He looked exhausted.

"Yes…if you don't mind."

"Of course not. Johanna will welcome the company. And Jamie will be happy to see you. She said to use her wagon. She left it hitched out front. One of us can take you back home later." His face remained stoic, his words spoken matter-of-fact. She pulled her coat tighter against the cold dismay that seeped through her.

How formal and unemotional his words sounded. *What about you? Will you be as happy to see me? Or would you rather I never return?*

CHAPTER EIGHTEEN

By late afternoon, Lorelei sat at Jamie's bedside mending a worn quilt that had seen much better days before warming numerous patients. He now slept after being awake for almost an hour.

Missy and Jessica sprawled on the single bed across the room engrossed in their dolls, obviously content after talking with their brother and knowing he would recover. Johanna lounged by the window and the brightest oil lamp for more light as she tatted a lace doily.

Outside, the sky had turned gray with heavy clouds. A marked drop in temperature forewarned of impending snow. Only a thin covering of white fluff remained on the ground from two days ago. Every now and then, winds gusted to rattle the window panes.

Jamie opened his eyes; a hesitant smile brushed his lips. His eyes looked tired and lacked luster. She wished she could say something to make them come alive as they did in the past.

What agitated this young boy? Did it stem from his father's drinking? Or could Miles be more abusive than anyone realized? Had Miles made Jamie feel so very useless or inadequate as a person that he chose to take his own life? A shiver ran down her spine. How could she ensure he would not try something again?

So many questions flitted through her mind that her thoughts spun in ten directions. Now was not the time for questions.

"How are you feeling?"

"Better, I think. I don't ache as much." His feeble smile seemed to cost him. He looked weak as a new born kitten. "Guess I'm in a pack of trouble, huh?" He looked down at his hands resting on top of the covers.

She had so much to say, felt desperate to make him realize his worthiness. She kept her voice at a whisper. "We have plenty of time to talk about it later. The important thing right now is for you to get well. That's all anyone wants at the moment. You gave all of us quite a scare."

He glanced at the wall, clearly evading further discussion. She accepted it. For now. She would probe when he was stronger and could think straight to comprehend his worth.

Johanna crossed the room, her eyes full of love as they roamed over Jamie. "I'll get some warm broth for you, love."

Lorelei grinned. Lord it felt good. "Don't fall asleep yet, your mother is as persistent as I am in getting fluids down you."

He made another sour face.

Lorelei laughed. "Doctor Taylor said we have to get as much liquid down you as we can." Jamie glanced across the room.

"He's not here. Mr. Miller was burned by some lit kerosene. I don't know exactly what happened yet."

"Yikes! Bet he hurts bad," he scrunched up his face, then yawned as his eyelids drooped.

****

While Johanna fed Jamie, the girls, curled around their dolls, napped. Allowing mother and son time alone, Lorelei paced the living room to work out the kinks in her legs.

As she peered through the window Seth came into view, his Palomino at a steady canter. He rode as if born to a saddle.

She noticed how his sinewy thighs hugged the animal. Just the sight of him sent her heart racing, her blood rising several degrees. Opening the door as he crossed the porch, she greeted him with a smile.

"Why, thank you, Miss Webster." He returned the smile and shut the door behind him. "How's our prized patient doing?"

"Better. Johanna is forcing down more broth." She chuckled recalling Jamie's scowl. "He doesn't like it very much."

Seth removed his coat and hung it on a peg beside the door.

125

Fascinated, she watched the muscles across his back flex under his frock coat, how his hair curled over his collar.

Seth's laugh joined hers as he turned to face her. "I'm sure he doesn't. We can start him on soft foods, if he likes." He massaged the back of his neck with his hand, twisting his head to and fro as if trying to work out fatigued muscles.

His nearness sent her heart hammering. She swallowed back the dryness of her throat. "How's Charles?"

For a moment as he canvassed her, the silence turned awkward. Why did he look at her so? She wished he found her as appealing as she did him. She released a held breath when his eyes lost that intent stare and he finally spoke.

"He's badly burned. Hands, forearms and chest. They'd blistered by the time I arrived. He tripped over his cat and landed right on top of the lantern," he said as he rearranged his black leather bag and then closed it.

"Dear God."

He shook his head. "Andy and Stan were coming into the store when it happened. It's a wonder they got the fire out before it burned down the whole place. He and his store would've fared far worse if they hadn't been there."

"Thank goodness they were there. But will Charles be all right?"

"I believe so. It's always hard to say when there's so much skin burned. I'll need to check him later, and every day for awhile to keep an eye on his progress. There was glass embedded in half the wounds." He shook his head again as if displeased by that fact.

Once more the silence stretched, making her ill at ease as he gazed at her with that baffling expression.

Each time they talked by themselves she became tongue-tied. What a complete fool.

"Mrs. Miller seems to have everything under control at the moment." He peered out the window and she was thankful he looked away. "You may want to check with her by tomorrow. She might use the help." He laughed, turning to face her again. "She said Charles is like a little baby when he gets sick and she'll probably lose her mind before he's well."

"I'll stop by tomorrow, even if it's just to relieve her for awhile from his complaints." She found herself relaxing as they both grinned, yet her pulse kept up its velocity.

"I'm sure she'd appreciate the respite." For the first time since his return, she noticed how tired his eyes looked.

She wished she had the right to embrace him. He had said he caught several hours sleep this morning. But how soundly had he slept? Then he had been busy with Jamie, followed by Charles. Even a robust man used to being on the go and under such tension needed more rest than he had grabbed in the past few days.

More than ready to avoid another puzzling stare, she went to where her coat hung. "I was about to go out for some fresh air to give Johanna and Jamie time alone. The girls are asleep."

She retrieved her wrap. Her fingers fumbled with the buttons. She needed more than fresh air. She needed distance to think straight. Did he hope she would leave and never come back?

What had she done now? Usually when people gawked at her she knew the reason, quite well, in fact. His eyes pierced her as if he were trying to see into her very soul.

You spent half the night in his arms, you ninny! Most likely he thinks you a hussy. But he said he pulled me against him. His glare rattled her more than her disturbing attraction to him.

"I'll go outside with you, if you don't mind." Without waiting for an answer, he crossed the room and grabbed his coat.

"All day I've been cooped up in here or at the Millers'. And you're right. Johanna needs time with Jamie." He pushed his arms through the sleeves and opened the door.

She doubted the cool air would calm her riotous nerves. She had thought she needed to get away from what she perceived as contemptuous glowers. Obviously, he did not detest her. Elation swept her mind, warmed her heart. *Maybe this is step two.*

"After you, Miss Webster."

As if Prince Charming had asked her for a dance at the grand ball, she grinned and sailed through the portal.

****

127

Seth followed. She had seemed pensive, almost uncomfortable in his presence. At first, he had thought he might be interfering with her privacy. He had been ready to retract his offer when her radiant smile had taken breath away.

He leaned against the porch support, enjoying the peaceful quietude, content to watch the thick clouds drift across the dull sky. More content to eye the pretty woman four feet away.

Leisurely resting a hip against the railing, she appeared lost in thought. A chilly breeze ruffled the stray hairs that had pulled out from the ribbon at her nape. How becoming she looked with the wisps brushing her soft cheeks.

Why did you come out here with her? Fool!

Yet, he knew why. She could hold an intelligent conversation, or at times like this, she remained silent as if sensing he needed time to think, or simply relax after the long, tiring day. He liked that in a woman. He liked it a lot.

You are a fool. Enjoy her friendship. Nothing more.

Then why do you long to taste those tempting lips? Why can't you forget how good she felt in your arms? Oh yes, he remembered her soft skin, the silkiness of her hair, her tantalizing scent. He tried to bury those disturbing recollections. They persisted until he thought he would bellow down the porch roof.

As another frigid gust swept passed, she wrapped her arms around her midriff.

"You cold?" he asked, breaking the silence.

"Not really. Actually, it's quite refreshing."

"Yes, it is," he agreed, noting how she worried her bottom lip with her teeth.

She remained focused on the lawn. "When should I talk to Jamie? I don't want to before he's out of the woods, but I don't think I should put it off too long." Her woeful voice tugged at him.

He took three steps to her side. The cool breeze carried her lavender scent to assail his senses. "Tomorrow's soon enough."

She turned and glanced upward, only inches separating them, her blue eyes mirroring sorrow and anxiety. He longed to kiss her trembling lips. He fisted his hands to halt their reaching out.

"I don't know if he'll tell me what drove him to do this. I'll try, but I'm afraid he may not tell me the whole truth. He's usually very reluctant to tell his most inner secrets." Her arms tightened around her waist. "It…must be something devastating for him to go to such lengths. For him to want to…"

She averted her gaze. He heard her slight gasp as if holding back her distress. He saw her shoulders quiver.

He knew better than to touch her. Not with the way his heart yearned. It longed to reach out to her more than his hands did. It ached as if it were breaking in two. It would be insane.

He lifted her chin with his index finger, catching a drop of wetness from her chin with the tip of his thumb.

Her eyes, wide and full of despair, met his. Tears spilled slowly down her cheeks, her long lashes glistening with moisture. This bold woman was not so bold right now. And it tore at him to see her so distraught. A tight fist twisted in his chest…

And for once in his life, he threw caution to the wind.

Possessed by a force stronger than gravity itself, he tipped his head to cover those trembling lips with his. Just one kiss to comfort her, to stop the pain she conveyed.

He'd known her lips would taste sweet. But God help him, they were more succulent than peach nectar, soft as a rose petal. His mind howled to pull back, to remember he had no right. Yet, it was far more difficult now that he had sampled the forbidden fruit. It'd be more than unfair to mislead her.

But she leaned into him, their bodies pressing together from chest to thighs. Dear God, but she felt good; like a downy soft angel he needed to comfort. Against better judgment, he deepened the kiss, and wrapped his arms around her to pull her tighter against him. A fire consumed him until he could not get enough of her. Her arms followed suit and embraced him.

His hips leaned inward of their own accord and he rubbed his hardened arousal against her soft mound. His mind sailed away, leaving him to only think with his racing heart, to feel with every sensitive fiber. She was, indeed, an angel; and he had just been granted the sweetest sample of heaven.

Like a man starved for sustenance, craving just the tiniest morsel of that prohibited fruit, he drank in her savory essence. Unable to arrest his riotous yearnings, unwilling to restrain himself, or to rationalize the consequences, he allowed his thoughts to soar on dreams, his heart to yield, and his lips to devour hers at free rein.

CHAPTER NINETEEN

Heady did not begin to describe what surged through Lorelei. She swayed and leaned further into Seth. If not for his forceful hold, she would have fallen to the porch on watery knees.

Michael had kissed her, well and good. She had thought. His kisses had been pleasant, filling her with sweet warmth. She had been a fool a hundred times over to think his had been, in any way, thorough.

No siree, ma'am! *This* was a kiss, or kisses. She couldn't be sure when one ended and the next one began. And by golly, it did not matter. She gave up further reflection of her past naivety, of Jamie's despairing predicaments, and lost herself to all the wondrous sensations rippling through her.

Heavenly days, this is what I've longed for.

Her light heart, her spiraling senses took flight

"Mm," she moaned, unable to withhold her pleasure and surrendered to the intoxication as he nibbled her lower lip. His tongue thrust deep into her mouth, sending torrid currents to the junction of her legs. Her tongue played with his, tasting the heated foreign grounds she had never experienced. And reveled in its erotic wonder.

She slipped her hands under his unbuttoned coat, roaming them up and down his broad back, across the corded muscles. She longed to touch every inch of him and cursed the barrier of his shirt. Currents of lightning bolted helter-skelter while warm ripples brooked their way downward to pool low in her abdomen.

Here was a man full of passion. A creator of magic who evoked an equal response that had lay dormant. Who could stir her senses, allowing the woman to emerge, who had been tucked away under the aggressive, strong facade she bore every day.

His lips abandoned her mouth to trail feathery kisses across her cheek, down the sensitive curve of her neck. Shivers skirted up her spine at the titillating sensations. She breathed in the woodsy aroma of aftershave, his masculine scent. Her fingers clawed his back. She finally understood the meaning of *swoon*.

So lost was she in her careening world, it took her a moment to realize he had stopped his ardent kisses. He stood stone still; his arms locked around her. Then he rested his chin on the top of head.

His breathing was labored as if he had run a race. She felt his heart galloping against her chest, matching hers. Should a woman say something at this point? Or remain silent and see what he held in store? Shoot! Of all the times to be inexperienced.

She would wait. She could wait like this forever, leaning against his solid strength, wrapped in his comforting arms, feeling his hard and swollen arousal against her belly. Yes, she could stand here a hundred years. And be quite content.

His arms fell away as he took a step back. The loss of contact left her feeling cold inside that had nothing to do with the evening's drop in temperature. She felt suddenly alone, though only inches separated them.

Daring a glance, she looked upward and sucked in her breath. He gazed at her, not with remorse, abashment, or even surprise. No, his eyes wore a coat of anger, so irate that she took a step back. Her hip thudded against the wooden railing.

His jaw squared, his cheeks flexed, while his hands fisted at his side. Her heart hit her feet with a crashing jolt. All her fallacious hopes and silly dreams toppled to join it, leaving her throat dry and constricted, and her mind in utter despair.

Fighting back tears that seemed to come readily since meeting this man, Lorelei spun on the balls of her feet to turn her back to his anger. How could he kiss her with such passion one minute then look at her so the very next? Numbness set in.

"I never should have done that. I knew better, yet I did it. Please forgive me for taking such liberties, Miss Webster."

His incessant use of her surname grated on her nerves, sliced her heart as if he had plunged a cleaver through it. An urge to turn and slap him as hard as she could besieged her. Yet, in the far recesses of her mind, his apology lent new meaning. Her hopes swelled, her pulse quickened.

Had he glared contempt because he was angry at himself? Her heart rose from her feet to beat frantically in her chest. She fought to think rationally. Without turning, she raised her chin and surveyed the moonlit lawn now bathed in hues of silver.

"I'll accept your apology only if you promise to call me Lorelei. We've been in each other's company enough times—and will most likely continue to do so—for us to be so formal."

Patiently, she waited for his response. If she assumed correctly, he would balk. And all because he, for some asinine reason, refused to allow himself to be drawn to her. It felt outrageously gratifying to know he shied away for reasons other than she lacked appeal or her meddling ways.

He came to her side, gripped the top rail and stared across the well manicured lawn. "It's not wise for me to be so casual with your name. I...can't allow myself that luxury."

He tightened his hold on the horizontal. His shoulders slumped forward. Stealing a glance to the side, she noted how defeated, how deflated, he appeared. She longed to reach out a hand, to wrap her arm around his drooped shoulders.

Did the same deep, dark secret that caused him to avoid community involvement also elicit him to resist her? She felt relieved there might be a logical reason, at least to him. The thought that he could not trust himself around her lightened her heart. She longed to know why.

Gaining courage, she asked, "Why would it be a luxury, Seth?"

Whether from her question or the use of his given name, he flinched. Would he tell her to mind her own business? Why, oh why, couldn't she think before she spurt forth such a question? She would never learn. Not in a hundred years.

Straightening, he withdrew his hands from their resting place, clasped them behind him, and looked directly at her. A faint smile curled his lips. Her heart tripped over itself.

"Miss Webster, most people appreciate the code of the west. A man's affairs, past and present, are his own. Most people respect that, and know better than to pry unless asked to do so."

She gave a nervous chuckle. "I guess that's my problem. I have nothing in my past or present that I feel I must hide, so I don't stop to think that my questions or actions will be offensive to others."

He smiled. "I should've realized you are not most people."

"No, I'm not," she confessed, warmed by his smile. "I apologize for intruding on your privacy. But I don't regret your kisses at all."

Even in the dimming light, she saw him blush. And she loved him all the more for it. Dear Lord, she had indeed fallen in love with this mysterious man. It was scary, knowing he would shun her attentions as best he could; it was exhilarating, finally admitting to herself how her feelings had grown toward this striking man.

Somehow, she would find out what made his mind and emotions work the way they did. If she had anything to say about the matter, he would not stand a chance against the bombardment of love she would throw his way. She would break down his defenses one by one, until she broke through that shield he had so ardently constructed.

"I already apologized for my behavior. It shouldn't have happened. It won't happen again."

"You're very good, do you know that?"

Anger sprang to his eyes as he stiffened. "I'm not the *good* person you think I am. Leave well enough alone. I do my doctoring, and that's it. That's all I want, no more, no less. It's nothing against you. You're a very attractive, well-meaning woman—but I don't want any woman in my life. Ever."

His words hit her like a bucket of ice water dumped over her head. They chilled her very soul. But she vowed she would not give up that easy. She was made of sterner stuff. Whatever demons he carried would not hold a candle to her head-strong persistence. He had best watch his flank and back, she silently laughed, for she intended to march strong, ready to converge from all sides if necessary. He was— simply put—inevitably doomed.

Giving him the most charming smile she could muster, she faced him with her head held high.

"Seth, you shouldn't put yourself down like that. Whatever is in your past can't be that bad. You *are* a good person, no matter how hard you try to convince me—or yourself—otherwise. But I wasn't implying that you were a good *person*. When I said you were very good…I meant you were very good at kissing."

He jerked back at her bold words. Fighting back laughter, she continued before she chickened out. "For a man who doesn't want any woman, you sure know how to kiss."

Damn her unruly tongue. With face flaming, she scooted inside to say goodnight to the others. She had not meant to be so brazen, but her willful mouth had run wild. For sure, he would shy away from her all the more. He most likely *would* label her a hussy.

Having hitched her horse to the wagon before returning to Seth's, she now had a way home. Thank goodness.

She could not leave quick enough.

CHAPTER TWENTY

The next morning, it took all of Lorelei's courage to return to Seth's. Her need to talk with Jamie fortified her as she knocked on the door. The brisk wind ruffled her scarf and whipped around her ankles, swirling up the snow that dusted the porch. She glanced at her horse and buggy at the hitching post. She longed to flee.

Footsteps neared the portal. Seth opened the door. Dark brown buckskins molded his long muscular thighs. The sleeves of his tan shirt were rolled up to his elbows, and the top two buttons were undone to reveal dark curls. The sight of him first thing in the morning, dressed so casually could force any woman to forego breakfast. He easily satisfied her hunger.

"Good morning, M...Lorelei. Please, come in out of the cold." His smile was warm and congenial, as if last night's trying episode had never happened.

She relaxed, though her pulse thrummed in her ears. She relished hearing her name on his lips. He held the door open and she passed through, making sure she allowed an appropriate distance between them.

"Thank you." Undoing her scarf, she strove to remain calm. "I hope I'm not too early. I wanted to talk to Jamie before I visit Hattie."

"Not too early at all. I've already redressed Charles's wounds. Hattie will welcome your visit. Here, let me help you."

Lorelei turned to allow him to remove her coat. His fingers brushed her nape and warm currents riveted down her spine.

"How did Jamie do last night?" She noticed how his eyes drifted over her well-fitting wool dress. She had never felt so conscious of her own person. Did he find her lacking?

When his eyes met hers, she knew by the sparkle in his eyes that he liked what he saw. Her heart beat a little faster. She had chosen the thin blue wool to compliment her eyes. He may not want a relationship, but she would not give up without a fight.

"He slept well, ate a good breakfast, and is begging to go home," he said as they started to amble down the hall.

Surprised, Lorelei paused and turned to him. "Today? This soon?"

His eyes twinkled. "I don't see why not. He's medically sound and I can't keep him in bed. He's pacing like a caged tiger."

"But emotionally...is he ready?"

He scowled. "I don't know. I haven't talked to him about why he did this again, if in fact the swimming episode was deliberate. But we have to trust him sometime."

Lorelei wondered how she would approach the subject. Could they trust him? How long before he might again try something and succeed at his determined goal? She shuddered at the possibility.

She took a deep breath. "You're right, but it's scary."

"I agree." They continued down the hall. Jamie stood gazing out the window, dressed and rubbing a finger over one foggy pane.

Jamie turned as they crossed the room, his smile a welcome relief. It was good to see him up, his face a healthy color.

"Miss Webster! Doc's going to let me go home today. Aren't ya, Doc?" Jamie grinned and stuck his hands in his pockets.

"I can't think of any reason why I should allow you to stay and eat me out of house and home. Can you?"

They laughed while Lorelei's abdomen tightened. She had no other recourse than to have a serious talk with Jamie first.

"I exercise every morning, so I'll trudge through it while you two visit. Then I'll take you home, son. That seem fair?"

"Sure thing, Doc," Jamie answered, his eyes leery as they focused on her. He knew her visit was not going to consist of mundane pleasantries. Jamie was too smart for that.

Seth excused himself and the silence in the room became almost tangible. No sense in beating around the bush.

Lorelei walked to the chair by the bed and sat. "Please, come over here and sit. We need to talk before you go home."

Grim-faced, he shrugged and walked over to the bed. The slats moaned as he sat. "I know what you're goin' to say, Miss Webster. And I know how stupid I was to pull a stunt like I did."

She leaned back, thankful he had started the conversation in the right direction. "You've thought about your actions and truly realize how foolish it is to do something that desperate?"

He stared at a spot on the floor by her feet. "Guess so."

That was *not* the answer she longed to hear. He didn't sound the least bit earnest. She grasped for the right words, something emphatic that would grab and make an impression to this troubled youngster. It was much easier to confront abusive men than to reason with a misguided teenager. Clasping her hands on her lap, she prayed her words would make an impact on him.

"Jamie, God gave each of us the most precious gift. Life. He intended for us to value it for the precious gift it is. Nothing, and I mean nothing, in our lives of troubles and woes is so terrible, so finite that we can't change it. And the death of one individual doesn't change or stop the wrong after they're gone. It only leaves friends and family suffering, and regretting such a senseless loss. It takes hard work to fight for what's right. To make a difference."

He stared at his feet. Her words were mere words, yet she prayed they would filter into his heart.

"It's not easy to change wrongs or injustices. Believe me, I know. I've made enemies and set this town on fire with my efforts. You know that. You've heard the men rant and rave. But I won't give up. My ways aren't very tactful. I can't seem to right the wrongs without causing havoc. But if I make a small headway in a few lives, or can lend a helping hand, then I can honestly say I've done God's work. I can be proud I made someone's life better. And that reward is so very gratifying that all the ugly words thrown my way can never hurt me. Do you understand what I'm saying?"

He glanced up and their eyes met. "I think so." He peered down at the floor. "But what if you don't know how to change things, what if…nothing you say, or do, will ever make it right?"

She had him thinking. "If you try one way and it doesn't work, you try another, then another—until maybe things haven't changed drastically, but hopefully, you've made some headway." She leaned forward to offer a listening ear.

"Will you tell me what troubles you enough that you want to throw your priceless gift away? I'm always here for you to talk to, Jamie. And others are standing by to help, too. We'll do anything to help you rather than see you harm yourself. There are so many who love you. And that love can help a person through the worst times. It can be your lifeline to hold strong so you don't sink. Always remember that."

He raised his chin. Unshed tears pooled in his eyes. His thin lips quivered as he clasped his hands on his lap.

Lorelei enfolded him in her arms, battling to restrain her tears. She was his rock. Later, she could fall apart. Her heart wept for his agony, for her distress at not foreseeing his utter anguish before it turned to such desperation that it nearly brought about his demise. He clung to her, his sobbed tears warm against her chest. She stroked his quaking back; he sniffled and gulped for composure. She rocked him, offering her strength, her love.

"Can you unburden your heart and let me help? Can you tell me?"

He pulled back as if reluctant to break contact. He looked her directly in the eye. "I can't. I know you want to help and you have. It's…it's not just my own life I'm unhappy with."

He wouldn't get off that easy. "Unhappy about what?"

He appeared rattled by her words. His eyes darted around the room as if seeking a quick escape. "Everything. We ain't got much money, my father ain't much of a husband, and he sure as hell ain't much of a father, if ya know what I mean. We're always working on the farm, but we never get done." He shrugged, avoided looking her way. "Guess it's just everything."

Lorelei's heart ached as if an auger were boring a hole in it. She cared not a whit that he had cursed or said ain't. Her concern centered on how despondent he sounded, as if there were no bright tomorrows to look forward to. How extremely sad for a boy of thirteen to carry the woes and weight of the world on such small shoulders. He perceived the world as one long journey of hard work with no rewards, no happiness and no better future.

"Jamie, there's always tomorrow. You're a very intelligent young man. Someday, you'll make your own decisions and carve out the life *you* want. You'll make your own happiness and find others to share your sorrows and joys. A person can never have enough friends and loved ones. It's up to you to find them, to enjoy them and the good life God wanted for you.

"It won't be easy, nothing of value and substance ever is. You'll have to work hard. But if you do, if you endure life's hardships, appreciate the God-given life you've been granted, you can have a life filled with wondrous fulfillment with a wealth of meaning. A happy, content life worth living."

He offered a weak smile as he brushed his hand over his wet cheeks. "I'll try. I really will. When you say it like that, it kinda gives a person some hope."

She took his hands within hers, their chilled digits a direct contrast to her warm ones. "There *is* hope, Jamie. A world sits out there waiting for young people like you to make their mark in society, to make a happy, meaningful life for yourself and others. Don't ever think there's not. Just reach for it."

"Thanks, Miss Webster. I'll try to make you proud of me."

"You do that, Jamie. But don't do it for me, or anyone else. Do it for yourself." She squeezed his hands, and hopefully gave a vote of confidence by her satisfied gaze.

His smile was the Jamie she cherished. He seemed to have cleansed his soul of the troublesome burden. For now. But how long could he maintain sturdy footing against the cruelties of the world before falling again? She prayed there would be no next time. Could she survive another go-around like this one?

"Why don't you wash your face? I'll go tell Se...Doctor Taylor you're chomping at the bit to go home."

"Sure thing, Miss Webster." He scooted off the bed and went to the washstand. Lorelei sighed in relief at his heightened spirit. Her heart felt lighter, her hopefulness uplifting. Yet she knew she would have to watch him with guarded eyes.

ALL FOR LOVE

****

The next morning, Lorelei hummed while doing dishes for Hattie. She smiled, content to know she had given Hattie a break from caring for her demanding husband.

Drying a plate with the linen towel, she moved to the bedroom doorway and peeked in. Charles remained deep in slumber since Hattie had given him a dose of laudanum before leaving.

She grimaced as she peered at the multitude of bandages wrapped around the man's face, arms, and hands. She knew more laid beneath the blanket. Thank goodness for the laudanum.

As she tiptoed back to the counter, Hattie and Bessie Langley bustled in, chatting about their purchases.

Hattie scanned the tidy kitchen. Her brows rose while her pleased grin crinkled the deep lines around her eyes.

"Land's sake, Lorelei, you didn't have to do dishes. You coming over to let me get out a bit was more than enough. Why did you think you had to clean up my mess? You'll never want to come back to visit." She placed her parcels on the counter then peeked past the bedroom door to assure herself Charles still slept.

Bessie laughed at Hattie's remark as she set a bag of flour on the table. "Hello, Lorelei. It's good to see you."

Lorelei smiled. She had met Bessie briefly at school programs. Bessie's gray-streaked brown hair and thick waistline attested to her ten children ranging from one to twelve.

"It's good to see you too, Bessie. Our paths don't often cross, but your children keep me well-informed. I understand your little Mary started running before she walked."

At Bessie's hearty laugh, Lorelei warmed to the woman.

"Yes, she did. I put nothing past that one. She's gonna be a living terror, more so than any of my boys ever thought of being."

The three laughed as Hattie hung their coats on a wall hook.

"It wasn't any bother to do your dishes, Hattie. I enjoy keeping busy. And I hope I'll be welcomed back for more visits. I checked on Charles several times, but he slept the whole time."

"You'll always be more than welcomed here. Why don't the three of us enjoy some tea and chat? That's why I dragged Bessie in here." Hattie's face turned serious as she headed for the kettle. "I told Bessie she needs to talk to you, Lorelei."

What would a happily married lady need to talk to her about? "The teakettle has plenty of hot water in it," Lorelei said, noting a faint blush surface across Bessie's cheeks.

"Wonderful." Hattie nodded, lifting the kettle. "I'll get out some spice cake to go with it."

The three gathered what they needed. In minutes, they were sitting down for a women's afternoon chat. As Hattie placed squares of white frosted cake on plates and slid them across the table, she did not mince words. "Go on now, Bessie tell her. I'm sure Lorelei knows all there is to know about such business."

Bessie looked as if she might pass out. Her face blazed crimson while her eyes nearly bulged from their sockets.

Lorelei leaned back against the tall slated chair, hoping to ease the woman's discomfort with her chuckle. "You might as well come right out with it, Bessie. Hattie won't stop until you do."

Bessie managed a wispy smile before a slight chuckle of her own surfaced. "You're right, there." She cast a sideways glance of mock annoyance across the table. Hattie burst out laughing.

With a lingering grin, Hattie cut a piece of cake with her fork. "Well, tell her. You don't have to be afraid to tell Lorelei anything. She hears more stuff in this crazy town than you or I could ever imagine. Isn't that the truth, Lorelei?"

It was Lorelei's turn to blush. She had listened to many private or intimate topics, willingly or otherwise.

"She's right, Bessie. I don't know if I can be of help, but there isn't much I haven't heard from women *or* men. What is it?"

Bessie fingered the rim of her cup. "I...I don't want more children." Her sorrowful eyes drilled into Lorelei's. Undoubtedly, she thought Lorelei would be horrified at her confession.

The poor woman. Lorelei's usual compassion and deep-seeded empathy went out to this woman who seemed worn out before her time. "I understand completely. Ten children in fourteen years is more than any man should ask of a saint, never mind a woman."

Bessie nodded, appearing a bit less flustered. "I love all my children dearly. Don't misunderstand me. I thank God everyday for each one. But I'm tired of being with a full belly for nine months out of every year. I don't think I can manage to take care of any more. The others help, but it's hard."

Bessie glanced down, and shook her head slowly. "Oh, Lord, forgive me for being such an ungrateful creature that I am. I'm sure He thinks I've sinned unmercifully for thinking this way."

Amazed at Bessie's notions, Lorelei said, "You're not a sinner and shouldn't feel guilty. I'm sure God didn't intend you to be a slave or to burden you with so many pregnancies."

Bessie's eyes filled with wonder. "But what can I do? Andrew…he…he has quite a…" The woman colored ten shades of red.

"Oh, hell, Bessie," Hattie spat as she pierced another piece of cake, "he has an appetite of an elephant when it comes to satisfyin' his male part. Just spit it out like it is."

If Bessie's situation wasn't so serious, Lorelei would have howled. Instead, she nodded in understanding. Reaching over, Lorelei covered Bessie's hand with hers and gave it a reassuring squeeze. "You can please your husband, yet avoid pregnancy."

Bessie gave a sheepish smile. "I tried washing right after, but it didn't work. I'd heard about skipping part of the month without…relations. But that didn't work either. I must be fertile all month." She looked defeated as she glanced at her cake.

"There are many ways more sound than those two, believe me. It's just a matter of which one is more suited for you."

Bessie glanced up, hope reflecting in her eyes. "Really?"

"Really." Lorelei leaned closer. "Does Andrew, though he wants to sate his appetite, know you don't want more children?"

Bessie slumped and squirmed in her chair. "I'm afraid not. Oh, he knows I'm tired out and sympathizes with me. But as long as he can…take me to bed he doesn't care about the outcome. He thinks we're blessed to have so many children."

"I see." And see, she did. Lorelei knew if her advice ever got out, all hell would break loose. The men, including gluttonous Andrew, would storm the town looking for her.

She noted the tired lines etched in Bessie's once pretty face. She looked haggard. While trying to appear content and happy, she trudged through each day encumbered by the fright of another pregnancy. She was a good wife, an excellent mother, a warm and caring woman. Her torment was far from fair.

Lorelei could not let this woman fall victim to her husband's over-zealous demands at the cost of her health and sanity. No matter the consequence, Lorelei could no more turn her back on this woman than she could stop breathing. If the men found out and turned on her, it would end any hope with Seth.

The thought jolted her. Tempted her to resist offering advice. Yet, knowing Bessie might suffer more pregnancies, could possibly lose her life from its taxing toll and leave ten children motherless, would be unthinkable...unbearable. No matter the cost, especially tossing Seth's possible love to the wind, she could not bring herself to turn her back on one in need.

Refusing to wallow over the price she might pay, she squared her shoulders against the pain within her heart.

For the next hour they sipped tea and giggled at the various, ridiculous concoctions Lorelei described. She covered everything from the ancient use of dried donkey dung, set into a woman's place—making Bessie shudder while the other two chortled—to dried tea leaves covered with gauze. In the end, the consensus boiled down to a small sponge saturated with strong vinegar.

"Thank you so much, Lorelei. I just pray it works." Bessie fairly beamed at her new found answer to her problem.

"The sponge can be very successful. But you must use it every time and insert it right before you go to bed. Do you think you can, and not have him know?"

Bessie giggled like a young mischievous girl. It warmed Lorelei's heart to be able to relieve Bessie's anxiety.

"Oh, yes. He always allows me privacy to use the chamber pot and wash before bedtime." Her eyes twinkled with new-found hope.

"Good." Lorelei stood. "I better leave so I can get a few things done before school tomorr—" Her words were cut off as Charles bellowed for Hattie from the next room.

Hattie pushed back her chair and shook her head. "The bear has awakened. Excuse me ladies."

Lorelei retrieved her coat and began wrapping her scarf around her head as Hattie returned to the room.

Hattie sighed. "He's hungry, thirsty, has to relieve himself, and is in a foul mood to boot. Men! They think all that can be done in two seconds flat."

"Do you need help? I'd be more than happy to stay," Lorelei asked, willing to put aside her own tasks.

"No, no," she insisted, taking a bowl from the cupboard. "You've done more than your share. You go along and get those lessons ready. I appreciate all you've done for me and Bessie. You've had one busy day, my dear. One you can be proud of."

Bessie joined Hattie at the counter. "She's right, Lorelei, and I again thank you, too. It was so nice getting to know you. And I hope we'll see each other more often. I'll stay a few minutes to help Hattie. I've plenty of time."

Elation swamped Lorelei. Bessie had more spunk than she had given her credit for. She wasn't the docile little lamb under her husband's thumb. The woman would do well for herself.

Lorelei smiled and opened the door. "I'm glad to have helped. I'll stop by in a day or two after school, Hattie, and see if there's anything else I can do for you."

"You do that, my dear, you're welcome anytime."

As Lorelei settled in her buggy and took up the reins, she wondered if she dared allow herself to feel so proud of her help with Bessie. In one way she did; in another, she cringed at the possible consequences if Andrew ever found out.

And what would Seth think if he ever knew? With a sense of uneasy foreboding, she clucked at her horse. The gray afternoon skies suddenly chilled her with gloom.

CHAPTER TWENTY-ONE

Two nights later, well after the sun had hidden below the horizon, Lorelei sat in her rocker in front of her woodstove reading papers from the day-before assignment. The stories were interesting, imaginative and well-written for the most part. A sense of pride beamed within her as she gazed down at the narratives each student had perceived as hopes for their futures.

Realizing she had been straining her eyes, she reached over and adjusted the oil lamp's wick. As she leaned back to peruse another paper, a jarring crash raised her clear off her chair.

Glass shattered like crackling thunder, flying through the room in all directions. Instinctively, she held up her arms across her face, deflecting bulleting shards as they whizzed past. She winced at hearing a solid thud as something collided with the wide bare floor boards. The object rolled over splinters of the panes, crunching and pulverizing the thin glass till it stopped not a foot from her on the rag rug.

Her pulse bounded in her throat, she quaked with sheer fright. The room turned deathly still. Cautiously, she lowered her arms. And stared at a rock enveloped by a piece of white paper and secured with brown twine.

She sat rooted in the chair and shook. Daring a glance at the near wall, she shuddered as she peered at a few jagged points of glass hanging precariously from the window frame.

Only then did she feel the raw sting of her left cheek, a warm trickle as it ran down her chin and neck, the smarting bite on her left forearm as she lowered it to her side.

She looked down at her arm and gasped. A triangle of glass had pierced her cotton sleeve, imbedding itself in her flesh. With her other hand, she raised it cautiously to her face. Gingerly she touched a finger tip to her left cheek. She felt warm stickiness, a slicing pain as her fingers pushed against glass fragments in the wound. Her finger sprang back.

"Dear God!" Tears rushed forth. Shaken and fearful, she slumped back in the chair. Brushing the chips from her clothing she eyed the rock. Angry, she pulled the wedge of glass from her arm and flung it. It shattered, bits scattering to tinkle across the floor. Her anger soared.

Again eyeing the window, feeling vulnerable and exposed, she listened for any further attack. Hearing no movement, she sighed in relief, yet wondered if it would be short-lived. Gingerly, still trembling and hesitant, she stood, walked to the rock and bent down to untie the twine. Her fingers fumbled as she tugged at the tight strings. Her left arm smarted; blood ran down in rivulets to stream between her groping fingers. Finally succeeding in loosening the thin cords, she lifted the paper.

Bold print leaped from the missive: KEEP YOUR DAMN NOSE OUT OF OTHERS' LIVES.

She sank to the rug and drew her legs under her. Her heart pounded, her trembling increasing until she had to brace her hand against the floor for balance. Andrew had found out.

She had met him briefly at school. She hadn't thought him vicious by nature. But maybe her meddling turned a placid man into a violent one. How had he found out?

She would worry about that later. Right now, she had to tend her wounds, to seal the open window space. With the cold weather pouring in, her woodstove would be useless. If snow started again, she would have more in her home than bits of broken glass.

She rolled back her sleeve. Blood ran in a steady stream. Digging into her pocket, she withdrew her hankie and dabbed the injury, only to feel sharp jabs. Obviously, tiny glass chips housed in the ragged cut. Three inches long, gaping at least a quarter-inch, it was much deeper than she had realized.

She would need it cleaned, then stitched. The blood dripped off her fingertips onto the carpet. Knowing she had to stop its flow, she scurried to her bedroom, grabbed a towel and wrapped it around her arm. She returned to the living room, grabbed the hateful twine and anchored the towel as best she could.

With the oil lamp in hand, she returned to her room and peered into the mirror. And gasped. An inch or so cut on her cheekbone ran parallel to her nose. Blood lay caked to her face, dried in a streak past her chin and down her neck, ending below her collar. At least, it had ceased its flow. She didn't relish the idea of having Seth probe for the glass.

As best she could, she draped a wool blanket over the broken window, stuffing its top behind the curtain rod. A harsh wind might blow the feeble barrier down. She headed to the barn.

Harnessing her horse aggravated her arm. No matter how hard she tried to use her right hand, she had to use the left. Even with the towel, she felt the bleeding persist.

After what seemed an eternity, she headed toward town. What would Seth say this time? He had been tolerant last time she sought help for herself. She cringed at the thought of his heated reprimand. His inevitable spurning.

****

Only a flicker of light lit Seth's front room. Her heart dropped to her feet. Was he out? Nonetheless, she pounded on the door. Nothing. She tried the door handle. Locked. In a quandary as to what to do, she thought of Michael. Maybe he would know where Seth might be.

Minutes later, she pulled in front of the sheriff's office. As she looped the reins around the hitching post, she caught sight of a man. He was descending the outside stairs from the second story of the Silver Dollar saloon across the street. The full moon illuminated him in silver.

She stood transfixed as he reached the ground and amble to his horse. Only one man in town rode a Palomino.

Despair, like she had never known, nearly dropped her to the ground. Tears gathered. He had rebuffed her, said he needed no woman, yet he had gone to one of them. Her chest felt as if one of the shards had imbedded itself within her very heart.

Maybe he had treated someone upstairs. Yet, he carried no bag. The answer was as clear as a spring morn.

Lorelei turned. She had to get inside. With a heavy heart, she cursed herself for being so foolish as to wish for anything more. Stupid, ridiculous dreams had made her wish for more.

At the top step of the stoop, Seth's voice boomed through the night's chilly air. "Lorelei?"

She froze, gathered her thoughts and refused to turn around. She heard the plod of hooves along with Seth's muffled footsteps, and then the wisp of reins as they were wound around the post.

"Lorelei? Is everything all right?"

She did not want to look at him. Yet, she needed his expertise. With faltering courage, she squared her shoulders and turned. Their eyes met on a level as he stood on the ground.

"I…went to your house, but you weren't there. So, I came to ask Michael for help." Lord, she was rambling.

His gaze fixed on her left cheek. Though darkness cast shadows between them, she saw his jaw flex. Was he angry because he knew she had again stirred up the town? Would he walk away and let Michael handle this? The thought pierced deep. She wished his disgruntled look stemmed from concern. What a fool she was! And she had always prided herself for being intelligent.

He glowered. "What happened now?"

Tears of humiliation threatened. She willed them back, wishing she could burrow under the walkway. He had held her in contempt as the others had the day they met, now seemed no different. Her heart lay in shreds at his unfeeling words.

"I guess you could say I did it again." At least, she had her honesty. They called her Miss Neb-nose, but she refused to add deceitful. She had some pride. Not much, but a smidgeon remained.

"Oh, Lorelei. What are we to do with you?" His hand settled on the stair rail, his eyes more exasperated than angered. "I'll be the next one ostracized out of town if I'm not careful."

His words wounded her tender heart. "And we certainly can't have that." She knew she sounded bitter, yet it was her only defense against breaking down in front of him.

"I'm sure Michael can fish the glass out," she went on. "You won't have to soil your hands on me, or put yourself in the line of fire."

She saw him scowl at the towel peeking out her coat sleeve. "Goodnight, Seth." She started to turn to gain sanctuary inside the office—anywhere other than to stay in his derisive presence.

He grabbed her right shoulder, stopping her. "Hold it right there. *I'm* the doctor. I'll treat you if you need treating. No matter what this town has to say."

Indecision as to the wisest choice zipped through her mind. She needed his help. Michael could no more suture her wounds than she could. Yet, she felt like a constant nuisance to him.

"I don't want to bother you. I know you—"

He took her by her shoulders. "I said I'll do it, dammit." His stare dropped to her left hand and he fingered the wetness covering her fingers. "Good God. This towel is saturated."

He actually sounded concerned. *Of course he does! He's a doctor, and you're bleeding like a stuck pig.*

But as his eyes pierced hers, she thought she read more than a doctor's concern for a patient. She reminded herself not to expect more than was actually there. Foolish dreams seemed to be what she lived on, lately.

With Seth's horse tied to the back of her buggy, the two sat silent while Seth drove. The gusts of wind hardly matched the chill of the prolonged silence. She sighed in relief and relaxed her stiff posture as they pulled up in front of his home.

He helped her down from the wagon. "Go inside; here's the key. I'll take care of the horses and be back in a few minutes."

She did his bidding, discouraged by the returned frigid attitude. She had definitely read more than she should have into his concern.

****

She lay on the exam table while he probed for glass fragments in her arm. Lorelei didn't mind lying flat so he could do what he needed to do easier. She was afforded the luxury of watching his handsome profile; his intense, dark chocolate eyes.

He again flushed the wound with an astringent. She gritted her teeth, yet dutifully held her arm still as he dug deeper.

150

"That's the last of it." He held up the forceps in front of her. A half inch sliver winked. His expression remained serious as he cleansed the skin around the wound and patted it dry.

"Take another swig of whiskey. You're going to need it."

She took a gulp from the bottle in her right hand. Its fire burned all the way down to her stomach. Yet the effects of four mouthfuls—or was it five now—spread a contented warmth through her limbs.

"I'm going to suture it now. It'll bite."

She gave a small smile, almost moaned as she inhaled his woodsy, clean scent. "Go ahead. I can stand it if you can."

He gave her a benevolent grin. She turned all toasty and knew it was far from being the effect of the whiskey.

"Here we go."

She flinched at the first prick of the needle. The following ones became less painful. The room took on a fuzzy haze as she laid silent, content to watch him hover over her.

Briefly, his nocturnal visit to the saloon drifted through her cloudy mind. She wondered if the woman he had sought appreciated his gentleness, his handsomeness, as much as she did. The thought of him making love to another clawed at her heart. She closed her eyes, tried to eradicate the pain within.

"Tell me what happened. It'll take your mind off what I'm doing if you talk."

She knew talking would not abolish the vision her mind conjured up of him with another woman. But for the duration of the stitching, she explained what had happened.

"Do you know who might have done it?"

Lorelei tried to blink the cob webs from her eyes. He looked far away, more blurry. "I think hit might haf been Andref Langey, buf I'm not sir." She nipped at her thick lower lip with her teeth. Goodness, they felt as numb as her fingers. She watched, fuzzy-eyed, as he held up a long strip of bandage, felt her arm raised and lowered. It all felt dreamlike.

"Andrew Langley? I can't imagine him doing that. He's a peaceful, God loving man. I've never heard him raise his voice above a soft monotone. Why would you think it might be him?"

She swallowed her giggle. Tonight's incident was far from being funny, yet picturing Andrew if he had discovered the bottle of vinegar in his bedroom struck her funny bone. Poor Bessie.

"What's so funny, Miss Webster?"

"I like hit bedder when you call me Lorelei."

He smiled. And though her mind seemed to float on a cloud, it set her pulse to racing. *What a pleasant smile he had.*

"I apologize, profusely, Lorelei. It won't happen again."

When he grinned, a warm current streamed through her veins. Oh, how very much she liked her name on his lips. She nodded in complete satisfaction.

"Now, what was so funny?"

She gasped as he probed her cheek. Mere inches separated their faces. She would love to pull his down, kiss those tempting lips. Would he like her kiss as much as the saloon girl's? She wished she was brazen enough to ask. Her coyness surprised her.

"Vinhegar in the behroom." Had he stuffed cotton in her mouth?

He stopped probing, dabbed her face with a pad, and peered down. Mm, yes, she could kiss him right now. Should she?

"Vinegar in *his* bedroom? It..." His eyes narrowed and he shook his head, the slow movement reminding her of a pendulum.

"And would he have found a sponge, maybe a wad of gauze like this one?" he held up the pad," if he'd looked further, *Lorelei?*"

Seeing the stricken look on his face, she had to stifle her laughter. Most likely, it duplicated Andrew's face at seeing the acidic solution.

Sheepishly, she mumbled. "I believe so." Darn it all, a giggle escaped.

"Do you know the Langley's have probably never quarreled? But I bet you a two-dollar gold piece they had their first, because of you. That's not funny, Lorelei."

His words sobered her long enough to realize the position she had put Bessie in. Remorse took hold.

"I know thath's not funny." Good Lord, she could hear herself slur and destroy words. Her lips felt swollen and numb. "And I yam truly sorry for Bethie if he founth out. But she asked my help and I gave hit. I don't regret I dith it. She needs some kind of prop...prothection." He

152

stared at her, and to her heart's delight, he looked as if tried to hide a grin.

"The funny part isth picturing him trying to fithure out why vinhegar was in hith bethroom. Can't you see hith face?"

He shook his head as he tended her cheek. Though his eyes reprimanded, she caught his smile. At least, she thought so.

"Yes, Lorelei, I *can* see his face."

As he gently dabbed her cheek, she felt moisture, cool and soothing against her skin. He leaned back, inspecting his work.

"There you go. All fixed up. You shouldn't have much of a scar on your face. I'll take the stitches out next week."

Lorelei would have preferred her time not over, but welcomed the thought of having to return next week. Lord, but he was a blur.

"Thank you, Sethh. If you'll help me harnath my horse, I'll be onth my way. I know I'f taken up a lot of yourth time."

His burst of laughter baffled her.

"Whath's so funny?"

"You are. You're stinking drunk. You can't go by yourself, and I'm too tired to take you and have to fix that window tonight. You can sleep in here. Tomorrow, I'll see to the window."

He helped her sit up. The room spun and her stomach flip-flopped. She wanted to argue with him as to her inebriated state, but as she swallowed down the taste of bile, she thought better of it. She really did not feel so good.

"Let's get you settled." He helped her to the bed, removed her shoes and covered her with the blanket. Their gazes met.

She knew she would be brash. The temptation was too great.

"I'll leave a light burning low. Sleep well, Lorelei," he said, tucking the covers snugly around her.

Before he could pull back, she reached out with her good arm, circled his neck with her hand and brought his face closer. "Good night, sweeth Seth."

Her lips touched his; barely a light touch…satisfying enough to send her into a contented slumber.

****

Jolted, Seth stared at her. She was out cold. Her kiss, like a whisper's breath, had sent an urge skyrocketing through his body.

"Damn you for making me want you." He lowered the lamp's wick and left the room.

Lying in bed, Seth craved her nearness. Lately, every stinking minute of the day, he thought about her; her shiny sun-spun hair, vivid blue eyes twinkling so full of life; her warm, sweet smile that sent his heart to racing at one slight glance.

He reflected on all the good she tried to do. She focused on helping others, to right the world of cruelties and wrong doings. All for the sake of others. Without a care for herself.

He had shuddered when he realized she was hurt. Had trembled as he inspected the jagged and deep injuries. She could have easily lost an eye, been maimed for life if she had been hit by the rock. His usual calm had been rattled to the core as she related what had happened. A growing need to protect her from further harm assailed him. He did not like it one bit.

What was he going to do about her? He could not fault her for helping others. He smiled as admiration wrapped around his heart.

Don't even think about more with her. He was insane to even fathom the thought that she could love a soiled degenerate.

He rehashed Lilly's words that he had been gentler than ten cowpokes put together. He liked her. Yet he always felt lonelier after using her for his purpose, though she insisted he pleasantly satisfied her. His mouth tasted bitter.

He only sought her out when he desperately needed release. She had chosen her profession. He paid her well, better than most from what she said. He had never felt guilty about going to her.

Tonight, he felt despicable.

He had used her as a substitute for the one he truly craved. For years, he had checked his feelings before they escalated. It had been difficult a few times, but he had managed to remember his unworthiness. Until Lorelei.

And tonight, he had been unable to sate his lust with Lilly. He swiped his hand across his face. Regret sliced deep. He had not meant to insult Lilly. But he had, by not responding.

"Oh, Lorelei!" Simply saying her name fired wretchedness as he had never known. With it came a ray of sunshine to his tormented heart. Just thinking about her made his pulse kick up a notch, his heart yearn for a future with such a woman.

"She could never overlook your past." He thrashed to his side. It failed to ease his torment. He winced at the thought of her rejection. If she knew, she would cringe at having his filthy hands on her even to treat her.

And filthy I am. The sardonic memories of his childhood never let him forget what he was. They festered in his mind like a swarming pool of maggots. The trembling started, as always, when he recalled those horrible years. Sweat surfaced, and yet, he shivered.

Oh, yes, he remembered. He remembered the pain, his tears, but foremost he remembered the complete humiliation. The sheer degradation that had etched his soul for all eternity.

Never would he be free from the solemn emptiness left inside. At his father's death, he had felt guilt, adding to his sins for he had neither shed a tear, nor felt any loss. Failing to comfort his mother at her time of need, he had borne guilt twice told.

But the past lay behind him. His parents were dead. Still, the imprint of tainted days gone by lingered like a sick legacy from his father, as if he mocked him from his place in hell.

Only he and his father, the scum of the earth, knew what an odious creature Seth truly was. No one need ever know; *could* ever know. And every time temptation rose, he forced himself to remember he did not deserve another's love. He hated the reminding; loathed all the recollections that surfaced from it.

He fought to bury the bitter past; had perfected burying it. If only it would remain dormant for longer intervals. He focused on the world's goodness. Lorelei, with her encouraging words for others, her benevolent will to protect. His torment quieted.

"Oh, Lorelei, even with your misguided ways, I'm falling in love with you. Damn you for making my life a living hell."

CHAPTER TWENTY-TWO

Lorelei's tender skull throbbed as if a hundred horses had galloped over it. Sunlight, dim and dismal, filtered through pulled curtains, yet its brightness stung her eyes.

Weary, she sat up and balanced on the edge of the bed. She braced a hand on each side of her head and leaned over to stare at the floor. Her belly rebelled, heaving up to her throat and back down. If she must die, she welcomed a quick demise.

"None too chipper this morning, I see."

Seth's voice reverberated against her eardrums as if tin cymbals clanged and banged in loud discord.

"Please," she whispered, without moving, "speak softly."

His boots came into her line of vision. He squatted down on his haunches and his knee came into view as it brushed her skirt.

"I did speak softly. We're actually whispering."

Wincing as his words rammed her temples, she closed her eyes. "Too much, shh…" His muffled chuckle rattled her brain.

"Please…it's not funny." Her belly churned again. "My head is cracking in two. My stomach…doesn't know which way to turn."

"That's why I brought you this tea. Drink it down. It'll help your head and stomach in a few minutes."

"What is it?" she asked, the few words sending another jolt through her skull. She eyed the pewter cup with a sideward glance, unwilling to move her head more than need be. Warm fumes of peppermint drifted upward.

He held out the cup. "Just drink it. It will soothe away your complaints. It has a nice taste to it."

Grateful for any help, she took the offering and sipped. It tasted of strong tea laced with peppermint, maybe something else. Again, she sipped. The warmth and peppermint did soothe.

He stood and then sat down beside her. The thin mattress shifted under her. Remaining bent over, she had to squirm to prevent toppling

156

onto him. Even so, she slid closer until her thigh rubbed his. Though layers of fabric separated them, the contact set her thigh on fire as if a hot poker lay next to it.

As poor as she felt, his nearness stirred her passion as easily as if he'd kissed her. Was she fighting a lost cause? Well, she wouldn't give up, not until he said it convincingly.

She took another sip. Could he hear her rapid pulse?

"All done?"

"Yes." As he took the cup, his fingers brushed hers. Her fingers turned light as feathers. Her heart flitted. Why, oh why, couldn't he feel what she felt? Only a minute had passed, yet the pain's intensity in her temples lessened, and her stomach started to calm.

"Thank you. I think I'm already starting to feel better."

"Good." He set the cup on the floor then placed his hands on her shoulders. "Let's sit you up. I'll see what I can do for you."

What he could do for her? Surely her pulse would burst through her skin. Oh, she could tell him many things she would like him to do. She had a tally as long as a child's Christmas list.

With the gentle guiding of his hands, she straightened. One obstinate pain knifed from temple to forehead, dredging up waves of angry sea within her belly. She closed her eyes and winced.

His fingers, gentle and warm against her skin, began to slowly knead her temples. Sheer heaven. She longed to lean against him, thought better of such a bold move, and resisted. Instead, she basked in the comfort of his touch. The throbbing gradually eased, her stomach settled.

His thumbs pressed into the back of her neck, massaging the tight cords. His fingertips caressed the back of her skull.

His tender ministration evoked a lulling of sweet serenity. So relaxed, so complacent, she wondered if she had drifted off to a state of light slumber for a time.

"Better?" His whisper fanned her face, warm, so sensual.

"Mmm, much better."

She turned her head. Their noses were just shy of touching. Their gazes locked. She recognized his passion, the fervid desire. Her heart trilled in delight. He might protest wanting her, but it was there as

157

clearly as she knew it mirrored her own. Maybe he protested too adamantly. Maybe he didn't know his own mind. She'd be more than happy to show him the way.

His gaze scoured her lips then swung back to her eyes. His hands slackened on her neck. A gamut of emotions clouded his eyes as if he was tormented by indecision. He wanted to kiss her. She'd bet her last two pence on it. *Please, just kiss me.*

"Lorelei." He shook his head. His eyes read like a book. Anguish conflicting with desire. "What am I to do with you?"

Do you really want to know? No well-brought up lady would reveal what she wanted to say. So she endowed a tolerant smile and tried to make light of the situation. He could only fight her so long. *Be patient if you want the outcome to be advantageous.*

"You're the one who gave me all that whiskey."

He nodded, his eyes full of regret, his hands falling to his sides. "Yes, I did. I thought I gave you just enough to lessen the discomfort from my probing and suturing. I'm sorry, I should've known you couldn't handle that much."

He stared at her intently. "I wasn't talking about your hangover. I think you know it."

"Am I such a dilemma?"

"You're more than a dilemma, sweet Lorelei."

Sweet Lorelei. Dear Heavenly Father. It was all she could do not to throw her arms around him and push him back on the bed.

Patience, my girl, patience. She was getting damn sick of patience. Patience might be a virtue, but she would just as soon lose a little virtue at the moment. Actually, if he wanted all her virtue she would give it. Wholeheartedly. And more.

Oh, my, but she had become brazen. The sobering thought compelled her to cling to the resolution to bide her time. If she pushed him before he felt ready, she could lose the battle before it began. Maybe his words of wisdom to always think situations through before riotously jumping in head first had started to sink in. She prayed it would work this time. But she didn't like having to wait, to play along slowly. Didn't like it one damn bit.

He took her hands within his. She looked down noting how tan, how very large his were compared to hers. His thumbs, scratchy with calluses, stroked her palms. She nearly toppled over as currents, sensuous and fevered, teemed through her veins.

"I don't have to be a…a dilemma."

His smile failed to reach his eyes. "No, you don't, but you are. I tried to make myself clear before. As much as I enjoy your company and appreciate your comeliness, I can never allow myself to be drawn to any woman. I live by that rule. I can't change."

"You mean you won't let yourself change." Though her voice sounded angry, she felt more hurt than angered. Could he not see what they might have together? Had some woman hurt him, soured him from allowing his heart to open? At the thought of him loving another, her chest constricted, almost cutting off her air.

He gave a slight squeeze to her hands. "You're right. I won't. There are reasons why I can't. Leave it at that."

"Is there another woman? Or *was* there another woman?" Why, oh why, had she asked? There it was again. Her and her big mouth. She could have kicked herself for being so forward.

He laughed at her stricken face. "My inquisitive, sweet Lorelei. No, there isn't any other woman, nor has there been. Does that satisfy your curiosity?"

Hell no, it doesn't satisfy my curiosity. And his answer only made her more confused. Her mind groped for a reason.

"You—" She stopped before she made an ass out of herself.

"I what?" His eyes now held the teasing twinkle she so loved. Her cheeks ignited into one big flame.

"I don't have the right to say anything. Please, let's just forget what I was going to say."

"You don't get off so easy. What were you going to ask?"

Lorelei prudently glanced at the floor. He had made it clear he wanted no relationship, so what did she have to lose? She could at least satisfy her curiosity. It begged to be fed. "You seek out saloon girls."

Good Lord, he actually blushed. He withdrew his hands and leaned his forearms across his thighs. "You don't mince punches."

"I never have. I thought you knew that."

He met her gaze. He looked none too pleased. "It's a job they're

159

paid for, one they've chosen. I occasionally visit them because they don't expect more. I'm a man, like any other. I have certain needs. Are you satisfied now, Miss Inquisitive?"

She looked down. "Yes." Her face felt as hot as a fry pan over an open flame. She was far from being satisfied.

"I better see you home. You've managed to stay here another night. Sooner or later your reputation, what little you have, as you say, will be torn to shreds if you keep this up."

She forced a meek smile. "I doubt it. My only reputation is for instigating trouble so I'm not worried.

Three nights she had stayed here. Each time consisting of more touching, talking and longing for each of them, if truth be told. Still, she wasn't any further ahead in reaching his heart than she had been on their first encounter.

Damn and double damn. There had to be a way. She simply had to find it. Undoubtedly, it would be as hard as trying to find that lost needle in a hay stack. Most likely, harder.

CHAPTER TWENTY-THREE

For the next week, Lorelei went about her teaching as if it were her only focus. But it wasn't. Not by a long shot.

More often than not, her thoughts dwelled on Seth's venture to the saloon. She itched to know if he made love with gentle caring or his detached attitude. What that might signify she could not fathom. But she had to find out. Plainly, something did not fit. She had witnessed his longing, sensed his inner battle. Oh, yes, the unknown question itched all right. It damn well prickled until she thought she would go mad from its incessant irritation.

Waving goodbye to the students, she gazed at the bright sun descending the cloudless Wedgewood sky. It glistened across the thin blanket of snow, painting the tall pines, poplars and giant oaks in pristine pearlescence. She needed to scratch that itch.

Without further contemplation, Lorelei buttoned her coat, wrapped her woolen scarf around her neck, pulled on her gloves, and hurried toward town. Such a pretty, crisp day for an invigorating walk. Hopefully, one for an interesting talk.

Approaching the saloon, second thoughts plagued her quest. She slowed her footsteps and almost laughed. For the second time, Seth's directive to analyze a situation before she charged forth sunk in. Maybe miracles did exist.

How did a bold teacher, shunned by half the town, ask a saloon woman such a question? How would she even start?

With a dignified high chin and a strut that belied her self-confidence, Lorelei suppressed her second thoughts and strode inside.

She marched straight to the long bar along the far wall. She heard whispers and snickers from the few customers across the room. Thank goodness, it wasn't as crowded as at night.

"Miss Webster," James Crawford, the bartender, nodded with a bemused smile as he wiped a glass with a terry towel. "What can we do for you? We don't have any sarsaparilla if you're wantin' to quench your thirst, ma'am." His eyes fairly danced. His attitude did not make this any easier.

Hearing more snickers, her gumption wavered. She swallowed, clutching her handbag more tightly with both hands.

"I would like to talk to one of the ladies, if I may."

The bartender's eyebrows arched as he hooted with laughter. "One of the ladies, huh? Don't think we have much use for *ladies* in this place. We got several *women* who work here."

Lorelei snorted in disgust and threw him one of her best exasperated looks. "That's exactly who I mean, sir."

He set down the towel and glass, giving her a once over enough to say she either bothered him or she had lost her mind. His attitude infuriated her clear down to her toes.

Leaning across the bar, he waved one hand in the air. "Hey, Pearl, this...*lady* wants to talk to you."

Lorelei wished she condoned violence. Then she could smack him but good. Did he think she might be seeking a job, or that she sought some trade secrets for her own use? To him, either would be quite hilarious. Her face flamed till her earlobes burned.

A redhead, dressed in a deep purple satin gown, revealing more cleavage than Lorelei had ever seen on one woman, glanced their way. She pushed away from the table and approached her. "Sure enough, Jimmy," she said with a grin.

Wide-eyed, Lorelei glanced sideways and stared at the middle-aged woman. Her lips were painted deep red, makeup and rouge caked her aging face. She walked as if she owned the place. Lorelei tried to picture Seth with her. Pearl could not possibly be the one. The thought of them together twisted her stomach.

"Hello, honey." She eyed Lorelei's attire and obviously found her it lacking if her smug grin said anything. "What can I do for ya? I'm not

162

used to being summoned by a woman. Guess I can accommodate anyone… if the price is right."

Pearl swirled the amber contents in her glass. James Crawford's howl rattled the fancy chandelier overhead. From across the room, whoops of laughter joined in.

Lorelei longed to run. Her feet were glued in place. She wanted to scream at the woman's vulgar insinuation. But she remembered her reason for coming. Perseverance rallying, she raised her chin and gave an impervious smile. "If you don't mind, I'd like to ask you a few questions. I won't take more than a minute or two of your time."

Pearl's smart smirk vanished for a split second before her ruby grin spread from ear to ear." Sure, honey. Let's us go over to a corner table and ya can ask away. Ya want a drink?"

"No…no, I won't be here that long. Thank you."

Pearl nodded and led the way. On shaky legs, Lorelei followed. She heard Pearl's muffled chortle. Resenting the fact that she served as Pearl's entertainment, she nonetheless felt thankful Pearl had chosen a table out of earshot.

When they sat, Pearl smoothed down her gown. She glanced at the men, smiled and boldly winked before she turned to Lorelei.

"So, what can I do for ya?"

Lorelei found it difficult to speak. Since Pearl's condescending looks had waned, Lorelei's nerves calmed. Somewhat. Why did women choose this kind of profession?

"Ya gonna ask me your question or not? I got ta be sellin' drinks, honey." Pearl's annoyance brought Lorelei back from her mental wandering. "That's how I make my livin'. Partly, anyway," she laughed, unashamed of her meaning. "Can't afford to sit too long while ya find your tongue."

If she meant to sound reprimanding, she failed. Lorelei surmised Pearl felt uncomfortable sitting with the likes of a schoolmarm. She appeared self-conscious, restless.

"I'm sorry. I don't mean to take up a lot of your time. I just wanted to ask…well—"

"Oh, for Christ's sake, just ask it. It isn't going to be anything I ain't heard before, ya know. I've heard everything, most likely more than any man has. Ask away, honey."

Lorelei swallowed and leaned toward Pearl, keeping her words at a whisper. "I wanted to know if you know Doctor Taylor."

Pearl's dark penciled eye brows rose and she leaned back with a grin. "Well, now, I know the doc, but I don't think ya mean just as an acquaintance, now do you?"

Lorelei blushed, yet found it less embarrassing than at first. "No, I don't. I believe he comes here to see...someone." If she weren't so embarrassed, why did her face burn so?

"Mm, mm, I'll tell ya something, honey. I'd give *him* the money if he wanted me for a night. But its Lilly ya want to talk to if your question has to do with that handsome gent."

Lilly? God in heaven, Lorelei had copied her hair style for the dance. Please, not Lilly.

Pearl laughed, a hearty laugh, at Lorelei's obvious dismay. The woman did not seem abashed by her statement in the least.

"Lilly's upstairs. I'll get her for ya."

Lorelei appreciated Pearl's help, felt guilty for putting her out. "I don't want to take up anymore of your time."

Pearl rose and set her drink down. "No bother. It'll only take a second. She should be on her way down with the others anyway. Ya wait right here. I'll be back in no time."

Feeling stares from the bartender as well as the men at the two tables, Lorelei focused on Pearl's glass. Whiskey fumes drifted her way and she sniffed at the not-so-unpleasant scent. Tempted to take a swig to calm her nerves, she recalled how she had felt after the brandy at Seth's. *No thank you.*

Lorelei glanced up at a scurry of activity on the stairway across the room. "Yes, siree. This is more like it," one of the men bellowed, his chair crashing to the floor as he jumped up.

Six voluptuous women, each dressed in different dazzling satin, their bosoms and cleavage equaling or rivaling Pearl's, paraded down the stairs.

Mouth-agape, Lorelei sat transfixed. And simply gawked.

They were all lovely in their own realm. Two brunettes, two redheads counting Pearl, and two very light blondes. Each with tiny waists, those well-endowed chests, and hair-dos from stylish upsweeps to dancing pulled-back curls. They all wore rouge, bright lip color, and dark kohl around their eyes.

They wore their profession like bright painted signs. She felt insignificant, frumpy and dowdy compared to them. Who was she kidding? She was older than most of them, and a spinster to boot. The truth pierced her soul.

Five of them flocked to the tables, two plunking down right on men's laps. Loud whoops and cat calls resounded through the place along with the women's laughter. Piano music burst forth, adding to the gay commotion. It wasn't even supper time and the sun had yet to set, Lorelei thought in wonder. She led a far different life. Very different, indeed.

Lorelei studied Lilly as she accepted a drink from James, then turned her way. She wore that fashionable upsweep with her wispy blonde curls bobbing along each high cheek bone. She was slender and petite, pretty with big dark brown eyes. Lorelei felt more than deficient. Naturally, Seth found Lilly ten times more appealing than her. Hopelessness gnawed her chest and left her feeling empty.

"Hello, Miss Webster. You wanted to see me?"

"Ah…yes. Yes, I did. But this obviously isn't a good time for you. You're supposed to be working too, aren't you?" The boisterous carrying-on became almost deafening. She wanted to get out of here before she made more of a fool of herself.

Lilly sat, her smile easy and kind. She seemed so different than Pearl. She had a sweet way about her, a quieter manner. Lorelei found her fascinating. No wonder Seth sought her out.

"I've a few minutes. What can I do for you?"

Lorelei felt the misplaced fool. It had been easier to talk to Pearl who was rougher, more brazen, and outlandish. Oh, what the hell, she was here. Her and her big mouth and neb-nose.

"You're the one Seth Taylor visits?" There. She had spit it out. She sounded like a wife checking on her delinquent husband. She could have bitten her tongue. Never should she have intruded like this. It was not right. *She had no right.*

Lilly's smile vanished, her hand curled tight around her glass. Her

165

wary eyes studied Lorelei. "I…don't want any trouble, Miss Webster. I can assure you."

"Please," Lorelei interrupted, feeling lower than a skunk's tail. "I'm not here to reprimand you, or to find fault. Your time with Seth is your own business. But I wanted to know…I need to know…" Lord, what could she say? She twisted her hands together, palms slippery with dampness. Their gazes met.

Lilly smiled, a gentle kind of understanding apparent. She really was quite lovely. Lorelei's chest tightened at knowing Seth surely viewed Lilly the same way.

"Just ask away and I'll try to answer your question."

"I want to know if…if when he makes…when he's with you… if he's detached, distant."

Lilly's eyes took on a dreamy, faraway look as she peered directly at Lorelei. "No, Miss Webster, he isn't. He's warm, he's gentle, and he's kind." Her smile seemed reticent as she leaned against the chair spindles. She hesitated and bit her bottom lip.

"I don't know why you're asking, but I'll be truthful. I've seen you in town. I've heard that you speak your mind plainly, so I'll speak mine. I'm not proud of the work I do, but it's a living. A living I chose, and that's the way it is."

Lilly folded her hands on her lap. "In my profession, I meet all kinds. Some rough, some tough. Some quiet, some talkative. Half of them are so cocky they make me sick. Some are just plain crude. But they all want one thing. Not many go upstairs offering more than their money. It's my job to see that they get what they paid for. Only a few care enough to give more of themselves."

Lorelei drank in every word. She had never talked to a woman like Lilly before. Lilly's self-recrimination humbled her. And in that instant, Lorelei realized she liked this woman. She found it gratifying that she was more non-judgmental than she had thought. Yet, Lilly's words baffled her.

"I see you're wondering what I mean." Lilly laughed, and Lorelei realized she must have frowned. "I do my job the best I can and receive money for it. I never count on more than that. There's little or no satisfaction in my line of work. The men take what's offered and away they go without a second glance until the next time. In other words, there's no meaning, no caring behind the actual act. It's strictly business."

"It sounds so cold and callous."

Lilly smiled. It looked strained and sad. "It is. It's not the kind of sweet kisses and gentle romancing of couples who care about one another. But, it's my job. I don't expect more. But, once in awhile, along comes a man who wants to reciprocate. He does more than just take. He makes it pleasant." She looked away.

"He makes me feel like I'm...worth more than a quick tumble on the tic. As if *my* pleasure is important to him." She turned wide eyes back to Lorelei. "He makes it seem like he cares about me because he likes me. You can't know how wonderful that feels, how seldom I'm made to feel like that."

Lorelei could no more restrain the tears accumulating than she could speak. She blinked them back. But Lilly had obviously seen them. Her eyes widened.

"Are those tears for me, or because he doesn't make *you* feel that way?" Lord Almighty, this woman spoke as boldly as she did.

Lorelei had blushed before. Now, her cheeks ignited. "Partly for you, partly because I know I'll never get that chance."

"What?" Lilly's eyes grew as big as saucers.

Though her relationship with Seth was far from being any laughing matter, Lorelei found herself chuckling at the woman's amazement. And as she did, her tension ebbed from between her shoulder blades. "We don't have that kind of relationship. I wish we did, but he resists any pull he might feel when he's around me."

For a moment, Lilly sat silent, tapping her long red index nail against the rim of her glass. "He must have mush for a brain. And here, I thought he was so smart."

They laughed like teenage girls who were best of friends. Lorelei recovered first.

"I thought he might have something wrong, physically or emotionally, so he couldn't...umm...respond to a woman. Now, I know I have a fighting chance to somehow whittle my way in. I'll keep trying, now that I know he's capable of more."

Lilly fairly beamed. "You do that, Miss Webster. I can't say that I'll be happy to see him not come visit me if you win him over, but I'll be content knowing it's you who has him."

Her sincere words touched Lorelei with a warm glow.

Lilly stood and grabbed her drink. "Good luck."

Lorelei followed suit, saddened to have to end their time together. She liked her, a lot. "Thank you for talking to me, Miss Tillman. You've been a tremendous help. I really appreciate it."

Lilly's sudden blush surprised Lorelei. "It wasn't anything at all. I was happy to help."

"It means everything to me. And besides, I should thank you for the wonderful hair style."

"My hairdo?" Lilly frowned, raising a hand to her upsweep.

"At the harvest dance," Lorelei explained, "I wanted to look my best for Seth. I had admired your hair several times when I saw you outside. I styled my hair like yours that night."

"Did it work?" Lilly's eyes twinkled with mischief. Lorelei hoped Lilly's elation stemmed from her praise.

"Yes, I think it did. To a certain extent. But just when I think he feels something, he pulls back. I'm not making much headway. I feel like an unruly yoyo. Or maybe *he's* the yoyo." She lifted her purse off the table.

Lilly grinned, rested her free hand on the chair back. "Now, Miss Webster, from what I hear, you won't stand for that very long. I expect I'll hear differently about the two of you quite soon if your reputation is all it's cracked up to be."

Lorelei laughed. "I believe you just might be correct. And please, call me Lorelei."

Lilly appeared appalled. "Oh, that wouldn't be right at all, you being a church-goer, a teacher, and all. Why, most folks would probably boot you out of town quicker if they knew you talked to me than they would for all your other doings."

As they laughed, Lorelei took Lilly's hands in hers, glass and all. "I don't care what this town thinks. I might've come here for answers, but I received far more than I counted on. I got my answers, but I hope I've made a new friend. And I hope you'll visit me, maybe for dinner when you're not working?"

Lilly's eyes did the swimming this time. Lorelei's contentment swelled. She was glad she had come. "Thank you, M…Lorelei. If you really mean it, I would love to. And please, call me Lilly. Miss Tillman is far too formal for me."

Lorelei nodded with a grin and squeezed Lilly's hands. "I most certainly do mean it, Lilly. I don't mince words. Ask anyone if my word isn't my decree. How about next week?"

"I'd like that. I have Thursdays free."

"Thursday it is. Can you come about six?"

Lilly fairly glowed. "Thursday."

CHAPTER TWENTY-FOUR

Snow wafted down in a lazy shower, large, lace-fanned flakes accumulating on the ground. The students ran through the foot of glistening fluff chasing each other with well-packed snow balls. Some darted to take cover behind the jolly snowman they had built, while others scooted around the sides of the schoolhouse to avoid being blasted by another attack.

Standing on the small landing above the steps, Lorelei chuckled at their shrieks of laughter. She loved watching them run and chase in the snow. Their afternoon break never seemed long enough.

She turned and spotted Seth riding past on the snow-covered road, his horse plodding at a slow, steady pace as flakes amassed upon both of them. Seth was bundled in a thick coat, a brown wool scarf wrapped around his neck, and a wide-brimmed hat upon his head.

He waved and smiled as his horse sauntered by. Lorelei waved back, her heart fluttering as it did every time she encountered him, no matter how briefly. The children's giggles and screams as they scurried to and fro faded in the distance. Another balled missile whizzed by and she reluctantly glanced away from Seth to see it hit and splatter against Johnny's shoulder.

Johnny laughed, brushed off his jacket, and scooped up a handful of snow for a return fire. Lorelei chortled as Johnny crouched down and took aim. Clearly, Jamie, who had turned and crouched down to gather ammunition, was his target. Johnny launched the ball; a direct hit to Jamie's backside. The children howled with glee as Jamie bellowed and made a mad dash across the lawn, ducking around the corner of the building for safety.

Glancing back at Seth, Lorelei's pulse quickened at seeing him laugh as heartily as the children. He shook his head, still chuckling while continuing past.

A little devil hopped upon Lorelei's shoulder. She just couldn't help it. She scurried down the steps, made a well-formed ball and hurled it at Seth's back. Her aim missed its target.

But it did knock off his hat.

The hat flew through the air, landing about ten feet to his left. The students' loud uproar filled the air like high pitched thunder. Her laughter joined in.

Seth halted his horse and peered over his shoulder. He appeared more than shocked that someone had sent a ball his way.

"Good shot, Miss Webster," Johnny's voice boomed through the crisp air, easily heard over other's giggles.

Undoubtedly, Seth heard Johnny's words, for his gaze scanned the yard until it fixed on hers. His shocked expression fled, replaced by a broad grin.

She watched him dismount, expecting him to retrieve his hat, and issue her a quick reprimand. Instead, he bent down, gathered snow in his gloved hands and turned in a flash.

"Turnabout is fair play."

Before Lorelei realized his intent, the ball sailed through the air. She darted to the steps. Her foot landed on the first step when the ball slammed against her back.

The children howled in glee. She could no more hold back her laughter than they could. As she reached around to brush off the snow, she turned to look at Seth. His eyes sparkled, rich with a devilment she had never witnessed before. He was already forming another ball. Another burst of mirth seized her.

"Do you give quarter, Miss Webster?"

She longed to continue their merriment, yet thought better of it. He definitely had a better aim and better packed snowballs, though she took pride in having removed his hat so well.

"I give quarter. But be prepared for a next time."

"Aw, Miss Webster," Johnny moaned, "don't give up yet."

They all laughed, Lorelei and Seth included. She might be surrendering a snowball fight, but she vowed not to give up on *him* as easily.

"I'll take warning, Miss Webster," Seth yelled. "But the things you teach these students." He shook his head as if disillusioned, yet his grin broadened. "I wonder if the board knows about these snowball fights. What would they say?"

Lorelei basked in his teasing. "I teach my students to defend themselves the best way they know how, Doctor Taylor. Let that be a lesson to you."

He nodded, his chortle shaking his shoulders. "I believe you have a good point there, Miss Webster." He retrieved his hat, mounted his horse and turned his attention to the children.

"Have fun," he said with a grin, "but just remember that Miss Webster is a sly one. You best watch your back when she's around." He nodded and cantered his horse down the road.

Lorelei watched Seth until he faded out of sight as the white downpour gobbled him up. Feeling light at heart, she turned and followed the children into the warm schoolroom. For the next hour, it became difficult to keep her mind on the studies at hand.

****

Thursday arrived before Lorelei realized a week had passed since talking with Lilly. She checked her roast, took out the apple pie, and set the table. After Lilly arrived, they chatted about everything from town politics to the latest hair fashions.

To Lorelei's delight, Lilly helped update a few of her outdated dresses. The woman had an eye for what and how to easily dress up the bedraggled plain dresses. By the time evening turned pitch dark, both women were reluctant to part company. They promised to keep in touch, Lilly accepting Lorelei's invitation to come back soon.

Though she took pride in being non-judgmental, it surprised Lorelei that she viewed Lilly without distaste. Lilly, indeed, was the warm and caring person she had believed her to be. It stymied her as to why Lilly had stooped to such a profession. If someday Lilly chose to offer why, she would not stand in judgment. She merely wanted to understand

172

what kind of life Lilly had endured so she might offer a shoulder to lean on; if, in fact, she needed or wanted one. And she desperately hoped their friendship would grow. A strong bond between two strong women.

Surprisingly, it did not bother her that Seth had been intimate with Lilly. He had sought Lilly's service for one purpose. She found no fault with either of them. In truth, Lorelei felt better knowing Seth sought out a person like Lilly rather than the outlandish Pearl. That Lilly had divulged Seth had not sought her out of late felt like a feather in her cap. Oh, how she prayed that feather stayed straight.

****

Saturday came with blowing snow. Lorelei wrapped the blanket tighter around her legs in the buggy as she drove to Seth's.

Last week, he had removed the facial sutures, informing her there would be little evidence fairly soon. The arm had not healed as readily because the wound had been deeper, so he had decided to wait another week as long as no inflammation set in.

She secured the reins to the post, and then shuffled through the six-inch snow. She knocked and waited. In mere seconds she heard footsteps. Despite the frigid temperature, her pulse quickened and her blood heated just thinking of seeing him again.

"Good morning, Lorelei. Please, come in out of the cold." He stood back, allowing her to pass, his friendly smile a tease to her heart. She inhaled his scent. Her pulse pattered faster.

She returned his smile, "Good morning." She stomped snow off her boots just past the entrance. Oh, how she would love to greet him with a good morning kiss. To have him return it with equal relish. That was probably the furthest thing from his mind.

"Here let me help." He reached out, taking her gloves, then the scarf after she unrolled it from around her neck and head. Next came her coat, as he slid it off and hung it next to his.

"Thank you."

"Come over by the fire and get warm before we take a look at your arm."

They walked to the large hearth glowing and crackling with long

173

yellow flickering flames. Lorelei held out her hands, feeling the warmth return to her fingers.

"Would you like a cup of tea, or coffee? Coffee's already made."

She longed for more than tea or coffee. *An embrace would do quite nicely, thank you very much.*

"No, thank you. I think the fire will warm me in a minute." Suddenly at a loss for words, she rubbed her hands together.

"Please have a seat until you get comfortable. That wind is vicious this morning."

Lorelei sat down on the davenport directly in front of the hearth and held out her hands again to feel the warmth. He sat in the chair to its side. She wished he had sat by her. By golly, she would have felt flames to equal those of the hearth.

"It's colder than I thought," she said, determined to hide how he affected her. Could he hear her hammering heart, her blood rushing like a spring brook? "Of course, we've had a mild winter so far, so we can't complain. It has to come sometime."

"You're right about that. Are you getting warmer?"

Oh, yes, I was warm the second you opened the door. "Yes, much better. Thank you." How awkward she felt.

Did he want to get this over with lickety-split and have her be on her way? The thought sent a chill straight to her chest.

"Just sit a little longer, then we can get to those sutures."

He was not trying to rush her. Her insides turned giddy with joy.

"Did you have any trouble coming through the snow?"

"No, not at all. John Hackley put wider wheels on my buggy this fall. Now it's much better in the snow and mud."

"That's good. I should do the same. I ride my horse most of the time so I don't get my carriage stuck. Of course, I prefer riding my horse to using the carriage, anyway."

She nodded. Their conversation lulled and she wondered how to restart it. They stared into the fire, the silence adding to her frustrations, as well as making her feel out of sorts.

Her mind groped for something to say. The Harvest Dance came to mind and how he seemed annoyed with Michael after they'd discussed Dan Purdy. "Was Michael able to close the case regarding Dan Purdy?

I meant to ask about it before."

"What made you ask about Dan? As far as the town is concerned, he died—and that was that." He seemed to watch her with renewed interest. An interest she did not think she liked.

"I don't know," she said, feeling like the neb-nose she had been labeled. "I just remembered you two spoke about it at the dance, and you seemed…rather annoyed with Michael afterward. I apologize if I asked something I shouldn't. I was only making conversation." She felt at a loss as to his reaction about Dan as she was over his keep-his-nose-clean attitude.

He leaned back, crossed one leg over the other so his calf rested on his knee. He had long, powerful-looking legs.

"I apologize. I shouldn't have questioned you like that. It's just that the case is puzzling."

Lorelei's brows shot upward. She leaned forward. He had tweaked her inquisitiveness to the hilt this time. She was dying to know. Oh good Lord, she *had* become a busybody.

"What do you mean *puzzling*, or can't you tell me?" He most likely would hedge at telling her, expecting her to run through town announcing it. Her chest tightened at thinking he believed the worst of her.

He studied her for a moment and then smiled. "Lorelei, the men have labeled you as a neb-nose, but in all honesty…I think you stick your nose in only where you believe it will do some good. I realized a long ago you're not fueled by petty gossip."

Lorelei's heart nearly bounded out of her chest. It mattered little if he agreed that she did, indeed, meddle. That he recognized *why* she did, triggered happiness equal to euphoria.

"Thank you." She forced herself not to jump up and hug him. If nothing else came of their friendship, she was learning patience with a capital P.

"You're welcome." When he glanced at the fire, she wondered if she would have to pry. He saved her from eating her words.

"Can you keep it to yourself if I tell you about Dan?"

Their eyes met. She could gaze into that deep dark richness forever.

"Of course," she answered, pleased he felt he could trust her. It had to be a step in the right direction. Her mounting intrigue fell shy in comparison to the joy she felt at his faith.

"He was murdered."

Stunned, she sat speechless for a second. "Murdered?" A chill crept up her spine.

"Yes." His expression said he was dead serious.

"How? And for heaven's sake, why? I can't imagine anyone in town doing such a thing. Was he robbed?" That had to be it. Some cowpoke from elsewhere had robbed him and fled. Her mind ran wild with a gamut of possibilities.

"Not that we know of."

Damn the man! She needed an explanation. Not evasive tidbits. And why had they kept it a secret?

"Can you tell me what you know?" He tempted her curiosity to the highest degree. His stalling infuriated her to no end.

Seth leaned back further, and chuckled. "My, you are the inquisitive one, aren't you? And here I thought you weren't the gossipy type. Was I so wrong?" His eyes twinkled.

He was teasing her! And she loved it.

"No, you weren't wrong," she answered, arching her brows and jutting out her chin to emphasize her dignity. "I may be many things, including a nettle in the seat of many pants, but I'm not the town gossip. This is something out of the ordinary, and you know it. It's devastating. I can't help but be curious. Why did you and Michael keep this a secret?"

A satisfied light shone in his eyes as he smiled his approval. She reveled in his open admiration, appreciating the sheer pleasure to sit and talk, even if it did pertain to a mysterious murder.

"There wasn't anything out of place. At least Michael hasn't found anything. That's what's so puzzling."

"And you're certain it was murder?" Good heavens, would he take offense at her questioning?

He did not seem to. "Yes, there's no doubt. By the time I arrived and had Dan brought here to inspect the body, the bruises around his neck were the first blatant evidence."

"He was strangled?" She failed to stifle her gasp, the eerie shiver that shook her. She rubbed her arms to thwart the goose bumps, yet leaned forward as curiosity got the best of her. "I thought he was found in bed. Everyone believed he died in his sleep."

"That's the impression we gave people until we could uncover some evidence. Michael purposely hid the truth, thinking the murderer might make a cocky mistake later on. And he *was* in bed, made to look as if he'd died in his sleep. The killer obviously doesn't realize the tell-tale markings of such an act."

Lorelei digested his words, as astonishing as they were. Somewhere out there stalked a murderer. Walking free, possibly lurking and planning another. Lorelei shivered from the grisly thought and again stroked her arms to ward off the sudden chill.

"You still cold?" His brow creased.

His concern touched her. Oh, how she savored this shared time with him. Her spirits sank as she realized she might never share more times like this with him, certainly nothing romantic.

"No. I'm fine. It's just so unbelievable. Scary, in fact." He nodded, and she remembered him mentioning evidence.

"What did you mean by 'the first blatant evidence'? Was there more?"

His brows arched, his eyes grew openly amused. She loved his soft laughter, his expressive eyes. "You're sharp. I wish Michael were half as sharp."

She felt like a breathless teenager at his compliment. His gaze traveled over her like a soft caress and she fought the urge to reach out and touch him. She marshaled her thoughts and grinned.

"Thank you, but what else did you find?"

He scowled and sighed. "His neck was broken."

Lorelei gasped. "I've been lax in locking my door, but I'll make sure I lock it from now on." The chills increased.

"Now I've frightened you. I didn't mean to."

"No," she insisted, "I'm fine. Really."

He sat up straighter. "I was too blunt. Maybe I should get you a brandy. It may make you feel better."

As she digested the shock of his disclosure she managed a tiny smile. "No, thank you. I'll be fine without any spirits."

"I'm not offering you the entire bottle, just a few sips." His grin said he, too, remembered her previous stupor.

She ventured another question despite how her cheeks burned. "Has Michael found out anything since the…murder?"

He shook his head and his lips thinned. "Not a thing. I know you and Michael are good friends, but sometimes he doesn't have the initiative to wholeheartedly pursue the issue."

She sighed. "No, he doesn't. He's really a good person. But at times he's too lackadaisical for his job. That's why…"

"That's why what?"

Oh, fiddle, what did it matter? Her relationship with Michael, platonic or otherwise, would matter as much as a speck of dust on a pig's behind to Seth.

"That's why I can never be more than his friend. I value his friendship, but I could never respect him enough to feel more. I can't abide his letting the world go off course and not do anything about it."

She wanted to swallow her tongue. Dear Lord, would Seth deduce she categorized *him* the same way? Well, facts were facts. At least, sometimes. Yet, she still felt attracted to the mysterious doctor while denying Michael a second thought—something she didn't understand about herself.

"I see." The tantalizing twinkle in those dark eyes evaporated. She wanted to kick herself right where it would it count. *Me and my big mouth.*

"If you'll remove my stitches, I won't take up more of your time." She needed to leave. It hurt to think about his flaw.

"Are you all warmed up now?" He seemed to question her sudden eagerness to leave. Or did he simply suspect her reason?

"Yes, thank you."

"Then come along, and we'll see what we have."

****

Proclaiming the wound sufficiently healed, Seth removed the sutures and redressed the wound. After instructing her to keep it covered for two days, she left with a bright smile.

He stared out his front window, knowing he should leave for the

178

Blair farm to check Silas's broken leg. The man had fallen from the barn loft a week ago and shattered the femur.

Instead, he glared daggers at the snow-covered lawn. Lorelei's words returned full force. Did she see him the same way? *Surely she must.* She wasn't stupid by any means; quite the opposite.

She most likely viewed him as lacking gumption to take a stand on certain matters. And for all accounts, she had every right to perceive him that way. He did step back when it came to offering his two cents to the community. He could not afford to give more than he did. And in her eyes, he would appear nonchalant, uncommitted. *As meek and unassertive as Michael.*

"Damn you, Lorelei!" He gripped the sill with both hands.

He felt the urge to shoulder the town's concerns. He'd become a part of this community far more than he had anticipated, especially since meeting Lorelei. Her efforts to rid abuse had increased his awareness that each person needed to take part to make the community work.

His fingers pressed hard into the wood. Standing back and allowing others to lead the way soured his stomach. It left him feeling inept. He longed to be part of the decision-making. For years, he had forced himself to take a second seat, convincing himself he needed to avoid the upheaval of involvement.

Oh, yes, avoiding his duty had always vexed him deep inside. Now, it did not sit right at all. And all because Lorelei Webster made his stance seem even more pathetic. Totally neglectful.

He felt like a heel. And he had no idea how to correct it. Or better yet, how to keep his sanity.

CHAPTER TWENTY-FIVE

For the next week, Lorelei threw herself into teaching and preparing for the Christmas pageant two weeks away. Yet, each day of hectic rehearsing and overseeing the students painting props distanced her further from Seth. That alone weighed on her heart far more than the accumulating snow drifts outside her door.

"Miss Webster. Come see what Elizabeth and Johnny and Jamie did." Missy Cooper's eyes danced to match her shuffling feet.

Having added another log to the woodstove to fight the dropping temperature, Lorelei turned to the enthusiastic girl.

"Lead the way, Missy." Lorelei smiled and held out her hand. "I can't wait to see." Hand in hand, they wound their way around desks that had been shoved to the front to provide the painters ample space.

Johnny and Jamie inched along on their knees, brushes in hands, at the top of the background prop for the manger scene. Elizabeth sat cross-legged at the bottom adding final touches to the strewn hay. Lorelei had not seen it for hours since she had been helping the younger ones make costumes.

As they neared, the boys added a few more brush strokes. The twelve-foot long, six-foot high board had been donated by Mr. Beebe at the sawmill. Lorelei had her concerns about the vast size and how the children would do.

The entire class had agreed it would be the barn's interior. She had envisioned upright boards, stacks of hay and maybe a tool or two hanging. That had been what they had discussed.

Now, viewing the students' talents and efforts filled her with pride so potent, she had to fight back tears. They had added a lamb lying down with its head held high and a cow standing at the right corner. Both animals were so well depicted, their eyes focusing intently upon what would be the manger, that she found herself anticipating a moo and a bleat.

She had recognized the artistic talent of all three, but never had she expected a masterpiece any professional would admire. It gladdened her heart to see them work together so well, knowing each coped with various family problems.

"What do think, Miss Webster? Are the animals too much?"

Lorelei laughed at Jamie's skeptical question. How could he possibly think she would not be pleased? The three had poured their hearts into their creation, demonstrating their expertise and expressing imaginative creativity to the utmost. There was hope for all of them if they chose to pursue their talents.

"I think the three of you have done more than a superb job. It's absolutely beautiful, a true piece of art." Other children came up behind Lorelei. Their "ooh's" and "ah's" filled the room.

"The three of you need to stand back and analyze your accomplishment. It's by far the best work I've seen any of you do, and you should feel as proud as I do about your abilities. I can't wait for the public to see this."

Jamie stood, brushed the dust off his pant legs and stepped back to view their finished product. Johnny leaned back on his haunches to inspect the large board. Elizabeth clasped her hands in front of her as she, too, looked on. All three grinned.

How good it felt to have them take pride in themselves. Especially Jamie. He needed every ounce he could grab.

"You really like it?" Jamie asked again as he backed up to eye it from a different angle. He looked very self-satisfied, more self-assured than he had in a long time. Thank goodness.

"I love it. As a matter of fact, I think we should have it nailed to the back wall after the pageant. It would serve as inspiration for other upcoming artists. What do you think?"

Three pair of eyes grew wide at her suggestion. Jamie glanced at the back wall. Devoid of windows, with the door offset, the wall could easily house the picture.

"You serious?" Johnny asked as he, too, studied the wall.

"I'm very serious."

"Wow!" Jamie whispered. Elizabeth beamed. Johnny grinned.

****

The rest of the afternoon flew by in a flurry. The older children assisted the younger ones with finishing costumes, filling the manger with straw, and making streamers and ornaments out of pinecones and ribbons for the walls and ceiling.

Lorelei fastened a bright red velveteen bow to the wreath that would grace the door outside. She listened as the three elated artists praised the younger children for their good work. When people felt good about themselves, they bestowed that feeling upon others. It would be a wonderful Christmas.

Seth came to mind. She wondered if she would dare give him the scarf she had started knitting. His brown one was quite worn. He needed a thick scarf for going to the surrounding farms in the fierce weather. Would he think her brazen to give him a present?

And where would he spend Christmas? She longed to invite him, yet knew that would be much too forward. Most likely, several families had already invited him to share the day. Her fingers faltered as she pulled the ribbon tighter. Her spirits dropped.

She did not expect any invitations. Oh, there were several families who might, but they lived quite a ways out. Those close to town, well, half the men would not want her around, so their wives would hesitate. Maybe Hattie and Charles would ask. Maybe she should ask Lilly to share the day. Now, there was a thought.

With that bright notion—and refusing to allow her spirits to be dampened, for Christmas was one of her favorite times—she forced herself to concentrate on the pageant. Better to be engrossed in the children than to brood. She would face the dilemma of the scarf another time.

Seth had called *her* a dilemma. She failed to understand exactly why. At least, she'd made some kind of impression on him. He'd thought about her.

Maybe she could label it step three.

****

Before Lorelei knew it, the night of the pageant arrived. She prayed each one would remember their lines so none would be embarrassed. She prayed harder that Seth would show his face. She needed to see him. Over the past week, she had caught a glimpse of him as he rode past the school, each waving their hello. It simply wasn't enough.

Lorelei arranged platters of cookies and pies that mothers had sent or she had baked. The Piedmonts had offered to bring fruit punch and cups, and Lorelei had thankfully accepted.

Jamie, Johnny, Elizabeth and Missy arrived as she was cutting the pies into wedges. They had insisted on coming early to help with any last-minute finishing touches. She more than welcomed their help.

By the time the pageant began, only standing room remained along the back. She all but glowed at seeing so many people; even the men who wanted her out of town. Delighted, she greeted everyone with a bright smile and sincere welcome.

Oil lamps, trimmed with red plaid ribbons and silver balls, hung along the walls every five feet. Candles, wreathed with pinecones and silver satin bows, flickered brightly on long serving tables against the walls. A golden glow filled the festive room. Everything was ready. Except for Seth Taylor.

Why hadn't he come? Walking to the front to stand before the beautiful scenery, Lorelei swallowed her disappointment. Jamie and Johnny had placed two small pines, their roots imbedded in dirt-filled buckets, to bracket the ends of the make-shift stage.

"Ladies and gentlemen, welcome to our first Christmas pageant. As..." She paused as the door opened. Seth eased through. She smiled. He nodded, looking uncomfortably apologetic, and closed the door. For a moment, she felt mesmerized as he removed his snow-covered hat, then leaned against the door.

Her heart slammed against her rib cage and her nerves jittered like cream in a churn. Lorelei mentally forced her thoughts to the captive audience who demanded she be the model of decorum this evening. The spell-binding gaze of the tall man in the back heightened her self-consciousness. She swallowed to clear her dry throat. Holding her head high, she restarted.

"As you can see the students have worked extremely hard to make tonight's event very special. We have magnificent scenery, and a talented cast of actors and actresses and carolers who are certain to bring soothing melody to your hearts. The students and I hope you enjoy the night's show, and that you'll stay afterward to talk and partake of the desserts offered. Thank you all for coming and making this first pageant a true success as I'm sure it will be. It's my great hope this will mark the first of many more to follow. Thank you again, and enjoy the evening."

With damp palms, Lorelei exited through the doorway to her living quarters where the children waited. They were using it as back stage to accommodate for more space. After each scene, they would return to her apartment until time to reenter the stage.

With a big smile and tender encouragement, she routed all of them out to begin the carols. She filed behind them as they paraded in front of the scenery until they had assembled, neatly as little toy soldiers, into two rows. Lorelei smiled in contentment then strode to the side so as not to block the audience's view. They sang *a cappella*, even the youngest hitting the notes with near perfection.

The harmony filled the room with sweet melody. Again, pride for them swelled in her chest, so full and rich it nearly burst through her bosom. They sang three songs, each giving their all, before marching back through the door at her cue. Lorelei followed, sniffling lightly to counter her blurred vision.

The pageant ensued, and for the most part, went extremely well. Only seven-year-old Caroline Jacobs, with panic stricken eyes, faltered with her lines. But as soon as Lorelei, from the sideline, whispered reassurance, Caroline continued on beautifully.

And of course, when Johnny's foot struck one of the buckets holding a tree and it nearly toppled, the crowd chuckled behind raised palms as he contorted like a jack-in-the-box in order to catch it before it hit the floor. What could have become a disaster, with the large scenic board collapsing backward, ended with a red-faced Johnny laughing along with the crowd.

The children finished with another trio of carols. As the students took a bow, the audience gifted them with a standing ovation while the round of applause shook the walls.

Lorelei took her place at the students' sides, pride at their achievement making her heart sing. "I think we can say this night has been a tremendous success. The students and I thank everyone for coming to share our Christmas gift to all of you. Please stay as long as you like and enjoy yourselves."

The crowd converged upon the children. Parents hugged their offspring and congratulated the many others. Even the adults who were not parents of any of the children lent their praises to each and all. Lorelei basked at all the happiness in the room. Goodwill permeated the air, filling her heart with sheer joy.

"I must say, Lorelei, you outdid yourself." Seth's breath fanned her cheek as he spoke at her side. "That was a wonderful show." Her adrenaline had been pumping since the beginning of the evening, now it surged through her veins at his praise.

She turned to him. "Thank you, but I merely directed the students. They're the ones who deserve the praise. They worked very hard to make this night special."

She meant every word she said, for the children had, indeed, put all their energy, their very souls into this event. A warm glow kindled inside her at seeing his pleased smile, the approval in his eyes, and knowing he appreciated her efforts.

Lorelei scanned the people milling around with cups of punch and plates of pastries in order to calm her racing heart. He always had that effect on her. Heck, he had that ability even when she *thought* of him. She almost laughed out loud.

"Yes they did, but you deserve some credit too. Excuse me while I congratulate the others." He smiled before he turned.

Her eyes followed him as he walked to where the children congregated in front of the manger. He greeted several with a pat on their shoulders. She could not hear what he was saying above the boisterous voices, but the children's eyes lit with pride and happiness as he spoke with each and every one of them.

Oh, Seth, you have it in you to give of yourself more than bestowing

185

your skill. Why can't you do it to its fullest?

Several people inspected the manger scene and commented on the skillful art work. Others headed in her direction, and she had to direct her attention to them rather than limit her perusal to Seth.

For the next hour, she conversed with those who she had only ever spoken to briefly. Tonight, everyone seemed to forget how she stuck her nose in others' business. It felt wonderful.

This one night, she was the teacher who had made parents proud of their youngsters. To the non-parents, she had held a community function bringing them together for a night of sharing and joy. It felt damn good for a change.

Hattie Miller went on and on about her delight at the evening's event. Then she started in about Charles's incessant demands from his sickbed. Lorelei continued to smile at the woman, lending an attentive ear to the woman's ramblings. While she listened, she stole a glance in Seth's direction.

He stared at her, his eyes unreadable. Unnerving, almost chilling. She pondered what caused him to look at her so.

What in tarnation had she done now to warrant that look?

CHAPTER TWENTY-SIX

When the majority left, several adults offered to stay and tidy the place. But when Lorelei insisted they should leave as most had a ways to go home, they turned deaf ears and pitched right in. She felt grateful; more delighted that Seth remained.

The women cleared tables, washed and dried every last dirty dish, and wrapped the unused pastries. The men dismantled props and long tables, swept up scattered straw and repositioned desks. She would have little left to do, come morning.

As coats were donned, Seth turned to the others. "I'll reload Lorelei's woodstove before I leave. She looks ready to drop."

Without waiting for comment, he turned and headed back into Lorelei's apartment. Lorelei's mouth fell agape at his thoughtfulness. Far be it from her to protest. She was too bone-weary, more than ready to collapse into her waiting bed. Still, her heart found the energy to beat a little faster at his gesture.

"What a kind man," Mable Gillis said as she ogled Seth's retreating back. "Some woman ought to snatch that handsome devil right up. Why if I were thirty years younger, I'd—"

"Come along, Mable, if you're riding back with me," Hattie scoffed, tightening her scarf. "If you were thirty years younger you wouldn't know what to do with a man like him." The others chuckled at her jest. Mable grumbled and stomped down the stairs.

"Good night, and thank you all so much for your help," Lorelei said as they filed out the door.

And Lord above, each man shook her hand! The women gave her

warm hugs, all of them reiterating their praises for a lovely night. Though her feet ached, her heart sang with delight.

She waved until the last carriage pulled away, then locked the door against the frigid wind. So Seth could leave by her door, she grabbed his belongings and blew out the oil lamps.

Shivering as she entered the apartment, she was more than thankful Seth had refueled her woodstove. She knew she would have forgone the chore to simply crawl into bed.

She latched the door to the school room and turned as Seth replaced the poker on the wall hook. He straightened and turned.

"Thank you for loading the stove. I don't think I would've had the energy to bother," she said as she yawned.

Seth chuckled, and despite the fact the fire hadn't yet flared to a good roar, she felt very cozy.

"You're welcome." He crossed the room and took his things from her. "You look dead on your feet."

Another yawn escaped as she smiled. "I am. But I'm elated about what happened tonight. The children can be proud of how hard they worked, and I believe everyone enjoyed the evening."

He set his hat, scarf, and gloves on the table and slipped on his coat. She watched him button it up, questioning his previous odd look. Tempted to ask, she thought better of it. It had been too nice of a night to ruin.

"You're too humble by far. You worked just as hard, so don't try to deny it." He wrapped his scarf around his neck, shoving the ends inside his coat. "I believe you made a step in the right direction tonight as far as half the town is concerned."

She surveyed his large hands, his long fingers as he pulled on his leather gloves. He picked up his wide-brimmed hat, held it in one hand. As tired as she was, she regretted his rushing off.

"I hope you're right. If I can button my lip until I think things through before acting on impulse, like you said I should, maybe I won't be booted out of town so easily." She laughed, feeling awkward at her words. How long she could curtail her wayward tongue and easy-to-flare temper, she just didn't know.

He fingered the hat's rim. "It's a very good start." He studied her as if reluctant to depart. *Oh, if that were only so.*

He chuckled at her third yawn. "Good night, Lorelei. You better go to bed before you fall asleep standing up."

He turned and walked to the door. Half awake, she followed. He stopped short of the door and abruptly turned around. She barreled right into him.

Seth grabbed her shoulders, righting her before she fell. "You're more tired than I thought. Did you lock the other side?"

Lorelei nodded and gazed upward, straight into his dark chocolate eyes. His hands held her gently; her palms rested flat against his chest. She might be half asleep, almost numb from fatigue, but she could feel. And, oh Lord, *how* she could feel the warm currents brooking through her limbs at his touch; the hard strength under her fingertips. She should thank him for stoking her fire. He stoked *her* fire all right. In more ways than one.

Without further contemplation about right or wrong—for in her mind, it was definitely right—she slid her hands upward to wrap around his neck, and rose onto her tip toes.

Her lips met his. She closed her eyes, but not before she witnessed his smoldering desire. Her heart thudded. The kiss was light, undemanding, and tender. Her lips clung to his, wanting more, needing more. Her blood rushed like a sun-bathed stream, soon turning to fervid rapids.

His hands tightened on her shoulders as he returned the kiss with more ardor than she had expected. His lips slanted across hers, pressure increasing. She soared.

Raw passion screamed for release. If he said the word, she wouldn't think twice about taking him to her bed. The thought shocked her, yet she knew he would offer no more while she'd be content to share this one night of bliss.

Her hopes fled the instant he drew his lips away. Still, he held her in a tight embrace. She rested her palms against his chest feeling his inner warmth, pressed her cheek to his chest and heard the rapid pounding of his heart. She basked in the knowledge her kiss could affect him. His shallow breathing matched her own. She inhaled his familiar scent. Of soap, sweet tobacco, and Seth Taylor. A potent mixture that released her sigh.

"Lorelei, what the hell am I to do about you?" His voice sounded pained. She knew what she wanted him to do with her, if that's what he was asking. *Oh, how shameless.*

"I only meant to thank you for helping."

She felt his chest rumble and realized he was laughing. "I've been duly thanked, my dear. And more." If he only knew how much more she wanted to give him.

He slackened his hold, separating them by mere inches, but kept his hands on her shoulders. She felt a mile apart, though her palms remained upon his chest. She damned the barrier of his coat. Their gazes held. "I better go before I forget myself."

"Would that be so bad?" Neither pulled away. And the same compelling temptation that fluttered her heart seemed to be mirrored in his eyes.

She held her breath in hopes he might weaken. But his eyes took on a wounded, wistful look. It tore at her heart, leaving her aching and floundering for understanding.

"I'd never forgive myself. And you'd hate me forever. I could never live with that, Lorelei. You may tempt me, make me forget promises I've made to myself, for an instant. But that's all. I'll never allow you, or anyone to suffer because of me."

Elation, poignantly thrilling, swept through her at his admission. His somber, determined rebuff baffled her. *Suffer because of him?* She searched his eyes for answers. There were none, only regret, maybe longing. What hideous demons held him at bay? If only he would confide in her, she might help him forget them. She would, by God. No matter how long or how hard a feat. "Seth, please tell me what's in your past. Let me understand why you feel you can't let anyone into your life. I—"

"Drop it. Lorelei," he snapped. He withdrew his hands as if scorched by her question, stepped back and jammed on his hat.

His eyes darkened, a muscle flicked at his jaw. "It's exactly that. In my past. I don't like to remember. And I won't. Otherwise, it would drive me insane. Leave well enough alone."

Lorelei knew better than to press. His expression bordered on surly, blatantly resentful. He stood rigid with hands fisted tight at his sides. She tried to fathom how painful his past must be…and failed. The room turned as frigid as the outdoors.

"Good night, then." She forced calm to her voice, fought to appear unfretted. Her heart ached as if she were saying a final good bye.

His features softened. "Good night. Lock your door."

She nodded, unable to speak past the lump in her throat. Any future with him seemed unattainable at this point. Too fatigued to think straight, she admitted she needed to wait to deal with all this in the morning, when she could think more clearly.

When the door closed, she allowed the tears free rein.

****

Saturday morning came all too soon for Lorelei. She rubbed the night's sand from her eyes and listened to the hollowing winds beat against the windows. She snuggled under her quilt, reluctant to flee her coziness. The room would be chilled, the woodstove in need of stoking. Her thoughts turned to Seth.

She wasn't surprised. Every night, she remembered how good his embrace had felt, the wonderful few kisses, until slumber took hold. Each morning she awoke to the stark realization of her farfetched musings. It damn well hurt. And this morning the pain twisted within her chest. So much that she cursed herself for being such a fool. Cursed him for his resolved obstinacy.

"Lorelei, you're not a fool, you're just plain stupid." Flinging the covers back, she shoved her feet into cold slippers and stomped to the stove. She added more wood, then jabbed angrily at the few coals with the poker as if she were thrusting a sword into a fire-eating dragon. Flames flared. She felt a small satisfaction at taking her anger out on something.

Her laughter filled the room. How silly to let her temper get the best of her. She would be better off redirecting her anger into energy. Energy needed to solve a very vital problem.

"A novel idea," she declared with renewed vigor and pulled her robe tighter against the chilled air. "Seth Taylor, come hell or high water, I'll find out what you're about. And when I do, I'll make you see it doesn't matter two hoots. I'll love you anyway."

Boosted by her renewed outlook, she hummed a lively tune, her steps light as she went to place the coffee pot on the stove.

Whatever Seth's reason for cocooning himself from her and others, she would find out. And then, he would not stand a chance. No obstacle was too great to overcome if you set your mind to it. And she fully intended for Seth to put his mind directly to it.

"You just wait, Seth Taylor. You just wait and see."

Her mood brightening, Lorelei dove into cleaning the school room then tackled her apartment. She added four rows to Seth's scarf while pies she intended to gift to others baked to perfection. One lemon meringue would bear his name. No doubt about it.

By late evening, the wind had settled down while light snowflakes steadily drifted past her window to cover the ground. Lorelei curled her feet under her as she relaxed on the stuffed divan, enjoying the warmth of the fire, luxuriating in finally having the time to be able to read *The American* by Henry James.

Her spirits ran high. She felt pleased by her day's accomplishments, still buoyed by the pageant's success and more than hopeful she could negate Seth's resistance. She squiggled into a comfortable position and turned to the first page, intent on one peaceful, relaxing evening.

Thunderous pounding rattled her door.

"Miss Webster, Miss Webster." Johnny's loud bellow shook her very soul.

Dear God, what now? Her heart lurched, her entire body tensed. As she flew to the door, she trembled with fear.

CHAPTER TWENTY-SEVEN

Lorelei flung the door open. Johnny's eyes were filled with panicked horror, his wan cheeks streaked with ongoing tears. He quaked, gasping as he steadied himself against her door frame.

"You got to come quick...he's done it good this time." He looked as if he might pass out. He shuddered and quivered.

His words registered. *Jamie*. Potent terror gripped her.

"Catch your breath, Johnny." She forced calm to her voice, belying her frantic frenzy. Johnny took a deep breath. His tremors continued. So did hers.

"Oh, God, Miss Webster...you gotta come. He...he...aw shit! He slit his wrists. He's gonna die." Fresh tears poured down his face as he nearly gagged to choke back tears.

His mournful wail tore at her heart. His words chilled her to the bone. *Numbing. Horrifying. Devastating.*

"Let's go," she said, not waiting for further explanation. She had to get to Jamie, to help.

As she grabbed her things from the coat tree, Johnny fell silent as if dazed. She turned him around and none-too-gently dragged him down the stairs to his winded horse. She fumbled with her coat and vaulted up behind Johnny.

They raced toward town. Undoubtedly, Jamie was at Seth's. Thankful he was in good hands, she sighed in relief, only to shiver when she found herself wondering how many times Seth could be asked to save Jamie's life. Was this the time he'd be unable to succeed? She refused to accept such a thought. Her heart pounded while trepidation nearly shook her off the flying horse.

Johanna's carriage stood outside Seth's home, her horse still blowing hard. The two leaped from the horse, ran across the porch and into the well-lit house.

Half-way across the living room, Lorelei skidded to a stop.

Johanna huddled on the couch, rocking back and forth, her arms clasped around her two sobbing daughters. Tears streamed down Johanna's ashen face while her eyes, so full of anguish, seemed to look right through her. Lorelei cringed at seeing the large patches of blood on Johanna's dress.

Oh, Jamie. Dear God in heaven.

So profound was her fear, her agonized remorse, words escaped her. She'd seen the signs this past week. His decreased appetite, his increased lethargy as he chased the others, times when he stared off across the school room in despondency. Oh, yes, she'd seen all of them. She had attributed them to a lesser evil, failing miserably at recognizing his degree of depression.

"Is Seth still in with him?"

Johanna rocked, her eyes a blank stare. The girls whimpered, their faces hidden as they pressed further into Johanna's bosom.

"Yes," Johanna said, her face expressionless, eyes haunted.

Lorelei rushed to the infirmary. The door stood open. She inhaled deeply then barreled through without hesitation. Half-way across the room, her courage wavered. She froze.

Wearing a white apron, shirt sleeves rolled back, his back to her, Seth leaned over the exam table. She stared at the top of Jamie's head, his lower legs covered by a sheet. Bloodied towels lay on the floor, a multitude of instruments on a stand to Seth's right. She recoiled.

Seth appeared so engrossed in his efforts that she debated if she should speak and break his concentration.

"Don't just stand there. If you think you can stand the blood, I sure as hell could use some assistance." Without turning, he grabbed a silver, long-nosed object.

She started at his clipped tone. She heard a click.

"If you're going to help, get the hell over here. Now! If not, before you pass out, get someone who's willing."

Indecision fragmented her mind. Could she handle this? She peered at the red towels at his feet. She shivered and took a step forward.

When Seth leaned to the right as he continued to race against the clock, she caught a glimpse of Jamie's face. His skin matched the sheet of bleached muslin. Jamie's life depended on help, now. Seth needed her. She had no choice.

Bracing herself for what she would see, Lorelei dropped her coat, squared her shoulders, took a deep breath, and walked the few steps needed to reach the table.

Jamie's left arm lay elevated on a pillow covered with a white cloth. A thick bandage encircled his wrist, ice surrounding it. Seth worked on the large, gaping wound on the right wrist.

Her breath caught, but she fought the sway that threatened. She tried to concentrate on the sheet directly where Seth worked. Copious amounts of blood altered the white field. It didn't sicken her as she had feared. It intensified her realization that she must give assistance. Three silver instruments much like thin scissors with serrations protruded from the injury, a rawhide tourniquet was pulled tightly around his forearm. Seth didn't look up. He kept his eyes focused on his suturing inside the wound. That arm lay packed on ice, as well.

She avoided eyeing Jamie's face again for fear she would falter. Instead, she cleared her throat. "What can I do?"

Without a glance, Seth pulled through a suture. "Apron's by the wash stand. Put it on. Use the green bottle to wash your hands. Don't dry them." His curt words set her in motion.

Returning to his side in a flash, she watched him snip off the fine thread, then unclamp one of the forceps. He dabbed around the wound with a square of white gauze as blood trickled slower than she would have expected.

He inspected his work. "Take this," he handed her the white gauze without glancing her way, "and hold the end of this clamp." He lifted up one of the clamps. She took it and held it upward.

For what seemed like hours, she knew not how long, he repaired the inside vessels, clamped, unclamped, probed, and sutured the wounds closed; she dabbed away the bleeding, cleansed and flushed out the wounds as instructed, handed him various utensils as needed, and held the clamps out of his way. She mopped beads of sweat accumulating across Seth's brow before they dripped into his sterile field of work.

Several times, Johanna or Johnny came to the doorway. Seth paid them no mind. Each time, Lorelei nodded that Jamie was still with them. Each time, they left without any words.

Exhaustion threatened to topple her. Her arms burned from holding them suspended for so long. Her back knotted while sweat ran in rivulets down her temples. Gritting her teeth, she held up Jamie's left forearm so Seth could wrap it. He pulled the bandage tight, going around and around to give extra padding.

He finally glanced up. "Go ask Johnny to bring more ice and snow. The buckets are under the table."

"Certainly." Neither of them smiled. There wasn't anything to smile about yet. But did the man never tire? Other than perspiring profusely, he just kept up his diligent labor.

Grabbing the buckets, she sought Johnny's help. The boy eagerly jumped at doing anything for his friend. She knew he also needed to do something besides sitting and thinking.

Johanna sat on the couch, somber and wide-eyed as Johnny went outside. Both girls leaned against her, sound asleep, their faces blotchy and streaked by previous tears.

"How...how is he? Can I go in and see him again?"

Lorelei took Johanna's hands in hers and gave them an affectionate squeeze. "Let's wait until S...Doctor Taylor has packed the snow around his arms, then I'm sure you can come in. He isn't awake, Johanna. Seth said he lost a lot of blood and most likely won't awaken for some time."

"I don't care, I need to see him, touch him before...before..." Johanna's sniffled back a sob.

Lorelei found her throat constrict as her own tears pooled. She willed herself to remain composed. "Don't even think such a thing. You have to tell yourself he's going to be all right. You can do that, Johanna. You have to."

For the first time all night, she was sure, Johanna managed a slight smile. "I'll try. I've said a hundred prayers already."

Lorelei forced a smile. "Then, surely, one of them will be answered.

He's a good boy, Johanna. We have to believe God knows that and will watch over him." Giving another squeeze to Johanna's hands, Lorelei prayed with all her heart that Johanna's prayers along with her own would indeed be heard and granted.

When Johnny returned with the buckets, he insisted on carrying them into the infirmary. Seth had carried Jamie to one of the beds and covered him with a blanket. Each arm rested atop pillows covered with large pieces of oil cloth. Each bandaged wrist was encased in oil cloth also.

Her eyes must have reflected her question.

"The bandages will stay dry with the oil cloth over them. The pillows will stay dry and the snow won't melt as quickly when wrapped in the cloth."

She nodded and watched Seth pack small chunks of ice and handfuls of snow around the bandaged areas. He folded the oil cloths so they encased the cold against the sites.

Seth placed a hand on Johnny's shoulder. "I'm not going to promise anything to you, Johnny. This time, Jamie isn't as strong as he was last time. He's lost a great deal of blood, and that isn't good. I've stopped the bleeding for now and repaired the damage as good as I can, but I can't predict the outcome. If you're a firm believer, prayers are what he needs now."

Johnny nodded, studying his friend from beneath his hooded gaze, his lips quivering, his shoulders slumped. Jamie looked so pale, so very ill. Lorelei closed her eyes and said another silent prayer. She would pray all night, if it would help.

Johnny, eyes tired and wary, turned to Seth. "Thanks, Doc. If anyone can save him, it's you."

Seth offered a tremulous smile. "Thanks, Johnny, I'll do my best. You want to go home, or would you rather stay? I don't mind if you spend the night here if it'll make you feel better."

Johnny's eyes widened at Seth's offer. He looked appreciative that Seth had made such an offer. "I better be gettin' on home. Ma will be worryin'. But thanks just the same. If it's okay though, I'd like to come and stay with him tomorrow."

Seth reached up and patted Johnny's back. "That'd be fine, son. You do that. Come anytime and stay as long as you like."

Johnny nodded, took several steps toward the door, paused and looked back. "Thanks Miss Webster. I knew Doc needed help and you'd want to be here. I...couldn't have done it."

Tears swam in Johnny's eyes. They invoked fresh ones in hers. "It's you I should thank, Johnny. Good night." Lorelei managed a smile while all she wanted was details of the night. But she figured she best wait for answers. Her composure wavered on thin ice at the moment. There would be plenty of time later.

"Night." Johnny turned and left.

In an instant, Johanna was at the door. "May I come in now?"

Looking awe-struck, Seth spun on his heels. He beat a path to the doorway. "Please come in, Johanna. I beg your pardon that I didn't have you come in sooner. Forgive me."

"I knew you were busy and I'd just be in the way. I didn't want anything to interfere with what you had to do."

Seth led a wobbly Johanna to the bed. Johanna leaned over and traced Jamie's pale face with trembling fingertips. When she stroked it, Lorelei felt her heart ache, raw and gripping, twisting and tormenting. She had to look away. *Would tonight be the night this mother would say good-bye to her only son?*

Lorelei tiptoed out of the room, tears spilling down her cheeks. She had fought her tears all night. She was entitled to shed a few now, wasn't she? Well, if she wasn't, they came anyway. Walking over to the girls, she checked to make sure they were all right. They both slumbered, Jessica sucking her thumb, undoubtedly her security for the night. Missy looked as if she slept fitfully, every so often twitching.

Lorelei swabbed the moisture off her cheeks with her hand. Most likely, Johanna and the girls would stay the night. Would Seth allow Lorelei to stay another night as well?

Under any other circumstances, she would be elated. But not when it meant Jamie and his family had suffered again. She would gladly trade a night at Seth's in a second if it meant Jamie's life.

Tonight would be very long, indeed. And only God knew the outcome. She wished she were privy to His knowledge.

CHAPTER TWENTY-EIGHT

After Johnny said he would stop at the Silver Dollar to tell Miles what had happened and that his family was staying the night at Seth's, Johanna and the girls settled down in the spare room.

Lorelei now stood watching Seth check Jamie's fingers and readjust the cold packs. She either needed to go home, or confiscate a place here. Though reluctant to leave, she knew she could not endure another rebuff from Seth. Not tonight.

"Would you mind if I sleep on your living room davenport? I won't be able to sleep at home wondering if I should be here."

Seth finished with Jamie, stretched his arms, and straightened. He looked more than exhausted. Had he heard her?

He turned and studied her a moment. "Take my bed."

In the aftermath of this night's trials, the furthest thing from her mind was executing Seth's downfall to her charm. His suggestion seemed too intimate for propriety.

"I can't do that. It's not right. The davenport will be fine." Thank goodness, her voice had not quivered to match her limbs.

He shook his head and appeared downright annoyed. "For the love of God, use the bed. You're tired and need rest. You'll not get much on that lumpy old thing."

"But—"

"No buts. There's nothing right about any of this. This is the third time Jamie has hurt himself, the third time you've spent the night, and now I've another woman and two girls staying. I'll probably even have an inebriated father shortly pounding down my door. Take the bed and go to sleep. I intend to do the same on the cot so I can check Jamie off and on."

His voice was loud enough to wake the entire town. Lorelei decided he'd had enough for tonight. But oh, what a handsome devil when riled. Even if his anger was directed at her.

She smiled as sweetly as she could. "Good night, then. Will you call me if you need any help?"

"You can bet on it. Let's hope I don't have to."

****

Seth went to his study, poured a good two fingers of brandy in the glass, and returned to the infirmary. He sat on the cot and took a good hearty swig. It burned all the way down to his belly.

He had not meant to sound gruff, but dammit, enough was enough. His fear of losing Jamie before he had a chance to save him had been paramount. He'd had to work faster than he preferred for true efficiency, the vessels so ragged he doubted his skills would be sufficient. Hell, he still wasn't sure. As he glanced at Jamie. Dismay weighed on his mind like a heavy cloud of doom.

"God, what a night." He leaned against the wall and swiped his face with his hand. He had pushed himself past endurance until he had accomplished all he could do.

To top it off, Lorelei had given her all tonight, and his admiration for her soared beyond belief. He wished he could forget her diligence, remain immune to her many redeeming attributes. Instead, they stamped their mark on his mind and wrapped around his heart. He felt surly as a wounded bear. He belted back the last of the brandy. And welcomed the burn.

But the fire did not eradicate the true problem. He longed to taste those delectable lips once more, inhale her lavender scent. God, he had needed the comfort of her embrace.

He had not meant to be curt, but needed her out of sight. Well, now she was out of sight. But definitely not out of mind.

****

Bright sunlight beamed through the partially pulled back curtains in

200

Seth's room. Lorelei welcomed the warmth on her face. Rolling to her side, she stretched and burrowed her face into the soft down pillow.

Seth's familiar scent that had finally lulled her to sleep invaded her senses. She sighed, content to lay all snuggled down and warm, and think of him. The night's horror sparked her instantly awake.

Her mind swirled with renewed apprehension of what the day would hold for Jamie. Dragging herself out of bed, she lumbered to the wash stand. The chilled water erased any lingering fatigue. She dressed in no time flat, then surveyed her hair in the oval mirror above the oak dresser. She laughed at the wild-woman staring back. Foregoing brushing out her hair last night, it looked like a pack of rats had stormed through it. Eyeing Seth's comb, she hesitated. Finger combing the tangled mop would have everyone running out the front door. She used his comb.

****

After checking on Jamie, who remained asleep and as pale as the night before, and with Seth using the necessary, Lorelei sat at the kitchen table and sipped coffee Johanna had made. She watched the woman butter three slices of bread while thick slabs of bacon sizzled in a pan.

"You sure you don't want anything, Lorelei?" Johanna's smile matched her quick steps around the room.

Lord, but the woman seemed bright-eyed and bushy tailed this morning. Lorelei felt anything but. Her arms and legs felt like they had been pulled through a wringer. The tension and assisting Seth for the long hours had taken their toll.

"No, thank you. Coffee's just what I needed. I might have a slice of bread later. You sure I can't help you with anything?"

"Good heavens, no. Took me a few minutes to find things, but now I'm doing just fine. And I need to stay busy. You look as if you could use some more sleep. You sure you don't want to lay back down for awhile?"

"Absolutely not. After I finish this cup, I'll be totally revived," she lied. She took another sip. As soon as she finished this one, she could start on number two. Ten might revive her.

"You don't look awake enough to drink it," Seth chuckled from the doorway.

Her cheeks burned. She knew her eyelids were puffy. The dark semi-circles below them were nothing to brag about either. She had pulled her hair back with a ribbon, but it left a lot to be desired. She was a mess. Felt worse. The crying she'd done over Jamie in Seth's room had left her with a whopper of a headache.

"I'm awake," she said, at an unfamiliar loss for words as she glanced his way. Did he always have to take her breath away? Oh my, her senses were alert now. As crisp and warm as toast.

He looked as rested as the springy Johanna. If Seth thought she always appeared so bedraggled every morning, for sure she would never make an impression.

****

Seth studied Lorelei discreetly as she broke eye contact and sipped her coffee. Obviously, she had not slept well. How many times had he been tempted to check on her? He knew if he witnessed her slumbering in his bed he would have curled up against her warm, luscious body.

He was a sick pervert to think about such things with Jamie lying at death's door. Between timed checks and ministrations to the boy and musing about Lorelei in his bed, he had acquired little sleep. He felt ready to fall on his nose.

"Sure smells good, Johanna," he said, forcing his mind from the fetching sight of Lorelei. Fatigued and disheveled, she could tempt a saint with those pouty lips and sleepy-eyes that twisted him inside out. And he was no saint, by a long shot.

Johanna turned, giving him a bright smile. "Your eggs will be ready in a moment." She turned and flipped them.

"No hurry."

"You sit right down, Doctor Taylor. They're all done."

Seth took a seat across from Lorelei, noting how intently she concentrated on her cup.

When she looked up, he wished he had the right to enfold her in his arms. She looked like hell; pale, red-rimmed eyes, a yawn escaping between swallows of coffee. Had she cried herself to sleep? Had she been thinking of him? Even a little? He dismissed that possibility. Most likely, she had only lamented over Jamie.

She had kept a stiff upper lip throughout the grueling evening; then, most likely, had broken down in privacy. That trait of hers reached out and caressed a corner of his heart. It warmed him all over. He should have allowed her to stay in the infirmary so he could have held her. For her consolation, of course.

You're a fool. You did exactly what you should have done. Be happy with your good sense. Yet he was anything but happy.

Johanna placed the full plate in front of him, bringing his attention back to the present. "Coffee's coming right up."

"Thank you. It looks as good as it smells. You'll spoil me with this kind of service."

Johanna laughed as she brought the coffee over and poured him a cup. She reached over and refilled Lorelei's cup.

"Thank you, Johanna," Lorelei said, offering a meek smile. He had noticed Lorelei's flinch at Johanna's laugh. He remembered the morning after she had drank too much brandy.

Johanna set the pot on a trivet in front of them. "I'll go sit with Jamie." Before either could say anything, Johanna fled. Lorelei, her head bowed till he thought she might burn her nose, spooned two teaspoons of sugar into her coffee and stirred.

"Are you not feeling well?" He spread the strawberry jam Hattie Miller had given him over the slices of bread.

She glanced upward as she set down the spoon. "I'm fine. A little headache is all. I'm sure it'll go away soon."

If Lorelei Webster said she had a just a little headache, it most likely was a doozie. "I'll be right back."

Returning a moment later, Seth uncorked the brown bottle and placed it in front of Lorelei. "Take a spoonful of this. Your headache will vanish in minutes."

He sat, picked up his fork and stared at his plate. A strip of bacon and slice of toast were missing. His gaze shot to her. She seemed overly attuned in pouring the medicine into the teaspoon. He watched her gulp it down. And burst out laughing.

"Where did you hide the rest of my breakfast?"

Her gaze met his, her face nothing short of bewilderment. "Whatever do you mean? Your plate is right in front of you."

"Lorelei, where are they?" He couldn't hold back a grin.

Neither could she. When she giggled, her eyes twinkled with that usual sparkle he found so appealing. Yet she held her head and shoulders stiff. Her headache hurt more than she had let on.

"Oh, all right," she laughed, bringing a napkin from her lap. On it rested the stolen goods. She handed them over.

"Thank you." God she was lovely, he thought, as she watched him place the items on his plate. Even with her looking so out of sorts, she fired his blood. He enjoyed her company first thing in the morning. Was he in trouble or what? The thought rattled him.

"Would you like some? I usually have a hearty appetite in the morning, but I don't think I'll be able to finish all this." Did his voice give away how unsettled he felt?

Their gazes met. Seth forgot to breathe.

"If you're sure. I might take one slice of toast."

He forced himself to break eye contact, lifted his plate, and offered her a piece. "Hope you like jam."

"I love jam, especially strawberry. Thank you." She took the slice and bit into it. "Mm, this is delicious. I didn't think I was hungry, but smelling your food changed my mind."

Frustration burst forth. The food on his plate could never satisfy the hunger he felt. He concentrated on his food. Mechanically, he resumed eating. One kiss from Lorelei would do it, though. Well, maybe two. Two long, sensuous, hot kisses.

Stop it. You're crazy! You can't have her.

"How's Jamie this morning? Really. I know you said he wasn't much different, but is there any change for the better?"

Seth glanced up, disheartened to think he could tell her nothing different, unable to give her a smidgeon of assurance.

He watched her take another bite and chew. A small dot of jam clung to the corner of her bottom lip. His heart thrummed. Yearning for what he could never have twisted in his gut. He longed to lick away the confection from her sweet lip.

"There's not much change. His pulse is still weak and thready from

204

the blood loss. He's suffered an enormous shock. Only time will tell. I can't offer much hope, not yet."

Her eyes mirrored the sorrow, the painful dismay within her heart. She nodded, glanced at her cup and toyed with the handle. He wanted so very much to tell her all would be all right soon. He regretted laying it on the line, but he knew she would not appreciate deceit. Instilling false hope in anyone was not his style. It only made it harder when the worst happened.

"How long does it usually take for a person to take a turn for the better…if they're going to recuperate?"

She didn't cry or tremble. Not her. She sat, asking questions, direct and as frank as his answer. She hid her apprehension well, though he sensed trepidation shook her inside.

She was one tough lady; one strong lady with a heart as big as the Grand Canyon. And he wanted her so badly his head felt as if it would spin off his neck. What the hell *was* he going to do?

"Two to three days. He's young, strong, and healthy otherwise. With luck, I should know by tomorrow. But that's not a guarantee. Complications could set in."

Her eyes became glassy. He watched her take a deep breath. His chest ached to match her sorrow. He longed to hold her.

"I'm sure you'll do everything you can. And I'm thankful you're the doctor." Her compliment boosted his own disheartened spirit. At least, she respected him as a doctor. If she ever knew about his past…He cringed.

"Lorelei, I'm human and can only do so much. I meant it when I said it's now in God's hands. I can watch for signs of infection or other complications and hopefully combat them. That's what I do. That's *all* I can do."

She nodded and sipped her coffee with downcast eyes.

He felt his resistance dissolve against her alluring charm. It scared the hell out of him. Never before had he experienced such weakening against his better judgment.

Lorelei, stay away from me. I'm no good. I'm worse than no good. And I don't know if I have the willpower or the strength to fight you any longer. Then, God help the both of us.

CHAPTER TWENTY-NINE

Having returned home, Lorelei made short work of bathing and donning clean clothes, then gathered an assortment of food to take to Seth's.

Eager to leave, she stuffed a stack of uncorrected tests and homework she had assigned several days ago into another basket. She would work on them while relieving Johanna, if she could concentrate on them rather than on Seth.

Satisfied she had all she needed, she went to the barn, loaded the carriage, and tied Seth's horse to the back.

Drawing up in front of Seth's, Lorelei recognized Johnny's horse. Another stood at the post. It looked familiar, but she couldn't place it. With a basket in each hand, she headed for the porch without giving the animal a second thought.

No sooner had she taken the stairs and placed one basket down to reach for the door than Miles Cooper loomed in the doorway. His barrel-chest, broad shoulders and protruding beer gut appeared much larger than she remembered.

Luckily, she took a step back as he flung the screen door open with raging force. It banged against the house with a loud clap. As it swung back, he caught it in his meaty hand.

He smirked, his sardonic mouth narrowing his gimlet-eyed glare. His eyes were blood shot, his face ruddy beneath a night's growth of dark stubble. By the looks of his disheveled, soiled clothing, it was apparent he had slept in them all night—if not longer. She did not like this man. She feared him more.

"Well, well, well. If it isn't the queen bee come ta see what trouble she can cause." His voice was nothing less than truculent, his attitude clearly antagonistic. She retreated another step. He looked ready for combat, and she, unfortunately, stood within his line of fire.

Lorelei glanced at the basket not a foot from his large boot. "Nothing to say?" He howled at his jest. His fetid breath collided with her mounting anxiety. Her stomach heaved.

"Not too often you keep yur trap shut." He took a step forward. Lorelei's feet froze.

"That's enough, Miles. Go home and sleep it off." The thunderous severity of Seth's voice made her jump. At the same time, it had never sounded so wonderful.

Miles spun around and glared. Would Miles light into Seth? Her heart banged against her ribs, her palms turned slick.

"You sniffin' at her skirts, Doc?" he sneered. "You won't get much for yur time. She can't shut her big mouth long enough to do much more. Yur wastin' yur time if—"

"I said shut your mouth." Seth stood in a broad stance, strong, unwavering. A force to be reckoned with.

Lorelei's heart fluttered at seeing this new side of him. She hated combativeness, yet this commanding, authoritative manner was more than she had thought he possessed.

His voice remained firm. "Miss Webster is here to help. I don't appreciate you stirring up trouble. Now, get off my property before we regret what might happen."

Miles's hands tightened into fists at his side, his face darkening a shade of red. His chest swelled up as if he meant to spew forth a rebuttal. Seth didn't allow it.

"Come back to see your son if you want. After you've cleaned up, are sober, and can keep your crude opinions to yourself."

Seth's hands were fisted at his sides, his face set with a dare-to-try-me expression. He reminded her of a lion, wisely assessing the prey, ready to pounce at one wrong move.

She watched Miles study Seth. He looked taken back by the change in the doctor's usual cool demeanor. Miles's bluster seemed to deflate as he faced a more-than-worthy opponent. His jaw flexed, and he issued a snort.

"I'll come back. And when I do, I'll take that snot-nosed kid of mine back with me along with my missus and other young'uns. You ain't got no right to stop me, neither."

With that threat, Miles kicked the basket. Papers flew in all directions.

Lorelei gasped at the malevolence he cast her way as he stormed past; she shuddered, knowing she had more than an angry father to contend with. She watched papers drift down onto the snow-covered porch.

Seth caught the screen door before it slammed. She trembled, and wondered if it was from relief, or the aftermath of fright.

Unwilling to have Seth see her wits rattled, she bent down, set the other basket to the side, and started scooping up the papers. She heard Miles's horse gallop away. The door snapped shut. Seth's booted heels thumped as he crossed the porch.

"You all right?" His concern nearly released her tears.

She scooted, bent-kneed, along the trail of papers, gathering them before a wind came along to snatch them.

"Ah...I'm fine. I need to get these before they get wet." She averted her face and blinked several times to curtail tears.

He helped retrieve the strewn sheets. When the last had been confiscated, Lorelei stood and brushed snow from her hem. Though she continued to quiver, she composed herself enough to face him.

His expression unreadable, he opened his arms. "Come here."

She needed no more encouragement. She didn't care that his intent was to console her. She crossed the five feet separating them without hesitation.

His arms came around her, pulling her tight against his chest. She laid her cheek against the hollow of his shoulder while her arms encircled his waist.

She inhaled his scent. He smelled so good, felt so good. Warm and strong. She welcomed the silence, of being held.

He gently rubbed her back, up and down, down and up. She could spend a lifetime like this and not have enough of it.

"Feeling better?" His breath fanned her ear, its tickling sending goose bumps up her arms, while a warm current of contentment simmered through her veins.

"Mm. Much better." Lorelei nuzzled her face into his chest. She felt his chest rumble and realized he was chuckling.

"If anyone passes by, we'll certainly give them food for thought."

It was early afternoon, and she knew he was right. Grudgingly, she pulled back, yet kept her fingers at the sides of his lean waist.

She looked up and recognized the burning desire in his gaze. It matched hers, she was sure. Her breath caught, her pulse quickened, and a heady feeling turned her knees weak. *He wanted her.*

"We'll both be damned," he whispered as his mouth covered hers. Warm and possessive.

Any reasoning to his remark flew from her mind as she basked in the glorious feeling of elation and warmth. He offered an uncommitted morsel of himself, and she willingly accepted it.

His lips slanted across hers, nipping, tasting, teasing.

"Part your lips." His words glided over her like a gentle caress. She didn't hesitate to do his bidding.

His tongue entered and explored, coaxing her to reciprocate. She'd never been kissed like this. The spiraling ecstasy made her sway; the escalating desire frightened her. Yet, she longed for more as she drank in the flavor of coffee, sweet jam. And him.

Her hands roamed up his well-corded back, across his broad shoulders and she gloried in the mere touch of his hardened muscles under his shirt. She longed to touch other parts of him and wondered if decent women did such things or if she was turning into a hussy. She really didn't care.

His lips pulled away. He reverently kissed her cheek, her forehead, before cradling her head against his hard chest, kneading the back of her neck with his hand.

"Lorelei, I made it clear there can't be more between us. But every time I'm with you, I fail to keep my hands off you."

She leaned back enough to look at him. "I don't expect more than you're willing to give." *But I want everything you can give. More.* "I'm not foolish enough to think I can change your mind." *But I won't give up trying.*

He scrutinized her. "I wish it were different. People can't always have what they want. I can't change, not even for you."

"I know. You've made that quite clear. And I accept that, Seth. I really do." She nearly choked on her dauntless words.

She couldn't bring herself to fully accept his strange reasons anymore than she could change how she loved him. And love him she did. Heart and soul. Even with his mysterious past, his refrain from community involvement, his resistance to her. She would most likely take that one-sided love to her early grave, grieving for something she had no business hoping for.

Yet, she wasn't done with her campaign, by golly. No matter what plagued him, she wouldn't give up. She may never uncover his secrets, but one thing she knew. He desired her.

And as long as she knew that for a fact, well and good, she would try to break down the defenses he kept hurling her way. Sooner or later he would have to succumb to her. *Wouldn't he?*

CHAPTER THIRTY

It was only right that Johanna take the girls home to gain some normalcy. Though the sisters' concern for Jamie haunted their eyes, the hours of quietude incited their restlessness. Johanna, though heaven only knew why, voiced her duty to soothe the disgruntled Miles. By evening, Johanna bundled up the two and promised to return after the girls left for school.

While Seth saw them to their carriage, Lorelei hung in indecision as she tidied the infirmary. She had a school to run. Christmas recess wouldn't start till Thursday. Until then, she had obligations. She felt the need to aide anyway she could in Jamie's care. And…maybe weaken Seth's opposition to her. *Damn.*

"Lorelei," Seth spoke as he strode across the room. "I appreciate all your help. But you need to go home, too."

She glanced at Jamie as he slept. "What if you need help?"

Seth smiled. "He'll probably sleep through the night. When I changed the bandages, the wounds looked good. I shouldn't have any problem. At least, until he awakens."

So, that was it. Go home; I don't need you or anyone else, now that the crisis has passed. She knew she was being childish. Seth *had* appreciated her help. He only meant well by sending her on her way. But reluctance at leaving nipped at her.

She focused on Jamie and fingered her skirt. "Are you sure—"

"Lorelei," he came to stand directly in front of her. She met his gaze. His palms cupped the sides of her face. *Oh, how she yearned for more of those potent, sweet kisses!*

211

His eyes bore into hers, his face taking on an almost pained expression. "Don't tempt me further. I told you before, neither of us will walk away without heartache."

Ready to deny any remorse she might feel, his next words stopped her cold.

"Don't make me hate myself more than I already do."

Lorelei swallowed a thousand questions. He hated himself? This confident, competent man whose skill kept half the people here alive? Her mind whirled with a jumble of disjointed thoughts. She could not make sense out of the small bits he slowly offered.

Her heart twisted. How he must suffer each and every day, trying to forget his tormented past, and despising himself. She wanted to weep, to throw her arms around him, to comfort him.

Instead, for once in her illogical head, she knew she best not push. The time was not right. His unflinching eyes voiced it all too clearly. She could not afford to have him shy away completely. *One step at a time, Lorelei, one step at a time.*

"I'll go. But I'd like to come back tomorrow after school."

He looked relieved she had not argued.

His thumb softly stroked her lips. It stole her breath. She trembled under the gentle caress. She fought to not kiss his finger, felt herself weaken as the calloused tip teased her.

He might have the willpower to hold back his feelings. She did not. Her resistance shattered. She kissed his thumb.

He pulled it back as if her lips had scorched it. When his hand drew away, she silently cursed her impulsiveness.

"You don't play fair, Seth Taylor. You say you have to stay away from me, yet you tempt me at every turn. If you're going to touch me like that, expect to receive equal pay back. I give you fair warning. I don't give up easily."

His face became animated, his smile warming her insides. "I'll remember, Lorelei. Indeed I will."

****

On Monday, the children did not want to be in school anymore than Lorelei did. Several children commented on her absence at church. She evasively explained that Jamie was very ill and she had been with his family and Doctor Taylor. The rest of the afternoon dragged more than the morning.

At three o'clock, self-conscious about her audacious statement about not giving up easily, Lorelei knocked on Seth's door. Johanna's wagon was nowhere in sight. When Seth appeared at the door, she found herself tongue-tied.

"Hello, Lorelei. Come in. Johanna just left a few minutes ago to be home when the girls arrived."

He seemed oblivious to her discomfort.

"How is he?" Jamie seemed a common enough ground to venture. After hanging her coat, she walked down the hall, him following.

"He woke for just a few minutes, then fell back to sleep."

"Did he say anything?" she asked, pausing half way across the infirmary.

Seth shook his head. "No, I don't think he had the strength. He did, however, take a few sips of medicated tea."

Lorelei nodded and drew up to Jamie's side. He still looked so pale, so sickly. "How's Johanna holding up?"

"She's doing fine. She's a tough lady, too."

Lorelei's eyes flew to his. "Too?"

Seth laughed softly, his eyes twinkling like polished chestnuts. "I know another tough lady in this town."

She smiled, accepting his indirect compliment for what it was. Her spirits rose. It was better than nothing.

****

Lorelei sat by Jamie's side for three hours, alternating reading with knitting. She had finished Seth's scarf since he had gone to check several patients, including Charles Miller. Hearing the front door open and booted heels tread against the hall runner, she set down her book.

Seth wore an amicable smile as he crossed the room. Oh, how he made her heart flutter. How easily her blood heated at seeing his mouth-watering physique, those take-your-breath-away good looks.

"Has he been awake?" He came to her side, rubbing the chill from his hands.

"Only for a few seconds. He mumbled something, but I couldn't make it out. He took a few spoonfuls of broth."

****

Seth looked down at her. Lord, would he ever get used to her loveliness? Every time he was near her, he yearned to pull the pins from her hair and run his fingers through its silkiness, to touch her soft skin, kiss those enticing lips. He remembered their honeyed taste. Yes, dammit, he remembered all too well.

He better pray for Jamie's rapid recuperation or he would find himself on the wrong side of his bedroom door with her there beside him. And feel more worthless. He cursed his father to hell and back for forcing him to avoid what he ardently wished for.

"Thanks for staying. When Johanna came, I didn't want to ask her to stay longer than it took to check on Jamie." *I shouldn't have ask you either. Not when I want to give in so easily.*

Lorelei stood and stretched her back. "I'm glad to have been here so you could leave. I'll come back tomorrow, too." She hesitated and glanced over at him. "If that's all right."

He should tell her to stay away. Watching her blouse pull taut over her breasts when she had stretched had sent an ache rushing to his loins. "That'll be fine. I'll look forward to it."

Her brows rose. Damn, he had not meant to sound so anxious for her return. Yet, he was. As much as he knew they should keep distant, as difficult as it was for him to fight his attraction, he knew he would miss her visits when Jamie fully recuperated.

He carried her baskets to the carriage, set them on the far side of the leather seat, then assisted her up. Large snowflakes steadily fell. He could barely see down the road.

"You be careful. It's already a foot deep. I should get you a lantern." He didn't feel right sending her out by herself.

She settled on the seat and smiled through the grayness of the night. His pulse raced like an eager young boy.

"I'll be fine. I'll be home before you know it."

He scowled and she laughed. And it sent a light-heartedness that tempted his very soul. His eyes devoured her smiling lips. He longed

214

for so much more. He was so engrossed in his unattainable desire, he failed to realize she had leaned down.

She kissed him. Sweet and gentle, and not nearly long enough. His heart raced. "You're too damn tempting for your own good, Miss Webster."

She laughed again. Her bright eyes twinkled at his frustration as she straightened and gathered the reins. "Oh, Doctor Taylor, I hope so. I certainly hope so."

She clicked her tongue and off she went through the field of white. He stood in the steady downpour, dumbfounded, yet unwillingly humored by her perseverance to break his will.

With any luck, maybe he would experience the ecstasy of really knowing her. Reality struck. He glowered at the carriage as it became a blur. He stormed into the house.

If he was really lucky, he would be able to stay away from her, and keep his sanity.

****

By Thursday, a routine had been established. Johanna and the girls visited Jamie after supper until Lorelei arrived. She stayed until Seth returned from calling on various patients.

Each night, like a ritual, Lorelei leaned down and kissed Seth goodnight. Illogically, he accepted it eagerly, knowing better than to lose his heart to this woman. Despite his good intentions, that's exactly what was happening. He relished her lips on his. Afterward, he damned them both. The hopelessness of the situation ate away at his very soul.

Each day, Jamie stayed awake a bit longer and took more nourishment, only to drift back into a deep sleep. Today, Lorelei arrived before supper and had brought Seth dinner. She checked the sleeping boy, then served Seth at the kitchen table. He ate every morsel on his plate and leaned back in his chair, finishing his coffee and cherry pie she had baked this afternoon, since there hadn't been any school.

"Jamie was awake most of the day," he said, knowing how pleased she would be by the news.

Her face beamed. "That's the best news I've heard in a very long time." Her expression turned concerned. "Does that mean he…is going to be all right?"

Now, he grinned. God, it felt good to know he had saved the youngster. "Sure does. He's well out of the woods."

Tears swam in her eyes and she put a hand to her trembling lips. She closed her eyes. "Thank God."

In that very moment, as he watched her digest the good news, he recognized the deep, abiding love she felt for Jamie. And realized he was in more trouble than he had thought.

He loved this brash, outspoken woman.

Despite all sensible reasoning, the battle he waged against her allure, he had fallen for this spunky woman who raised the hackles on so many; who so often incited outright scorn.

He had no choice other than to repress his feelings unless *he* wanted to feel *her* scorn. That thought tore at his insides, twisting like a tight rope, suffocating and crushing.

It would be worse than death itself to witness revulsion in her beautiful eyes. And that's exactly what he would see.

CHAPTER THIRTY-ONE

Due to Christmas recess, the routine in Jamie's care changed drastically. Johanna and the girls came midmorning and stayed until mid afternoon, which gave Seth time to see patients either there or at their homes.

Lorelei knew mother and siblings deserved time with Jamie. Therefore, she visited before supper, tempting Seth with her cooking, no matter if Johanna had brought something, as well as with her body. Anything was fair play. And she needed it all.

She had not often paid much attention to sprucing up. But today, it had taken her half an hour to choose the right outfit and fashion her hair. And heaven forbid, she had even pinched her cheeks until they blushed becomingly.

Saturday evening, Lorelei sat at the bedside and played checkers with Jamie while Seth mixed various potions and decoctions he might need for others in the coming weeks.

"Aw, Miss Webster, you're too good for me," Jamie grumbled as she kinged another of his men.

Seth turned as they both laughed. "You mean she doesn't allow a sick young man to win? She's heartless, Jamie. I'd watch out, if I were you."

Jamie chuckled good-naturedly. "Yeah, she packs a dynamite snowball and plays one hel...heck of a game of checkers too, Doc. No tellin' what else she can do."

Seth's gaze fixed intently upon her. "No telling at all, young man, no telling at all."

Pulse humming, Lorelei wondered if his words held a double meaning. Jamie yawned and slumped back against his pillow.

"Are you tired? We can finish the game tomorrow if you are."

Jamie glanced at the board, then at her. His woeful eyes tore at her heart. *What troubles you, Jamie? Tell me.*

"Yeah, I'm pretty worn out, Miss Webster. Maybe tomorrow I can save the rest of the men before you king all of them."

Lorelei glanced across the room. Seth had left. The time seemed right to ask a few questions. Whether he was tired or not, he couldn't rely on that excuse any longer. She picked up the board, carried it to the next bed, and carefully set it down so as not to disturb the pieces. She returned to her chair.

"Jamie, what you did was wrong. You know that, don't you?"

His eyes widened. He looked shocked she had broached the subject. He glanced at the covers and squirmed his feet.

"Yeah, I know." His attitude bordered on flippant.

Her determination soared at his frivolity.

"You said the same thing after you took your mother's pills. And then there was the swimming incident that you denied." She regretted her clipped words, but knew she needed to plunge head first into deep water. Last time, she had handled him with kid gloves. And it had only led to further trouble.

He remained quiet as he fingered the blanket.

"Jamie, trying to end your life, isn't the answer. We had this talk before, but I'll say it again. You have to deal with life's problems the best you can, even if it's the hardest thing you've ever had to do, even if it seems hopeless. And if the approach you take fails, you have to seek other avenues until you succeed. If something can't be significantly changed, then at least there may be room for compromise. There's always a solution to be had, no matter how big the obstacle."

He stared at the blanket, fingered it. She wanted to rip it out of his hands.

"I'd like to know why you felt you had to do what you did."

Eyes averted, he tugged the folds as if agitated. At least she had invoked a response. Agitation was better than avoidance.

"I'd appreciate you looking at me. Please, tell me what makes you do such things." She damned herself for softening her voice.

He slowly raised his head. His gaze collided with hers. She nearly gagged on the gasp she held back. She had never thought to see such an expression on his face. His eyes bore fierceness more savage than mere anger. Whether it was directed at her or at his torment, it sent blood-curdling chills down her spine.

She swallowed back desire to withdraw her pursuit. "Jamie?" She touched his arm, surprised by her courage. This was a very troubled boy. If she gave up now...

Refusing to harbor thoughts of easing up on him, she took her own advice. She would coax, compromise and deal with whatever bedeviled his logic until he only saw future hope.

She thought of Seth. Memories plagued him, prohibiting him from seeing a brighter tomorrow. How similar they were. For them, obstacles existed everywhere, demons haunted until both suffered more than they deserved. Were her shoulders big enough to accept the weighty load of Jamie and Seth at the same time?

When he blinked, she thought she caught a glint of remorse surface in his eyes before he glanced back down to the covers.

"I'll help you all I can, Jamie. But you have to let me in on what's going on. There are so many people who want to help you work this out. You have to believe that."

He shrugged, as if to imperviously say he couldn't care less. But tension roiled. She felt it. He tried to act heedless, yet she could almost feel the testy outrage storming his mind, battling with reluctance. Possibly fright?

He lifted his chin, met her gaze. His face resembled a lost little boy's, so full of conflicting feelings she wanted to cry.

"I told you, I hate my life. I hate every day and every stinking night. I...I can't talk about it. No one can help me."

For a moment, Lorelei became lost for words at hearing the finite attitude. She wasn't doing any good going around in circles with him. She'd give it one last shot for the evening.

"Jamie, is it because of your father? I know he drinks far too much. And that he yells at all of you. Does he hit your mother or you children?" There, she had opened the door.

His jaw squared as his focus pinned the far wall. "Yeah, he throws his weight around. I can take it...but he shouldn't take it out on...ma." His softly spoken words trailed off.

His tone lacked the vehemence she had expected. Oh, he resented Miles's brutality, but he had definitely skirted the true problem. She would let him rest. Tomorrow, she would change tactics, force him to talk. Find a way to help him.

"Tomorrow we'll talk more." She covered his hand with hers and gave a light squeeze. Hoped it would tell him he had a friend who cared, who would listen and who was willing to help. She tucked in his covers and then turned down the wick to a dim glow.

"Good night, Jamie." Dear God in heaven, she had almost blurted out "sweet dreams". How childish it would have sounded to a mind that had the weight of the world bogging it down.

"Night, Miss Webster," she heard as she left the room.

Her fury mounted fast and fierce. She cursed Miles Cooper. Did he know how troubled his son was? Would he even care?

A hideous, heinous idea stormed her mind.

Could he be doing more to Jamie than verbally or physically abusing him? Could he...could he be sexually abusing his son? It was vulgar, despicable, unacceptable to even consider. But consider the possibility she must.

Disheartened and nauseated, Lorelei shuddered. She leaned against the hallway wall and took a deep breath. It couldn't be. Yet, as chills ran up her spine, the possibility grabbed hold. Where *had* such an idea sprung from? She wished she could dispel the notion. But the more she reflected on Jamie's bottled-up anger and reluctance to reveal the catalyst, and then recalling Johanna having said Miles would never forgive him for trying to defend her, the more believable the idea became.

Dear God. No. Not Jamie. Her stomach twisted in knots. She needed to leave, to think clearly. No, she corrected her thinking. She needed to talk this through with someone. Seth.

As she entered the kitchen, Seth stood at the counter pouring a solution from a small tin pan into a funnel atop a short-neck brown bottle. She took a seat at the table and remained silent so as not to

220

disturb him until he finished. He set the pan down, removed the funnel and corked the bottle.

"Is he sleeping again?" he asked without turning around. He always seemed to detect her presence. She watched as he lifted another pan from the stove, positioned the funnel in a taller, long-neck green bottle, and poured the liquid into it.

Distress swarmed her mind, clawed her heart till it ached unmercifully as her assumption regarding Jamie reached new heights. She sat and admired how the cords across Seth's back rippled under the shirt with each pivotal movement. In the same instant, her mind spun back to her useless talk with Jamie and took precedence over her willful emotions.

"I think so."

"Who finally won?" He grabbed another bottle the same color and repeated the process.

"We didn't finish. He seemed so tired I decided to let him rest. We can finish tomorrow when he's fresher."

"Smart boy." Seth laughed, corking the last two containers. He placed a label on each and started writing on one of them.

"He's smart, all right," she said, unable to hold back her exasperation. "I tried to get him to tell me why he had done this, but he won't open up."

Seth glanced over his shoulder, his hand stilled in writing. "I'll be done here in a minute. Don't be discouraged yet. It'll take time for him to open up."

If only his words were true. She had more than an inkling that Jamie would never tell her what she needed to know.

It seemed essential at the moment to run the horrid thought by Seth. She bit back the urge to blurt it out and see his reaction. Would he agree her suspicions held any basis at all? Or would he think her impetuous, an extreme alarmist? His repeated advice of reasoning out situations before acting on them held her tongue in check once again. She marveled at her reserve.

"There." He set the last bottle down and wiped it with a cloth. "You want some coffee? It's fresh. I thought I'd have a cup while I relax a few minutes."

Lorelei started to rise from her chair. "I'll get it for both of us."

He turned and flashed a smile. "No, you sit still. I'll wait on you, for a change. I think I can handle two cups of coffee."

Lorelei sat back down, unable to force the meekest of smiles. She watched him take two mugs from the cupboard. He seemed so comfortable in his domain, capable and confident. He was intelligent and skilled, not only as a physician, but in all phases of life. He possessed the common sense of ten men, willing and able to do the normal everyday tasks from keeping his house in order to planting trees in his front lawn.

From the very first time she had met him, she respected his knowledge. The second time she had marveled at his precise expertise, his steadfast composure. Over time, her admiration for his other abilities had raised a notch. Of course, his handsome face and muscular physique did more than send her heart quivering. Simply thinking about him did the same blasted thing.

She wasn't any different from the few other single women in town. She had seen them coyly bat their lashes his way, and if that hadn't drawn his attention, they'd tried other tactics. Would one of them eventually win his heart? The thought tore through her like a ragged piece of steel.

"How many sugars?"

Lorelei started at his question. "A…just one, thank you." He added one teaspoon, stirred.

"You like cream too, don't you?" He didn't wait for her answer as he went to the large oak icebox.

"Yes, please."

"Freshest cream going. Mrs. Harris brought me a bottle of milk and a jar of cream just before you came. She's determined to pay me twice over for treating Jethro's measles."

He set the cups on the table. "Here you are."

She loved to look at his large hands. Hands, so skillful, so gentle when they had touched her. Would she ever be able to get the hot coffee past the stricture in her throat? He sat down across from her. Her racing heart would surely burst through her chest wall.

She managed a smile as she lifted the cup. "Thank you. It smells wonderful."

She knew better than to hope he would return her feelings. And why did her unruly heart insist on overlooking his detached attitude to others and to her? It infuriated her to no end. She would be wise to remember his flaw that stuck in her craw till she wanted to scream come Sunday and just go on her merry way.

"So, what *did* Jamie say?"

Lorelei fingered the handle of her cup and raised her gaze to his. Maybe she prayed for the day when she could make Seth deal with his past and change his attitude. Yes, that's what she was waiting for. Would that day ever come? She doubted it.

"He said he hated his life. Every part of it."

His jovial mood faded into a scowl, his thoughts apparently as troubled as hers. He leaned back, stared at the thin vapors rising from his cup. He raised his chin. Their gazes locked. She thought she might swoon.

"You think Miles treats them worse than we suspected?"

How well he read her mind. Could he read how much she longed to make him hers? The thought rocked her.

"I asked if he beat them more than a few slaps. He said no."

"And you believe him? After he duped us twice?" He sounded incredulous at her acceptance.

"No, not really. But…"

He leaned forward. "But what?"

Her heart failed to take flight. No passion existed between them. Only Jamie and his problem. Easily, she buried her fanciful notions and focused her full attention on Jamie. The lost soul needed her more in the next few days than she needed passion. Her mind's eye saw Jamie's eyes. Cold and ruthless. She shivered.

"Oh, Seth, if you could have seen him! The look in his eyes—" She rubbed her hands along her forearms to stop the chills.

"What look?" He rested his forearms against the table while searching her face for answers.

He was so easy to talk to. Maybe *he* should be the one to talk to Jamie. The idea sprang to life like a bright flame. Could she coax him into it? It might work.

In all honesty, though she strove to right the wrongs in this blasted town, she admitted she was far from being any great counselor. She didn't say the right words.

"When I asked Jamie to look at me, to tell me what makes him want to harm himself, he looked at me with the…coldest, most vicious eyes I've ever seen." She read disbelief on his face.

"Jamie? Vicious? Now, Lorelei—"

"He did. He looked more ferocious than when the men wanted to do me bodily harm. He looked…Oh, God, he looked savage. It scared me. Really scared me." She watched his eyes widen. Blankness glazed his eyes before a stark intensity drew his face taut.

Whatever jolted him for that split second seemed to ease away as he took a long deep breath. He surveyed her with a critical squint. What had flashed through his mind?

A fine sheen of perspiration glistened across his forehead. Had his past been conjured up by something she had said? She would store this incident in her mind to be dealt with in the future. Had she somehow hit on some piece of the puzzle?

"What did he say after that?"

Again, he was all business, self-assured. She liked that about this man. The confidence, the determination, to analyze a problem through and then deal with it.

She struggled to remember their conversation. "I told him I'd help him anyway I could. That's when he said he hated his life. That there wasn't any help for him. When I asked him if Miles hit him or the others, he confessed he did."

"And?" When he covered her hands with his, her gaze flew to his. Her pulse quickened. His touch gave her strength.

"That's the strange part. When he admitted Miles hits them, he didn't have that fierce look. He seemed reconciled to his beatings, though annoyed Miles hit the others. That's when I suspected there must be something else."

His thumb brushed lightly back and forth across the top of her hand. Was he conscience of the movement of his thumb? She certainly was! Her heart flitted and fluttered within her chest like an excited bird caught in a cage. Her hand flamed wherever he touched. Jamie might

224

have been in the forefront of her mind throughout their discussion, but right now, Seth Taylor took the ring side seat. Her entire body ignited.

His sincere gesture of offering comfort during her frustrated ramblings touched her heart more than anything else he could have done. As if realizing what his thumb was doing, he pulled back reluctantly. Her heart soared. Could his defenses be weakening? She prayed they were.

"I better check on him." When he walked out of the room, she wanted to scream. One minute he seemed drawn to her, the next, he rebuffed her. *I'll bring you down yet, Seth Taylor.*

She chided herself for such selfish feelings. She had no right to expect Seth to come over to her corner at a time like this. His concern for Jamie equaled hers. She should be thankful Seth's full cooperation and undivided attention focused on Jamie. She was a hopeless, thoughtless woman to want anything less.

****

Seth cursed his weakening resistance toward Lorelei as he studied the sleeping boy. Bending down, he pulled up the blanket that had worked its way down to Jamie's waist. Tucking it around the youth, his hands shook from fear of almost losing control.

He had never come so close to succumbing to the forbidden. Even now, rattled by his near slip, he felt tempted to throw caution to the wind. Say to hell with logic.

He craved just one night. A night of fulfillment in the arms of the woman he loved. He had heard love was painful. Now, he understood; as if a fired branding iron had been plunged into his chest. And God help him, he did love her.

Why shouldn't he be allowed to glory in her passion for a few moments? He knew she would welcome it. Hell, at every turn, she hinted she wanted more. Tonight, he had seen it in her eyes. Eyes like fields of cornflowers, brighter, bluer than the most precious lapis. He could drown in them and never want for air. He had felt it in her trembling hand as he rubbed its baby-soft skin, saw her cheeks flush with desire.

As temptation beckoned the forbidden, his mind sprang back to subdued reality. His dreams crashed at his feet. His body quaked as he pictured the repugnance in her glare. If she ever discovered how ugly his soul, how soiled his body was, her eyes would be no less than condemning and repulsive.

Seth closed his eyes and willed away the vivid horror. His fists tightened at his side as he struggled to push his desires back where they belonged. Hidden, buried.

He dared not let down his guard. Not for one second. Fantasizing was one thing, but yearning for the unattainable equaled sheer lunacy. Thank God his mind over-powered his heart. Otherwise, he did not know what direction his life would take. Yet, his heart begged his mind to yield. He fought a gruesome battle. Could he win against such pull?

"I've done it before. I can do it again." He literally shook from suppressing the potent feelings. Tears sprang to his eyes.

"God help me, Lorelei, I pray I can bury these feelings." His whispered sorrow wrenched the air as he scrubbed the moisture from his cheeks. He longed to give his feelings free rein, to feel, to give of himself, to receive her passion and her love.

He wanted…

He wanted Lorelei Webster. He wanted all her love.

Choking back anguish, he swiped at the tears that threatened to spill again. Taking a deep breath, he squared his shoulders and turned to leave the room.

Damn you father. Damn your black-hearted soul.

CHAPTER THIRTY-TWO

Much to her chagrin, Lorelei knew she had no further excuse to linger. Intending to take a peek at Jamie and bid Seth a good night, she entered the infirmary. She watched Seth swath his hand over his face, heard his deep sigh. Knowing he must be exhausted, she wished she could embrace him, comfort him.

He turned, took one step, and halted. Their gazes met. His eyes widened as if startled. The lantern's glow reflected off his moist lashes. Her breath lodged in her throat.

Fearing Jamie had taken a turn for the worst, she struggled to find her voice. "Is he all right?"

He blinked several times, obviously trying to hide what she'd already seen. "He's fine." His voice sounded choked.

She sighed as relief washed over her. Yet, seeing him so distressed, his pain became her pain, twisting taut within her chest. Dare she hope that his grief stemmed from resisting her? Dubious as to what to say or do, she let her heart lead. If she had any chance of breaking his resistance, it might be now.

Dear God, let me be right. If she wasn't, she would merely add being a fool to her list of transgressions. But whatever plagued him, she needed to let him know she would stand behind him.

She sailed across the room. Without hesitation, she wrapped her arms around him and laid her head upon his chest. He stood rigid, arms straight at his sides, his heart drumming against her ear. Her heart wept at his reluctance. Despair tore at her soul.

His arms moved with such speed she flinched. His bone-crushing embrace was painful. His fingertips dug into her flesh through her thin blouse. Yet, she welcomed it.

"I can't let this happen." He trembled.

Tilting her head back, she gazed upward and felt stunned by the haunted agony in his eyes. Lovingly, she caressed his cheek, the fine dark stubble. She needed him to reciprocate her feelings. Craved it, even knowing it might be for one brief moment.

"What we feel is very right, Seth. We can't deny it. We shouldn't have to. If for only tonight, don't fight it. With all that's happened I can't bear your rejection tonight."

He placed his hands on her shoulders, his troubled eyes boring into hers. "I won't deny the charge between us, but if I give into it I'd only ruin your life. I can never give you any more than one night. I've tried to make that clear. I can't ruin your future with some other man more deserving than—"

She pressed a finger to his lips. "Don't say it again, please. My life is mine to do as I wish. I hold little hope of finding any man who'd want me as his wife."

"That's nonsense," he said, removing her hand from his lips, yet capturing it within his.

"It's the truth," she retorted. "If I ever find someone, he'll have to accept me as I am. I'd never regret tonight."

His eyes widened. She denied him time to reinforce his stand. "Make love to me, Seth. If only for tonight, so be it."

He closed his eyes and his hand tightened on hers. When he opened his eyes, stark despair bore into her.

"Lorelei," he inhaled raggedly, "you're enough to tempt a saint. And I'm far from that. If I didn't care about you or have sense to protect you from making a foolish mistake, I'd make love to you in one second."

Disheartened by his refusal, her ardor cooled abruptly. Still, his earnest words raised her hopes for a time when he would be unable to resist. Her heart sang with renewed faith.

Her gaze dropped further, and she beamed at seeing the obvious evidence that he was, indeed, affected. Bold with revitalized self-assurance and heated blood, she peered upward.

"Be warned, Doctor Taylor. There *will* be a next time. And you won't be able to say no. You can't always have your way."

At her audacious words, his eyes twinkled as he grinned. "I'll be sure to watch my back at all times. You're quite the woman, do you know that?"

She laughed as tension eased. Though he had refused further intimacy, their relationship had taken a decided direction upward. It had strengthened so they were comfortable being honest with each other. Surely, it was a good sign.

"You knew that the first time you met me. I don't pull any punches, so be well warned. I won't give up." She gave him a purely sassy grin. Next time, he wouldn't stand a chance in hell.

She pulled away and walked over to Jamie. After placing a light kiss on his forehead, she returned to Seth's side. His eyes held an appreciative glimmer. Maybe admiration? And by golly, she basked in it. If she could turn that look into smoldering that couldn't be contained, she would be quite happy. Quite happy, indeed.

****

Seth followed her to the front door. She was some lady, all right. He had almost thrown caution to the wind. And damn if he was not still tempted. His insides remained fully inflamed, his arousal uncomfortable as he walked. He longed to drag her by that silky hair, throw her down on his bed, and taste those luscious lips until he could no longer think straight. He yearned to touch every soft inch of that milk white skin until…

He reached for her coat and held it open while she donned her gloves. At least, it covered his throbbing desire from her view. Lorelei turned and pushed her arms through the coat.

When she turned, their gazes held. Desire sizzled through him like a lit dynamite fuse. She smiled, a sweet, I-know-what-you're-feeling grin of satisfaction. He wanted to throttle her for making him feel, for knowing the effect she had on him. He wanted to make sultry, sensual love to her, over and over again.

"Thank you for the delicious dinner. And for your time with Jamie." *And me.* He had to stop thinking like that. She had made him crave something he had to deny. That, and the pain between his legs that would take a very long time to subside.

"You're welcome. I'll bring more food tomorrow when I come back to talk to Jamie," she said with an all-knowing smirk.

"It'll be appreciated. Be careful going home." He hated having her out in the dark by herself.

"I'm always careful."

Dan Purdy's image flashed before his eyes. A sense of panic washed over him. And a potent protectiveness he had never experienced before. "Do you carry a gun?"

"A gun? Good heavens! Whatever for?"

"I just thought about Dan Purdy. Whoever did him in may still be out there. How would you defend yourself?"

She smiled and her eyes just about danced at his voiced concern. He could have bitten his tongue. It was hard enough to resist her. No need to give her any more ammunition against him.

"I have a gun at home. I'll carry it with me from now if you really think I should."

"I think it would be wise. You never know who might be coming through from another town."

"Of course."

She looked pleased as punch.

You're a damn fool, Taylor. He reached for his coat.

"Please, stay inside, Seth. I'm quite used to hoisting myself up. There's no need for you to see me off."

He shrugged and returned his coat to the peg, respecting her wishes. He would miss her light goodnight kiss she always bestowed upon him from her carriage. It would be better to forego that touch of sweetness tonight. Any night, for that matter.

"Well then, goodnight." He opened the door and held the outer door open. The cold rushed past to cool his ardor.

She took two steps to bring herself directly in front of him. Before he realized her intent, she rose on tiptoes and planted a tender kiss square upon his slightly parted lips. He smiled beneath her luscious lips, accepting what she offered, returning it willingly. He should have realized she would do it.

Its feathery light touch sent his heart to pounding, his blood rushing within his ears. It was not the quick peck she bestowed each night from the carriage. It was hardly forceful, demanding, or seductive. Just tantalizingly slow and full of succulent sweetness. It shook him to the core. He braced himself against the door casing, fought the urge to embrace her.

She stepped back. "Sweet dreams, Seth Taylor." And the bold Miss Webster winked and proudly ambled out the doorway.

After watching her leave, Seth closed the door, doused the lights and headed for his room. And grinned like a fool. How easily the brazen woman filled his heart with humor and a lightheartedness he wanted to go on forever.

No, she wasn't brazen. At first he had thought her crass and insolent. But she was spunky and outspoken and unfortunately, impulsive half the time. And lately, she showed restraint and acted only after cautious reasoning.

But she was determined as hell to have him make love to her. How would he fight her? Day by day, he felt his attraction increase, his willpower weaken. He had to resist her lure. Yet, how did one love intensely, yet withhold that emotion?

The answer drew blank in his weary mind as he lay on the lonely bed. "Lorelei, Lorelei. Stay away from me."

He closed his eyes and willed his aching loins to relax. Lorelei possessed more determination than he had resistance. If he gave in...

They would be doomed to forever live in a separate hell.

CHAPTER THIRTY-THREE

Lorelei glared at Jamie, her anger so fervent she had to gulp down the nasty lashing she wanted to deliver. The youngster, in a flannel nightshirt, lay atop the bed covers and stared at the wall. Tight-lipped as usual.

After supper, Lorelei had again trounced Jamie at checkers. She had, as tactfully as she could, approached the subject of his troubles. As determined as she was to discover the underlying cause, he remained as resolute to withhold answers.

She trembled from the effort it took to cage her anger. Anger at him for refusing to divulge the source of his woe; anger at herself for her ineptness to extract the answer. Frustrated beyond belief, she deposited the game pieces on the other bed.

"Rest for now, Jamie," she said, forcing irritation from her voice. "I'm going to get some coffee. Do you want anything?"

Jamie focused on the wall. "No."

Wanting to lay into him, she fled the room. Fists clenched, she stormed into the empty kitchen. The aroma of fresh made coffee tantalized her dry mouth. It did little to set her agitation to rest. Her hands shook as she poured herself a cup. Would Seth know what to do or say?

Cup in hand, she strode to the living room only to find it vacant. Disappointed, she took a moment to survey the room, sip her coffee and calm her frustrations.

How refined, yet relaxing this room was with its Eastlake furniture. She liked the spooled furniture, from its ornate chairs to the comfortable, large davenport.

"You all right?"

At Seth's soft voice, Lorelei spun on her heels. He stood in the doorway to the den. Respecting his private domain, she had never gone into that room.

"Yes...no," she said, rubbing the cup's handle with an agitated thumb. "I'm not all right. Jamie won't tell me a thing." She knew she whined. Her frustration returned full force.

"Poor, Lorelei," he said, slowly shaking his head. "Come in here where we can talk."

He didn't have to ask twice. She marched past him before he could fully get out of the doorway.

The room spoke masculinity, very cozy, very much Seth Taylor. A floor-to-ceiling bookcase along the entire back wall housed books of every size. In front of it stood a large mahogany desk cluttered with stacks of papers and books. To her left sat an overstuffed dark brown leather chair, bearing the deep indentation from much use. Its matching ottoman had been pushed to the side. A mahogany table with more books, the top thick volume lying open, hugged the arm of the chair. Three hanging oil lamps bathed the room with a radiant, soft golden glow that illuminated paintings of ships and seas. A small woodstove in the far right corner crackled as it spread its warmth. The missing glass panels of the barrister to her far left stood out like a sore thumb.

"This is where you spend most of your time."

He laughed. "Most of my time is on my horse or at neighboring farms. But when I'm home, this is where you'd find me. Please, have a seat."

She set her cup on the table, sat down on the ottoman, and caught the scent of tobacco. She noted a brass ashtray with several half finished cigars.

"I occasionally enjoy a cigar with a brandy while reading. Not often, but it relaxes me."

She nodded, feeling as if something warm, almost intimate passed through her. It felt so right to be in here, with him.

"It's very nice in here. Are you sure I'm not intruding?"

"Not at all." He sat down and stretched out his long legs. "You look as though you need to talk."

For the first time all evening, she found herself smiling. She sighed, not knowing where to begin.

"Tell me what happened after you trounced him at checkers."

He was so easy to talk to. She had known that from the first time she had really talked to him, when he had told that story to Jamie. He had a way with words, an eager ear to listen, a knack of making another feel they could pour out their soul to him. Maybe he *should* be the one to talk to Jamie.

"I tried to get him to open up. I…I feel like he's about to spill it out, then he closes me out."

"You still think it's more than Miles beating them?"

"I know it is. I can feel his frustration at times when we're not discussing the man's brutality."

"What's your next step?"

Would he think her intuition without merit? But before she told him, she would see if he might be willing to help. She had learned to be patient with her thinking before moving ahead as he had encouraged her to do. Yes, it would be better to get him to consent. Then, she would lay the ball in his lap.

"I don't think he'll confide in me. He needs someone else, maybe a man, who he respects and feels more comfortable with."

He stiffened, his eyes fixing on her, his expression as stoic as the austere faces in the living room pictures.

"Lorelei, I know what you're suggesting. I've doctored the women and children you've brought to my door. I appreciate the business and the vote of confidence you have in me. And I'm very fond of Jamie. He's a terrific young man. I've fought three times to save his life and each time I've been thankful I succeeded. But don't ask me to become involved in his family's affairs."

Lorelei leaned forward. "Seth, I'll say this point blank. I'm quite aware that you avoid becoming immersed in civic matters or hot issues in town. You've made that quite clear."

He looked contrite. "I have my reasons. That's the way I am. That's the way people must accept me."

She straightened, unruffled by his clipped words. "I know and that's

234

fine." *For now.* "I wish you would let me understand those reasons so I could maybe make it easier for you, but this isn't the time for me to get into that topic. Jamie needs our help, Seth. I can't give it if he won't let me." She watched his jaw flex, felt his tumult brewing inside.

"How can you turn your back on him?"

"I'm not turning my back. For Christ's sake, Lorelei, I saved that child's life three times. I love that boy."

"Then don't let him try again, Seth. Because he will, you know. Can you let that happen? You might be his only chance."

Seth closed his eyes, his hands fisting on his thighs. He stood, glared at her, then turned and stomped toward the desk.

Lorelei remained silent, wondering if he would kick her out of his house. Holding her breath, she prayed he would relent.

He turned. His piercing scowl was enough to send her flying off the ottoman. She flinched, yet sat poised as if unfretted.

His broad shoulders slumped. Giddiness took hold, and she longed to throw her arms around him. He was softening. She wished it were as easy to weaken his restraint when it came to her.

"I'd never hurt that boy or wish for him to be hurt, Lorelei. You know that." He walked to her side.

She held his gaze, positive the love she felt for this strong man radiated from her very eyes. "I know."

"I might not be the one who can make him talk." He smoothed the leather across the top of the chair with his palm.

"Maybe not. But it's worth a try, isn't it?"

His eyes studied her, with not the damning glower, but more of an ill-at-ease look. She never thought to see this big, intelligent man quaking in his shoes at the thought of confronting Jamie. It felt as if she was trying to read a book with blinded eyes.

"I'll try. And I'm only doing this because it's Jamie. I'll not do this on an ongoing basis, Lorelei. Know that right now. Not for you or anyone else. Do you understand?"

"Yes," Lorelei said, placating him with sugariness. God forbid, she had almost said, *yes, sweetheart.* She stifled a giggle and conjured up a serious face in light of his glower.

He sat, looked at his timepiece. "It's eight-thirty."

"Yes?"

"You want me to talk to him now?" She knew he hoped to postpone the dread. She also knew he would not sleep tonight thinking about it if she pegged him right.

"Yes. Before he starts thinking of harming himself again."

"I'm sure he only feels totally inadequate in Miles's eyes. Hopefully, he'll admit it to me. Then you can deal with the rest. Agreed?" He seemed pleased with his easy reasoning and solution.

"No."

His eyes rounded as if someone had yanked his hair. Oh, there was that scowl again, except now, he looked shocked.

"What the hell do you mean *no*? I'm not going to continue to counsel him. I'll try and find out what devil chases him, then he's all yours. Got that?"

Now he was angry. Good and angry.

"I didn't mean that. I meant I didn't agree that Miles's attitude toward Jamie is the basis for his agitation."

His brows rose. "What *do* you think?"

"Promise me you'll talk with him?"

"I…" His eyes narrowed suspiciously. "I promise."

"I think…Miles might abuse him in other ways."

He gasped as if the wind had been knocked clean out of him. He stiffened. His eyes drilled into hers. "What are you insinuating?" His words were cold as ice water.

"I think Miles may be sexually abusing him."

Bracing herself against the harsh bite of either his denial of such an absurdity, or his out and out laughter at her vivid imagination, she found herself ill-prepared for his reaction. She watched the blood visibly drain from his face, his face void of all expression. His fingers clawed into each arm of the chair like curling talons. He sat motionless as if he had stopped breathing. Sweat beaded his forehead. He trembled.

Stunned, Lorelei scrutinized his eyes for answers. He seemed to stare through her. Eyes so full of pain, raw and tormented, glazed over with something she did not want to identify.

Suspicion exploded in her mind, twisted her stomach in gut-wrenching knots. She felt her own blood congeal.

No! Dear God, no! The possibility he had suffered such abuse as a child waxed too heart-wrenching to contemplate. She closed her eyes against its ugly picture torturing her heart.

Desperate to deny such a probability, she reminded herself he was a doctor, a skilled, intelligent professional, a robust man full of self-confidence, self-assurance to boot. Yet, his one flaw scraped at her disavowal. Her mind grabbed for straws.

He was a tower of strength. He would never let such a past dictate his life. Surely, his resisting her wouldn't have been...

Oh, God, what have I done?

If she had not pegged it exactly, she had hit on something very close. Did he even realize she remained in the room? She needed to snap him out of the other world he had careened into.

"Seth." She covered his hand with hers, noted how clammy his had become. "I know I shocked you. I'm probably wrong." She hoped her voice did not sound as rattled as she felt.

He blinked then scanned her face, her hand. He inhaled, stood and strode to the door.

"I'm fine" He said with his back to her, his voice gruff and short. "I'll talk to him."

Lorelei slumped against the wall, her heart aching for whatever pain she had caused him and more baffled than ever. Would a man who appeared so self-assured, so in touch with the world, allow an abusive past to discolor and distort his mind until he believed he had to shy away from others? But why?

He had asked her not to make him hate himself *more. My God.*

It didn't make any sense. He gave of himself every day. He always had a smile for others, treated their ailments because he deeply cared. He had admitted he loved Jamie, felt attracted to her. Still, he pulled back at every chance he got. Certainly, he did not refrain from relationships because of his tainted past. He was too smart for that. Wasn't he?

She might have more to deal with than she had known, or even bargained for.

CHAPTER THIRTY-FOUR

Seth approached the infirmary feeling as if he were walking a gangplank. How could he draw out the boy with the right words when he could not even handle his own thoughts or feelings concerning sexual abuse? Rape. Incest. The very words made him cringe, soured his stomach until it twisted in unbearable knots.

Jamie lay on his side, reading a book. As Seth crossed the room, the boy looked up, smiled, and set aside the book.

"Hi, Doc. Your game of checkers any worse than Miss Webster's?"

Seth laughed, though his troubled mind hammered with a headache. "You better believe it. After seeing how badly she beat you, I'll never play checkers with her." *I won't do a lot of things with her I'd like to.*

"Maybe tomorrow, if you have time, we could play a game. 'Course, you said you might let me go home tomorrow, didn't ya?"

God, how he loved this boy. If ever he could be blessed with a son, he would want one like Jamie. His heart ached with that usual knife-slicing pain whenever he thought of never being a father.

"If the sutures are set well and you hold down more food, I may let you go." Knowing Jamie might again try something scared the pants right off him, tore at him, deep inside where he had tried not to let anyone reach. He could not hold him here much longer. Jamie and his family were eager for his return.

"How about a game right now?"

"Sure thing, Doc. The board's right over there." Jamie pointed across the room at the other bed.

In minutes, the two were sliding their wooden discs around the board.

Seth knew he could not postpone his talk. If he did, he would not only disappoint Lorelei, but he would suffer lingering guilt if he did not try to prevent further harm. He slid his red piece to a safe square and leaned back as Jamie contemplated his turn. The boy loved the game.

"Your father is a hard man to live with."

Jamie's breath hitched as he eyed the board. "Yeah."

"You want to talk about it?"

"No." Jamie intensely perused the board.

Damn, he hadn't worded that right. "We *need* to talk about it." There, by God.

"I'd rather play checkers." He slid his man to a square where Seth knew Jamie would eventually get one of his.

"We can play while we talk."

"Miss Webster already talked to me."

"She wasn't convinced you won't do anything again."

Jamie frowned. "Yeah? Well, that's her opinion."

Around and around they went with Seth probing, Jamie evading. Seth failed to gather any new light on the subject. Jamie kinged two of Seth's men. The boy was good.

Seth was hard pressed to concentrate on the game. When beating around the bush failed, he plunged in with directness. Nothing drew out the youth. Lorelei was right. Jamie's anguish stemmed from more than just having Miles drink and use his fists.

Seth studied Jamie as the boy intently inspected every possible move available. He could almost hear his mind analyzing his counter attack. The kid was sharp. Seth held back a smile.

Lorelei's claim slammed through his mind. He would rather not think about Jamie's sexual abuse…or his own. He winced at the likelihood of Miles's pathetic perversions. It ripped his heart apart as if someone had reached in and torn it out of his chest. As usual, bile churned in his stomach, and his gut twisted. He remembered his humiliation, the overwhelming helplessness and anger potent enough to want to lash out and kill the tormentor. It all collided in a tumult within his spinning mind.

His damp hands trembled. Cold sweat beaded his brow. He wanted to vomit, to punch his fist through the wall, to scream every vile name at his deceased father. He couldn't do this. Recalling his past reinforced how tainted he was.

"King me!" Jamie laughed, despite his vexation at Seth's persistent questions.

Seth tried to pull his roiling thoughts together. He shook his head at Jamie's cleverness and kinged his man. Their gazes met. Seth's heart contracted.

And he knew then, no matter how agonizing it would be for him, he couldn't let Jamie's abuse go on, if in fact, that was the case. Jamie was a good, intelligent boy, sensitive, caring and a hard worker. He had a bright future if his sadistic father didn't ruin it. How many years had it taken him to deal with his painful burden? Could he make a difference in Jamie's life if he stepped in, put a stop to the warped, malicious injustice?

He could neither allow Jamie's abuse to continue, nor have the boy try to end his precious life again. Not and live with himself. Seth clasped his hands on his lap to stop their shaking.

"Jamie, I want you to listen to something I have to tell you. I can only say this once, *if* I can even manage it."

At Seth's serious tone, Jamie glanced at him with questioning eyes. *God, give me strength.* He trembled.

"When I was your age…a bit younger in fact, my father drank too." Seth found it easier to stare at the wall. He'd never shared his past. Now, it became the hardest thing he'd ever done.

"He didn't drink as much as your father. And he didn't do it often. But he was a mean son-of-a-bitch when he did." He felt Jamie's eyes bore into him. "Unlike your father, he was just as mean and hateful when he didn't drink."

The whip's sharp crack lashing across his back, the painful sting from its vicious blows, stormed Seth's mind. His throat clogged with horrid memories. He fisted his hands, gulped.

Thrusting his own anxiety aside, he cleared his throat. "I took a lot of beatings, mostly with a switch or whip, for no good reason most of the time. But I took them to spare my mother. I figured if he didn't beat me, she'd suffer."

"Did...did he beat her too?" Jamie's whisper almost made him cry.

Seth dared a glance at the boy. "Yeah, the bastard hit her, usually with his fists. And they were meaty weapons, let me tell you." Lorelei would have a fit if she knew he swore so much in front of Jamie, but he couldn't corral the hate. It came with its telling. Jamie most likely had heard worse from Miles.

"I tried to stop him once when he was beating her. I jumped him from behind, punching him for all I was worth." He swallowed, desperately wanting to forget that day's horrors. "That was the day I learned my lesson to never cross my father."

Out of the corner of his eye he saw Jamie stiffen. "He dragged me by my hair to the barn like a sack of potatoes. I knew I'd get a good whipping. If I'd known what else he'd do, I would've run when I had the chance, or knifed him in the kitchen."

Jamie gasped. Seth inhaled, struggled to continue. *If you hesitate, you'll never finish. You're doing this for Jamie.* He shook all the more.

"What...what'd he do?" Again, Jamie whispered as if hoarse.

"He whipped me all right. He tied my wrists to a pole, slashed my back till it felt like raw meat." How inconsequential that beating had become in a matter of seconds. He must have sat dwelling on that day until Jamie spoke.

"Did ya pass out?"

Seth turned and studied the boy. He sat still, his eyes round as saucers, his obvious concern apparent. Would Jamie's attitude toward him change the minute he told him the rest? Would he look at him with disgust, total revulsion? *Of course he will. But if it'll help him...*

"No, unfortunately I didn't. He stopped before I got to that point." The room became an inferno, sweat streamed down his temples to his neck. It became harder to breath. "He wanted me conscious, but helpless as a lamb."

He looked Jamie in the eye. *I can't do this. God help me.* Tears clouded his vision, yet he blinked them back with more determination than he thought he had.

Jamie leaned forward, his face fearful. "What'd he do?"

Silence hung in the air as man and boy stared at each other; one with alarming fear, the other with humiliation, regret and stark fear of losing the boy's respect and admiration.

"He..." Seth looked down, unable to bear witness to Jamie's contempt. "He raped me."

Seth closed his eyes against the thunderous roar in his head. He grabbed the edge of the chair in both hands as vertigo threatened to topple him. Bile rose to his throat.

"Geez."

One single word, so softly spoken, so innocently said, brought Seth back to earth. He opened his eyes.

Jamie appeared unrattled, a wide-eyed look of pity and sadness all wrapped up in one small face. Seth sat in wonder. He saw none of the emotions he had thought he would initiate.

It took Seth a moment to deal with his spiraling turmoil. Could Jamie hide his own humiliation that well? Not hardly.

"Is that what your father did to you, Jamie?"

Jamie scurried back against the wall and curled his legs under him. He bunched the blanket in his tightened fists and stared at it. "No. He didn't touch me like that."

"Jamie, it's okay for you to tell me."

Silence.

"I told you about me so you'd know I'd understand. You can say it, son."

Jamie's chin flew up, his eyes blazing with hatred. Seth stared, taken back at witnessing such an incredible change, the savage look Lorelei had seen. But it was good, he reminded himself. Jamie was dealing with his frustration. He'd gotten this far, couldn't stop now. Not until Jamie dealt with it openly.

"He beats you," Seth taunted, purposefully antagonizing him to lash back.

"Yeah. What of it?" he fired back, his eyes drilling Seth.

Seth went on, unmerciful in his drive to draw him out. "He touches you, hurts you, humiliates you. He rapes you." Seth found himself shouting back at the boy, his own raw emotions soaring.

"No, no, he doesn't do that to me. He does it..." The boy blanched to match the pristine snow outside. His face contorted with agony, his eyes reflecting pain so distressing, Seth found his own eyes stinging.

He mentally repeated the boy's words.

"He does it to whom, Jamie? Who does your father do it to?" Seth reached over, covered the boy's hands with his.

Jamie's lips quivered, his shoulders shook as tears streamed down his sorrowful face. "Nobody. Nobody, you hear?"

"I'll ask you again. Who does he do it to? Your mother?"

No response. Seth's blood ran cold. He shivered with dread. "Missy?"

Jamie stiffened, his fists tightening their grip. The trembling escalated until his entire body quaked.

"He touches Missy," Seth scoffed to egg the boy on. He had to harness his own rage at the thought he had struck home. "He touches her, makes her do things no little girl should even know about. He does things to her that hurt her. He—"

"Stop," Jamie bellowed through an onslaught of fresh tears. His fists clutched the blanket in a death-grip. "It's not her fault. He makes her do those things. I tried to stop him. I did. I tried..." The child broke down sobbing and trembling violently.

"I...I...hate him," he panted through heart-wrenching sobs. "I...wish...he...were dead."

Seth lunged from the chair, sat on the bed and enfolded Jamie in his arms. He held him against him, his own tears escaping down his cheeks. His heart ached, wept for this boy who longed to protect his sibling and couldn't, for the little girl who endured such vile wickedness from her heinous father.

He wept for the boy back in San Francisco who had been left feeling unworthy of anyone's respect, and who had wished his father dead, only to bear the guilt of that very wish ever since.

He rocked Jamie as a father would an infant. He rubbed his back with one hand, offering the security he needed.

Seth heard a sniffle from beyond the half closed door.

Dear God, Lorelei.

How much had she heard? Dread swamped him as if someone had covered him with an icy shroud. He focused on consoling Jamie. He would deal with Lorelei later; know how much she had heard when he looked into her eyes. He loved looking into her deep blue eyes. Now, he feared what he would see.

He would call her in later. She would want to help heal Jamie's wounds as much, if not more than he. But who would heal his own?

"It's going to be all right, son. We'll help Missy all we can." He stroked Jamie's back, offering comfort and to calm the boy down. And felt an overpowering urge to lambast Miles Cooper.

God, just let me get my hands on you, you slimy pervert. He wanted to break his nose, push it into the manure in the barn, and let him wallow in the filth that suited him. Actually, that would be too good for the rotten, sadistic bastard.

"Nobody...can help her, Doc. My father...would kill anybody who'd try." His muffled words against Seth's shoulder, only served to heighten Seth's desire to flatten the man. His adrenaline surged. He would do it for Missy, for Jamie, and, by God, for himself. And come away a very satisfied man.

"We'll deal with it soon enough, Jamie. Your father will be made to pay for all the wrongs he's done. And Missy won't suffer anymore. As God is my witness, I promise you that."

Jamie pulled back far enough to look up at him. He batted the moisture off his face with his knuckles. "You think you can really do something?" His eyes were filled with so much hope that Seth knew he could never let this boy down.

"I always keep my promise, son." He smiled, and Jamie's face lit up with more elation than he had seen on it in a very long time. In the same instant, Jamie grew serious.

"I won't tell nobody about what you told me, Doc. It's between you and me. I promise."

Seth experienced a love for this boy so powerful it turned painful within the confines of his chest. He could not understand how Jamie could look at him and not feel he was unworthy of his friendship. But he was not about to question the boy's reasons. He grabbed what he offered and savored it within his tender heart.

"Thank you, Jamie. I appreciate that."

Jamie beamed. "My promises are as good as yours. I always keep them. Except...except with Missy." Jamie pulled away and Seth allowed the boy to gather his dignity.

"How so?"

"I told her I'd not let him take her to the barn again. I didn't keep my promise to her, Doc. I tried, but I couldn't do it. He laughed at me when he last took her to the barn."

Seth's hands itched to feel Miles's skin break under his blow. "Well, now, I think by you telling someone about this, someone who can help, you kept your promise. Don't you think?"

Jamie grinned. "I like your way of thinkin', Doc. I knew you were a smart man."

Seth found himself laughing at Jamie's compliment. "And you're one heck of a young man yourself."

Shuffling in the hallway reminded Seth that Lorelei hovered nearby. She most likely was chomping at the bit to come in. He braced himself for the disgust he would see in her eyes. Or would it be pity? Either would rip his heart apart; it did now merely knowing she knew. He swallowed and buried his ego.

"Miss Webster, you might as well come in."

CHAPTER THIRTY-FIVE

Lorelei swiped her cheeks with her hands and entered the room. She was a bundle of nerves. No two ways about it.

Hearing Seth's agonizing past had stunned her until she thought she might never again breathe. After Jamie's revelation, she felt strung tighter than a bow string. The two men, so important to her, had suffered unmercifully. And so had Missy. Her heart went out to all three.

Plastering on a bright smile, she crossed the room. Empathy for Seth, Jamie, and Missy swamped her. But now knowing of Seth's tormented past, Missy's humiliation, and Miles' vulgarity regarding his own daughter fired her blood.

"I thought you two were going to raise fists." She noted Seth's perusal from hooded eyes. Did he think she would scorn or pity him? *Foolish man.* She admired him for rising above his past.

Seth sat stiff, his eyes avoiding contact. "Our voices rose a bit, did they?" Oh, how he tried to make light of the matter. His effort shot an arrow right into her heart. A cupid's arrow.

Jamie laughed. Lorelei shook her head. "'A bit' wouldn't begin to describe it." Seth scrutinized her every move, and gave a good attempt at concealing his apprehension.

While listening to Seth's past, she had put together most of the pieces of his puzzle. Found it hard to believe a man so confident in everyday life and in his profession, having more intelligence and common sense than most, could harbor such self doubt. Clearly, he thought himself less of a person than any one man should be made to feel. So unworthy that he separated himself from others. She found such a fact too devastating to comprehend.

But why did he hesitate from becoming involved with civic matters? One piece of the puzzle still didn't fit.

"You heard what I said?" Jamie asked, scowling and almost cringing at the fact she knew his secret.

"Yes, I did." She sat on the chair. "You should be proud of yourself for finally letting us know. Now, as Se…Doctor Taylor said, we can do something about it. Missy won't suffer anymore."

Jamie's eyes turned troubled, yet he held her gaze. He had grown up in the last few days. What a lousy way to mature.

"You…you don't have to tell anyone else about Missy, do ya? She…she feels real bad about it, Miss Webster. She'd never be able to face them if they knew."

If she ever had a son, she hoped he would mirror this wonderful, empathetic young man. She could only pray the rest of Jamie's life would be less harrowing than what it had been up until now.

"Only those directly involved or who need to know so we can stop your father from hurting her again. And those people would never think any less of Missy. I assure you."

With a hopeful, yet wary glint in his eyes, he nodded.

For a few minutes, the three discussed Jamie's family. Miles did quite often hit them, even little Jessica. Lorelei became incensed; Seth's fists clenched. Jamie told all now that the weight of the world had been lifted from his shoulders.

Throughout their talk, Lorelei stressed that Jamie shouldn't feel guilty. Seth, bless his heart, reinforced all she said, phrasing it differently to make Jamie realize he wasn't at fault.

"You two keep talking, it's good for you, Jamie," Seth said as he stood and stretched. "I think you've learned that when there's a problem, you need to seek help from someone older and wiser. Even if it's only to shed new light on the subject."

Jamie nodded, a tentative smile surfacing.

Seth glanced at her. "I'm going out. I'll be back shortly."

She wanted to ask where he was going, but thought better of harping like a wife and nodded. In all likelihood, he needed to deal with his own demons. Noting his purposeful stride across the room, she realized he just might be going to the Cooper's.

"Should I say *be careful*?"

He paused at the door, glanced back, yet avoided eye contact. "I will. If I'm not back soon, get Michael."

His words instilled the fear of God. Would they argue? Would Miles shoot him? How long was "soon"? Temptation screamed she should fetch Michael now.

After a half hour, allotting time for Seth to get to the Cooper's and back, Lorelei paced the infirmary in agitated stomps.

"Doc's great. He isn't any dimwit, Miss Webster. He'll know how to handle the bastard."

She appreciated Jamie's attempt to console her, yet reprimanded him for using language no better than that of the so called "great Doc."

For the next fifteen minutes she tidied room."I can't stand it any longer, Jamie. I've got to get Michael."

"Sure thing, if it'll make you feel better, Miss Webster. But I think you're gettin' all riled for nothin'."

Of course he did. He thought Seth Taylor could walk on water. But the man was not more invincible than any other. And she worried about Seth far more than any other man.

"You'll be all right while I'm gone?"

"Sure thing. Give my regards to my pa when you see him."

She burst out laughing. "Jamie, you're terrible. I think you've been around Se…Doctor Taylor way too long."

"That can't be all bad, can it? You might as well call him Seth. You almost call him that every time you speak."

Red-faced, she shook her head as she crossed the room. "You, young man, are too full of confidence by far for your own britches. And we have to do something about your English. You murder several words by cutting off their endings."

"But Miss Webster, you both just got done telling me to hold my head up and speak my mind. I'm just followin' your advice."

"Yeah?" She laughed, using his slang term. "Well, don't take it to heart so well next time."

****

Finding Michael's office vacant, Lorelei's anxiety mounted. Tom

Burdock meandered out of the saloon as she turned to leave.

"You lookin' fer the sheriff?"

"Yes…yes I am."

"He be up at the Cooper's. Little Missy came a-runnin' to tell him there was a ruckus at her house. They took off like lightnin' was scorchin' their back sides. Just left awhile ago."

With a nod of thanks, Lorelei flicked the reins. "Hah!"

The horse bolted, swiftly covering the ground, the buggy bouncing over uneven ruts as if there was no tomorrow. Fearing Seth lay hurt, Lorelei's heart galloped to equal the horse's hooves. She'd strangle the man if he had let that happen.

****

Lorelei leaped from the carriage before the wheels had fully stopped. As she flew across the lawn, Michael's horse side-stepped at the rail. Without bothering to knock, dreading what she might find, she barged through the doorway.

And halted in midstride.

Miles sat on the floor, leaning cock-eyed against the wall, groaning between deep gasps and holding his left arm. His left eye and cheek were swollen and turning purple, his skin gaped open at the cheekbone. Johanna, kneeling by his side, held a bloody towel beneath his crooked nose. She looked none too pleased. Was Johanna more infuriated at Seth or at Miles?

Her heart hammering, Lorelei fearfully spun around in search of Seth. She didn't have far to search.

He sat, leaning back on a wooden chair, holding a towel to his own jaw while Michael scowled at the two. Seth's eyes sparkled above ruddy cheeks. He grinned like a cock-sure idiot.

"Hello, Lorelei," Seth said, his voice surprisingly composed after such a fight. "Nice you could join us."

Despite the small cut above his right eyebrow and the apparent injury to his jaw, Lorelei longed to throttle him. She fumed. How dare he sit so content after he had scared her half to death? But her brief anger dissipated into thin air, replaced by an overwhelming sense of delight. Seth had put Miles in his proper place. And Miles's moans sang like music to her ears.

"You all right?" Michael asked Seth, his lips thinning. He looked and sounded more perturbed at the smiling man than concerned, apparently no happier with the situation than Johanna. He paid no mind that she had joined them.

Only then did Lorelei realize Michael sounded far more short-winded than Seth. Blood dotted the front of his shirt and sleeves, most likely from pulling the two apart. It amazed her to think Seth had bested Miles when the brute attacked him.

"Yeah, I'm fine. Better than fine," Seth gloated as he dabbed the corner of his curled lips.

For the first time since entering, Lorelei relaxed and scanned the room. The other chairs lay overturned, strewn throughout the room. One, broken beyond repair. Missy and Jessica stood in the bedroom doorway, their eyes round and astonished.

Thinking of how frightened they must have been—still were, by the looks of them—Lorelei rushed over to them with open arms. "It's all over now, girls. Your papa will be all right. And so will Doctor Taylor." She didn't give two figs about Miles. He deserved a lot more than Seth's few, lucky punches.

"Arrest that…that crazy bastard, Sheriff," Miles managed to bellow through his continued panting. "If ya don't…I'll see to it he never…comes in here like that again."

Astonished at Miles's outburst, Lorelei gaped at the three men. You couldn't arrest a man for coming to say his piece. She would have been behind bars long ago if that were the case.

Michael's jaw squared, his hands clenched into fists as he straightened. He glared at Seth. "Let's you and I go outside. You can tell me what the hell got into you before I lock you up."

Lorelei's mouth fell open. What was he thinking?

"Michael, for heaven's sake, it should be *Miles* you lock up! You don't know the whole story. He came here to speak with Miles, to reprimand, yes, but—"

"You got that ass-backwards, *bitch*," Miles cut in with a hiss, groaning as he tried to turn to his side.

Johanna got in the midst of it then. "Miles, I'll not have you curse like that in this house. Not in front of the gir—"

"You shut up too, you nagging old bitch...they've heard worse before, and ya know it."

Johanna blanched. It was hard to imagine she could be so stricken by his foul mouth after so many years. She tossed the towel to the floor, rose, and regal as a queen ushered the girls further into the bedroom.

When the bedroom door closed, Seth stood and strode to the kitchen door. As the two went outside, indecision thwarted Lorelei. She did not want to stay in Miles's presence another instant. She would not pass in front of him to get to the bedroom, either.

"Can't even call the damn sawbones to patch me up." Miles tried to sit up straighter, cursed a blue streak, and sank back down to the crooked sitting position. "Bastard broke my leg, my nose and most of my ribs. He's crazy I tell ya. Crazy bastard. I'll see him pay. Pay good, he will. For all my broken parts and the mess he made of my house." His profanity soared in volume as well as obscenity until Lorelei's ears flamed.

She had no choice but to leave. He might be hurting, angered beyond reason, but he had no right to be so crass. She eyed him, distaste turning her mouth sour as the image of him abusing Missy fired revulsion in her stomach. He could not reach her, but she did not have to listen to his foul mouth. And, she wanted answers. Her feet took flight.

Michael and Seth stood by the barn. She crossed the porch, flew down the three steps and approached them. The cold night air bit her cheeks. She sunk her hands in her pockets.

"Lorelei, go back inside. This has nothing to do with you, and I need some answers."

Michael treated her like a little girl. Well, she needed answers too.

"I can't stay in there and listen to him. He's disgusting. And I'm well aware of why this happened. I won't interfere."

Michael glared, yet gave no argument. He turned to Seth, who nonchalantly leaned against the barn, his arms at his sides.

"You gonna tell me why you tried to destroy their kitchen and make mince meat out of Miles? Or, do I just lock you up?" Michael scowled as he broadened his stance. "This isn't like you. Didn't you have enough patients without creating another one?"

Seth looked Michael right in the eye. "I had good reason."

Why didn't he tell Michael he was the victim? Lorelei lost her patience. "Tell him how you came to talk—"

Seth chuckled, glanced her way and pushed away from the barn. "I didn't come to talk, Lorelei. I came to beat him to a pulp. And I would've, if Michael hadn't pulled me off him."

She stood dumbfounded. Was this the same Seth Taylor she knew? "What did you say to him to start the fight?"

He grinned like a little boy, one with a brand new toy that he had coveted for a very long time. "Didn't. Just walked through the door and took the first swing."

His chest puffed up like a proud rooster's. Maybe he *could* walk on water. "Not one word?"

"Nope." His eyes twinkled in the silver moonlight, his grin as pleased as a cat with fresh warm milk. Lorelei couldn't, for the life of her, find fault with what he'd done. And by gosh and by golly, she was tickled pink that he had finally shown his true colors. Her pride in him matched his. Her heart seemed to want to join the stars that now dotted the dark sky.

"He deserved everything you gave him, and more," she said, unable to hold back her smile. They shared an understanding grin.

Michael snorted. "I thought Seth had lost his mind. But you're no better, Lorelei. He can't just walk into someone's house and bust it *and* the owner up. I want answers. *Now*."

Seth explained what had fueled him to beat Miles. Michael stood silent, his face somber. When Seth finished, Michael's hands fisted at his sides and his eyes bore no less menace against the broken man inside than what Seth or Lorelei felt.

Michael exhaled a huff. "I almost wish Missy *hadn't* found me so soon. Maybe you could've finished him off. He—"

"God forgive me," Johanna's anguished voice broke through the darkening skies. In unison, they turned. Tears trekked down Johanna's cheeks, glistening like pearlescent ribbons. "I had no idea. The times he took her to the barn I thought...I thought he was teaching her about the horses. She...she loves them so. I...I..."

Lorelei's heart ached for the distraught woman. She scurried to her side and hugged her, intent on comforting a mother's worst nightmare. To her amazement, Johanna pushed away, her face a mirror of loathing and anguish, courage and determination.

Johanna pulled her coat closed against the chilled wind. Straightening her shoulders, she brushed away the wetness on her face. She faced Michael, her eyes void of any sorrow.

"I came out to tell you something I dreaded. But now, hearing his other sin, I've no regret in telling you."

Michael shuffled from one foot to the other. "I'm sorry you had to hear what Seth said, Mrs. Cooper. I—"

"Please, hear me out," she held up one hand. "I'm not sorry at all." Her words were direct, curt, and laced with ice. "It makes it easier to tell you what he just confessed."

Michael's brows arched, but he nodded. For once, Lorelei had to credit Michael for his good sense.

"He was slurring Doctor Taylor when I returned to the kitchen. He said he'd get just what he gave Dan Purdy."

"What?" All three asked at the same time.

A chill, much more frigid than the night air, scurried up Lorelei's spine.

"That's what he said. I knew he'd been very angry at Dan for not giving him more time to get the cash to buy the old Griffin land. When Dan told Miles he was going to sell it to Fred Harper because Fred was good for the note and he wasn't, Miles argued with him for weeks. He tried to convince Dan his credit was as good as Fred's. But of course, Dan knew better."

Michael took a few steps closer to Johanna. "Mrs. Cooper, Miles is your husband, no matter how bad he's mistreated your child. I need to warn you whatever you say can be used in court. I wouldn't want you to have regrets later. Think before you tell me what he said. I don't think you realize what this might mean."

Johanna laughed, disgust making it sound like a snort. "Oh, but I do. I didn't before. I had no idea Dan had been murdered. But I know now. He did it, Sheriff. He admitted it."

Lorelei felt the blood drain from her face, her heart thud to her feet. She detested Miles for mistreating his family, for his crass, drunken state half the time. She loathed him since finding out about Missy. But never had she labeled him a cold-blooded killer. The night air pierced like an iced shard.

Michael stood rigid, feet braced apart. He looked every bit the sheriff. "I'll remind you again, Mrs. Cooper. He's your husband. Think before you say anything else. He's done your daughter a terrible injustice. And for that, he'll pay dearly. But what you're telling me will earn him his death."

Johanna issued a tight smile. "He is my husband. And I damn each day since I took his name. The only thing good he's ever done is to give me my three beloved children. Other than that, Sheriff, he's been a torment, a misery I've had to bear with regret and agony each second of every day." She drew in a long breath, continued as if they were discussing the weather.

"I want him out of my house. Take him away. I never want to see him again. He flat out told me he killed Dan. He actually laughed before he realized what he'd said. Then he tried to make light of it. But I heard him. Loud and clear."

Michael withdrew his gun, his face grim and stern. "I'm real sorry, Mrs. Cooper. You've been through hell with Jamie, Missy, and now this. But the town'll stick by you. You're a good woman. Your children are real—"

"Just get him out of my house," Johanna spat, her voice raw with bitterness. "I can almost feel sorry for him being pressured by Dan. But I'll never, never forgive him for what he did to my daughter. For what he almost did to my son. For that, he can rot in hell or die hanging from a tree. It matters little to me. I told the girls to stay in the bedroom. If you don't mind, I'll stay out here until you take him away."

Lorelei's eyes burned as tears gathered. She blinked rapidly to curtail their escape. If Johanna could remain tough through this whole atrocity, so could she. Her heart twisted in anguish for what the woman now carried upon her shoulders, for all the agony and sorrow Johanna had suffered. But she felt relief so poignant for Johanna that she wanted to rejoice.

This woman, with her fierce pride, her devoted love for her children, would do well without the miserable Miles Cooper. Yes, this woman had a new life ahead of her, and Lorelei knew she would do well. And so would her children under her steady, understanding guidance. Lorelei's tears started anew. But they didn't hurt or drain her heart. Oh no, they only made it sing for thankfulness. Thankful for a brighter future for the Coopers.

Michael turned to Seth. "I'm taking him in, but I'll need your help moving him. You'll need to patch him up first."

Seth nodded and trailed in Michael's footsteps. As he passed Lorelei, he gave a wink and smiled. Despite the horrible situation, Lorelei's heart did triple time at his gesture. The man surprised her at every turn. And whether he knew it or not, she was not done with the good doctor. Not by a long shot.

****

Inside, Seth gave Miles a scathing look. His right shoulder was sore; but oh, what a *good* sore! Having bashed Miles satisfied him to no end. If Michael had not stopped him, he would have finished the pervert off. Thank God, he hadn't. The lowlife would have escaped too easily for all the crimes he had committed.

As Michael lit a cigarette and idly watched him splint Miles's leg with a chair slat and strips of towel for binding, Seth smiled as he recalled Lorelei's adamant defense. She was quite a lady. Yet, he cringed as he thought about facing her again; thought of the scorn she would cast his way when she finally realized he was a piece of dirt.

His elation over Miles faded, replaced by chilling dread.

CHAPTER THIRTY-SIX

After Seth secured Miles's leg and arm, he and Michael carted the foul-mouthed man to the Cooper's flatbed wagon. Though obviously disgruntled to accompany Michael to the jail, Seth did so in order to further repair the damage he'd done to the sot. But before they left, Lorelei extracted Seth's approval for her to bring Jamie home to be with his family.

As her horse plodded along back to the Coopers', Jamie bundled in a blanket, she expounded on the fight between his father and Seth. Jamie seemed more than pleased punishment had been doled out to Miles for whatever he had done to Missy.

Johanna had asked her not to tell Jamie about the Purdy murder, and she felt honor-bound to grant her wish. Anguish seared her heart at knowing though Jamie detested his father, he would again suffer more agony. And then, there would be a hanging.

Though eager to be on her way home, Lorelei complied with Johanna's insistence to have a cup of tea. It was pushing eleven by the time she left. But instead of going home, she headed toward the house she had frequented so many times of late.

Since she would not gain sleep anytime soon, she might as well check on Seth. By the time she arrived, her body screamed fatigue, yet her mind worked overtime. She had so many things to sort out. Especially where Seth was concerned.

Her heart wept for the young boy who had been unjustly abused. She would have to bury any pity she felt when she faced him. He would not want it, would cringe from it, in fact. He would need understanding and insight on how to bury the past. She was unsure what would blot out the reminders. But she was more than willing to try.

Unsure if he had returned, she bypassed knocking and boldly went inside. "Seth are you here?" Nothing.

Light streamed from the kitchen. There had been none when she had retrieved Jamie. Her hopes rose. Shedding her wraps, she scurried down the hallway. Finding the kitchen vacant, her enthusiasm faltered. She turned and glanced at the open infirmary door. Excitement stirred as she approached.

"Seth?"

Seth jerked around. He stood at the counter holding a cloth to his forehead, a medicine bottle in the other hand. He wore the same blood-smeared shirt, sleeves rolled up his forearms.

"What are you doing here?" Though his words sounded more surprised than annoyed, his scowl was far from happy.

Lorelei questioned her good sense in coming. "I wanted to make sure you were all right." *How lame her excuse sounded!*

"I'm fine." His lips thinned, and he glared.

He sure was out of sorts. And why not? Mildly put, it had been a hellacious night. The antiseptic, tinged pink from blood, ran down his face and neck to soak his collar.

"Damn." He swiped his cheek and neck with his hand.

Lorelei smiled. "I believe you need doctoring, Doctor."

She crossed the room and reached for the cloth. His scowl turned more irritated, and he gripped the soggy wad tighter. The liquid streamed from it like a compressed saturated sponge. It splattered his already-soiled shirt and dripped onto the floor, forming a small puddle. "I think I can handle a small cut."

She laughed harder at his rising frustration. Ah, if only he were that rattled by her presence, she mused on a wish.

"You sir, might be a competent doctor to others, but you're making one hell of a mess here." She grabbed the cloth before he had time to do battle. "Sit down, and let me wring this out."

He looked ready to explode. Was he embarrassed by her knowing his dark secret? Did that, plus confronting Miles cause him to be so churlish? The thought had merit. She would go gingerly with this proud man. Proud? No, he tried to act proud, while all the time feeling embarrassed, ashamed and more than unworthy.

With a will of steel, she vowed she would make him forget.

"Sit." Her voice matched the severity of his. Though his eyes glared, she caught the slight curling of his lips. He sat on the chair and shook his head. Then grinned.

The awkward tension broke. And her heart lightened with the knowledge she had made him relax, if even just a morsel.

"You're a very pushy lady, Lorelei Webster."

"You've known that all along, Seth Taylor." She wrung out the cloth over the pewter basin, folded it in a square and returned to his side. When he relinquished the bottle to her, she poured a small amount on the liquid on the pad.

Handing back the bottle, she gently dabbed the gash over his right eye brow, then held the cloth over the wound to soak off the congealed blood.

"Do you think you'll need stitches?" She glanced down at the swollen, purple jaw and winced. It had to hurt like crazy.

"Don't even think about it." She felt him flinch from the thought and had to apply more pressure as he pulled back. "If I need sutures, I'll do it myself."

Lorelei laughed at his obvious reluctance. "Coward."

He grinned. "You're damn right. Be happy I let you do *this*."

"You weren't doing so great when I arrived, *Doctor*."

It felt good to banter. Maybe it would take his mind off all his troubles. *In a pig's eye.* His past was ingrained in granite.

"I could've managed."

Her breath hitched as she gazed into his twinkling eyes, nearly swooned on their familiar gaiety. Oh, how good it felt. She longed to kiss him.

"But not half as well." She lifted the pad and was pleased to see most of the dried blood had loosened. She wiped off the debris, dipped the cloth in the basin of water, wrung it out, applied more antiseptic, and set it to his wound.

"How's your jaw?"

"Hurts like hell, if you want the truth." Maybe she should kiss that, too. Could he hear her blood hum, feel her pulse bound?

"I'll get some ice for this as soon as I'm done here."

He smiled and her heart fluttered as it always did when he looked at her that way. She read appreciation in his expressive eyes. It warmed her insides and curled the tips of her toes.

His brow furrowed as he rested his palms on his thighs. "You really didn't have to come. You must be dead on your feet."

His concern touched deep, wrapping around her heart as if he had tucked a warm blanket around it. She loved this man so much. She would walk ten thousand miles in a blizzard if it meant helping him. How could she not be here tonight for him?

"I couldn't have slept without knowing you were all right."

Pain streaked over his face, his eyes dulled. It literally tore at her chest, gripping and twisting. How would she ever make him come to terms with his past enough to let her into his life? The odds of doing that seemed so farfetched, so hopeless; she found her throat dry as a bone baked in the sun.

"Did you fix up Miles?" Safer ground. *That's good, Lorelei.*

"Yeah," he scoffed as she rinsed out the cloth and repeated the process. "He'll mend. Long enough to face his demise." He looked ever the formidable foe he had been back at the Coopers'. She could feel the tension return as his body stiffened.

"You really gave it to him. I'm very proud of you. And I'm sure Johanna was after she realized what he'd done to Missy." Her heart wept for Johanna's suffering.

Despite his intensity, he smiled. "I believe you have another side to you, Lorelei. One that relishes battle. You best be careful. That's not always good."

"I don't like fighting, especially physical combat. But I don't deny I appreciated every blow you gave him. He deserved it for Missy, for Jamie *and* for Dan." She glanced at him and caught him studying her. She didn't mince her next words.

"I never thought I'd see the day when it'd be *you* to hurl punches. You're quite good. As Jamie would say, you have a mighty powerful swing, Doc. Working out with that equipment sure pays off." She gave him a small smile.

He looked her straight in the eye. "I don't like fighting either. But I swore years ago...after that one night, I'd not ever let myself be unprepared to defend myself if need be. Tonight, I wasn't defending myself, but Missy. I did what I felt was right."

"Yes, you did. And a fine job too." Could he recognize her love through her appreciative eyes? She didn't care. She'd made it obvious before that she wanted more of him than he offered.

He nodded, said nothing. They were at a standstill. She had hoped they would delve into his past. If they didn't, most likely the topic would never surface again. Then, where would she be? Without any way to reach into his soul, that's where.

"Jamie was pleased to go home." *Let's get the ball rolling.*

"Did you tell him I beat his father?" He looked like a little boy who had lost his best friend.

"Yes. He's very pleased you avenged Missy's honor. Johanna wants to wait until tomorrow to tell him about Dan Purdy."

His lips thinned as if he also regretted what the family would be put through because of Miles. Lorelei pulled the cloth away and swabbed the injury clean. "It looks pretty good. Do you want to check it?"

Seth got up and peered into the small mirror on the wall. "It won't need sutures. A bandage on it will do fine." He gathered up a pot of salve, a small pad and a roll of inch-wide binding and started to apply the salve to his forehead.

"I'll get you some ice." In a few minutes she had ice secured within a linen towel and a snifter with two fingers of brandy placed by his chair in the study.

Returning to the infirmary, she watched him secure the bandage. "You look like an Indian with a headdress."

He laughed, peering into the mirror. "It'll stay on through the night better this way. Tomorrow I can apply a smaller bandage." He glanced over his shoulder. "Where's the rest of the ice?"

"I put it in your study. I thought maybe you'd be more comfortable there."

"Thank you," he said, stepping aside for her to lead the way. Was he wondering when she would leave? She didn't want to at all. She skirted to the side of the leather chair, feeling unsure as to what to say.

It was not often she felt so ill-at-ease. But her future, his future, maybe theirs together hinged on the precarious next few minutes. At least, she hoped they did.

Seth stopped by the overstuffed chair as if waiting for her to take a seat. She sat on the ottoman two feet away. As soon as she perched, he sank down into the overstuffed seat. He smiled at the brandy at his side. "Smart lady. Thanks. Would you like some?"

"No, thank you. I'm fine." That liquor had muddled her mind the last time. She needed a clear head for the next attack.

She handed him the ice pack. He placed it against his jaw and winced. He exhaled, leaned back, and with his free hand took a sip of brandy.

She dug right in. "Thank you for talking to Jamie. He never would've confessed to me what was bothering him."

He tilted the snifter from side to side in a circular motion and watched the amber liquid swirl gently up the glass. Silence hung in the room like a weighty cloud.

"You were wonderful with him. We would have never known about Missy if you hadn't drawn him out like you did."

His gaze rose to hers. She expected to see anger that she knew his past. She could deal with that, re-route it. She had prayed to see longing. *That*, she would relish. Instead, she read such haunted anguish that her heart felt wrenched from her chest. She blinked back tears, trembled with uncertainty as to how to proceed.

"I never wanted anyone, especially you, to know my past. If Jamie's life hadn't depended on me finding common ground that might get him to open up, I never would've divulged it."

Didn't he realize his past wasn't his fault? After her praise, how could he remain humiliated? Obviously, he did.

She had hoped he would share his bitter memories so he could deal with them. Determined to ease his discomfort and get on with what she hoped might be a future between them, she plunged in.

"We all have things in our past we'd rather not remember."

His laugh was bitter, his eyes skeptical, almost incredulous.

"Lorelei. I know you came here tonight out of pity. I don't want it. I don't need it. You go your way and I'll go mine." His hand tightened

261

around the glass.

"Pity? I didn't come here out of pity. I came here because I was concerned about your wounds, about how distraught you might be after fighting Miles, and then having to treat him."

He glared at her as if he didn't believe a word she said. He needed the truth. "Yes, at first, I felt pity. Pity for the young boy who had to deal with a sick, unfeeling father. A boy who suffered the worst kind of abuse possible. But that's where I left my pity, Seth. You had a horrific time when you were a child, and that was beyond shame. But that's all in your past."

Seth's eyes glared, his brow etched deeply. His hand squeezed the glass till his fingers blanched white. She shuddered as she waited for the glass to shatter. Why was he so angry?

"If you didn't come out of pity, then I thank you for not offering it. And I'll thank you for not spreading my sordid past about town before I have time to leave."

Her chest tightened as it were clenched in a vise. Her hopes and dreams plunged to her feet. She searched for understanding. *Leave? He could not leave. He could not just walk out of her life.* She trembled at the thought.

"Why would you leave?" she managed to whisper through tears clogging her throat. "Seth, say you won't leave."

He set down the glass and the ice pack. He rose from the chair, walked to the desk and kept his back to her.

"I can't face you and Jamie every day." His voice was so soft she had to strain to hear him. He sounded so forlorn. She longed to jump up, scurry to his side and enfold him in her arms. To hug away all the pain inside him. She forced herself to remain calm, to offer him a chance to unburden his soul.

"Why not?"

He snorted. "Lorelei, for Christ's sake, how do you expect me to go on like nothing has changed? You and Jamie will look at me with..." She saw his shoulders quake, his hands grip the edge of the desk. He needed to keep talking, to rid the demons.

"With what, Seth? How will I look at you?" Her pulse thudded in her ears. *Come on Seth, let it spill out, open up.*

He didn't answer immediately, merely stood with his head tilted down. "With disgust." His shoulders slumped.

Disgust? He thought she would be repulsed because of what had happened to him? Stormed by a potent urge to run to him, to throw her arms around him, to crush him to her chest and…

Her actions would only temporarily soothe, she realized. Only postpone his need to reject. He needed to speak of his past, to become cleansed from inside out. She had to keep him talking.

Oh, God, he was so wrong, so very, very wrong. How could she convince him otherwise?

His demons were far more dangerous than she had realized.

CHAPTER THIRTY-SEVEN

Seth shook. He couldn't help it. And he couldn't turn around to witness her scorn-filled stare, the absolute revulsion in those lovely eyes once she realized how soiled he was. Oh, she had cleansed his wound, given him an ice pack and offered him a brandy, but soon her expression would be filled with scathing rejection. His heart would never survive it. Even now, a fist clenched his chest until it felt squeezed into a tiny ball, his heart too constricted to pump.

"Seth, I could never feel disgust—"

"Don't." He hated barking at her, but he had no choice. He had to fight his attraction. For his sake, as well as hers.

"Don't fool yourself, Lorelei. Just leave so I don't have to see it when it finally registers. We both know I'm no good. I've lived with the knowledge of my filth for years. I can continue to do so. It's my own damn fault for being persuaded to talking to Jamie. For once, I thought with emotions instead of logic."

The weight in his chest became unbearable. He took a needed breath. Hell, he'd even let his imagination run wild about her.

He heard her sigh. "Maybe that's good. Maybe you needed to finally deal with it."

"And maybe I can live as if none of the past ever existed." He snorted at the absurd jest. "Be sensible. I'm scum. The lowest vile form on the earth. I try to remember that every day, so I don't falter. I made a mistake in getting caught up in Jamie's problems. But I'll not make that error again. I usually avoid anything like that." God, why wouldn't she just leave so he could drown in his sorrows? He had come so close to making a bigger mistake where she was concerned. And that would be a monumental disaster over time, when she started resenting what he *really* was. He leaned sweaty palms harder against the desk.

"That's why you hold back from the community. You don't want to strongly care about anyone or anything because you don't think you have the right. My God...now, I understand."

Her words hurt. But she had it wrong. *Might as well set it all straight. What the hell difference did it make?*

"You don't understand a damn thing. I avoid getting involved because of the havoc. Havoc and heated discussions make me remember days of old. The fear, my pathetic inability to get away from him; the pain, the humiliation. All of it comes back. I can't sleep, can't think straight. But I have my profession, and feel proud of what I do. That's the only thing I *am* worthy of. And I'll be damned if I'll let anyone take that away. When the memories surface, I can't think coherently enough to treat a swollen-bellied cow. I won't let that happen."

Why the holy hell had he spilled his nightmarish fears out to her like that? He needed to calm down. *She had to leave.*

"You better leave, Lorelei. Walk out that door and don't come back. Soon, you'll acknowledge what I am; that I'm right in sending you away. You'll thank me, in the end."

"Oh, I realize what you are right now," she bellowed as she moved up just behind him. "You're an *idiot.* A blubbering, foolish *idiot.*"

When she stomped to his side, he glanced sideways. Her fists dug into her hips. He remembered their first meeting when her dander had risen. And right now, her dander was flying high.

"So you think you're unworthy of anyone's caring," she taunted in a sing-song tone. It damn well scorched his ears. "That's the most ridiculous thing I've ever heard. Well, hear this, Seth Taylor. I care. I *more* than care. *I love you.* Don't you know that?"

His heart must have stopped. He couldn't breathe. When he finally managed to inhale needed air, his blood surged with elation. At the same time, he longed to crawl in a hole and bury himself deep. He didn't have the right to accept what she so foolishly offered.

He couldn't look at her. "If I'm an idiot, you're twice the fool. You don't know what you're saying. When you think this through, you'll come to your senses. I'm dirt. I'm not fit for you to walk on." He wished things were different. Craved it with every fiber of his heart.

"Oh, for heaven's sake, stop saying that. When I look at you, I see an extremely handsome man, strong, powerful, and confident in his competent skill of doctoring and in a hundred other facets. I see a vastly intelligent man who could lead others, teach them and befriend them. I see a man who is more worthy of leading a life of happiness than ten others. You're a good, caring, loving and respectable person, Seth. Just look at yourself, the person you are now. You can't deny that."

"I'm scum. Don't forget that." Tears burned his eyes as he refuted her words. Words he wanted to believe. Words he wanted to reach out and cling to. Words that pierced his very soul.

"Your *father* was scum. *Not you.* You were a *child*. A manipulated, abused child. He sinned. You were a victim. But you rose above your anguish. Because of the goodness within you, you chose to help others. Doesn't that tell you how noble you are? How considerate, how caring? That's what makes a person worthy, Seth. What's in their heart and how they express it. You have a heart worth gold. You give of yourself every day. That's a worthiness that can't be denied. It's a humble expression of one's self, and that's why God put us here—to share our knowledge with others, to help those in need, to warm the hearts of many. You do that whether you want to admit it or not."

Her words bathed him in warm nectar, so compelling, he longed to believe. Yet, unworthiness lingered inside. Yes, on the outside he willingly gave to others. On the inside... lurked a hidden criminal. Dirty, soiled by greed and cruelty by his father. He could never forget. It shadowed him every step of the way. He had mentally sinned. And that was just as foul.

"My body's not only soiled, but my mind is corrupt too, Lorelei. I can't change that."

She touched his arm, and he yearned crush her to him. Hold on tight and never let go. He should pull away. He couldn't.

"Please, tell me. Let me in." Her voice, so sweet, so persuading had him unburdening his soul before he realized it.

"I wished him dead." He had never admitted it to anyone. Not even his mother. But every day it hammered in his mind, tormenting. And for that, he was condemned to his own hell.

"A person can't will anyone to die, Seth. You know that. You're a doctor."

"I wished him dead, and by God, the next day he fell down the saloon steps and broke his neck."

The walls seemed to move in on all sides. The air became thick, too thick to breathe.

"You were a child, Seth. You saw that through a child's eyes. You may have wanted him dead, and God knows you had good reason—but your wish had nothing to do with it. He fell, and that's what caused his death. Not your wish, not anything else."

"You make it sound so simple."

****

Lorelei watched tiny beads of sweat surface on his face that contorted with agony. She empathized with how difficult this conversation must be, but so were the days and nights he spent torturing himself. How burdensome, how painful it must be to harbor horrible memories of sexual abuse, as well as the guilt of believing he killed his father.

He believed himself a poor excuse for humanity. She struggled to find words to disclaim his misconception. *Show him.* The thought echoed like a tolling bell. *But how?*

As if a light flashed before her eyes, she knew. She would let him hear his own words. And when she did, he would fire back in defense. She prayed her logic would work.

"You know, Missy most likely should leave with you."

The change of subject obviously threw him. "What?"

He looked as flabbergasted as Charles Miller had the day a pig ran through his store, pots and pans flying like confetti.

"I said, Missy should leave with you."

"What the hell are you talking about?" His glower should have sent her running. But that's just what she'd wanted. Him fired up. Responding. Too frazzled to see straight for a second.

"She'll be ostracized if word gets out about her. And if not, she'll still feel others know what she is." She prayed for God's forgiveness for her holding back what she now knew as the truth regarding Missy.

"She'll walk around thinking how soiled she is, self-conscious with her head bowed down for the rest of her life if she stays here. She has no future here. You have to take h—"

True to form, Seth turned livid. His cheeks reddened, his eyes grew round and fired daggers at her.

"She's the sweetest, most precious little girl I've ever known aside from Jessica. Good God, Lorelei, she's only eight. She might be ill-used by Miles, but it wasn't her fault. She's still innocent of a man's touch and you know it. It…"

Lorelei beamed, had to fight back the laugh about to erupt. "Yes, you were saying?"

Seth pierced her with another scorching glare. His face blanched, his expression turning troubled as he glanced at the desk. She could almost hear the workings of his mind.

"It wasn't her fault, Seth. You just said it loud and clear. Think long and hard about that. You feel no different toward her now than you did yesterday. She's still the same sweet, adorable little girl she was yesterday. We love her, her family and friends love her just as much. She believes in the same values she had before Miles abused her. She was a pawn to a sick and depraved man. And so were you. You had no more choice in the matter than she did. You're no less of a person than she is for the hideous acts committed against you."

Seth stood stone still, his face a wooden blank. Imagining what turmoil crashed through his mind tore at her heart. But she had him where he needed to be. Hopefully, he would see himself through different eyes. Had she reached him?

She felt the muscles of his forearm flex taut under her hand, saw his knuckles turn white as he dug his fingertips into the edge of the desk. He shook his head as if to dispel the changing of his mind. She could not let that happen.

She would go in for the kill.

"Seth," she whispered, rubbing her fingers lightly upon his forearm. Good, he didn't pull away. "I thought better of a relationship with you because you shy away from civic commitments, but somehow, I knew you had a reason. I was willing to wait to find out why, and then decide if you were the man I thought you were. It's definitely been worth the wait."

His fingers relaxed their grip on the desk. Her pulse surged. Was his strong conviction of believing him worthless weakening? She swallowed the lump of agony that rose each time she thought of how sad, how senseless it was for anyone, especially Seth, to feel such a way.

She needed to bombard his swaying defenses. "Knowing your past hasn't changed my opinion of you one bit. Actually, I admire and respect you more because you lacked self-esteem, yet pursued such a meaningful career. It takes a man of great mental strength, sheer dedication and super-human fortitude to do what you've done. And for that, I love you all the more."

For the first time in so very long, he turned his head to meet her gaze. His glassy eyes were filled with longing, stringent pleading. He wanted to believe, she could feel it, see it in his skeptical, yet beseeching expression. He was so close.

Again, she plundered his fragile state, keeping her hand on his arm to offer him security, to give her the strength to go on. "I've looked long and hard for a man who might come close to possessing the high qualities I set my bonnet for. I never thought I'd find one who could possibly have all of them. But you proved me wrong. You possess every one of them, Seth. You heal physical wounds of others with your skilled hands. Let me heal your emotional wounds with my heart."

"Lorelei," he breathed. He trembled as his gaze bore into hers. Dear God, how she loved this wonderful man.

"Make love to me. So I can finally know the touch of a very special man. So you can chase those demons from your mind forever. Let me cleanse your soul and purify your mind."

Turning toward her farther, he placed his large hands upon her shoulders. She felt the blazing heat of them through her thin blouse. His intense eyes searched hers.

"Take me to your room and make me a woman. A woman who has longed for your touch since the first day I met you."

His face bore witness to the pain, the doubts still lingering.

His hand caressed her face; his callused thumb stroked her cheek reverently, as if he were afraid she might break. She felt cherished by his gentle touch. His rough skin stirred her senses; its tenderness evoked a riot of flames through her veins.

"Love me, Seth. Please, please, love me."

His arms came around her, fierce and forceful. He crushed her to his chest as his face burrowed into the curve of her neck. "God help me, I do. And you're the bigger fool for wanting me."

"Never," she gasped, joyful tears springing to life at his long-last declaration. His mouth sought hers, searing and devouring. She drank in his heady essence, her senses reeling as his eager hands glided across her back. Heart bounding, her skyrocketing libido steamed in all directions. She clung to him.

He hadn't a chance in hell.

CHAPTER THIRTY-EIGHT

Without further words, he took her hand and led her to his bedroom. A shaft of silver moonlight beamed through the window, silhouetting them as they faced each other by the double bed. Lorelei held his gaze and released his hand to undo her blouse.

She wanted this more than anything in the world, yet her fingers shook as she struggled with the top button. How very strange and awkward to stand here and simply disrobe. She had never thought about how one went about this part of it.

"Let me," he whispered, gently brushing her fumbling fingers aside. His husky words skimmed across her face like warm silk.

Her pulse quickened and her heart drummed staccato. Their gazes clung as he undid the first button, then the next and the next...

He pushed the garment past her shoulders and she shivered as cool air collided with her heated skin. Her nipples pebbled against her silk chemise. She felt sensuous, potently erotic. And longed to do the same to him.

As he unfastened her waistband, she undid buttons of his shirt. She heard his indrawn breath, felt his chest expand, his abdomen suck in. Her heated frenzy soared.

His fingers left a blazing trail wherever they touched. Hers tinged as they brushed his taut muscles, his smooth skin. When her skirt puddled at her feet, she kicked it aside and reached for his belt buckle. Her fingers turned to butter. Totally useless. Her face flamed at the swift onset of shyness.

Chuckling, he cupped her quivering hands in his and pressed them against his chest. His warm skin felt like soft steel. When she brushed her fingertips through the dark curly hairs, she nearly swooned. She basked in his smile, in his eyes so full of heated desire.

"I better do this part, or it'll be daybreak by the time you get through. And I can't wait that long."

Unable to mutter a word past the dryness in her throat, she nodded. How utterly embarrassing to be so inept at something she craved. He must think her a naive ninny. Withdrawing her hands, she retreated a step. And regretted she had broken their contact.

Without the slightest chagrin, he shucked his trousers and drawers in one clean sweep. Having never seen a naked man before, she became absolutely fascinated. Her embarrassment fled out the window. Her blood raised ten degrees. No one had to tell her he was the exemplary ideal of the male body.

His arms and chest bulged like a fierce warrior's. Silvery beams bathed his broad shoulders, narrow hips and wash-board abdomen. Her eyes trailed past the thick mat of chest hairs, down to where it tapered into a straight line. His manhood, erect and quite impressive, jutted out from a dark forest. Her throat constricted, her mouth watered.

"Let's get rid of this," he said, raising her chemise. His fingers grazed her skin in their ascent, scorching every inch along the way. The silky garment slid tediously upward, eliciting titillating heat waves that converged at her throbbing womanhood.

Resisting the urge to cover herself, she allowed him to take in his fill. She'd done no less to him. As his eyes slowly devoured her, her desire soared and her blood surged. Her knees weakened and headiness had her swaying.

"You're more beautiful than I ever imagined." He embraced her as his mouth claimed her lips in fervent possession.

She clutched him just as vigorously, wishing her hands could absorb his relentless doubts that plagued his mind.

His kisses spiraled from sweet to demanding to unbridled...sweeter, more dear to her heart than she had thought possible. His tongue lunged past her parted lips, hot and teasing. She followed suit, hesitantly at first, then seeking with the greed of one starved. Any further thoughts of how she could slay his past demons fled. In its place rushed an intense yearning to offer him all the love she had to give. And she trembled from it.

She had no idea when or how they'd reached the bed. But she welcomed it; his weight upon her, slick skin against slick skin, chest hairs tantalizing her over-sensitive breasts, ravenous kisses and magical hands, his heated erection pressed against her belly. She inhaled his woodsy scent, the heady musk of passion an aphrodisiac that heightened her senses and invoked her blood to rush hot and wild.

With a boldness she didn't pretend to hide, she ran her foot up and down his leg, loving the feel of the coarse hairs, the sinewy strength of his calves. Her hands roamed the corded back, splaying her fingers over his lean hips and across his buttocks. Her pulse thrummed as if ready to burst through her skin.

His ardent kisses sent her desire swirling. He kneaded her breasts, teasing her nipples to hard kernels. The flaming sensations sent Lorelei spinning head over heels. She arched her back, thrusting her breasts upward, eager and begging for more.

When his lips withdrew, she nearly cried out at the loss. When he laved her nipple and circled the areola, she cried out.

"Oh, Seth, Seth..." She bowed further, seeking more of the wicked deliciousness he stirred inside her. His mouth covered her breast, sucking, licking, nipping.

Frenzied, in need of touching every inch of him, her hands roamed non-stop. She dug her fingers into the firm cheeks of his buttocks as she climbed higher.

"Easy, sweetheart. I know. But it's just begun."

Just begun? His words vaguely registered. She didn't know how much more she could take. She needed...She needed...

Just when she thought the sensations would drive her mad, his fingers trailed down across her belly to fan through the triangle of hair. Her heart drummed.

"Open for me sweetheart. Spread your legs."

His words, so erotically stimulating, fed into her veins like the finest warm mulled wine. Willingly, she answered his request, eagerly seeking whatever he offered, desperate to stop the intense ache where her juices now flowed.

He stroked the sensitive nub of her desire with his thumb until she flailed upon the bed like a wild woman. His finger delved deep. Then two. She shuddered.

"Oh, heavenly stars!"

"That's it, sweetheart. Let go. Don't hold back."

She couldn't have held back if she tried. She lost all thought of her surroundings; spasm after spasm claimed her. He held her, kissing her with tenderness and deliberate slowness, until the mindless wonder eased and she could take a long breath. He moved atop her, entered her just enough for her to feel the fullness of him. He withdrew ever so slightly. Then plunged past her maidenhead.

She flinched at the stab of pain, her muffled cry absorbed by his nurturing lips. "No more pain, sweetheart, only pleasure," he whispered, gently kissing her eyelids, her cheek, her neck.

He held still as if waiting for her discomfort to subside, then began moving in a slow, stroking rhythm. Instinctively, her hips gyrated to meet each deeper thrust. An escalating pressure burgeoned until the flames of passion consumed her. Her mind, her body splintered; lost once more to his masterful touch. They reached fulfillment together, her shuddering, almost convulsing, as her climax sent her to somewhere outside the universe. He plunged once more, touching her very womb, and she felt him quake within her arms.

They lay for several minutes, each spent from the exhilarating ecstasy, too breathless to speak. Their moist bodies fused together as they cooled down, their hearts gradually returning to normal beats. Seth rolled off her and pulled her to his side, wrapping his arms around her. She snuggled into the length of him, resting her head on the hollow of his shoulder, content to just lie in his warm embrace and listen as his racing heart returned to a steady beat.

Complete contentment nestled within her. Somehow, she'd known it would be this way between them. And not only this potent physical force, but in mind and soul.

****

Seth lay in sheer wonder. Satisfaction that he had never hoped to attain seeped through him. And it was not just being physically sated. A

274

serene peace, an inner happiness, settled within him to the likes he felt no man deserved. Lorelei had given that to him. A feeling of love, of true giving of one's self, of total acceptance by another. He wanted it forever.

This bold, outspoken woman had broken through his long-established defenses and had somehow made him trust her enough to let down his guard. To allow him to believe himself worthy enough to touch her, to love her. It was not "*somehow*", he realized. It was because of her steadfast, unselfish love.

For years, he had convinced himself he was dirt. But he had been insecure and clinging to misplaced guilt. Now, he knew it and saw himself differently. This sweet, loving woman had changed his views of himself. A lot of things would change from here on out. And those changes would enhance his life as never before.

She had made him realize that no one, including him, would condemn Missy for what had been unwillingly thrust upon her. And he could now appreciate his worth, despite his past. He had a life worth living, not only to serve others, but a life of his own. And warm and caring Lorelei deserved a life of happiness and contentment. If she could overlook his past, he would give her what she deserved. And he wanted to do that, more than anything he had ever wanted before.

He bent his head and kissed her forehead. She pulled back far enough to look up at him. Her candied smile melted his heart.

"I love you, Lorelei. I love you so much it scares the hell out me." It felt so good to finally to say those words out loud, to be proud to say them.

Her smile was dazzling, her eyes reflecting her love. He felt ten feet tall; confident he could master the world.

"And I love you with all my heart. I have for so very long." Her eyes filled with tears. He felt her tense and knew she expected him to say they could never be. *Silly woman.*

Before he could set her fears to rest, she spoke. "Even if you feel you can't make a commitment to me, it's all right. I..." Her voice cracked and her lashes glistened like iced spikes.

"You what?"

She looked so unsure of herself. So scared he might say this one night was it. And God love her, she acted ready to accept it if need be. He loved her all the more for it.

She blinked three times to check the tears. "I'll understand if you want no more to do with me." The tears trailed down her cheeks despite her valiant effort. With his thumb, he lightly brushed the drops away, then cupped her face within his palms.

"But I *do* want more." He watched her eyes widen.

"You...do?" She looked more like a vulnerable little girl than the brazen, feisty woman who ranted at the town. Now, she had become the one to doubt her own worth.

"Yes, sweetheart," he whispered, and watched her eyes fill with dreaminess at his endearment, "I do."

"We can be most discreet." Oh, how hard she tried to act stalwart. He fought back a laugh.

His chuckles caused her to pull back. A troubled frown marred her lovely face.

"We won't have to be discreet if you'll say yes."

She literally stopped breathing and he wondered if she would ever take another breath. Their gazes locked; his reflecting all his love for her, hers full of hope, yet skeptical of what his innuendo really meant.

"Will you stay by my side and give me encouragement to see each day through so I can I live with myself? So I can stay by your side, love you for all eternity and be a contented man?" She swallowed and trembled within his arms.

"Will you marry me, Lorelei Webster?"

He had always compared her smile to warm sunshine. But never had it glowed as brightly as it did now. And his love for this woman spilled from his heart, overflowing as if a dam had burst.

She kissed him with a force strong enough to send them through the thin mattress.

She pulled back enough to look him in the eye. "You may not want to marry me when I tell you I've kept something from you."

Taken off guard, he stiffened and frowned. "What is it? It can't be bad enough to not answer my question. I thought you'd be pleased at my proposal."

Her lips trembled and her eyes glistened in the moonlight as she met his gaze. "When I said how others would condemn Missy if they found out what Miles had done to her, I wanted you to realize how unjust it would be to Missy."

"And your point was quite clear. I heard what you said and realized she...and I, were victims. It worked."

She swallowed and he braced himself for the unknown.

"When I took Jamie back home, Johanna explained that she didn't want Missy to suffer alone any longer and had already had a heart-to-heart talk with her."

Trembling, Seth tried to hold himself in check, as stiff as a board. He did not want to hear what she had to say. Especially, not now. Before he could waylay her, she persisted.

"Three times Miles tried his best to molest Missy, but each time he put his hands on her she shied away and pleaded with him not to touch her. It seems Miles had the decency, or more likely he only bided his time, until he could coax her to let him do more." She gulped and her eyes turned woeful.

"Even putting his hands on her is disgusting, sinful abuse and can never be overlooked. They should hang him by his toes for that alone. And sooner or later, he would've lost patience...but you stopped him before that could happen."

Seth lay still, absorbing what she said. His mind reeled from the truth. She had known Missy had not suffered further abuse. And had withheld that truth. He wanted to rage, to scream she had been unfair to let him believe otherwise. But his elation at knowing that the little girl had evaded the beast's attempts were so profound, he could not find fault in what Lorelei had done. By God, she had forced him to realize— or, at least think—Missy was no more than a victim than he. And she had been right. Miles *would have* lost patience sooner or later. And that would have been...he would not think of the horrific results.

"You lied to me by not telling me."

Tears spilled down her cheeks. "I know. And it broke my heart not to tell you right then. But I realized I had to make you see—"

"Shh...don't say anymore." He gathered her in his arms, held her tight. "I know what you felt you had to do. And it worked. And I thank God you made me see the light. I don't agree with your method, but I understand. And I thank God Missy didn't suffer any more than having his meaty, rotten hands on her."

She squiggled back in his arms to peer up at him. "You understand? You don't hate me?"

His kissed her tenderly. "Lorelei, I love you. Again, I may not always agree with your methods, but you're learning. Just promise me you won't lie to me again. Or, I should say, keep the truth from me in the future."

"I promise. I'll never withhold the truth, ever."

He flashed her a grin. "I ask you again. Will you marry me?"

"Oh, good gracious! Yes! Yes, yes, yes. I'll marry you tomorrow, if you want," she squealed with delight before wrapping her arms around him and bestowing another bruising kiss.

"Today wouldn't do, huh?"

CHAPTER THIRTY-NINE

The wedding took place on Christmas Eve. Seth scanned the crowd as he impatiently awaited his bride.

It was a lavish affair. More than half the town turned out in their better-than-Sunday best to wish them well and listen to their vows. If part of the men had been dragged by their wives, they didn't let it show. Only smiles and joy filled the church. Pews were decorated with greenery and deep red bows and a hundred white candles burned brightly. By the time the pipe organ heralded the wedding march, there wasn't any standing room left.

Only the knowledge that Miles Cooper would be hanged the week after Christmas had put a somewhat dim cloud over the past several days of excitement. The hanging had been delayed in observance of the holiday. Yet no one seemed to think twice about that gruesome outcome at the moment. Seth, too, repressed it, refusing to let it overshadow this special night.

Jamie, honored to be best man, stood proud and tall at Seth's side. Michael, more than pleased for Seth's good fortune— though he'd clearly pointed out what Seth would be in for with such a strong-willed woman—flanked Jamie's side as groomsman. Lilly glided down the aisle, beaming proudly at having been asked to be maid of honor. Tears streaked down her smiling face. With pleased grins, Jessica and Missy scattered poinsettia petals from their baskets as they passed the well-wishers.

It was a hodge-podge wedding, to say the least. And it suited Seth just fine.

Seth's breath hitched as Lorelei walked down the aisle in a snow-white satin creation. She looked like an ethereal princess.

He had never felt such pride as he did at that moment. He felt awed at seeing her sparkling eyes, her radiant smile. He was a proud man indeed. As his soon-to-be bride joined him at the small altar, he smiled, remembering how he had vowed to stay away from this meddling woman. Now, a hundred buffalo in his path couldn't stop him from reaching out to her.

As they held hands, exchanging their vows, he knew no one could deny the happiness or love between them. Both smiled as if there was no tomorrow. But only this moment existed for the two of them, and he didn't care who saw it.

As he promised to love, honor, and obey and gazed into her eyes brimming with the deep love she bore him, Seth realized he had found happiness dearer to him than anything possible. He had found a love he would cherish until the end of time. He had found inner peace, self-worth and new-found esteem, stronger than life itself. And all because of one meddlesome woman.

As they prayed, asking God to bless this union of hearts, he felt humbled by the sheer beauty of their unity. He silently thanked the Almighty for allowing him to find her, and for her adamant tenacity. Lorelei Webster was one hell of a woman.

****

Lorelei gazed into Seth's warm loving eyes and an incredible pride swelled inside her. Resplendent in a black long-tailed suit and red silk ascot, he nearly took her breath away. Never had she dreamed she could respect, admire and love someone as deeply as she loved this man. For all his previous doubts and fears, his avoidance and resistance to her, she had persevered. And it had paid off. She felt not only a deep-seeded love for him, but an inner contentment at his own acceptance of himself.

She would love him till death did them part. She would cherish him for always. As far as obey...

Must she really have to obey in *everything*?

She still had her work cut out for her regarding the community.

Seth would most likely balk and try to persuade her otherwise. At least, at some of the fiascos she would create. And create them she would. She knew herself all too well. But she would think before leaping. She had been instrumental in his finding his self-worth again, and he had taught her better ways to deal with others with more finesse.

She would obey him. To a certain point. He would have to love her despite the turmoil she would set afire.

She smiled. Yes, they loved each other deeply. And that undeniable love meant accepting each other, *despite* the other's faults or transgressions.

They would do very well together. Because of their love, they would conquer the future, endure rocky roads—no matter the many pitfalls they might encounter. They would give their all in order to make their marriage a true success, each one of them striving for a harmonious, compromising union.

Because of their unconditional love they had found true happiness. It would be all because of love, *all for love,* that they would have a life of sheer and full contentment.

Bending to kiss her, Seth winked, as if he had read every thought.

Author's Note

No one likes the thought of abuse, neglect, or sorrow. Whether it's regarding adults or children, especially children. I, for one, would much prefer a world where all is happy, good, loving and peaceful. A place where everyone helps their friends, neighbors and those in need.

Unfortunately, such a perfect world doesn't exist. Many of us have encountered victims of such crimes that pierce our very souls.

But we can strive to make our world a better place, the best place for all. Each and every one of us, each and every day of our lives. And because we hope for that better world, we are extremely fortunate to have those who devote their best efforts in helping others who truly need that very special attention and assistance. Thank goodness.

To all the devoted, dedicated and caring people who have given tremendous time, valiant effort, and diligent, professional expertise to those abused or neglected, you have my praise.

From our forefathers and fore-sisters who persisted in righting the wrongs, to the people today in Social Services, Protective Agencies and the like, I thank you.

ABOUT THE AUTHOR

For years Beverly Wells worked a hectic pace as a Public Health Nurse in Homecare while serving on the Medical Reserve Corps for Homeland Security. Little did she know when she decided to escape from reality and try to write a historical romance it would set another whirlwind to swirling. With the help and guidance of RWA, her local writing chapter LCRW and many rewrites, the award-winning author now devotes her full time to making writing her career. "It's my new chapter in my life and I'm lovin' it."

Living with her own hero and rescued dog Jamie in the Finger Lakes Region of NYS, she enjoys writing humorous, sensuous Historical Westerns while including a lesson learned or raising awareness of a heartfelt issue. Her debut novel Only When the Loon Sings, published by TWRP, has captivated readers far and wide. Her second book, All For Love, published by Prairie Rose Publications, is sure to follow suit. She's busy finishing her third.

For more information regarding Bev, visit her at her Prairie Rose Publications author page, her website @www.beverlywellsauthor.com, FB, twitter, blog @beverlywellsauthor.wordpress.com or gmail her @beverlywellsauthor@gmail.com She'd love to hear from you.

DRINA'S CHOICE by Agnes Alexander. To get away from an abusive home, Drina Hamilton answers an ad for a mail-order bride, not knowing the only reason Aaron Wilcox agreed to marry a stranger was to save his ranch.

HOME FIRES by Kirsten Lynn. Cord Matthews sets his sights on the open Montana Territory when the War Between the States rips everything from him. Olivia Bartlett, the only woman he's ever loved, has been killed—a cross marks the place where she lies buried. Cord builds a new dream, but a ghost from his past won't let him forget what his heart wanted most.

LASSOING A BRIDE by Livia J. Washburn, Gail L. Jenner, Sarah J. McNeal, Tracy Garrett and Sara Barnard. Some brides are hard to get a rope on, for sure! But in these wild west romance tales, being married is like sugar and lots of spice—with a dash of pepper in the mix! Ain't nothin' tame about these brides, who have a delicious story of their own—each falling under the spell of a handsome devil she thought was out of her reach. Unanswered prayers, broken dreams and unexpected circumstances are sometimes the best way for a groom to get the gal he loves when he's looking at Lassoing a Bride!

LASSOING A GROOM by Kathleen Rice Adams, Jacquie Rogers, Kirsten Lynn, Tracy Garrett and Kristy McCaffrey. How is a woman supposed to catch a husband? In the wild, wild west, she's got to find a way to Lasso a Groom! Some of them are lawmen...some are outlaws. Ranchers and homesteaders are fair game, as well—none of 'em safe from love's lariat, or the women who finally manage to rope 'em in!

LASSOING A MAIL-ORDER BRIDE by Cheryl Pierson, Tanya Hanson, Kaye Spencer, and Kathleen Rice Adams. A woman would have to be loco to become a mail-order bride...wouldn't she? Leaving everything behind and starting fresh in the untamed west is the answer to a prayer for these ladies! A beautiful socialite needs a husband fast— but her husband wants a bride for life. A pregnant young lady becomes desperate—almost as desperate as her soon-to-be husband, who just inherited his sister's kids. A man is in love with a woman he can't have—or can he? A woman's reputation is tarnished and professional career compromised—she runs, but she can't hide. Will they all find love with strangers they've never met who are set on LASSOING A MAIL-ORDER BRIDE?

www.prairierosepublications.com